A MUCH NEEDED HOLIDAY

"Is There Something Wrong With Your Food?"

"Not at all." Kate assured him. "There's just too much of it! And wanting to set an example for our baby, I've been trying to clean my plate."

"*Our* baby?" Until Trace murmured the question, Kate wasn't even aware of her odd choice of words.

"Our? Did I say our? I didn't mean to say our! Really, I meant *your* baby!" Kate knew she was chattering. The slow smile lifting the edges of Trace's lips didn't help much, either!

Casually leaning back in his chair, Trace slid an encompassing glance over Kate, then his daughter, Kathy, then Kate again. As if he'd come to an important decision, he nodded once.

"Kathy's beautiful," he said in that same low tone. "But you and I would make an equally beautiful child together."

SEASON OF MIRACLES

"I've Never Been Able To Forget You."

Sloane heard her gasp at his words, and he searched her face. "Don't get the wrong idea," he said, smiling cynically, "I haven't been carrying a torch. Except..."

"Except what?" she demanded angrily.

"Except that I want to be completely free. And I couldn't be until I knew you were happy. Tell me you are."

"No, Sloane, I can't." Elise felt like an open wound, but she willed herself to sound calm.

"I'm exactly what you see. An old maid living in an old house. But I've taken more risks than you'll ever take, even though I stayed while you went off to see the world. I've given love, with absolutely no guarantee of having it returned. I may be weak, afraid of change, as you say. But I'm not afraid to give myself. Will you ever say the same?"

Dear Reader,

At this special season we bring you a very special book. This is our editors' most exciting choice of two full-length memorable holiday novels by two of your favorite and award-winning authors.

We hope your own much-needed holiday will be full of joy.

Best wishes for a Happy New Year,

Candy Lee
Reader Service

Christmas Classics

Harlequin Books

TORONTO • NEW YORK • LONDON
AMSTERDAM • PARIS • SYDNEY • HAMBURG
STOCKHOLM • ATHENS • TOKYO • MILAN

CHRISTMAS CLASSICS © 1989 Harlequin Enterprises Limited

ISBN 0-373-15130-6

A Much Needed Holiday © 1985 Joan Hohl
Season of Miracles © 1986 Emilie Richards McGee

All the characters in this book have no existence outside the
imagination of the author and have no relation whatsoever to
anyone bearing the same name or names. They are not even
distantly inspired by any individual known or unknown to the
author, and all incidents are pure invention.

® are Trademarks registered in the United States Patent and
Trademark Office and in other countries.

Printed in U.S.A.

CONTENTS

Joan Hohl

*

A MUCH NEEDED HOLIDAY

For Rita Clay Estrada,
for introducing me to San Antonio.
And for Kay Garteiser, Parris Afton Bonds,
Linda Lucas, Tate Mckenna, Gayle Link and Kathie Seidick
for their delightful company at dinner
along the San Antonio River walk.
Remember the Alamo!

One

Kate Warren never knew her parents. It wasn't as if Kate was an orphan, or that her parents had abandoned her when she was an infant. Kate merely never had the opportunity to get to know the two people who had made her birth possible. When it came right down to it, Kate's parents didn't know each other all that well either.

Since Kate had faced the fact that her parents were strangers, well over ten years ago around her thirteenth birthday, it no longer bothered her except during this time of the year—the season of goodwill, peace on earth, and strong family unity.

Slowly threading her way through the shoppers thronging to the mall on the Saturday after Thanksgiving Day, Kate smiled wistfully at a snowsuited toddler impeding her progress. The blond child's dark blue eyes were as wide as saucers as she gazed in wonder at the twinkling decorations on the Christmas tree that rose majestically into the air, thirty feet from its base in the center of the mall.

Sublimely unconcerned with the foot traffic of the giants scurrying around her, the child came to a dead stop, her tiny red lips forming a silent *oh* at the magical sight of animated animals and carollers dressed in Victorian garb at the foot of the mighty pine.

Enchanted by the toddler's rapt expression, Kate came to a halt only inches from her. Momentarily forgetting how pressed for time she was, Kate observed the child as she examined the man-made winter wonderland.

The child, little more than a baby really, was beautiful. Blond curls cascaded around her small shoulders and pooled into the tossed-back hood of her pink jacket. A tiny, not quite pointed, chin was raised as the child lifted her head to stare at the huge star at the very top of the tree. Her cheeks were downy soft and flushed with pleasure. Her blue eyes were bright from the reflection of the sparkling lights.

Sighing, Kate snapped herself out of the spell cast by the little girl and moved to walk around the child. At the same instant, the toddler blinked and gazed up trustingly. Before Kate could take a step, the expression on the tiny face changed from delight to terror, and her little lips parted to emit a wailing cry.

"Daddy!"

Her mouth soft, Kate glanced around, preparing to smile in understanding when her gaze encountered the child's anxious father or mother. Her smile turned into a frown when all she saw were curious looks from the people rushing by.

"I want my daddy!"

The now tearful sound of the child's high-pitched voice drew Kate's gaze back to her terrified little face. What the devil was she to do, Kate thought frantically, suddenly mindful of the time and the fact that she was already late for her lunch date. She simply couldn't walk away and leave this child standing all alone!

"It's all right, baby," Kate said soothingly, stooping to be on a level with the sobbing child. "Don't cry, honey."

Revealing incredibly long eyelashes, the child blinked again. "I want my daddy!" she cried loudly. "Where's my daddy?"

"I…I don't know, love." Uncomfortably aware of the stares she was receiving, Kate tentatively raised a hand to brush at the tears rolling down the small face. "I think he's lost."

Strangely, Kate's observation magically silenced the sobs. Frowning in a comically adult manner, the child stared at her.

"Daddy's lost?" she asked solemnly.

"I'm afraid so, baby. But don't worry, I'll help you find him," Kate promised reassuringly. "Come along, love." Standing, Kate held out her hand to the girl. "We'll go to the mall office." As the child slipped her small hand into hers, Kate smiled again. "I wouldn't be surprised if we found your daddy already there."

The child gazed up at her with innocent eyes. "Is that where lost daddies go?"

"Usually." Kate nodded. "And then, the lady or man working in the office will give a description of the lost daddy over the public address system."

"Oh." Wide blue eyes gazed at Kate uncomprehendingly.

Muffling a groan, Kate bit on her lip. How in the world did one go about explaining a public address system to a child three years old at the outside, she wondered, carefully guarding the little person as she wove in and out of the shoppers.

"Do you ever listen to the radio?" Kate asked hopefully.

"Yes." The little girl nodded eagerly.

"Well, the public address is something like the radio," Kate smiled. "You'll see when we get there, baby."

"Kathy."

Startled by the blandly delivered information, Kate stopped walking to stare at the child. "Your name's Kathy?" The girl nodded again. "That's a beautiful name," Kate complimented. "And my name is Kate." Beginning to move again, Kate paused when the child tugged on her hand.

"Is my daddy crying 'cause he's lost?" Kathy's lips trembled.

If he's not he ought to be, Kate thought, inwardly outraged at the very idea of a man being so careless with his daughter. Even in their disinterest her parents had never lost *her*! Hiding her feelings behind a smile, Kate shrugged helplessly.

"Does your daddy cry a lot?" she probed.

Kathy frowned in that oddly adult way. "No." She shook her head decisively. "Not ever."

Then perhaps he should, Kate declared mutely, picturing Kathy's father as a typical swaggering machoman.

"Daddy don't like Christmas." Kathy offered the unsolicited information sadly. "Or Santa Claus," she added on a sniff.

"Daddy *doesn't* like Christmas," Kate corrected automatically.

"I know." Kathy sniffed again, louder this time. "He said he'd just as soon forget the whole blasted thing."

Kate's sense of outrage grew into consuming anger. Kathy had obviously quoted her father verbatim. What sort of man would say such a thing to a baby, she mused irritably, especially a beautiful, alert baby? Trying to keep her smile, Kate squeezed the small hand gently. *She* wasn't particularly wild about the holiday either, but she'd never dream of spoiling it for an innocent youngster.

"Why doesn't daddy like Christmas or Santa Claus, honey?" Kate inquired.

Kathy's shrug was as oddly adult as her frown. "He says he needs Christmas like he needs a case of the flu. And that it's nothing but a damn waste of time and ... and ... ah ... espense!" She beamed at Kate with pride for having managed the unfamiliar word.

Kate felt a sharp catch in her throat and her heart; she had never even laid eyes on the man, but she disliked him immensely! Kathy had to be *the* brightest child Kate had ever encountered, and the fool that had fathered her was not only teaching her to curse, he was robbing her of one of the joys of childhood! At that instant, Kate longed for the opportunity to give the insensitive brute a large piece of her mind, along with the sharp edge of her tongue!

"What's espense mean?" Kathy's question shattered Kate's vision of a certain male's chastisement.

"The word is *ex*pense, darling," Kate explained softly. "And it means to cost a lost of money."

"My daddy has a lot of money," Kathy said seriously. "Lots and lots of pennies ... and even quarters!"

"That's nice, love." Kate's smile was tinged with genuine amusement; how simplistic children were, equating wealth with lots and lots of pennies and even quarters!

And it had required quite a few of those quarters to outfit the child, Kate decided, running an encompassing glance over Kathy's sturdy figure as they stood in the midst of the hubbub of shoppers.

The child's snowsuit alone had very likely been exorbitantly expensive. Beneath the open jacket, Kate could see and evaluate the cost of the luxurious velour smock and corduroy slacks the girl was wearing. The supple fur-lined, leather boots encasing her tiny feet hadn't come from a bargain counter either!

At least the absent parent was scrupulous in the child's physical well-being, Kate conceded grudgingly. But that certainly didn't compensate for his dereliction of duty as far as the girl's emotional security was concerned. And, if anyone had firsthand knowledge of the lack of emotional security, Kate did!

"I'm hungry, Kate." Kathy's whimper drew Kate away from the unpleasant memory of her own barren childhood.

"Are you?" At the girl's nod, Kate asked, "Didn't you have any lunch?"

Kathy's blond curls bounced on her shoulders with a negative shake of her head. "Daddy said I could have a hamburger and French fries at McDonald's." Her lower lip quivered, "And now daddy's lost, and I'm hungry."

Her gaze was captured by the trembling rosebud mouth, and Kate sighed in defeat. Oh, well, she'd simply have to explain the whole thing to David later—surely he'd understand why she'd had to stand him up. But to be honest, Kate wasn't all that positive that he *would* understand; David had been displaying an uncomfortable tendency toward possessiveness lately.

Pushing thoughts of the man waiting to have lunch with her from her mind, Kate grinned at Kathy.

"You know what? I'm hungry too." Tightening her hold on the child's hand, Kate walked determinedly in the direction of the mall office. "So, let's go tell the authorities that your daddy is lost, and where we're going, and then we'll both have a hamburger and French fries at McDonald's. Okay?"

"Okay!" Kathy agreed, smiling all over her adorable little face.

Some thirty-odd minutes later, Kate and Kathy were ensconced in a booth inside the fast-food restaurant, happily munching on Big Macs and golden slices of deep-fried potatoes, washing it down with large cups of cola.

Though Kate had hoped that she and Kathy would find the negligent parent pacing the mall office, she had to admit that she wasn't devastated that they hadn't. In fact, she had to admit that she was having a great time with the intelligent little girl.

Endearingly at ease now with Kate, Kathy rambled on about how she was going to see Santa Claus, even though her disgruntled father was vocal with disapproval, and that afterward she was going to visit her grandparents for the rest of the weekend.

"You like visiting your grandparents, don't you?" Kate asked, knowing the answer by the gleam in Kathy's eyes.

"Uh huh," Kathy nodded vigorously. "Gramma plays games with me, and grampa takes me for long walks." She chewed methodically a moment then added wistfully, "Sometimes my mommie is there—" she sighed "—and then everybody just yells a lot."

Kate felt an actual stab of pain in her chest at the too-wise expression on the youngster's face. Back off of this subject, Katie my girl, she advised herself ruefully. Still, she couldn't help but deplore how people managed to tangle up their lives and hurt their children in the process.

"Ah . . . what are you going to tell Santa Claus?" she asked with forced brightness. "What do you want him to bring you for Christmas?"

"A new mommie," Kathy said emphatically, stunning Kate into stillness for several seconds.

"But—" Kate shook her head "—but, Kathy, you already have a mommie! Why do you want a new one?" Kate blurted out without thinking.

"That is none of your damned business!"

Kate jumped at the harsh male voice coming from behind her left shoulder. Shifting around on the plastic-covered booth seat, she found herself staring into glacial green eyes just as Kathy squealed:

"Daddy!"

A chill invaded Kate's spine as she gazed into the harshly etched face of the cold-eyed man. *This* was Kathy's father? Instantly the image Kate had formed of the man dissolved: this man was definitely not a swaggering young macho-man. Oh no, this man exuded an aura of arrogant self-confidence that was so palpable that Kate fancied she could feel its rays enveloping her, smothering her with their force.

In a mere moment that seemed to last forever, the man's entire appearance was impressed upon Kate's mind and memory.

He was not exceptionally tall, perhaps an inch under six foot, yet every one of those five feet eleven inches was solidly packed with large, angular bones covered tautly with lean, hard-looking muscles. He was attired in a casual, ordinary fashion—tan brushed-denim jeans, a dark brown-and-white striped bulky knit sweater, desert boots and a Western-style, sheepskin-lined jacket, both in buff suede. On him the clothes looked neither casual nor ordinary!

But it was his facial features that caused the chill in Kate's spine to spread insidiously through her entire body. Made up of hard angles and smooth planes encased in wind- and sun-roughened skin, nose long and straight, cheekbones wide and high, jaw line uncompromisingly hard, all framed by a thick mane of chestnut-shaded hair, he was devastatingly handsome in a thoroughly masculine, almost brutal, way.

The mere sight of him scared Kate! But, of course, she had no intention of allowing *him* to see it!

"You're Kathy's father?" Kate infused a hint of contempt into her cool tone.

"That's right," he snapped, moving to stand beside the bright-eyed child. "Who the hell are you?"

Heat raced through Kate's veins, and she felt a surge of warmth rush into her cheeks at his insulting tone. Of all the ungrateful...! Kate's mind groped for words strong enough to indict the brute and went blank in the process. Never before in her life had she encountered such arrogance!

"*I* am the woman who has been looking after your daughter," Kate gritted furiously. "The one *you* mislaid!"

His narrowing eyes spoke of his own rising anger. "*I* mislaid? I'll have you know—" he began roughly when Kathy cut in excitedly.

"Daddy, this is Kate, she was helping me find you when you got lost!"

"I got lost?" he exclaimed incredulously. "Young lady, I told you to stay beside me while I paid for your shoes!" The hard-eyed stare he leveled on Kathy aroused Kate's maternal instincts, but before she could voice a protest, he went on icily, "Get your jacket, we're leaving."

"But, daddy," Kathy cried, "I just started—"

"And you're not seeing Santa Claus today," he cut in brusquely.

Kate gasped, stunned by his cruelty. But when she saw the large tears welling up in Kathy's eyes, she flung caution to the wind and, regaining her voice, she launched into a defensive attack.

"Your behavior is unforgivable, *sir!*" Kate sneered the term of respect. "Kathy has barely started her lunch!"

"The name is Sinclair," he said much too softly. "Trace Sinclair." A chilling smile twisted his lips. "But you may call me sir." An arctic stare was raked over what he could see of Kate's body, lingering an insulting moment on her high, full breasts. Then, dismissively, he turned his attention back to his daughter.

"Daddy, I'm hungry!" Kathy wailed pleadingly. "Can't I finish my hamburger and French fries?"

Her blood near the boiling point, Kate bit her tongue against the tirade choking her and glared at his profile, willing him to show the child patience and compassion. When he relented, Kate knew it was because of the tears now running freely down Kathy's flushed cheeks, and not from her silent urging.

"All right," Trace Sinclair said abruptly, "I did promise you lunch at McDonald's." His less than enthusiastic glance swept over the food in front of Kathy. "And, since I have to wait for you," he sighed, "I may as well eat too."

Kate aimed visual daggers at his back as he swung away to stride to the order counter. The man was an absolute tyrant, she thought, trembling with anger. What sort of life must this poor baby have? Her fighting spirit awakened, Kate was determined that Kathy would see Santa

Claus after lunch even if she had to make an embarrassing scene to bring the visit about!

"Why is daddy mad at me, Kate?" Kathy's tremulous voice drew Kate from her fuming thoughts.

Withdrawing a tissue from her handbag, Kate reached across the narrow table to wipe the tears from the small face. "I'm sure your daddy was more worried than angry, darling," Kate smiled reassuringly, not particularly assured herself. "I suppose that when he was lost, your daddy was afraid you wouldn't be able to find him."

"My daddy's not afraid of anything!" Kathy blurted, wide-eyed. "Not even snakes and crawly things!"

"Really?" Kate contrived a note of awe.

"Yes, really." Trace's drawl surprised Kate. She hadn't noticed him approaching the booth. "Not snakes or crawly things or anything else." A mocking smile curved his hard-looking lips. "Not even afraid of intrepid young rescuers of disobedient children." His eyes gleamed as he noted Kate's soft gasp. "May I join you, Miss...?" One dark eyebrow arched tauntingly.

"Kate," Kathy volunteered.

"Warren," Kate said repressively. "And please do," she waved a negligent hand regally, "join us, I mean."

"How gracious," he murmured in a near growl before slanting a glance at Kathy to order, "Slide it over, kid."

Kate's heart ached for the child as her expression brightened at the teasing note in her father's tone. How very little it takes to make her happy, Kate sighed inwardly, watching as Kathy scooted to the end of the bench seat, her face glowing with a delighted smile. Shifting her gaze, Kate silently renewed her vow to see Kathy sit on Santa's lap as she observed Trace place his food-laden tray on the table. He then shrugged out of his jacket and eased onto the seat beside the child.

"So, *Kate*," he drawled, his taunting tone underlining her name. "Where did you run into my wandering off-spring?"

Kate didn't even realize she was gritting her teeth until her jaw began to ache. "Gazing wide-eyed at the tree," Kate somehow managed to drawl back. "Right in the center of the mall," she paused, then added sweetly, "*Trace*."

A brief flicker in the eyes that Kate could now see were a clear light green acknowledged her deliberate use of his first name. "Not thirty feet from the store where we had just purchased her shoes..." he shot a grim glance at Kathy, "...while I was frantically searching the entire mall." His features hardening, Trace caught the child's tiny chin in his strong hand and lifted her head to face him directly. "If you ever walk away from me like that again, Kath, I'll tan your rear with my belt. Do you understand?"

"Yes, daddy."

The quiver in Kathy's voice and the wounded expression that seemed to crumble her face sent a bolt of sheer rage through Kate. In her mind's eye a vision rose of Trace wielding a belt on the beautiful child, and common sense gave way to her protective urges.

"Over my dead body!" Kate exclaimed in a grating tone.

An uncommon stillness gripped Trace, then he slowly turned his head to pierce her with glittering green eyes. "I beg your pardon?" he murmured ominously.

"I said, the only way you'll ever take a belt to this child is over my dead body!" Kate reiterated, incensed and not thinking rationally. "I'll see you in hell first!"

Amazement transformed Trace's features for an instant, then a curtain was drawn, concealing emotion—

except in his eyes. A contemplative watchfulness gave his eyes a gemlike gleam.

"Indeed?" His food ignored as if forgotten, Trace regarded Kate with cool consideration. "And how do you propose to carry out this ferocious guardianship?" he gibed in a deceptively soft tone.

Stark awareness shuddered through Kate, not only of her inability to back up her hastily blurted challenge, but of an uncomfortable sexual awareness of Trace as a man. All kinds of sensations went zigzagging through her body, leaving her hot and cold at the same time. Her breathing was suddenly shallow and painful and she stared at Trace helplessly.

Immune to the electric force field of currents shimmering between the two adults, Kathy's plaintive interruption shattered the raw intimacy humming between Trace and Kate.

"Daddy, please, please let me see Santa Claus today," she whined, sniffing loudly. "You promised!"

"That's very good." Drawing his gaze from Kate reluctantly, Trace smiled wryly at Kathy. Kathy returned the smile sheepishly. A frown line marring her smooth brow, Kate glanced from father to daughter in confusion; Trace's follow-up observation clarified his seemingly unrelated remark ... at least partially.

"You're becoming quite the little con-artist with your begging routine; you should take the show on the road." His lips flattened into a forbidding straight line. "Picked that little whining number up from your cousins, did you?" he demanded coldly.

Kathy hung her head abjectly. "Yeah."

"Excuse me?" Trace rapped at her terminology.

"Yes, daddy," Kathy corrected.

Removed from the exchange, Kate continued to shift her glance from one to the other. From what she could gather, Kathy was acquiring some habits from relatives that Trace firmly objected to.

"Maybe your Aunt Barbara and Uncle Fred will put up with your cousins' behavior," Trace continued, confirming Kate's speculation, "but I certainly will not." His tone hardened, "Is *that* understood, Kath?"

"Yes, daddy," Kathy whispered.

"All right." Lifting her head with one long finger, Trace smiled so gently at her that it caused a dry tightness in Kate's throat. "Now finish your lunch," he ordered softly, "before it gets completely cold."

Silence blanketed the table for the following fifteen minutes as the three concentrated on their food. Kate utilized those minutes devising ways to change Trace's mind about Kathy's visit to Santa Claus, studying her adversary from the protection of her lowered eyelashes.

And Trace Sinclair did make an interesting study! The first descriptive word that sprang to Kate's mind was arrogant—swiftly followed by self-confident, rugged, virile, and supremely male.

Feeling uneasy by the strange, new sensations whirling through her body, Kate shifted on the seat. Through the veil of her thick black lashes, her gaze touched then became caught on the thin masculine lips. His lips moved as he murmured something to his daughter, and a sigh of longing to feel those lips moving on hers shivered through Kate.

The longing, spawned from blatant sexual hunger, shocked Kate to the marrow of her delicate bones. What in the world was happening to her, she wondered, frantically shifting her gaze away from temptation. Never in her life had she experienced such a strong physical attraction to a man!

Clutching the paper cup of cola with trembling, achy fingers, Kate gulped at the cold liquid in a futile attempt to quench the flames of desire licking her senses into hot arousal. Observing her trembling fingers as if they belonged to someone else, she felt a sinking feeling in her stomach.

Did those fingers really belong to the woman who had earned herself the title of "the unresponsive one" while she was still in college? How many frustrated men had called her that? Kate had lost count of the number. Yet, now, sitting in a public place with a man she'd met less than an hour ago, she found herself responding to everything male in him.

What was happening to her? With the silent cry ringing in her mind, Kate exerted every ounce of willpower she possessed in an effort to appear coolly composed as she raised her eyes. The heat in the eyes that met hers sent a delicious tingle of sheer anticipation skittering along her spine.

Good Lord! A man could lose his soul in the depths of those smoldering smoky-gray eyes!

A rush of hot desire swept through his body as Trace stared, with a sudden intense hunger, into the eyes of his daughter's beautiful champion.

And Kate Warren was beautiful . . . breathtakingly so! Not even bothering with the effort of concealment, Trace devoured Kate's face and form with a fiery gaze, from the riot of gleaming black waves that fell softly to her shoulders to the narrow waist he could discern just below the table edge. And every luscious inch revealed during his inspection made his lips ache with the need to explore the inviting satin skin hiding under her clothes.

Shaken by the intensity of the desire raging inside his mind and body, Trace frowned fiercely at the woman who'd created the blaze.

What was it about Kate that had sent his libido into overdrive, he railed irritably. So she was beautiful with all that silky black hair he ached to dig his fingers into. So she was alluring with enticing smoky-gray eyes surrounded by unbelievably long, thick lashes set in a patricianly boned face he longed to touch. So she was sexually exciting with that slender, delicately wrought body with gently sloping shoulders and high full breasts he burned to imprint with his own angular strength.

So what? He knew many women with equally beautiful faces, enticing eyes and exciting bodies. Why then, Trace brooded, did he feel he had to possess this one woman above all others?

Merely admitting the compelling need to himself made Trace uncomfortable. Damn it! The last thing on earth he wanted was to feel a *need* for anybody…especially for a woman. The disintegration of his marriage and subsequent desertion of his wife had cured him of the ills of *needing* another person.

At least Trace had convinced himself he'd been cured. In the four years since his wife had walked out of their home, Trace had experienced countless hours and situations during which his body had tormented him with the demand for physical release.

Imposing a will forged out of the fire of devastated pride into the tempered steel of determination, Trace had ruthlessly denied the demands of his body, submerging them in the celibacy that had begun with Kathy's birth.

Never again, he'd vowed, would he allow his emotions to dictate to his mind. And, until now, Trace had steadfastly adhered to that vow.

Actually trembling, as much from his thoughts as from the passion searing his body, Trace stared into her smoky-gray eyes and cursed the circumstances that had brought him into contact with Kate Warren.

Reminded of those circumstances, Trace relived the stark fear he'd felt with the realization that Kathy had disappeared from his side. Slanting a glance at the child, he allowed himself the luxury of a sigh of relief. This tiny, exquisite daughter of his was the one and only person in the world that Trace loved. If he lost Kathy... Trace angrily pushed the consideration from his mind, unwilling to even think of it.

In a toss-up between remembered panic and renewed passion, Trace opted for the latter, sliding a thoughtful glance over Kate's delectable body. A twitch of a smile lifted the corners of his lips as he heard again the outrage in her tone when she issued her challenging statement "Over my dead body!"

Strange, he mused, how very protective she was of a child she barely knew. But, then, Kathy *was* an exceptionally attractive, bright child, with the ability to wrap all kinds of people around her small finger.

Trace grimaced inwardly, qualifying, all kinds of people except her own mother.

Bitterness ran as hot as passion through Trace's veins. Damn all women and their lack of integrity!

Deciding at that moment to get away from Kate as soon as decently possible, Trace narrowed his eyes when she once again had the temerity to question his authority.

"If you don't want to take Kathy to see Santa Claus, Trace," she said hesitantly, "would you have any objections if *I* took her?"

Kate's tone told Trace clearly that she fully expected him to refuse. And, in truth, he fully expected to. When he answered, it was hard to judge who was more surprised.

"I'll take Kathy to sit on Santa's lap, Kate," Trace stunned himself with his reply. "But you may come with us if you like."

Two

How did I get into this?''

Slanting a glance at Trace out of the corner of her eye, Kate hid a smile behind a manufactured cough and made believe that she hadn't heard his complaint. When her expression was once again serene, she surveyed the cause of his impatience.

The line of children waiting to chat with Santa Claus was very long and very noisy. And, as they'd arrived on the scene mere moments ago, Kathy was near the end of that long, noisy line.

Flanking Kathy on either side, Kate and Trace moved in unison as the line advanced one child length.

"I hope you had no plans for this afternoon, Kate," Trace said mockingly over Kathy's head. "At the rate this line is moving, we're liable to be here until dinnertime."

"I'd planned to do a little shopping," Kate admitted calmly. "But I can do that another time."

"Can Kate have dinner with us, daddy?" Kathy gazed up at her father imploringly. "Please?"

Kate's cheeks grew warm at the flash of annoyance that sparked Trace's eyes. "I'm sure Kate has a previous engagement, Kath," he said coolly. "Am I correct, Kate?" Raising his head, he challenged her with a glittering green stare.

That Trace couldn't wait to be rid of her was more than obvious. And she was equally anxious to get away from him, Kate assured herself firmly. But a retaliatory, devilish imp took control of her tongue.

"Actually, I'm free this afternoon." Kate smiled gently, relishing the flush that crept up over Trace's rocklike jaw. Your move, Mr. Sinclair, she thought wryly, amused by the telltale narrowing of his eyes.

"You're free to spend the rest of the afternoon *and* the evening with us?" Trace baited the trap so casually that Kate walked into it without a care or thought.

"Yes, I am." She smiled tauntingly, confident that she wouldn't have to break her date with David. Her confidence ebbed as Trace began to smile.

"Good." The softness of his tone gave it the distinct sound of a purr. His smile twisted warningly.

A warning tingle trailed down Kate's spine.

"I detest shopping." Plunging a hand into his pocket, Trace produced a crumpled piece of paper. "Women are so much more efficient at this sort of thing." He held the slip of paper out to her. Frowning her confusion, Kate automatically accepted it. "That's my Christmas list." Now the smile that had lifted the corners of his lips was almost feral.

"You want me to do your Christmas shopping for you?" Kate asked blankly, once again moving in unison with him as the line advanced.

Trace nodded decisively. "In exchange for dinner—at the restaurant of your choice, of course."

Kate could have happily hit him; he was so smug! A cutting refusal sprang to her tongue. As if sensing what was coming, Kathy tugged on her skirt. Her lips tightly compressed, Kate glanced down at the child impatiently and immediately felt the fight drain out of her seeing the pleading expression in the round, innocent blue eyes.

"Please, Kate," Kathy begged, "it'll be fun."

Berating herself for a fool, Kate swallowed the refusal. Sighing in defeat, she managed a gentle smile for the child, mentally echoing Trace's earlier complaint of "How did I get into this?"

"I can't possibly do this all by myself." Ignoring the disgustingly complacent expression Trace was wearing, Kate stooped to Kathy's level. "You're going to have to help me with this." She waved the shopping list under the girl's button nose.

"Oh, yes!" Kathy enthused. "I know just what I want to get for everybody!"

And I hope every single purchase is enormously expensive, Kate thought sourly, raising her eyes to glare at Trace.

By the laughter dancing in the green gaze Kate encountered, it was quite evident that Trace was neither intimidated nor impressed. It also quickly became obvious that he read her intent with amazing accuracy.

"Planning to relieve me of a good deal of the weight in my wallet, are you?" he chided softly as Kate straightened.

"It will be a pleasure," Kate assured him sweetly.

If Kate had expected any response at all, it certainly wasn't the warm laughter that rippled from his throat, stabbing at a soft spot in the vicinity of her heart. Her breath catching in her throat, she glanced away quickly to hide her reaction. Fortunately at that moment the line moved again, and Kate was surprised to see Kathy walk confidently up to the man decked out in red velvet and white fur.

When had the line advanced, she wondered, observing Kathy as she conversed animatedly with Santa. Kate saw the man frown, then say something to the child. Whatever he told Kathy, it must have been what she wanted to hear for a glow sparkled in her eyes, and her face lit up brighter than the huge tree behind Santa's chair. Feeling ridiculous for her reaction, yet powerless to prevent it, Kate felt her throat grow tight and her eyes become misty at the sight of that happy little face. As she slipped off of his lap, Kathy waved gaily.

"What a shame life robs us of that innocence."

Startled by the bitterness in Trace's tone, Kate looked at him sharply, then wished she hadn't. His face appeared locked up, devoid of all expression, and frightening because of the absence of emotion.

This man has been very badly hurt. For some obscure reason Kate wasn't even tempted to examine, the realization of Trace's vulnerability touched that same soft spot in her heart.

"Trace?" All the compassion that Kate held within was contained in that solitary word. Trace rejected it with a cold stare.

"Save the maternal understanding for Kath," he snarled under his breath, stretching out a hand for his approaching daughter. "I don't need or want it."

"That was neat!"

Kathy's excitedly high-pitched voice covered the gasp that escaped Kate's lips at his unbending tone. Had she really felt sympathy for him for an instant? How positively naive of her. The man was as vulnerable as a spitting tiger.

"So, did you give the old boy your list of gimmes?" Trace teased Kathy in a chiding drawl.

"I only asked for one thing," Kathy replied seriously.

"My bank balance rejoices." Trace grinned. "Or is that one thing going to wipe me out financially?"

"I don't think so." Kathy frowned. "But, even if it does, it'll be worth it."

"To whom?" Trace retorted.

"To me, acourse." Amazingly, Kathy's grin mirrored her father's.

Her gaze flashing from one to the other, Kate could only stare, transfixed by the exchange. She had realized almost at once that the little girl was very bright, but now Kate had the odd sensation she was listening to a miniature adult. Except for the occasional mispronunciation, Kathy's vocabulary was as good if not better than some teenagers Kate knew, and the intelligence she displayed was that of a much older child.

"Don't let it throw you, Kate." The softly drawled advice indicated that Trace had correctly read her reaction again. "Kath has been around adults for every one of her four years. But your thinking is on target. She is an exceptionally bright child."

"Four!" Kate looked at Kathy closely. "I'd have thought she was less than three."

"Her mother is very small—" Trace grimaced "—and delicate."

"And she has blond hair, just like me," Kathy piped in.

"Ah . . . that's nice, honey." Feeling out of her depth, and going down for the third time, Kate gazed helplessly into the child's innocent blue eyes. There were currents here that she had no desire to get caught up in, yet she could already feel the tug of the undertow. And, if she was being completely honest with herself, Kate knew that the tug came as strongly from the rough-voiced man beside her as from the sweet-faced child she was gazing at.

"So, are we going to shop, or are we going to stand here blocking traffic?"

Jarred from her uncomfortable introspection by that same rough-voiced man, Kate pulled herself together and forced a smile for Kathy.

"We're going to shop," she declared, winking at the smiling child. "Right, baby?"

"Right." Kathy nodded her head vigorously.

"Kathy is not a baby." The flat statement was issued from a frowning Trace as they strolled away from the milling youngsters. "As far as that goes," he continued instructively, "Kathy was never called 'baby' even when she was an infant."

Kate felt her face grow warm for the second time in one hour. Embarrassed, she smiled ruefully at the girl.

"I'm sorry, Kathy!" Kate wasn't sure if she was sorry for having called the child "baby," or for the fact that no one ever had.

"I'm not!" Kathy yelped. "I like it!"

Unable to resist, Kate tossed a superior glance at Trace before laughing down at the child. "I'm glad, because *I* like it too."

The only response Trace made sounded suspiciously like a snort. Grinning unrepentantly at each other, Kate and Kathy clasped hands as they entered the first of many stores.

Some three and a half hours later, Trace called a halt to the frenzy of shopping Kate and Kathy had indulged in. Hands planted on his hips, he scowled at the two females.

"I've had it." His tone brooked no arguments. "I'm tired of the crowds. I'm tired of the pushing and shoving. I'm tired, period." His eyebrows drew together as if warning either child or woman not to voice a protest. "I'm hungry, and I need a drink." A long-suffering sigh moved his chest, "In fact, I need several drinks." He indicated the exit doors with an imperious wave of his hand. "Move out." Trace bit the order out tersely.

"Yes, sir!" Straightening her spine and squaring her shoulders, Kate pivoted on her heel and marched toward the doors, Kathy's muffled squeal of laughter following her.

Kate remembered her date with David as she marched past the bank of phones near the exit. Spinning around, she held up her palm like a traffic officer.

"I have to make a call," she explained, rooting in her bag for her wallet. Before her fingers made contact with her change purse, a hand was extended to her. "Thank you," she murmured, accepting the coin Trace offered.

"Kath and I will go get the car. We'll pick you up out front in a few minutes." Grasping Kathy's hand he strode off.

Strange man, Kate mused, studying his retreating back. After the way he'd spoken to her when they'd met, then manipulated her into doing his shopping for him, the very last thing Kate had expected from Trace Sinclair was sensitivity to her need for privacy while making her phone call.

Shrugging, Kate dropped the coin into the box and dialed David's number. Breaking her date with him wasn't going to be easy, especially with the pangs of guilt that were already stabbing her conscience. David didn't make it any easier.

"What!" he shouted after she'd explained she couldn't go out with him. Holding the receiver away from her ear, Kate winced as he continued. "What do you mean, you have to break our date? And where were you at lunchtime?" he went on angrily before she could answer. "I waited an hour and a half for you!"

"I *am* sorry, David," Kate said contritely. "But, you see, I ran into this little girl who was lost, and I simply couldn't leave her standing all alone and frightened."

"Well, why didn't you take her to the mall office? They'd have kept her until her parents showed up." Exasperation sharpened David's voice.

"I did take her to the office," Kate explained patiently. "But her—" She caught herself just in time. Biting back the word father, Kate began again. "But there was no one there for her and she was hungry, so I took her to lunch. I knew you'd understand," she finished quickly.

"Well, I'm sorry, but I don't," he snapped. "The kid was not your responsibility."

Suddenly Kate's guilty feeling gave way to anger. She hated the way he said the word kid! Odd, but she hadn't minded at all when Trace had called his daughter that.

"I couldn't leave her, David." Kate repeated grittily.

"Okay, you couldn't leave her," David sighed his frustration. "But what has that got to do with our date tonight?"

"I...ah..." Careful, Kate, she cautioned. "I've been invited to have dinner with her as a reward." Closing her eyes, Kate prayed for forgiveness.

"Oh, come on, Kate!" David was obviously at the end of his limited supply of patience. "Why didn't you simply accept a check and say a polite goodbye?"

"I couldn't accept money for staying with Kathy!" Kate protested on a gasp.

"Why not, for heaven's sake?" David demanded. "It's done all the time."

"Not by me," Kate shot back. "Kathy is an adorable little girl, David. I spent the entire afternoon with her, and I loved every minute of it." Well, perhaps not *every* minute, she qualified silently, remembering several sticky moments with Trace. "And I have agreed to have dinner with her," she continued adamantly. "I'm not sure why, but I gather that she's not from around here, so I'll probably never see her again."

"And you can see me anytime. Is that it?" David grumbled.

Not if you whine more than a four-year-old, Kate advised him mentally. A flashing image of a moment at lunch brought a smile to her eyes and a retort to her lips.

"That crushed act is very good, David," she paraphrased Trace. "Perhaps you ought to take it on the road."

There was a tense silence for a few moments, as if David was holding his breath. And, when he finally responded there was a breathless quality to his voice.

"Are you trying to tell me something?"

Not wanting to hurt him, Kate had agonized for weeks over how to break off their one-sided relationship. Now, thoroughly disgusted with his childish possessiveness, she drew a deep breath and ended it.

"Yes, David, I am. I've tried to tell you before that I don't want a deeper relationship with you."

"Kate, listen—"

"No, David, not this time," Kate cut him off ruthlessly. "You've applied too much pressure, much too
quickly. I'm not ready for that kind of involvement. I'm
sorry, David. Goodbye."

Kate replaced the receiver gently, then turned to hurry
through the exit to the car that waited opposite the doors.

The passenger door was hanging open, Kathy was ensconced in the back seat, and Trace was at the back of the
car, ready to stash the bulging shopping bag Kate was
carrying into the already crowded trunk. Walking up to
him, she silently held the bag out.

"Trouble with your call?" Trace searched her face as
he relieved her of the bag.

"No!" Aware of the abruptness of her response, Kate
managed an unconvincing smile. "No, of course not.
Why do you ask?"

Trace didn't return the smile, "Because you have the
same rebellious expression Kath gets when things don't
go her way." His glance lowered to her lips. "The same
pouty look to your mouth, too."

"I don't pout, Mr. . . . ." Kate forgot what she was saying. Her breath growing shallow, she watched a light flare
in his eyes as his gaze clung to her now trembling lips.

"Strange," he mused, slowly, reluctantly raising his
eyes to hers. "When Kath gets that look, I have to fight
the urge to reprimand her. On you, that pouty look pro-
duces an altogether different urge."

"What?" Kate could barely breathe, let alone speak.
The sensual expression that softened his rugged features
dried every bit of moisture in her mouth and throat.

"You know very well…what." Trace arched one brow
mockingly. His voice went very low and disturbingly sexy.
"And, at some point before this evening's over, I fully
intend to indulge that urge."

"I . . . I think not," Kate muttered, moving away from him.

"Think again," Trace advised adamantly, slamming the trunk lid for emphasis.

Buckled into the bucket seat beside Trace, Kate's imagination ran rampant with speculation. At the same time, her blood rushed through her veins and pounded loudly in her temples.

Trace meant that before the night was over he was going to kiss her. Well, that was nothing to get bent out of shape about—was it? Of course not, Kate assured herself. She'd been kissed before—many times. No big deal. But, suppose he'd meant something else? Biting her lip, Kate gave Trace a swift sideways glance. What else could he have meant? Who are you kidding, she chided herself. His expression, combined with the way his eyes had seemed to darken, had definitely been what is commonly referred to as that "bedroom" look. A streak of something she refused to identify as excitement flashed through Kate. Good grief! Was she crazy? She didn't even know the man!

"Where are we going to eat, daddy?"

Kate sighed with relief as Kathy's question snapped the tension singing along her nerves. Waiting for his reply, she turned in her seat to look at Trace and immediately wished she hadn't.

Reflecting her thoughts, Trace's lips curved sensuously. The gaze he quickly ran over her ignited flash fires all over her body. "It's up to Kate," he finally answered. "I told her she could choose the restaurant."

"Kate?" Kathy nudged.

Shifting around as far as she could within the confines of the seat belt, Kate smiled at Kathy. "It really doesn't matter to me, honey. Is there somewhere special that you'd like to go?"

"No." Kathy shook her head. "We don't know too many places around here," she confided, reinforcing Kate's hunch that they were not local residents. "We've only been to one fancy restaurant and a pizza place."

Kate caught the wistful note in Kathy's voice as she mentioned the latter establishment. She also caught the smile that eased Trace's lips as he shot Kathy a warning glance in the rearview mirror. The warning said: this is Kate's choice.

"Pizza is fine with me," Kate laughed, amazed at the level of silent communication between father and daughter.

"Where are you two from?" Kate had held her curiosity at bay until they were seated in a booth at the restaurant.

"Texas," Kathy said proudly.

"Outside San Antonio," Trace supplemented.

"I thought I detected a drawl." Kate smiled at Kathy. "I just couldn't decide whether it was of the southern or western variety." Turning to Trace, she probed, "You're a rancher?"

His soft laughter did strange and wonderful things to her equilibrium. "Why do all easterners imagine that all Texans are ranchers?" Trace grinned. "Even Texans need medical help on occasion."

"You're a doctor?" Kate blurted out artlessly.

"Blows your mind, does it?"

Avoiding his mocking eyes, Kate studied the flickering candle on the table. A doctor! Kate hadn't the vaguest idea why it should, but the information *did* blow her mind! Trace Sinclair simply looked too earthy to be a physician.

"Daddy's a very good doctor, Kate." Kathy's aggrieved tone snagged Kate's attention.

"I'm sure he is, honey," she soothed before returning her gaze to Trace. "Do you specialize?"

"I'm a neurosurgeon, Kate." Observing her with eyes gleaming in amusement, Trace waited for a reaction to his coolly intoned statement. He didn't have to wait long.

"Oh!" Kate's mouth and eyes opened simultaneously. His roar of laughter brought her to her senses. "I'm sorry." Kate's smile was sheepish. "I didn't mean to be rude. It's just that—" she shrugged helplessly "—you don't look like a doctor, let alone a neurosurgeon!"

"Really?" Trace frowned mockingly. "What exactly does a neurosurgeon look like?"

"I...I don't know." Kate searched her mind for a way out of her dilemma. Trace's movement as he raised his beer mug to his lips caught her attention. "You do have the hands of a surgeon."

Trace was off again, his rich, rumbling laughter drawing reciprocal smiles from Kathy and the other patrons in the restaurant. "Oh, Kate!" Pausing to catch his breath, Trace shook his head. "You're a gem. I can't remember the last time I laughed like that." His gleaming eyes danced with amusement as he watched the flush tinge her cheeks dark pink. "How would you like to come back to Texas with me?" Kate's gasp went unheard as he continued, "You'd be just the person to come home to after long, grueling hours in the operating room."

She was being teased and she knew it, yet she had to hold back on the automatic "yes" that sprang to her lips. Stunned by her uncharacteristic, spontaneous response to Trace *and* his ridiculous offer, she stared at him through eyes that betrayed her desire. Distracted with trying to figure out her own conflicting emotions, Kate was blind to the light of hope flaring in his eyes.

For the length of a heartbeat, their entire attention centered on each other's eyes. Trace and Kate were beyond noticing another pair of eyes, sparkling blue, set in a small intense face.

"Come to Texas, Kate." Trace broke the visual thread binding her to him.

Blinking herself back to reality, Kate glanced around the room, as if wondering where she was and how she'd gotten there. Never before had she experienced the sensation of being lost inside a man's compelling gaze, and this particular man's eyes held the allure of a cool, green glade on a hot summer day.

"Oh, yes, please, Kate! Come with us to Texas!" The high-pitched excitement in Kathy's young voice tugged at Kate's heartstrings.

"But that's impossible, baby!" The light laugh Kate attempted didn't quite come off.

"Why?" Kathy's rosebud lips curved down in disappointment.

"Honey, you must understand. I have a job here, responsibilities, a family! I can't simply uproot myself. I . . ." Kate's voice trailed away and she shrugged. Who was she hoping to convince, she taunted herself. Kathy and Trace Sinclair, or Kate Warren?

"What do you do, Kate?" Trace asked in a tone devoid of inflection.

"Do?" Kate frowned her confusion revealingly.

Not unaware of his effect on women, Trace smiled. "You said you have a job. What sort of job?"

"Oh!" Kate shook her head at her own incredulous density—what *was* wrong with her, anyway? "I'm an insurance rater," she finally managed.

"Ah, yes," Trace drawled. "I've dealt with a few insurance raters."

Kate winced. She didn't need a code book to decipher his sardonic tone. She was in a position to know the enormity of the current malpractice insurance rates.

"I'm...I'm sorry." Kate sighed. How many times had she apologized since meeting him? *That* was another new experience!

"What for?" The gentle smile that curved his lips shook Kate to the very center of her being. "I didn't think you were personally responsible for the rates."

"What are you talking about?" Kathy demanded, obviously put out at being excluded from the conversation.

"Nothing very interesting, kid." Reaching out, Trace ruffled her blond curls. "Where's our dinner?" He frowned ferociously, coaxing a giggle from Kathy. "I wouldn't want my best girl to fade away to a shadow!"

Suddenly feeling left out, Kate listened to the teasing banter exchanged by Trace and Kathy until the arrival of their meal ended it.

All through dinner, Kate mulled over her reaction to both the situation and the two people who'd precipitated it.

Along with the pungent aroma of spicy tomato sauce and garlic bread, her senses swam with the whirlpool of events she'd been caught up in since lunchtime.

Carefully twirling spaghetti onto a fork, Kate readily acknowledged that she'd completely lost her heart to the blue-eyed, blond child happily digging into a slice of pizza across the table from her. As to the man next to her, Kate was ambivalent—a state which by itself was unsettling.

Observing Trace surreptitiously while sipping her glass of wine, Kate attempted to sort out her own conflicting emotions.

Most definitely there were more facets to his character than were apparent at their first meeting. Though certainly strong-willed and more than a little arrogant, Trace had revealed glimpses of a capacity for deep understanding and sensitivity as well. While owning his fair share of self-confidence, he'd shown moments of uncertainty and doubt. As if he could not bear the sight of her, he had growled at her one minute, only to confound her the next by teasing her as gently as he did his obviously adored daughter.

How was a woman supposed to be anything *but* of two minds with such a complex man, Kate wondered, sighing softly.

"Is there something wrong with your food?" Trace asked, hearing her sigh and misinterpreting it.

"Not at all," Kate assured him, smiling to emphasize her words. "There is just too much of it!" She improvised the excuse. "And, wanting to set an example for our baby, I've been trying to clean my plate."

"Our baby?" Until Trace murmured the question for her ears alone, Kate wasn't even aware of her odd phrasing. Having it pointed out to her, even in a whisper, made her grow hot with embarrassment all over again.

"Our? Did I say our? I didn't mean to say our! Really, I meant *your* baby!" Kate was chattering, but she simply could not stop the flow of words. The slow smile lifting the edges of Trace's lips didn't help much either.

Casually leaning back in his chair, Trace slid an all-encompassing glance over Kate, then Kathy, then Kate again. As if he'd come to an important decision, he nodded once.

"Kathy's beautiful," he said in that same low tone. "But, we'd make an equally beautiful child together."

Kate gave fervent thanks that she was sitting down because if she hadn't been, she'd have collapsed from the shock of his softly voiced assertion. The suggestion set loose a series of disturbingly exciting visions...every one of them erotic!

Swallowing to restore moisture to her suddenly parched throat, Kate choked, "As chances are slim to none of that ever happening, we'll never know—will we?"

"Won't we?" Trace murmured before turning his attention to Kathy, who'd stopped eating to stare at them curiously. "Beginning to stall, Kath?" he asked blandly.

"Are you and Kate fighting in whispers?" Kathy demanded.

"Fighting? Kate and I?" Trace grinned. "Ridiculous!"

"Are you sure?" Unconvinced, Kathy's little face puckered into a frown.

His eyes bright with a devilish glow, Trace swung his gaze to Kate. "Are we fighting, Kate?" His tone was laced with contrived confusion.

The onus was now on her and Kate squirmed in her chair. The beast, she thought, exerting all her willpower to control the smile tugging at her lips. Trace Sinclair deserved a thorough shaking up! Allowing the smile free rein, she reached across the table to grasp Kathy's hand.

"Yes, we are fighting." Her smile flashed momentarily at Trace, then returned to the frowning child. "But, don't let it upset you, baby. It was only a word fight." She squeezed Kathy's hand gently to let her know she was only teasing. "You see, now that I know the rules of this word game, I can beat your father at it with one lip tied down." As she finished, Kate winked at Kathy conspiratorially.

"She thinks!" Trace retorted, chuckling softly.

"Boy! This is fun!" Slipping her fingers from Kate's hand, Kathy clapped her palms together gleefully. "I really, really love you guys!"

Three

___

"Where have you been?"

Trace stiffened at the imperious demand in the voice that flung the question at him. His arms tightened reflexively around the sleeping child in his arms—his child, the single good out of a thoroughly bad marriage.

"I asked you a question!" Annette's voice rose impatiently.

"I heard you." Trace didn't raise his voice from a murmur, only his eyebrows went up—mockingly. "Do you think you could save the third degree until after our daughter is settled?" A shiver skipped the length of his spine as inside his head a soft voice echoed—wanting to set an example for our baby, I've been trying to clean my plate.

Turning abruptly, Trace mounted the open stairs in the ultramodern town house of his former in-laws. Annette's mother met him in the wide hallway.

"Let me help you with her, Trace." A gentle smile curved the older woman's lips as she preceded him into the room kept exclusively for Kathy.

Working swiftly and silently, they got Kathy out of her clothes and into her nightie without waking her. Trace brushed his lips over her soft pink cheek as he drew the covers up to her tiny chin, then followed her grandmother out of the room.

"Did you have a nice day?" Ruth asked softly as Trace quietly closed the door. "Did Kathy talk to Santa Claus?"

"Yes." Trace smiled at his daughter's grandmother, wondering, for perhaps the thousandth time, how she'd managed to produce a child so unlike herself. "We had a very nice day." A vision of a young, dark-haired beauty tantilized his memory and body. "And Kath did talk to Santa." A frown darkened his brow. "I'm sorry if I inconvenienced you by not having Kath back for dinner, Ruth." He shrugged. "She wanted pizza."

"I wasn't inconvenienced, Trace!" Ruth protested softly. "Regardless of what Annette might say to the contrary." A spasm of pain rippled across her still lovely face. "She's waiting for you. You'd better go down." Her narrow shoulders moved with the sigh of regret that lifted her chest. "I'm sorry, Trace." As she moved away from him towards her own bedroom, she whispered, "Sorry for everything."

His green eyes stormy with emotion, Trace watched as Ruth slipped inside her room before turning to the stairs and the confrontation waiting for him below.

Annette was standing in the center of the narrow living room, one tiny, slender foot tapping an impatient tune on the honey-colored hardwood floor.

His features locked into an expressionless mask, Trace sauntered into the room. Shrugging out of his jacket and tossing it onto a delicately wrought, satin-covered chair in gold and green stripes, he arched one eyebrow at her quizzically.

"Something bothering you, Annette?" Trace contained a smile of satisfaction at the frown his coolly unconcerned tone elicited from his former wife.

"Mother expected you to have Kathy back in time for dinner!" Annette's perfectly fashioned lips twisted over her daughter's name—a name she had resisted from the beginning and still detested. "She was very upset."

All too aware of how she felt, had *always* felt about bestowing his mother's name on their child, Trace narrowed his eyes warningly. "You're a liar," he said brutally. "I spoke to Ruth upstairs and she assured me she was not in the least upset." Moving into the room, he dropped lithely into a padded club chair. "You're up to something," he said disinterestedly. "Let's get it over with, Annette."

It was going to be bad, Trace knew it. His muscles tightened, he watched her closely, waiting for the verbal blow to fall. At that instant, Trace could have sworn he could feel the tension shimmering in her petite body.

"I'm seeing my attorney Monday, Trace." Annette's slim heels clicked as she moved to stand militantly in front of him.

"Good for you, or him, or whoever." Not by the slightest tremor did his tone betray the sudden clenching sensation Trace felt in his gut. "But what does that have to do with me?"

"You're so superior!" Annette hissed, her blue eyes flashing with hate. "Well, we'll see how damned superior you feel after you've lost custody of your precious child!''

Staring at the ugliness twisting her classically beautiful face, Trace felt suddenly sick to his stomach and cold to his very soul.

"You signed the papers nearly four years ago, Annette. You have never been a mother to Kathy." Trace leaned back into the chair with a deceptive ease; he'd die before showing weakness to this woman, or any other, ever again. "You can't take her from me."

Annette's body shook with impotent fury at the cool note of confidence in his tone. "We'll see about that!" she snapped, pivoting on her heel to walk jerkily away from him. When she spun to face him again her features were composed, her eyes gleaming maliciously.

"You're all threat, Annette; you always have been." Trace lifted his lips in a pitying smile. "Hot air and no ammunition," he concluded softly.

"Oh, really?" Her laughter was not a pleasant sound in the quiet room. "How's this for ammunition? Round one: you are a bachelor. Round two: your work necessitates your being away from home quite frequently. Round three: your home is located in an isolated area. Round four, and probably the most lethal of all: Kathy's only companion while you're away is an aging Mexican woman with a limited command of the English language." She smiled smugly. "I happen to think that's quite effective ammunition."

"Against the fact that you voluntarily gave up custody to Kathy?" Trace smiled wryly. "And the added fact that you've failed to take advantage of your visitation rights and have not even been here on several occasions when I've brought her east?" He shook his head. "I'd say your ammunition is about as effective as a pea-shooter against a mountain lion."

"We'll see, won't we?" Annette was now shaking with anger. "We'll see what *effect* my suit has after my witnesses, very well known and respected Philadelphians, have testified to my distraught, anguished state." Annette strolled arrogantly to him, sneering down at his sprawled form. "And after I testify how confused, rejected and unhappy I was feeling after Kathy's birth."

A tightness invading his chest, Trace slowly straightened in the chair. "All right, Annette, what do you want?" Even though he refused to let it show, asking the question cost him dearly in pride.

"Want?" Annette laughed in his face. "I'll tell you what I want. I want to make you suffer."

"Why, for God's sake?" Trace sprang to his feet, forcing Annette to retreat. "You accomplished that while we were married! It's been four damned years! You don't want Kathy, you never did. You know it as well as I. So why are you doing this? Why claim you want her now?"

As if she knew what his reaction would be, Annette backed farther away from him. "Because I know you *do* want her. And I know what it will do to you to lose her."

"But why should you care?" Frustration thickened his voice.

"Because I could never reach you, never touch you!" she shouted. "You were so damned self-contained inside your hotshot surgeon image. You gave me nothing!"

"Nothing?" Trace was so angry he had to whisper to keep from exploding. "Nothing? I gave you my love, my trust and my honor. What the hell else did you want?"

"My rightful place in society as the wife of San Antonio's leading neurosurgeon, that's what I wanted!" Annette was now trembling with fury. "*Your* love, *your* trust, *your* honor—'' she spat the words at him ''—I didn't want any of those any more than I wanted *you* or *your* brat!''

''You bitch!'' Trace actually took a step toward her before he caught himself up short. ''You position-hungry bitch!''

''Why don't you strike me?'' Annette's eyes glittered with anticipation. ''I wish you would. It would give me more evidence of exactly how unfit you are to have custody of a child!''

''I wouldn't waste the effort.'' Swinging away, Trace strode to the doorway where he paused to level a narrow-eyed glare at her. ''You are not getting Kathy away from me, lawsuit or not.''

Annette suddenly had a wild, frantic look. ''I will get her! I must! Randall wants her!'' As her own screamed words hit her, she clamped one fragile-looking hand over her mouth.

''Randall?'' Trace repeated the name softly. ''Randall who?'' he began walking slowly toward her.

''Get out of here!'' Annette shook her head wildly. ''Get out of here before I call the police and have you thrown out!''

''Call them!'' With a wave of one hand, Trace indicated the gold filigree French-style phone on the end table. ''But, I give you my word you'll answer me before they can get here. Now, who the hell is this Randall?'' Walking to within an inch of her, he glared directly into her frightened eyes. ''And what does he want with *my* daughter?''

''I—I—''

His control breaking, Trace grasped her by the arms and shook her. ''Answer me, damn you!''

"I'm going to marry him!" Annette blurted out jerkily.

"He has my condolences," Trace snarled. "What does that have to do with Kath?"

"Ran...Randall cannot father a child. He needs an heir." Annette cringed away from the expression on Trace's face.

"He can't have mine." Trace said each word distinctly. Dropping his hands as if touching her sickened him, Trace wheeled away from her. His hand was on the doorknob when Annette's voice stopped him.

"Randall can give me everything I ever wanted!" Her tone was strident. "He's very wealthy and prominent, and has an established place in Philadelphia society." Her eyes glittered with fervor. "I refuse to let you interfere with my plans. By the time my suit goes before a judge I will be Randall's wife." Her lip curled. "Which one of us do you think the judge will award Kathy to?"

Not bothering to reply, Trace pulled the door open. Annette's laughter followed him to the car.

His mind seething with impotent rage, Trace slammed the rental car into gear and tore away from the town house. Emotions churning, he handled the car recklessly on the narrow streets in the quaint restored section. Too stirred up to go back to the hotel he was staying in, he drove aimlessly for several minutes, searching his mind desperately for a way to thwart Annette.

Damn her! Cursing his former wife silently, Trace eyed a bar on the corner when he was forced to stop for a red light. He wanted a drink. No, what he really wanted was to hit something or someone! But he'd settle for a drink. As the light flicked to green he sent his gaze skimming the street for a vacant parking space and cursed again when he found none.

Positive that if he returned to his hotel room he'd pace the floor for the rest of the night, he slowed the car to a crawl, looking for a watering hole and human companionship.

Kate!

Even as her name popped into his mind Trace had a vision of her as she'd appeared earlier that day, her eyes smoky and her body taut with anger as she championed Kathy.

Without pausing to consider, Trace turned the car in the direction that would take him to the suburban community where he'd dropped Kate at her apartment building less than two hours before.

Dressed for bed in a very sheer, slip-style nightgown and a robe that had seen better days, Kate sat staring sightlessly at the TV screen while replaying the events of the preceding ten hours in her mind.

Well, one certainly couldn't say her Saturday had been dull, she thought wryly, stretching her arms over her head to flex tired muscles. There wasn't one thing dull about either one of the two people she'd spent the majority of her day with. And the smallest of the pair was an absolute doll!

A soft smile curving her lips, Kate drew her feet up under her robe and rested her head against the back of the sofa. Of all the children she'd ever met, Kate decided she liked Kathy the best. She'd never run across a child who was quite so impish and charming at the same time.

A low chuckle whispered through Kate's lips as she recalled Kathy's methods of soft-soaping her father—or attempting to!

Kathy's father—Kate's chuckled trailed away to a sigh—now there was a different story altogether. Trace Sinclair. What was one to make of a Trace Sinclair?

Impressions, some shadowy and unclear, others sharply defined, drifted in and out of her mind. Hard—gentle, impatient—forebearing, self-assured—hesitant. Electric! Exciting! Sexy!

Kate shivered. Trace was very much a man, and she was not immune to his masculine attraction. Strange, she had been seeing David for over six months, yet never in all that time had she felt the sensual fascination she'd experienced after only a few minutes in Trace's company.

Kate's bare toes curled at the memory of the alluring spell he cast. And he had more or less promised to kiss her before the evening was over—but he had not kept his promise.

After dinner, Trace had driven her directly home, bidding her a polite "good night" while she'd hugged and kissed Kathy. Now, over two hours later, Kate was amazed at the depth of disappointment she was still feeling because of his failure to keep his promise.

"Silly girl!"

Chiding herself, Kate slid off the sofa to flip through the TV channels in search of a good, late-night movie. What a way to spend a Saturday night, she thought wistfully, frowning at the flickering screen. Thanksgiving Day weekend and I'm faced with watching Cary Cooper ride off into the sunset!

Feeling restless and moody, and not even certain why, Kate turned the television off just as the doorbell rang.

David! Oh, no! Kate glanced at the digital clock on the TV, then at the door as the chime sounded for a second time. She didn't want to see David tonight; she didn't want to talk to him. As if the visitor was growing impatient, the ring peeled again, shrill, imperative. Sighing softly, she crossed the small room to the door, leaning forward to peek through the tiny hole.

The taut figure standing in the hallway was definitely not David Kendall. His shoulders hunched inside the suede jacket, his hands jammed into the deep pockets, Trace looked cold, impatient and more than a little angry.

Her breath suddenly erratic, Kate fumbled with the night chain and deadlock. Conscious of her appearance, she opened the door a few inches and peered around the edge of it.

"Trace, what are you..."

"May I come in, Kate?" Trace cut her off tersely.

"Trace, I'm not dressed!" Kate felt her cheeks flush. "I mean, I'm dressed for bed."

"Sounds good to me," he muttered. Slipping a hand from his pocket, he pushed gently against the door. "I came to talk, Kate, not to take you bar-hopping."

As he applied pressure to the door, Kate had little option but to let him in. Drawing her robe around her tightly, she retreated back to the sofa as Trace quietly closed and locked the door. The sound of the chain rattling into place caused a tingle along the length of her spine.

"Ah..." Kate had to pause to clear her throat. "What did you want to talk about?" she finally managed, watching him warily as he took off his jacket.

"The cold weather here in the east, the high cost of nearly everything—" Trace smiled slowly "—the fact that we both realize we want each other."

Kate's heartbeat seemed to come to a shuddering halt while a lump grew in her throat, making breathing difficult—if not completely impossible. Her mouth open in shock, she could do no more than stare at him for long seconds. During those seconds Trace moved to stand in front of her, his gaze steady on hers.

"I...ah...mmm...Trace, I, really...I..."

"Don't panic, Kate." Shaking his head at her feeble attempt at speech, he reached out to glide the tips of his fingers across her now flaming cheek. His smile grew decidedly sensuous at her shivery response. "I'm not going to force any issues here," he murmured.

Kate's breathing resumed as he removed his fingers and settled himself on the cushion beside her. Nervously smoothing her palm over the worn material of her robe, she studied his profile out of the corner of her eye.

"Well?"

"What?" Kate had become so engrossed in the unrelenting male beauty of his features that the sound of his voice startled her.

"I merely said 'well?'" Though his face remained impassive, his eyes gleamed with amusement. "You've practically dissected me with your eyes." Trace allowed his amusement to lift his lips in a smile. "Have you made a diagnosis?"

Embarrassed, Kate sniffed disdainfully. "I'm positive you're fully aware of how attractive you are." With an ease she was far from feeling, she turned to face him.

"Yes, I'm aware." His tone conveyed self-knowledge, not conceit. "The question is," Trace arched one brow rakishly. "Am I attractive to *you*?" Before she could begin to form an answer, he added, "As attractive as you are to me?"

Flustered by his directness, Kate lowered her eyes. "Trace, we've only just met!" she protested softly.

"Which means absolutely nothing, and you know it."
Though his tone was low, it held firm conviction. "There
is that indefinable 'something' flowing between us. It's
been there from the first moment our eyes met." Leaning toward her, he brushed his parted lips very lightly
over her cheek. Kate couldn't suppress the gasp of pleasure that burst from her lips. "You see what I mean?"
Her gasp became a moan when he teased the corner of
her mouth with the tip of his tongue. "Ah, Kate," he
whispered enticingly, "I want to kiss you so badly my
entire body aches."

Her breath coming in shallow little spurts, Kate closed
her eyes. What should she do? What could she do? He
was too close. The musky male scent of him aroused
everything female in Kate. Her senses greedily drank in
the essence of him as she moved the fraction of an inch
necessary to slide her lips under his.

In the quiet room, Kate heard his breath hiss as he
drew it in sharply. For an instant his lips lay against hers
in breathless stillness. Then, with a sweet tenderness, his
mouth moved, slowly molding her lips to his. Surprisingly, there was no demand in the kiss, no urgency.
Gently, as if he was holding a fragile flower, he explored
the taste and texture of her lips.

Sighing softly, Kate leaned into the kiss, her body beginning to tremble as her breasts touched the hard plain
of his chest. She heard him groan, then the wonder of his
mouth was withdrawn.

"You're very new at this—aren't you?" His warm
breath caressed her lips. Kate shivered. "Have you ever
been with a man, Kate?"

"No." Raising strangely heavy eyelids, Kate stared up
at Trace in bemusement. "At least not in the way I think
you mean."

"I mean exactly what you think I mean." The tiny lines radiating from the corners of his eyes deepened, and Kate knew he was smiling at her. "You've never made love before?"

Kate shook her head mutely.

Trace expelled his breath very slowly. "I want to love you, Kate. You know that, don't you?" He drew his head back just far enough to gaze down at her. His eyes darkened as he watched her moisten her dry lips with her tongue.

"Trace, I . . ."

"You're afraid?" he murmured gently.

"Yes." Kate closed her eyes.

"Yet I can feel how you respond to me." One hand moved to capture her breast, fingers testing the hard readiness of the nipple. "Why are afraid?"

"When I opened the door for you, you looked so angry and—" she shrugged "—and so frustrated." Her lip caught between her teeth, Kate opened her eyes to stare up at him in mute appeal.

With a heaving sigh, Trace moved away from her to rest his head on the back of the sofa. "I was." Rolling his head to gaze at her, he smiled derisively. "Very angry and very frustrated," he admitted with dry self-mockery.

"Why?" Kate asked bluntly. "Were you angry at me?"

"No," Trace laughed softly. "But, I suppose I must have thought you might be the cure for both the emotional upsets."

Of course, Kate was consumed with curiosity. Wanting to know, yet hesitant to ask, she gazed at him indecisively. Trace gazed back, a tiny smile curving his lips— lips that Kate ached to feel pressed to hers again. Certain he could read the longing in her eyes, she glanced down at her hands.

"What upset you, Trace?" Surprised at her own temerity, Kate kept her eyes averted. She could feel Trace stiffen and was on the verge of recinding her question when he sighed deeply.

"I had an argument with Annette," he said tersely.

Annette? Kate frowned—as much from the sudden dart of jealousy she felt as the confusion the name caused. Who was Annette? Lifting her head, she managed a cool stare.

"Annette?" Kate felt rather proud of her detached tone.

"Kathy's mother." Trace smiled grimly. "My ex-wife. She's been living with her parents since the divorce." His smile faded. "She was waiting for me when I took Kath back."

"And the argument made you angry," Kate concluded softly.

"No, the argument made me furious." Trace bit off a curse with a sharp shake of his head. "She's going to try to take Kath away from me." His lips twisted in a way that sent a shaft of fear through Kate. At the same time his eyes grew dark with pain so intense, Kate's heart ached for him.

"Oh, Trace, no!" Remembering Kathy's own words about her mother, Kate was powerless against the protest that rushed from her lips. "Kathy is so obviously happy with you!"

The flicker of understanding that moved across his face registered her concern. "I said she was going to *try*, Kate." His voice lowered dangerously. "I have no intention of letting her win . . . and I don't give a damn what I have to do to stop her."

At that moment, violence, terrifying in its intensity, seemed to flow from him, crackling the very air around him. Thankful she was not the one responsible for all that enmity, Kate shrank back into the corner of the sofa, actually feeling sympathy for his former wife. Her movement did not go undetected.

"I'm sorry, Kate." Raising his hand, Trace brushed the back of his fingers over her cheek. "I didn't really come here to dump my problems on you."

His hand still stroking her face, Trace shifted to lean over her. His lips hovered tantalizingly close to hers. Caught off guard by the lightning change in him, Kate gazed uncertainly into his eyes.

"In all honesty," he whispered, "I came here for very different reasons." Now the force field crackling around him was sensuous in origin and twice as potent. Turning his hand, he cradled her face in his palm. "I've been wanting to make love to you since lunchtime."

"But we only met at lunchtime!" Kate croaked, shuddering as his tongue moistened her dry lips.

"I know." His gliding tongue slid between her lips to trace the ridge of her teeth. "Strange, it seems I've been wanting you forever."

How she'd have responded to his observation, Kate was never to know, for with the last word, Trace crushed her mouth with his. This time there wasn't a hint of tenderness in his kiss. His lips were hard and urgent, demanding full participation from hers.

Thrilling to the sensations coursing through her body, Kate curled her arms around his tensely corded neck and kissed him back hungrily. Within seconds she was lost to reason and all sense of self-preservation.

Blindly, eagerly following his murmured urgings, Kate stretched out fully on the sofa, clinging to him as he moved to lay beside her. His chest crushed her breasts between them as his mouth sought hers. Drawing her lower lip between his own, Trace taught Kate things she'd never even imagined about kissing.

Kate was so warm, so very warm, yet shivering from the riot of sensations, which awoke desires that she'd thought existed only in imagination. Her breathing reduced to shallow little gasps, she speared her fingers through the silken strands of his hair and pressed her fingertips against him, urging him closer.

Drowning in a molten sea of hot pleasure, Kate was barely aware of Trace opening her robe. When his long hand enveloped her breast she moaned softly and arched her back. Accepting her silent invitation, Trace swiftly slid the robe from her. His gaze burning into her skin, he followed the motion as his hand slowly glided the narrow shoulder strap of her gown off her shoulder and down her arm, baring one full, taut breast.

"You're so very beautiful." Raising his eyes, Trace observed every nuance of expression on her face as his long fingers stroked her silken skin. "Haven't you ever been caressed like this before?" he murmured hoarsely.

Her head thrown back, lips parted, Kate could barely breathe, let alone speak. Moaning softly deep in her throat, she shook her head. Her silent denial was the truth. Never had she allowed a man to touch her like this.

"Has a man ever kissed you here?" Trace touched the aching tip with his finger.

Trembling in reaction, Kate again shook her head. Her breath escaping as mere puffs, she watched as Trace, a satisfied smile curving his mouth, lowered his head to her breast. An exquisite pain uncurled in her body when his lips closed over her aroused nipple.

"Oh!...oh, God, Trace!" The cry burst from Kate's tight throat at the flicking touches of his tongue. She heard herself whimper when he gently began suckling.

Kate was no longer warm; she was burning. A rush of feelings, wild, crazy, swept her away. Murmuring little, incoherent sounds in her throat, she arched into his hungry mouth, her body undulating sensuously against him. A soft protest whispered through her lips when he withdrew from her breast only to become a sigh of delight when Trace fastened his mouth to hers.

Passion building, Trace coaxed her lips apart, then plunged his tongue deeply into the honeyed sweetness of her mouth. With a low, growllike rumble, he plundered her mouth in an evocative rhythm.

Restless with the tension coiling in her body, Kate skimmed her hands down his back, kneading his taut muscles with the tips of her fingers, scoring his shirt with her nails.

"Yes," he urged raggedly, sliding his lips from her mouth to the curve of her neck. "Touch me, Kate. Love me with your hands." Drawing back, Trace practically tore the shirt from his body. "Please, touch me, Kate!" His tongue etched erotic designs on the sensitive skin at the curve of her neck. His hair-roughened chest brushed tantalizingly over the tips of her breasts.

Kate needed no further urging. Loving the feel of his heated skin against her palms, she stroked and caressed his back and chest. Her own excitement went spiraling out of control at his sharply indrawn breath when her nails scraped his flat male nipples.

Sweet, hot desire flowed through her. Kate parted her legs when his hand stroked the quivering flesh of her inner thigh, and she arched into his touch as his palm cupped the heart of her desire.

"Kate. Kate. Kate." A whisper. Her name. Nothing more. Yet, inside her head, the need contained within those whispered words became a shouted plea.

Reacting instinctively, Kate moved to accommodate him as Trace slid his body between her thighs. Even through his clothes the extent of his arousal was evident. When Trace thrust his hips into hers, Kate gasped with surprise and shock.

Four

What was she doing? The intrusive thought pierced the fog of passion clouding Kate's mind and cooled the heated response of her restless body.

She did not know this man! Why was she reacting to him with such intensity? Did she really want to offer him the gift of herself? Kate shivered from the force of her doubts.

The shiver turned into a shudder of exquisitely renewed pleasure as Trace again sought her breasts.

Helplessly obeying the urges controlling her body, Kate moved sensuously beneath him. She wanted Trace badly, ached for the fulfillment he could give her, and even as her mind argued for a cautious withdrawal, she could not deny the craving she felt for him.

Sensing her conflict, Trace lifted his head to gaze at her soberly.

"What is it, Kate?" The strain in his voice was a barometer, indicating the control he was exerting over his own clamoring body. "You're only with me halfway now. What's going on inside your head?"

Kate moved her head distractedly on the sofa cushion. "I . . . Trace, I . . . don't know but, I'm . . ."

"Scared?" Trace finished for her, his lips curving in a surprisingly understanding smile.

"Yes." Embarrassed by the intensity of her unbridled behavior, Kate lowered her lashes to conceal the gleam of tears in her eyes.

"There's no reason to be, you know." Sighing, Trace moved to lay beside her, still touching, but less intimately.

Kate opened her eyes in time to see Trace close his. Her lip caught between her teeth, she watched as his chest heaved in deep, controlled breaths.

"God, I want you, Kate!" he muttered hoarsely, opening his eyes to stare into hers. "I want you so very much." His lips twisted derisively. "But not so much that I'd take you like this." His smile gentled as he tapped her temple with his forefinger. "I want you willing and eager for me . . . in your mind as well as your body."

Heat suffused Kate's face as Trace carefully slid her nightgown into place. Feeling utterly stupid, she stammered into an apology. "Oh, Trace, I—I'm sorry!" Raising her hand she stroked his beard-stubbled cheek. "I want you too. I really do! But . . ." Her voice trailed away to nothingness.

"But you're not quite ready," Trace again completed her faltering explanation. "I know." Lifting his hand he captured hers, holding it against his face. "You're very young, my lovely Kate. So very young," he murmured sadly.

"I'll be twenty-four on Christmas Day!" Kate protested. "That's not *very* young!"

"In comparison to my thirty-five it is." Settling more comfortably beside her, he propped his head on his hand and gazed down at her, a teasing smile playing at the corners of his mouth. "I've got eleven years and eons of experience on you, kid."

"But I'm a fast learner!" Kate blurted rashly. "Don't give up on me, Trace!"

"Oh, Kate, you're priceless!" His laughter began as a low rumble in his chest, then exploded into a roar, warming Kate as it swirled around her. "Come to Texas with me, Kate." Trace's half-joking plea tugged at her heart.

"You know that's impossible, Trace," she chided softly.

"Nothing's impossible, innocent one." His smile crooked, Trace rubbed his nose against hers. "If you won't come to Texas, come to breakfast with me tomorrow morning, and stay for dinner." His teeth nipped playfully on her lower lip. "And maybe even longer," he whispered enticingly.

"I did have a previous engagement." Kate was suddenly finding it difficult to breathe again. Holding her breath she endured the mind-scattering sensation of his tongue stroking the spot he'd moments ago caught between his teeth. "I'll . . ." Kate gulped. "I'll break the date!" His tongue darted teasingly into her mouth. "Oh, God, Trace! What time do you want me?"

"A very inviting question," Trace murmured against her lips, soft laughter evident in his voice. "I ache to give the obvious answer . . . but I'll contain myself."

"You're laughing at me." Try as she might, Kate could not prevent the hurt from tingeing her tone.

"No, darling, I'm laughing at myself." Giving her a final, hard kiss, Trace swung his legs to the floor and stood up. "I'm going to get out of here before I laugh myself into trouble." A tender smile tilting his lips, he held his hand out to help her up. "Do you trust me enough to come to my hotel for breakfast?"

"In your room?" Kate paused in the act of pulling on her robe to blink at him.

Shaking his head at her, he chuckled again. "No, funny Kate, in the hotel coffee shop." His gleaming eyes held both question and challenge. "I'm staying at the Hershey. Will you come?"

"Yes." Noting his satisfied smile, Kate followed him to the door. It was not until she'd agreed to meet him in the coffee shop at ten, and he'd stepped into the hallway that she added, "I'd have come to your room, Trace." When he arched his brows mockingly, she said softly, "I trust you that much already."

"Thank you, Kate." Leaning toward her he brushed his mouth over hers, then turned away abruptly. "See you at ten," he called as he rounded the corner at the end of the short hall.

A smile of bemusement on her soft lips, Kate closed and locked the door. Absently switching off the lights, she drifted into her bedroom. A glow of warm anticipation tingling through her, she tossed her robe onto the foot of the bed, then slid between the covers.

What was one to make of a Trace Sinclair? Kate asked herself dreamily, forgetting to switch off the bedside light as she sank into a reverie of the time they'd spent together.

Trace was almost back to his hotel in the city when he realized that for the past few hours he'd completely forgotten Annette and her threat.

Reflectively, his grip tightened on the steering wheel. Damn her! The only way she'll get Kath from me is over my dead body. The silent vow still rang in his mind when memory sent a smile to his grimly set lips.

"The only way you'll take a belt to this child is over my dead body!"

Trace could still hear the outrage that had quivered in Kate's voice when she'd thrown the challenge at him. His smile grew wider, then he frowned as pain registered on his conscience. Glancing down at his hands, he was amazed to see his knuckles were white.

Trace cursed his former wife as he loosened his death grip on the steering wheel. There had to be a way to stop her from getting custody of Kath. A way that would not mean depriving Kathy of the genuine love of her maternal grandparents.

Anger again began churning through his body. Trace turned the rented car over to the hotel's valet parking attendant and went to his room only to pace the floor in restless frustration.

How had he ever convinced himself that Annette would be the perfect lifetime partner for him? Shaking his head in disgust, Trace flung his body into a chair. How many times had he asked himself that same question since Annette had revealed her true colors?

God! Were all females scheming and dishonest in their quests to attain their goals in life? When he'd first met Annette, seven years before, she'd appeared the most gentle, understanding woman he'd ever run across.

The memory of that meeting and the subsequent ugliness of their marriage twisted Trace's lips as though with a bitter taste.

At twenty-eight Trace was already being praised throughout San Antonio for his skill in the operating room. His hands and mind were sure and incisive, his methods innovative. He was well on the way to carving a name for himself in medical circles throughout the country.

His success had not come without cost. Long hours of work and short respites for rest had left Trace numb to the ego trip that usually accompanies sudden adoration. Trace was simply too weary to be impressed—either with himself or anyone else.

That is until the afternoon he was introduced to the house guest of a colleague of his. The occasion was a barbecue at the home of the head of neurosurgery.

Trace had not wanted to attend the affair; even when he had no surgery scheduled he had time-consuming paperwork to do. The chief neurosurgeon had not extended an invitation, he'd issued an order: "You'd better be there." Trace went, muttering imprecations all the way.

From the moment Trace sauntered onto the patio of his chief's home, he saw little but the exquisitely lovely young woman seated with his colleague's wife. The woman was small, dainty, and the most beautiful woman he'd seen in years. There was a soft, gentle look about her that drew him like a homing device.

As he approached the two women, Bette, his colleague's wife, smiled widely.

"Oh, here's our glory-boy now!" Laughing at his frown of disapproval, she extended one plump hand to him. "Trace, come meet a friend from my college days."

Her name was Annette Parker, and her voice was as beautiful as the rest of her. Within half an hour of their polite greetings, Trace had learned that Annette was from a moderately well-off Philadelphia family; that she had graduated from University of Pennsylvania; that she belonged to the Junior League and did volunteer work; and as she had no burning desire for a career, worked part-time for the firm which employed her father as a vice-president.

Soft, bitter laughter shattered the silence of the dimly lit room. Resting his head against the back of the chair, Trace reflected on how perfectly clear hindsight was. Now, seven years removed from their first meeting, he sardonically applauded Annette's consummate act of assumed gentleness. Of course, now Trace knew too well that Annette was as gentle as a black widow spider—the only difference being, she didn't want to devour him, merely his social position in the community. And it had taken less than three years for her to reveal her true colors.

Growling a curse of disgust, both for himself and Annette, Trace surged to his feet to pace the impersonal room, one hand agitatedly raking through his hair.

What an utter fool he'd made of himself over her! Though unpalatable, Trace faced the truth squarely. True, he'd nearly worked himself to the point of exhaustion in the months preceding her advent into his life and had very probably been ripe for picking by cleverly directed feminine fingers. But that in no way excused his behavior, or his tolerance of hers. He'd behaved like a love-sick teenager in the throes of first passion.

Made uncomfortable by his reflections, Trace prowled the room, finally coming to a stop at the window that overlooked the broad center city street.

Trace didn't want to look back, didn't want to remember, yet the fury coursing through his veins would not allow relaxation. In an effort to purge his system of Annette's poison, he deliberately unlocked the door he'd slammed on memory four years before.

Playing her role to the hilt, Annette had insisted on a very proper courtship, even after she'd returned to her home two weeks from the day Trace met her. Since she'd aroused him unbearably, yet left him frustrated, he'd continued his pursuit long distance via phone calls, and flowers with little notes, and long, impassioned letters.

When, after four lonely, fantasy-filled months, she agreed to marry him, Trace had practically worked himself to a standstill. Tired but triumphant, he journeyed east to meet his future in-laws, Ruth and William Parker. Expecting to spend a few days in Philadelphia before whisking Annette back to Texas with him, Trace had his hopes dashed again when she informed him she wanted to have a large wedding at home.

Beginning to feel desperate, Trace agreed to all her demands and went back to Texas alone. Annette kept him abreast of the ongoing, elaborate wedding plans by lengthy, long-distance calls.

There were times during the intervening months when Trace felt on the verge of climbing the walls. He hadn't been with a woman since weeks before meeting Annette, and he wanted her so badly that merely thinking about her gave him the shakes.

Then, finally, the day came for him to fly east. After what seemed like an endless round of parties for the couple, Trace at last stood in the old, stately church the Parkers attended and watched in bemusement as his bride slowly walked down the aisle to him, his heart swelling with the pride of realization that the beautiful woman was his.

Following a lavish, endless wedding reception, Trace escaped to Hawaii for two weeks of bliss with his bride.

Harsh laughter bounced off the cold windowpane—a raspy sound from a tight throat. Well, Trace thought wryly, his plan had been for two weeks of bliss when he'd made the reservations for their honeymoon. From the way Annette had responded to him before the wedding, he'd every reason to expect an ardent bride in his bed. Her frigid attitude soon put a damper on his expectations. Though not completely cold, her response could only be described as lukewarm at the best of times. And then only after he'd debased himself by begging.

"Oh hell!"

Swinging away from the window, Trace began pacing again. Why *had* he allowed the memories to surface after all these years? He didn't want to remember the times he'd swallowed his pride to coax and cajole that unresponsive, cold-hearted witch! God! Why, how had he continued to love her?

Because out of the bedroom she was so charming, that's why, Trace jeered. At least, he qualified, Annette was charming until he cut her ration of social functions. And that was when she'd revealed her true self. Up until that point, though hating it, Trace had squired Annette to as many functions as he could manage with the schedule he maintained. It was at these affairs that Annette was at her most shining, charming best.

Always a loner, Trace had shunned the many social gatherings he was invariably invited to. His rare, free hours were precious, and he preferred to spend them quietly. While waiting to claim his bride, he'd eagerly looked forward to spending those quiet moments with her. On their return to San Antonio, Annette had quickly changed that idea. She made no bones about demanding the glittering social whirl his position entitled her to.

Disillusioned, but still wildly infatuated with her, Trace had indulged her for almost two years. He even rented an apartment in the city, conveniently near both his office and the hospital. Then one night while dressing to go out to yet another of the endless affairs, tired beyond belief and sick with self-disgust, Trace had stopped dead in the process of buttoning his elegantly pleated shirt to stare at Annette with eyes that had lost the glow of adoration.

"The hell with this," he said tersely, shrugging out of the shirt. "I'm beat, and I'm not going anywhere. You may go alone if you wish."

Exquisitely gowned in a Paris original, Annette had merely gaped at him in shock for several minutes. Then she gave her best performance to date. First she tried anger. Then she tried tears. And then, when the realization dawned that it wasn't moving Trace, she tried sex.

Perhaps it was understandable that Trace's firmness wavered, then crumbled; he'd waited so long, wanted so badly.

The very sad thing was that, even before the loving was over, Trace felt nothing but crushing disappointment. And, more sadly still, he was forced to admit to himself that he no longer cared.

But the final, irrevocable blow fell when Annette first suspected that she was pregnant a few weeks later.

Up at his usual early hour, Trace had surprised her in the bathroom, being violently sick. Moved by compassion, he'd supported her until the shudders had subsided. When he stepped back she turned on him, her eyes frantic, her lips twisted with fury.

"Damn you!" she'd shouted. "Damn you for getting difficult at the exact time I had to stop taking the pill! Now look what's happened!"

Stunned, Trace had stared at her blankly, his mind digesting her accusation with incredulity. He was a doctor—and he hadn't even known his wife was taking birth control pills!

"Is it so terrible?" he finally asked. "We've been married for two years, Annette." Trace smiled tenderly—after all, she was very likely a little scared . . . and *he* was going to be a father! "It's not too soon to start a family."

"Never is too soon!" Annette cried shrilly. "I have just established myself in the best San Antonion circles! I'll lose ground—I can't be pregnant now!" She raised one delicate hand imploringly. "Trace, you're a doctor. You can do something, you've *got* to do something!"

A chill pervading his body, Trace said carefully, "What, exactly, do you want me to do?" He knew the answer she'd give; he could feel it in his bones. Yet, when it came, it wrenched his heart just the same.

"Get rid of it!" Annette wailed. "Admit me to the hospital and take it out. I can't bear the thought of it!"

It was dead. The love, or infatuation, or whatever it was that Trace had felt for her was suddenly completely dead; Annette had killed it with her whining plea.

"No, Annette, I won't do that," Trace said with a steadiness he fought to maintain. "Nor will I allow any other physician in this city to do it. The child is mine, and I want it."

"Well, I don't!" Annette screamed. "I don't want either you or your brat! Do you understand that?"

A low growling noise broke the silence of the night. Standing rigid in the middle of the Philadelphia hotel room, Trace shrugged, as if freeing himself of a burden. As if he'd forgotten where he was he glanced around the room. A wry smile touched his tight lips when his gaze settled on the bed.

Trace had walked out of the bedroom the morning Annette had screamed that she did not want him or his "brat." He had not shared a bed with her or any other woman since then. His celibacy was self-imposed. Trace was determined that never again would he be vulnerable to any woman.

* * *

With a bright smile and a cheery "hello" to the doorman, Kate breezed through the wide hotel doors at two minutes to ten the following morning. Her lustrous black hair bouncing on her shoulders in time with her jaunty step and her gray eyes gleaming with good health, she looked thoroughly relaxed and carefree. Her appearance was a facade; inside her stomach, a million nerve-endings she hadn't realized she owned were busy tying themselves into hard little knots.

How would Trace behave with her this morning, she wondered nervously, crossing the spacious lobby to the coffee shop. Would he be warm or cool, friendly or distant ... would he show up?

The questions which had tormented her from the moment she woke up were answered as she entered the coffee shop. Trace was already there and, as if he'd been watching the doorway for her, he got to his feet and pulled the chair next to his out for her, a dazzling smile of welcome enhancing his attractive face.

"Good morning, Kate," he murmured as she slid onto the chair. "From the color on your nose and cheeks, I'd hazzard a guess that it's cold outside."

Smiling her thanks as he slipped her jacket from her shoulders, Kate nodded. "There's a brisk wind." Her nostrils flared as she inhaled the inviting aroma of freshly brewed coffee. "It bites at the exposed areas."

"So do I," Trace teased softly, settling himself close beside her. "And the covered areas too."

Embarrassed, but pleasantly so, Kate glanced around the half-filled room. Satisfied that there were no patrons within hearing distance, she brought her quelling gaze back to him, her head moving back and forth in despair.

"Trace, really! If anyone heard, they'd think—"

"But never in public places," his laughing voice over-rode hers. "If anyone heard me they'd think—what?" Arched eyebrows demanded she finish what she'd started to say.

"That..." Kate looked directly into his eyes. "They'd think that we were lovers," she said softly.

"They'd be close to right." Trace shrugged his uncon-cern. "And, before too long, I fully intend making sure they *would* be right." His gaze noted the renewed color in her cheeks. Gliding his hand over hers, he entwined their fingers. "I want very badly to be your first lover, Kate," he said distinctly. Then, very softly, "And I think you want that too."

"Trace, I...I..." Flustered by his bluntness, Kate searched for a response—*any* response. She could hardly admit that his assertion was correct, and that she *did* want him to be her first lover. Lost for words, she shook her head distractedly.

"Don't go spinning off into space, smoke-eyes." Trace's eyes darkened to the shade of jade with amuse-ment. "I did say I wouldn't make an issue of it." His lips curved appealingly. "In fact, I'm going to let you decide when and where." The smile faded as he grew serious. "Okay?"

"Yes." Kate gave him a trembly smile of relief. "And...thank you. You could easily have...ah, re-solved the issue last night, you know?"

Trace smiled in understanding. "Yes, honey, I do know. But, thank *you* for being so honest with me." His smile curved wryly. "I find honesty in a woman rather refreshing."

A tingle of unease slid down Kate's spine; what *had* gone wrong with his marriage? More importantly—what was she getting herself into here? She had problems of her own; she wasn't sure she was up to handling bitterness and cynicism from him. And yet, unaccountably, she felt an overwhelming urge to reassure him.

"I will always be honest with you, Trace."

A subtle change altered his expression from wryness to appreciation of the somber steadiness of her tone. "And I promise I will always be honest with you, Kate," he returned her vow quietly.

As had happened over the dinner table the night before, Kate got lost in the beckoning lure of his cool green eyes. Unaware of the passage of time, or the bustle of activity as a large group of people entered the coffee shop, she stared into those cool depths, her lips parted slightly with the wonder of the longing tugging her toward him.

"I think we'd better order breakfast."

"What . . . ?" Kate blinked, shook her head fractionally, then refocused on his austerely set face. Even as a flush of embarrassment warmed her throat, she realized that Trace had been affected by that strange, trancelike moment as well. The echo of his passion-roughened tone whispered through her mind, and his eyes were bright with heat from within. As the flush mounted to her cheeks, his lips tilted in a heart-stopping, tender smile.

"I said, I think we'd better order breakfast," Trace repeated softly, his smile growing into a teasing grin, "before we get thrown out of here for indecent exposure."

Indecent exposure? Kate's blankness lasted only an instant, then her face blossomed with understanding. Had she been that transparent? Had the yearning she was feeling for him blazed out of her eyes?

Of course it had. Catching her lower lip between her teeth, Kate found little comfort in the knowledge that Trace's eyes had revealed an equal measure of desire.

"Don't, honey." Strong fingers applied reassuring pressure to hers. "There's nothing to feel embarrassed about." Lifting her hand he brought it to his lips to bestow a warm, brief kiss. "The feeling is mutual." As Trace lowered her hand to the table, his eyes began dancing with devilry. "The hell with the rest of the world." Rakishly raised eyebrows invited her to join in with his devil-may-care attitude.

"Is that any way for a physician to talk?" Feeling suddenly free and feather-light, Kate grinned at him, shaking her gleaming hair back with an abandoned toss of her head.

Trace's soft laughter flowed over Kate like warm honey. "There you go again," he teased as his laughter subsided. "Exactly how is a physician supposed to talk?"

"In deep, confident tones," Kate shot back, reflecting his light mood. "In a manner befitting his serious occupation."

"No kidding! Befitting even?" Trace contrived to look amazed. "I never knew that. I'll have to practice—befitting, I mean."

Although they seemed to be laughing constantly, both Kate and Trace managed to consume an enormous breakfast, beginning with fruit cups and ending with blueberry blintzes.

"Good heavens!" Kate groaned, replacing her empty coffee cup on the saucer. "I don't think I'll be able even to think about food for at least a week!"

"I'll bet you the price of a movie ticket that you'll be moaning you're starving by dinner time." Trace issued the challenge with a grin.

"We're going to see a movie?" Kate asked hopefully.

Trace chuckled at her eagerness. "After dinner, if you like." He tilted his head questioningly. "Is it a bet?"

Positive she wouldn't want as much as one more bite of food for the remainder of the day, Kate smiled smugly. "You're on," she agreed, then qualified, "on one condition."

"Name it," Trace said expansively.

"I get to pick the film."

"You drive a hard bargain, woman," Trace frowned. "But, okay, you get to pick the film."

A twitch at the corners of his lips ruined the effect of his frown as he stood up and tossed an over-large tip on the table for the waitress. Then, after scooping the check up, he nudged Kate into movement with a gentle taunt.

"I think we've taken up space in here long enough." Tipping his head he drew her attention to the restless line of people waiting for tables. "Perhaps we'd better leave before we're asked to vacate the premises."

It was not until Kate was patiently standing beside Trace at the cash register that she noticed the rain-spattered look of some of the people waiting in line and the dripping umbrellas in the hands of others.

"Trace, it's raining outside," she murmured as they made their way around the line and strolled into the hotel lobby.

"So I see." Carrying her jacket over one arm, Trace curled the other arm around the back of her waist, gently propelling her to the wide windows that faced the street.

In communal silence they stood for several minutes, staring out at the rain, sheeting at an almost horizontal angle from the force of the wind. A shiver feathered Kate's shoulders and arms at the sight of the few pedestrians she watched, hurrying along, huddled beneath umbrellas buffeted by the wind.

Feeling the tremor that ran through her, Trace tightened his arm to draw her close to the warmth of his body.

"Not exactly inviting—is it?" He voiced her thoughts correctly.

"No," Kate sighed. "Had you planned anything for today?"

"I was going to suggest that you show me the sights," Trace shrugged. "But it's hardly the weather for sight-seeing."

Seeing the prospects for a day spent in his company dwindling, Kate looked up at him dejectedly. "Would you prefer to take me home?"

"Home?" Trace repeated hollowly. "Do you want to go home?"

"Oh, no!" Kate cried, shaking her head. "But, what else can we do?"

A satisfied smile curled the edges of his lips. "We could go up to my room and play doctor," he suggested wickedly.

Five

Kate tried very hard to appear both shocked and affronted. But even with her teeth clamped together, the bubbling laughter his outrageous suggestion elicited burst through her lips.

"But Trace! There's not a thing wrong with either my head or back!" she gasped through her fit of giggles.

"Brat!" His low growl was muttered close to her ear as he bent over her shaking body. "Okay, let's go up to my room and talk." Tightening his hold on her waist, Trace turned them both in the direction of the elevators. Before striding out, he paused to glance down at her. "Okay?" Though his voice held firm, there was a shadow of uncertainty in his eyes which tugged at Kate's heart.

"Okay," she agreed softly. The tug in her chest curled happily as the uncertainty in his eyes was banished by a glimmer of undisguised pleasure.

Since the elevator held three other people, they rode up to his floor in silence. It was not until they were standing in front of the door to his room that Trace leveled a solemn look at her.

"You don't have to be at all nervous, you know," he said reassuringly. "I'm not going to ask anything from you that you are not prepared to give willingly."

Kate fully realized that she could be acting very foolishly; after all, she hardly knew the man! Yet, for reasons incomprehensible to her, she trusted him to the marrow of her bones. Foolish? Perhaps, but there it was.

"I'm not nervous, Trace." Kate's voice was soft with honest simplicity. A teasing smile lit her face. "Had I been nervous, I'd have bolted for safety when you made the suggestion."

For an instant, Trace stared at her as if held in breathless stillness. Then, a devastatingly beautiful smile transformed his face and he flung his arm around her shoulders, hugging her close to him.

"You know," he observed softly as he inserted the door key and pushed the door open. "Every overworked doctor should have at least one Kate in his life." His arm still clamping her to his side, Trace shepherded Kate into the room, releasing her as he turned to shut the door quietly behind them.

Deeply affected by the meaning contained within the deceptively casual compliment, and not quite sure how to respond, Kate walked slowly to the wide window. A glowing warmth seeping through her, she stared sightlessly at the rain-washed pane, her mind revolving with the echo of the words: *In his life. In his life.*

"Kate?"

The confusion in Trace's low voice drew Kate away from her bemusement over an emotion too tenuous to name. Blinking her eyes as if emerging from a trance, she slowly turned to face him.

"Hmm?" Kate was unaware of the dreamy, faraway sound of her voice.

"Is there something wrong?" Eyes narrowed, Trace scrutinized her expression.

"Wrong?" Kate frowned. "No, of course not." She waved her hand as if waving aside the very idea. "Why do you ask?"

Trace tilted his head, one eyebrow arching quizzically. "Why? I asked because you suddenly seemed to withdraw into yourself." His lips curved ruefully. "Are you having second thoughts about being alone with me?"

"Not at all!" Kate denied at once. "If I seemed to withdraw it was just..." She smiled self-consciously. "To tell the truth, I was just very flattered by what you said."

"About every busy doctor needing a Kate!" he exclaimed. "Honey, if that's your idea of thought provoking flattery, you've been hanging out with the wrong guys!"

"Trace Sinclair! I have not been *hanging* out with any guys!" Kate protested laughingly.

Trace grinned. "Yeah, I know." Walking over to her he caught her hand to lead her to the settee beside the window. "I have...ah, proof of that." His grin widened. "You're so innocent it scares me."

On examination, Kate decided Trace didn't look at all scared. As a matter of fact, he looked as bold as brass and equal to anything—especially a twenty-three-year-old virgin. Curling into the corner of the settee, she drew her legs up under her and grinned back at him.

"Well, in that case," Kate drawled the curve, then fired the fast break, "maybe I can scare some answers out of you."

With his long legs stretched out, booted ankles crossed, head resting on the amply padded back of the settee, Trace had the appearance of a completely relaxed man. His easy smile reinforced the appearance.

"Maybe," he drawled lazily. "Why don't you give it a shot?"

Kate's hesitation lasted only long enough to marshal her questions into order.

"Okay, here goes. I know you're thirty-five, about six feet tall, and more attractive than is probably good for you...or any member of the opposite sex." Kate managed to keep a straight face when Trace laughed softly in appreciation of her description. But her lips trembled with a smile at his calm acceptance of her evaluation.

"Too true." His shrug was casually elegant; his eyes danced with amusement. "But I do love hearing it." He worked his features into an avid expression. "Please, do go on."

Kate lost the battle of control with her mirth. "You're retiring attitude underwhelms me!" she gasped. "I think you missed your calling. You should've gone into acting."

"Hey, yeah! I never thought of that." In all seriousness, Trace went along with her silliness. "Gee, not only would I have made a lot more money, I'd have all those delectable aspiring actresses crawling all over me." He produced a leering grin. "Damn! Where were you when I was making a career choice?" he demanded with mock gruffness.

"Very likely still in diapers," Kate retorted.

Trace grabbed his ribs as if he'd been injured. "Oh, cheap shot, kid!" he objected. "That barb caught me where I live—right on the ole ego."

Suddenly the laughter died on Kate's lips, and she gazed at him wistfully. "You think I'm too young for you, don't you?"

Trace became abruptly serious. "Aren't you?" he asked tautly.

Regretting her gibe, Kate stared into his eyes, which had taken on an emerald hue. "No," she answered very simply.

"The span involves more than mere numbers, Kate." Trace attempted a smile, failed, then gave up the effort. "It encompasses a great deal of painfully earned experience and maturity."

"I realize that, but..." Kate groped for words that would exactly define her position. "I may be inexperienced, Trace, but I do consider myself a mature adult." Her smile grew sadly reminiscent. "One tends to mature very quickly in a family of forever young advocates."

"That's a teaser, honey," Trace said quietly. "Let's have some clarification."

Kate was immediately sorry she'd offered the explanation. She wanted to learn about Trace, talk about him...not herself. She especially didn't want to elaborate on the whys and wherefores of herself. She started to shake her head in denial; Trace wouldn't accept the motion.

"Spill it, kid," he ordered gently.

And spill Kate did. Though she began slowly, hesitantly, the story poured out of her with increasing swiftness until she was empty, drained by the barrenness of the years she chronicled.

"I suppose my family would be classified as average—middle class. One husband. One wife. Two children. The obligatory first-born son, my brother Scott, and yours truly, the baby daugther. There is, of course, the required ranch-style house in a planned suburban community. Nothing posh, you understand, but acceptable."

As she was now looking inside herself, Kate was immune to the waiting stillness gripping Trace. It was at this point in her narrative that Kate's words began racing off her tongue.

"My parents arrived at this middle-class station via the mass transit of individually pursued careers. To maintain it, my mother continued on in her chosen field—with short absence leaves to give birth."

"A common enough practice in today's economy," Trace inserted carefully.

"Yes, unfortunately it is," Kate agreed cynically. "As is the running, faster and faster, merely to maintain the place or status." Her smile was devoid of humor as she explained. "You know, the constant jockeying for position." Her lips twisted into a grimace. "What's that?" Raven-wing eyebrows arched. "You say the neighbors two streets down had their patio flag-stoned? Well, it must be time to have the rec-room remodeled into a facsimile of a twenties speakeasy."

"It's called keeping up with the Jones'," Trace murmured.

Kate laughed bitterly. "I'll say, and then some. But completely harmless, unless children are neglected while the adults are playing their funny little games."

Trace frowned. "You were neglected?"

"Oh, not in the physical sense," Kate said hastily. "Scott and I were well cared for in that respect; well fed, well dressed . . . very well dressed. We were taken for medical and dental check-ups regularly." She smiled widely to reveal perfectly even, white teeth. "The orthodontist's bill was a dandy—and my teeth weren't even very crooked to begin with.''

"Well then?'' Trace moved uneasily—as if becoming uncomfortable with his thoughts.

"Emotional poverty,'' Kate said distinctly. "Too many hours spent in the company of uninterested nursery school employees and baby-sitters. Too many birthdays and holidays spent with all the 'right' people, who were not necessarily friends. Too many achievements ignored or overlooked because of a dinner party that absolutely couldn't be missed, or an opportunity to move up the social ladder that simply could not be passed up.''

"Kate...'' Trace began sympathetically.

"Do you have any idea what it's like to watch your parents flirting outrageously with near strangers?'' she went on as if she hadn't heard him. "Can you imagine what it does to an impressionable teenager to observe her mother give the come-on to a man she barely knows simply because it's an accepted part of the game of staying-in-place?''

"No,'' Trace said quietly.

"Emotional poverty—in capital letters.''

Trace's eyes narrowed thoughtfully. "And that's why you were so bristly at our first meeting,'' he mused softly. "You thought I'd 'mislaid' Kathy by sheer carelessness.'' When Kate averted her face, Trace caught her chin to make her look at him. "You believed I was caught up in the moves of those 'funny little games'—didn't you?''

"No,'' Kate admitted. "I thought you were even worse. I was sure you were completely careless of your daughter.''

"Ah, Kate, protector of lost children,'' Trace murmured, the expression on his face heart-wrenchingly tender as he gazed down at her. "Is that your mission in life—looking out for emotionally poor kids?"

The hand gently cupping her face moved caressingly along her jaw line, long fingers stroking, testing the satiny texture of her cheek. Kate's skin tingled, sending shock waves all the way to her toes.

"N-not at all!" she exclaimed on a quickly drawn breath. "I...I..." Kate's voice faltered as the fingers slid sensuously down the length of her throat.

"You...you...what?" Trace murmured, exploring her collarbone with the tips of his fingers. "What do you want out of life, Kate?"

Kate trembled as his fingers drew a gliding pattern on her skin from her collarbone to the fluttering pulse at the base of her neck.

"I want to be a wife and a mother," Kate answered with all the honesty she'd promised him. "A *full*-time wife and mother." She smiled deprecatingly. "An ambition not at all in vogue, I know. But that's what I want out of life—eventually."

"Emotional security?" Trace queried softly, denying the urge to send his itching fingers to trace the edge of her blouse.

"Yes," Kate answered simply. "I don't know if I'll ever really attain it, but I know I must try."

"And is there a special man right now?" he asked casually. "One you think might be suitable to play the role of husband in your plans?" His eyes were coolly remote as he watched her with unnerving steadiness.

Trace was silently demanding Kate live up to her promise of honesty. She gave in to his demand without hesitation.

"No," she replied with equal steadiness, "there is no special man."

"You're not seeing *any*one?" Trace asked skeptically.

"I didn't say that," Kate corrected blandly. "I have been seeing a man the past few months, but I decided to end the relationship because he was getting too possessive." Her smile was sadly gentle. "He wasn't at all special, you see."

"Very clearly." Trace didn't smile, but his fingers moved with nerve-jarring slowness, gliding erratically along the edge of her blouse lapel. "You weren't at all tempted, hmm?" His fingers came to a stop at the first fastened button, an inch or so above the valley between her breasts.

There wasn't a chance he'd miss her responding quiver, and Kate knew it. Not even bothering to hide her reaction to his touch, she murmured, "Not even a little bit."

"And now?" Trace was no longer looking at her. His eyes darkening to dense forest green, he observed the pattern his fingers were tracing on her flesh. "Are you tempted now?"

Tempted? Had Kate been able to spare a shallow breath she might have laughed. As it was she could barely speak.

"You know I am."

A tiny, exciting smile lifted the corners of his lips. "May I open the button?" Trace flicked at the small pearlized stud with his index finger.

Kate paused for a breathless moment, during which her mind raced with conflicting emotions. Without a shred of doubt she knew that were she to ask him to stop he would do so immediately. She also knew she didn't want him to stop...at least not yet. If only for a moment, she yearned to feel again the sensations his stroking fingers had evoked the night before. With unconscious deliberation, she pushed caution to the farthest reaches of her mind.

"You may open every button," Kate whispered through dry lips.

There was no pause or hesitation in Trace. Swiftly, expertly, he slid the small buttons through their corresponding holes, tugging the blouse gently from beneath the waistband of her slacks to get to the last two. Then, his touch a caress, he drew the panels apart to expose her lace-covered breasts.

"Lovely." His voice a barely audible murmur, Trace praised the perfection of her pale skin. One deft movement and the clip on the front of her bra was unfastened. Trace caught her breasts in his palms as they spilled from their lacy confines. Cupping them, lifting them, he slowly lowered his head.

"Tr-Trace?" Even as she whispered his name, Kate was arching her back in invitation.

Pausing inches from her body, Trace raised his eyes to hers. "You have beautiful breasts, Kate. Silky and exquisitely formed. Let me love them." Holding her gaze, he remained absolutely still, waiting for her response.

"Yes." A breath. A sigh. Then, as his thumbs teased the tips into readiness, a shuddering moan. "Yes, please Trace, yes!"

This time, prepared for it, the thrill that went spiraling through Kate's body at the touch of his mouth on her breasts was doubly intense and exciting. Blindly following passion's lead, she raised her hands to clasp his head, holding him to her, urging a deeper intimacy.

The flickering movement of his warm tongue sent a shaft of delight cascading along her nerves from her aroused nipples to the very tips of the fingers she pressed into his thick hair.

"Oh, Trace. Oh, Trace!" Kate was barely aware of repeating his name until his teeth gently closed around one rigid nipple. Then the throaty sound of her voice registered as she encouraged him in an impassioned plea. "Oh, Trace . . . yes, yes, yes!"

Without breaking the attention he was lavishing on her breasts, Trace grasped her waist and slowly slid from the settee, positioning himself on his knees on the floor between her thighs.

"You're so soft, so very soft." Trace murmured the words against her skin. "Like shimmery satin warmed before a fire."

Palms flat, fingers splayed, Trace moved his hands slowly over her rib cage, then down. When his palms brushed the waistband on her slacks he slid his hands along the material to her sides, outlining the curve of her hips before gliding inward to the front zipper.

His breath now an uneven moist cloud sensitizing her quivering flesh, Trace whispered raggedly, "May I pull the zipper, Kate?"

Why was he asking? What was he asking? Her mind spinning from the heady sensations exploding throughout her body, Kate moved her head restlessly against the back of the settee. What should she say? What should she do? Struggling against the fog of sensuality she was sinking into, she writhed agitatedly, thrusting her body artlessly into his. His reaction to the contact was instant and devastating.

"Kate!" His sharply indrawn breath was followed by a hoarse demand. "May I?" The electrifying sensation of Trace's tongue curling around one aching nipple robbed Kate of breath as well as what was left of her rationality.

"Yes! Yes! Yes!" Inside her head her words resounded like a shout; the sound that whispered through her parted lips was little more than a whimper.

As Trace continued to drive Kate senseless with his tongue, his hands were busy slipping the waistband button through its slot and releasing the zipper. With swift, economical movements he eased the material over her hips then, leaning back, off of her slender, shapely legs. Her slacks still clutched in one hand, he got to his feet. Swiftly stepping out of his jeans, he tossed both garments aside with careless abandon.

As Kate's eyes were shut tightly, she didn't see Trace divest himself of his jeans. But, in the moments he was away from her, she felt a coolness on her heated skin, and a glimmer of alarm piercing the fog of passion.

"Sweet Kate, you *are* beautiful."

The husky sound of Trace's voice closed the gap of alarm in Kate's mind. The feel of his hard thighs sliding between hers banished the growing chill. Tumbling back into the furnace of desire, Kate moaned as his hands grasped her thighs tightly to his hips, then gasped with pleasure as his fingers trailed fire from her navel to the edge of her brief panties.

Not even conscious of the fact that the soft, whimpering sounds she heard were coming from deep inside her own throat, Kate trembled as Trace slid his fingers beneath the elastic band and cried aloud when he found, then stroked, the moist heat of her femininity.

"Trace. Trace." Mindlessly murmuring his name, Kate arched her body into his touch, instinctively seeking release from the excitement and tension building to an unbearable pitch inside her.

His breathing a harsh labored rasp, Trace chanted her name like a prayer for salvation as his hands moved to grasp her sweetly rounded derriere. A visible tremor quaked through his body when Kate clasped his hips tightly with her thighs in an impassioned lover's embrace.

A wispy pink patch of nylon and a swatch of navy-blue cotton were the guardians that prevented complete unity when Trace compulsively thrust his hips into hers.

There was an instant of utter stillness as Trace held Kate's body to his with desperation. Eyes closed, he drank in the sound of her throaty murmurings while his palms absorbed the feel of her quivering flesh. Then, with a shudder, he released her and sprang to his feet.

"Oh, God!" His face a mask of strained agony, he spun around and strode unsteadily to stand before the window.

Startled, confused, and frightened by the suddenness of his violent action, Kate lay staring at him out of widening eyes, her body sprawled in a position of wild abandonment.

What had she done wrong? Had she appeared too eager for his touch? Too abandoned? Why, why had he flung himself away from her like that? Had she filled him with disgust? Unable to bear her own clamoring thoughts, she centered her attention on his hands, clenching at the sides of his tautly held body.

"Trace?" Kate whispered his name questioningly when the silence in the room stretched into long seconds. She winced in pain when his body flinched at the sound of her voice. Feeling shamed, she sat up, drawing her blouse closed protectively over her breasts.

"I . . . I'm sorry if I displeased you." The choking apology hurt her throat.

"You didn't displease me, Kate." Trace murmured the reassurance without turning. "The truth is, you pleased me too well.'' Leaning forward, he rested his forehead against the cool windowpane.

"But I don't understand!" Kate cried brokenly, drawing her legs up to clasp them with her trembling arms. "If I pleased you, why did you turn away from me like that?" Even in her agitation her gaze appreciated the sight of his masculine beauty. His deep sigh drew her gaze to the back of his well-shaped head.

"You are so unbelievably innocent!" Trace's strained laughter held the sound of splintering glass. His chest expanding with a deeply drawn breath, he turned to face her, his arousal still very much in evidence behind the flimsy covering of his briefs.

Unable to tear her gaze away from him, Kate stared, wide-eyed until, embarrassed by the realization of what she was doing, she lowered her eyes to the carpet under his feet.

"Kate, look at me," Trace commanded softly. "*Looking* at me—all of me—is nothing to be ashamed of," he chided gently when she raised her eyes hesitantly. Very deliberately he ran his gaze over her slowly. "There should be no shame in enjoying the attractions of the person you've been making love with." A tiny smile quirked the corner of his mouth. "I think you're beautiful and looking at you excites me." His quirky smile turned rueful as his gaze skimmed the length of his own body. "Obviously," he muttered.

"But then—why, Trace?" Kate blurted out in confusion.

"Honey, I've been a long time without a woman," Trace explained carefully. "A few minutes ago I was on the very edge of losing…ah…control." His lips twisted into a sardonic smile. "Had I *lost* it we'd have both been embarrassed, and my pride would have suffered for it."

Kate stared at him uncomprehendingly for a moment, then blinked as understanding dawned. What an idiot she was, she thought on a wave of fresh embarrassment. But how was she to know? Now longing to reassure him, she rushed into stuttering speech.

"Oh, Trace! I...I'm so sorry! Please forgive me. I...I didn't know!"

"Of course you didn't know," Trace inserted when she paused for breath. "I'm relieved you didn't know." He took a step toward her then stopped, a self-derisive smile curling his lips. "I wanted you very badly, Kate. I *still* want you very badly." Taking another step, he scooped his clothes from the floor. "I'm not running any more risks today." Leaning toward her he draped her slacks over her drawn-up knees. "As long as we stay here alone we're sitting on a potential powder keg." He smiled as he pulled on his jeans. "Rain or no rain, honey. I think we'll both be a lot safer if we get out of this room."

Ten minutes later, her appearance restored to at least a semblance of what it had been when she'd left her apartment that morning, Kate stood quietly beside Trace as they waited for the elevator to ascend to his floor. Not one more word had passed between them since he'd decreed that they leave his room. Now, armored by clothing and fresh makeup, Kate broke the uneasy silence.

"Trace?" she ventured tentatively.

"Hmm?" he responded mildly.

Encouraged, Kate rushed into the question that had been driving her crazy.

"You—ah—said it has been a long time since you've been with a woman." Kate paused to wet her suddenly dry lips. "Ah...well...*how* long has it been?" She stopped breathing the moment the words were out of her mouth.

Moving slowly, almost lazily, Trace turned to look at her, his eyes gleaming gemstone bright with amusement.

"A very long time, Kate." He hesitated, as if considering if he should elaborate, then he shrugged. "Since before Kathy was born, as a matter of fact."

Trace hadn't been with a woman in almost four years? The pent-up breath eased out of Kate's constricted lungs in a soundless whoosh. There were implications here that did not bear thinking about, yet Kate knew she had to obtain some answers.

"That's not very complimentary to me," Kate observed in a shaky tone. "Is it?"

"What?" All the humor fled from his eyes, leaving them as dull looking as an unpolished stone. "What are you cooking up in that inexperienced little head of yours, kid?" he demanded in an ominously soft tone.

"Well, I mean, after four years, almost *any* woman would do." Kate's throat tightened at the flash of anger that brightened his eyes, and she finished in a dry whisper, "Isn't that true?"

"No, dammit! Listen, Kate, I . . ."

Trace broke off as the ping announcing the arrival of the elevator car sounded. Staring ahead he followed her into the crowded elevator when the door wheezed open.

"We'll continue this conversation in the car," he muttered warningly, sliding a protective arm around her as they jostled for position.

His anger a palpable force radiating from him, Trace maintained his grip on her waist as they waited for his car to be brought to the front of the hotel. Even after they were in the car and moving, his forbidding expression warned her against breaking the silence between them.

"Now, Kate, I want you to listen very carefully to what I have to say," Trace gritted after they'd cleared the worst of the city traffic and were in more open country. "The reason I haven't been intimate with a woman all this time is not because of a lack of feminine interest; I know many willing and eager females." His lips curved cynically. "And I'm not interested in men."

"I never for one second thought you were!" Kate exclaimed in a shocked squeak.

"Thank you for that, anyway," Trace drawled, failing entirely to mask the anger still clawing at him. "I've remained celibate for one reason, and one reason only."

Suddenly swerving the car onto the shoulder bordering the highway, Trace pulled on the hand-brake then shifted on the seat to face her squarely.

"After the debacle I laughingly refer to as my marriage," he said coolly, "I made up my mind that never again would I allow myself to need or be vulnerable to any woman." Lifting an arm, he ran his fingers through his hair. "There have been times—many in number—when I've been tempted to indulge myself merely for the purpose of physical gratification." A derisive smile played over his lips. "In other words, Kate, there have been times when I ached like hell."

"Oh, Trace . . ."

"I'm not finished," he cut her off harshly. "Until yesterday, I've managed to work myself through those...shall I say, hard times?" He met her quick flush with a shake of his head. "By late yesterday I knew I would not be celibate too much longer," he said bluntly.

"Because of me?" Kate asked hopefully.

"Yes, Kate, because of you." Reaching out to her he stroked her cheek with his fingers, smiling when his touch drew a shiver of response from her. "I could have had a woman, a *body*, any time, Kate," he admitted without a hint of male vanity. "I chose not to. Last night, and again a short time ago, I didn't want a woman, a body, I wanted *you*, Kate, *your* body." With a final, lingering caress, Trace let his hand drop to the car seat. "I still feel the same, Kate. I will never allow myself to need you. But I do want you, as you had ample proof of earlier."

Moving so quickly Kate didn't even realize what he was doing, he leaned to her and touched his lips to hers; their mouths fused hungrily. Before the kiss could deepen, Trace pulled away from her.

"You're trembling with urgency for me, Kate," Trace murmured. "And I'm trembling, too. Eventually, we're going to be trembling in a bed, as close together as any two people ever get. I'm warning you now, in case you want to run for the hills, don't build any expectations around me, honey. I can't fulfill them."

Six

Trace was gone. Glancing away from thé computer screen, Kate's gaze came to rest on the tiny watch circling her slim wrist. The digits pulsed out nine-seventeen. Trace and Kathy had reservations on a flight scheduled to depart from Philadelphia International at 9:05 A.M.

Detached from the usual workday activity and chatter around her in the large office, Kate sighed while fighting back a yawn. Feeling the effects of a sleepless night, her shoulders drooped tiredly. Dragging her gaze back to the computer she stared sightlessly at the information presented on the green screen. In her mind's eye she was reviewing the events of the preceding day. With her inner ear she heard the hard finality in Trace's voice.

"I'm warning you now, in case you want to run for the hills, don't build any expectations around me, honey. I can't fulfill them."

Had she begun building expectations around him, Kate wondered, automatically touching keys requesting additional information from the computer. In a secret place in her mind, had she begun weaving dreams around Trace Sinclair?

Frowning, Kate stared incomprehensibly as the data lines changed on the screen.

"Kate?"

For one thrilling instant, Kate imagined the male voice belonged to Trace. Had he somehow missed his plane, she thought fleetingly. Had he deliberately missed his plane? Hope rose like a phoenix only to die again as she swiveled around on her chair.

"Are you feeling all right, Kate?" Mr. Denunzio, the office manager, asked, a concerned frown wrinkling his forehead. "You're pale and you have dark circles under your eyes."

"I ... I'm fine." Kate strove to mask the disappointment in her tone; Mr. Denunzio had always treated her with kindness and consideration. "I didn't sleep too well last night," she added truthfully.

"Too much holiday weekend?" he teased.

"I suppose so." Kate managed a weak smile thinking, too much Sinclair weekend!

"Well, don't overdo it today, and try to get a good night's sleep tonight," he advised gently. "We don't want you coming down with that flu that's been making the rounds."

"I'll take care, sir, and thank you."

With a final word of encouragement the office manager strolled off in the direction of his own office.

Though Kate ruthlessly applied herself to the business of rating insurance policies, memory flashed at odd, unsuspected moments during the day, bringing to mind brief, flickering scenes of the hours she'd spent with Trace.

The strongest of these scenes was the one that followed Trace's warning to her.

Attempting to assimilate not only what he'd said, but also what he'd left unsaid, Kate had stared at him mutely for some time; his impatience made it clear it was too long.

"Do you understand, Kate?" he'd demanded.

"Yes." Kate nodded her head once.

"Do you have any questions?"

"One," she murmured. Actually, Kate's mind seethed with questions but, since she was positive he'd prefer not to hear them, she kept them to herself.

"Well?" Trace prompted when she again fell silent.

"Will you drive me to the mall where we met yesterday?" she finally blurted.

Kate's request appeared to stun Trace. Regarding her from eyes opaque with confusion, he asked wonderingly, "You want to go shopping? Today? Sunday? In the rain?"

Kate might have laughed at his blank expression... if her eyes hadn't started to sting with the threat of tears.

"No, I don't want to shop, Trace," she assured him in a suspiciously husky tone. "I've got to get my car. It's been parked there since before noon yesterday."

Trace's brow drew together with further bewilderment. "Your car was parked there when you left the mall with Kath and me?" he exclaimed.

"Yes."

"Coffee break, Kate."

The call from the young woman who sat at the desk next to hers snapped Kate out of introspection. Frowning, she gazed up at the smiling woman.

"Boy, you're really into it today," Lisa grinned. "I haven't heard a word from you all morning."

"I'm working at staying awake." Kate's return smile lacked sparkle. "Holiday weekends tend to leave one a little groggy—don't they?" Slipping off her chair she followed the other girl to the lunch room.

"I guess that depends on how you spend the holiday weekend," Lisa laughed as she carried her coffee to an empty table. "Other than eating too much on Thanksgiving, I had a boring weekend." She eyed Kate as she seated herself across from her. "What did you do that was so very tiring?"

In a bid for time to form an answer, Kate took a deep swallow of her steaming coffee, scalding her tongue in the process. "I was Christmas shopping," she blurted with a sharply indrawn breath. "And you know how much I enjoy that!"

"Yes, I know." Lisa nodded once, then shook her head despairingly. "There are times, Kate, when I think you're an unnatural woman."

Not at all offended, Kate merely smiled and arched one questioning eyebrow.

"Well, I mean, you just aren't like other girls I know," Lisa insisted.

"Really?" Kate laughed softly. "In what way am I different?"

Lisa frowned. "You won't get angry? I mean, I don't want to hurt your feelings or anything." Her small white teeth gnawed on her lower lip. "I like you, Kate. I don't know anyone in the office that doesn't like you."

"But?" Kate prompted, curious to learn how the others felt about her.

"Well, you know." Lisa lifted her narrow shoulders in a helpless shrug. "Even though you're always dressed fashionably, you really don't seem to care about clothes like most women.''

Kate's shoulders reflected Lisa's shrug. "That's right, I don't. Go on."

"Well, then, there's this job." Lisa indicated their surroundings with a limp wave. "To the rest of us it's just that—a job. But you seem to really love it!"

"I do," Kate admitted, thinking that she'd probably scream if Lisa said "well" one more time.

"And you don't bother with men," Lisa stated flatly. When Kate blinked in surprise, she added hastily, "I mean like the rest of the single girls. I know, I know, you date occasionally, but you certainly don't seem all that interested in going out, and you never party like the girls I know."

Kate wasn't quite sure whether to feel flattered or insulted. Every one of Lisa's assertions held validity. Other than the desire to appear presentable, clothes didn't concern Kate. She *did* enjoy her work, which was not only interesting, but financially rewarding as well. And she had never felt desperate if she found herself without a date on the weekend. As to Lisa's final point, Kate knew exactly what she meant by the term "party." And, of course, it was quite true. Kate never drank more than a glass or two of wine; she did not "do" drugs; and she definitely didn't indulge in sexual games!

At least, she hadn't before Trace Sinclair had barged into her life! Kate writhed inwardly at the thought.

Suddenly uncomfortable, she pushed her chair back and stood up. "Break time's over," she said with forced brightness.

"Now I've hurt your feelings!" Lisa wailed.

As the conjecture about Trace had blanked all thought, Kate wasn't even sure what Lisa was talking about.

Frowning, she paused to gaze at the girl. "Hurt my feelings?" She smiled as Lisa's character analysis came rushing back. "No, you haven't. Everything you've said is true." Her smile softened with genuine amusement. "I guess I must be a female freak."

"Well, I never said that!" Lisa protested as they walked back to their desks.

Kate laughed aloud, drawing looks of surprise from several of the young women in the room.

"I know." Sliding onto her desk chair, Kate grinned. "I was only teasing."

Was she something of a female freak? The question nagged at Kate's mind intermittently throughout the remainder of the morning. At intervals, she thought about Trace and the evening they'd spent together.

Trace had driven her to where her car was parked on the large mall lot, then had followed her to her apartment building. As the rain was still coming down pretty hard, Kate had very carefully, very casually asked him if he'd like to spend the rest of the afternoon in her apartment.

"Are you crazy?" A rueful grin robbed the query of any insult. "One close call a day is about all I can handle, thank you."

Feeling somehow both inadequate and responsible, Kate gazed bleakly at the hands she was twisting in her lap. His covering hand stilled her agitated action.

"Honey, it *was* a close call," he murmured. "And all my fault." Releasing her hands, he lifted his index finger to her chin, raising her head. "Look at me, Kate," he demanded softly. When she opened her eyes, Kate's breath caught at the tenderness shining out of his eyes.

"I wanted you very badly." Trace expelled his breath with a weary sounding sigh. "Too badly. By continuing, by rushing you, I could have hurt you.'' The tip of his finger outlined her trembling lips. As if that visible tremor gave him pain, he groaned, "Honey, the last thing in the world I want to do is hurt you!" Dropping his hand, he sat back. "Do you understand?"

Kate nodded. She might be inexperienced, but she wasn't *that* innocent! From the things she'd read and the confidences she'd unwillingly listened to from friends, Kate was well aware that a woman's initiation to sex could be painful if not handled delicately.

Kate knew she should be feeling grateful to Trace at that moment; instead, all she felt was rejection and frustration. As if Trace could read her thoughts, he shook his head at her, smiling sadly.

"You'll be relieved when you've had time to think about it," he assured her softly. "For now, I think a change of plans is called for." Turning back to the steering wheel, he twisted the key in the ignition. "How do you feel about afternoon movies?"

"Ambivalent." Kate grimaced. "You can't hear the sound track for the kids."

"We can circumvent that." Trace slanted a teasing glance at her as he drove away from the curb. "We'll go to a film that doesn't attract a lot of kids."

Kate had loved every minute of it. Not that the movie Trace chose was great, it wasn't. In fact, it was a poorly made film. But the theater was nearly empty and they had one whole section to themselves, and Trace not only held her hand the entire time, he drew it to his lips repeatedly to press tiny, moist kisses on her palm and fingers. His kisses made it worth the price of admission.

During lunch Kate blocked the images of Trace from her mind by scrupulously attending to the conversation of the four young women she shared a table with. Since most of the talk was concerned with how the others had spent the weekend, Kate added very little to it.

By the time she went back to her desk Kate's mind boggled with the amorous exploits revealed by her co-workers. Maybe she really was something of a female freak, she reflected, amused at her shocked reaction to their frank discussion of their bedroom adventures.

Mulling over the lunchtime roundup of the weekend sexual indulgences of her table companions, Kate decided that, at almost twenty-four, she was pretty dumb. And considering the manner in which he'd left her, Trace Sinclair probably thought the same.

After leaving the theater they had gone directly to a nearby restaurant for an early dinner. For all her earlier disclaimers to the contrary, Kate was surprised to discover that she was hungry again. Strangely, considering the breakfast he'd so effortlessly consumed, Trace displayed little appetite, merely playing with the food on his plate before shoving it aside.

He drove her directly home from the restaurant, again declining her invitation to come in.

"I think not, honey." Trace smiled wryly. "Let's not tempt fate . . . or the devil in me." His gaze clung to her face as if to burn her likeness into his memory. "I've arranged to pick Kath up early. Our plane is scheduled to depart at 9:05."

"Give Kathy my love," Kate murmured, fighting a raspy thickness in her throat, "and tell her to write to me."

"May I write to you, too?" Trace asked, leaning across the seat to her.

Kate's heart seemed to leap at the request. Was he serious? She hoped so. "If you like," she replied wistfully.

"I do like." Moving slowly, Trace brushed his mouth over hers. "And I will." For a millisecond his mouth clung to hers. "You'd better go in now, honey." A derisive smile cut across his face as he moved away from her. "While your innocence is still intact."

Sighing, Kate glanced at her watch, groaning at the realization that only an hour and a half had passed since lunch time.

You came close to making a fool of yourself this time, Sinclair! Trace moved uncomfortably in the confines of the seat and stabbed impotently at the egg mixture in the oval plastic container. This morning his appetite was nonexistent.

Trace's normally smooth movements became awkward because of the tension that was humming through his body. His hand shook as he lifted his cup and drained the surprisingly good coffee. The instant he replaced the cup on the small tray a flight attendant materialized in the narrow aisle, glass coffeepot in hand.

"More coffee, sir?" The handsome young man smiled, his even teeth a startling white.

"Yes, thank you." A tremor ran through the long body of the plane, and Trace watched in admiration as the young man, body erect, poured the steaming liquid in a steady stream. "That's very good," Trace complimented as the attendant set the cup back on the tray.

"It goes with the job, sir." White teeth flashed again as the man moved away.

A wry smile curving his lips, Trace settled back in his seat. He could appreciate the flight attendant's insouciance. There had been times when Trace had performed not only adequately, but some claimed brilliantly, in the operating room under adverse conditions. Though he'd never put it into words, Trace's attitude mirrored the attendant's—it goes with the job.

More than one of his contemporaries had voiced the opinion that Trace was "cool under fire." A sour taste rose to sting his throat. Dr. Trace Sinclair, he thought mockingly, the cool, calm, collected whiz in the operating room, and a trembling basket case when confronted by the pale skin of a twenty-three-year-old virgin!

Shaken by the truth behind his thoughts, Trace grasped the small cup, gulping the hot brew in deep swallows. Instead of drowning the sour taste, the coffee burned his tongue and throat.

"Dammit!"

Though Trace had muttered the curse under his breath it reached the child sitting in the seat next to him.

"Don't you like your eggs, daddy?" Kathy asked, more like a concerned parent than an inquisitive child.

His set features softening, Trace turned to gaze lovingly at his frowning daughter.

"The eggs are very good, sweetheart," he replied. "I'm just not very hungry this morning." A smile easing his tight lip line, Trace indicated Kathy's breakfast with a nod of his head. "Apparently the pancakes were excellent."

Grinning impishly, Kathy glanced down at her food container, empty except for a few traces of dark maple syrup. "Yeah, they were. So were the sausages, and the cookies, and the juice." Her bright eyes sparkling with contentment, Kathy gazed up at him trustingly.

Trace didn't have the heart to chastize her about the use of the slang "yeah." Chuckling softly, he used his own napkin to wipe a dab of syrup off her chin.

"Would you like more juice?"

"Oh, no!" Kathy shook her head. "If I drink any more, I might need to go to the bathroom." Her pink lips twisted into a grimace. "And I *hate* when I have to go to the bathroom on an airplane!" She grinned when his chuckle gave way to a soft burst of laughter. "I think I'll take a nap," she said seriously. "If I sleep the time will go faster."

"Good thinking," Trace nodded solemnly. "Maybe I'll do the same."

After the breakfast trays had been cleared away Trace, following Kathy's example, released the seat to a reclining position and closed his eyes.

Though his eyes ached with a gritty sensation, Trace held out little hope of losing himself in sleep. He hadn't slept at all the night before, so why should this morning prove any different? It didn't. With conscious effort, Trace was mildly successful at relaxing the taut muscles in his body. But while his body rested, his mind raced.

What *had* happened to him?

The question had nagged at him throughout the seemingly endless night with boring regularity. Trace was almost accustomed to the question and the fact that he could find no answer to it.

Not in all the years since he'd imposed his own rule of absolute abstinence had he been so sorely tested. The realization that he'd been within a hairsbreadth of failing that test shook him to the core.

Trace was no fool. He knew, had always known, that the day would arrive when he'd consciously decide to lift the ban on physical gratification. He was a strong man, mentally as well as physically—but he *was* a man. How long could a healthy man, with an equally healthy sexual appetite, suppress the natural demands of his body?

Being a physician, Trace was aware of the effect of physical exhaustion on the libido. In consequence, he had maintained a work schedule that kept his body in a constant state of near exhaustion. His maneuver had produced two positive results. It had enhanced his reputation as a surgeon and had smothered all but the faintest twinges of sexual desire.

Those faint twinges had occurred on the rare occasions when Trace found himself in relative privacy with a woman.

Shifting his long legs to a more comfortable position in the small space between his seat and the one facing him, Trace examined the proximity as an excuse for his loss of control the afternoon before. The time required to examine the theory came to all of thirty seconds. The theory couldn't hold air, let alone be an excuse, and Trace knew it.

So, Trace charged himself scathingly, what the hell had happened to him with Kate?

Trace didn't like the answer that swirled around the edge of his consciousness. And not liking the answer, he mentally dodged it, refusing to give it substance throughout the majority of the flight west. The jet was making an approach to the landing strip when the answer formed into words that seared Trace's mind like a branding iron.

Kate Warren had happened to him.

Kate had the flu. Confined to her bed and hating every minute of it, Kate changed position for the umpteenth time since waking that morning. It was Monday, the third day of her confinement, and exactly two weeks since Trace had returned to his home in San Antonio.

Trace.

Sighing softly, Kate wriggled in an effort to ease the discomfort of her aching body.

What, she wondered moodily, was Trace doing at this minute? Was he in consultation with a patient in his office? Or, perhaps, proving his expertise in the sterile environs of the operating room?

Feeling out of sorts, slightly neglected and just a little sorry for herself, Kate made no attempt to stem the tears that slid over the edge of her eyelids to roll hotly down her face.

Trace had said he would write to her; he hadn't. Had he given as much as a passing thought to her in the past two weeks? Probably not, Kate decided, sniffing loudly.

Irrationally, the thought occurred that her illness was all Mr. Denunzio's fault, simply because he'd made a point of cautioning her to take care of herself. In her more serene moments, Kate admitted to having been careless with her health while running around in the freezing rain the previous Saturday. The really galling thing was, she'd been doing, of all things, her Christmas shopping.

Christmas.

The mere thought of the swiftly approaching holiday brought a groan to Kate's lips, a frown line to her brow and, most annoyingly, a fresh surge of stinging moisture to her eyes.

On the very day before Kate finally admitted she was sick, she'd acquiesced to her mother's request that she join the family for dinner that evening to discuss plans for the holiday.

Already uncomfortable with the achey, feverish symptoms of influenza, Kate sat mutely while the rest of the family chattered incessantly around the dining-room table.

"What do you mean—you won't be here for Christmas this year?" The shocked voice belonged to Kate's mother, Arlene. She was speaking to Kate's brother, Scott.

"Now, mother," Scott's tone was soothing, but firm. "We'll be here Christmas Eve, and that's really when all the holiday action happens around here."

All the holiday action. Kate sighed wearily. Some action.

"But I still don't understand why—"

"What's to understand?" Gina Warren interrupted her mother-in-law coolly; Gina had never allowed Arlene to intimidate her. "Scott and I decided to give the kids a trip to Disney World for Christmas. We're going on an arranged tour. It leaves early on Christmas morning. It's as simple as that." Her eyes gleaming with challange, Gina sat back, fully prepared to outstare Arlene.

Arlene was fully prepared to attack in another direction—sibling loyalty.

"But, Scott!" Arlene's tone was a delicate mixture of sadness and reproach. "You'll miss your sister's birthday!"

Oh, brother! Too tired to feel more than slightly amazed, Kate turned to stare at her mother out of dull, disbelieving eyes. Since when had anybody worried about *her* birthday? Other than as an addendum to the holiday?

Scott's thoughts were obviously running along the same vein. "Mother, honestly." He expelled his breath in a sharp sigh of impatience. "We've always incorporated Kate's birthday celebration with the usual Christmas Eve festivities. Why should this year be any different?" Scott frowned. "I really don't understand what all the fuss is about. Christmas Day has never been much more than a time to recuperate from the Christmas Eve hangover.''

"Do you object, Kate?" The ostensible head of the house, Paul Warren, inserted his question in a tone that clearly said it didn't matter one way or the other what she thought.

Object? Kate tried to corral her feverish thoughts. What was the question, she wondered. Was there a question? Her sister-in-law saved Kate the effort of forming a suitable denial.

"It makes no difference whether Kate objects or not, Paul." Gina had adamantly refused to address her in-laws as mother and dad from the very beginning. Gina had also never made a pretense of putting Kate's feelings ahead of her own either. Kate admired Gina for her honesty if nothing else. "The arrangements are made. The trip is paid for." Gina lifted her head defiantly. "We leave Christmas morning."

Although Kate heard every word spoken, she was not paying much attention to the adults at the table. Her bleary gaze was busy studying the expectant expressions on the faces of her six-year-old nephew and five-year-old neice. Very little perception was needed to realize the children could almost taste Disney World.

"Oh, I think it's a wonderful plan." Kate's smile was normal, even if the reedy sound of her voice was not. "I'll bet Disney World at Christmastime will be a lot of fun."

Kate's soft observation and the children's enthusiastic response had ended the debate.

Now, feeling alternately hot and cold as the fever waxed and waned, Kate groaned aloud as the final exchange between her mother and Gina came back to haunt her. The confrontation occurred as they were all milling around at the front door—Scott and his family intent on making their way to their home in Media, Kate desperate to reach her own apartment and her bed.

"How many—ah—*close* friends will be in attendance at your Christmas Eve open house *this* year, Arlene?" Gina's tone just barely escaped being labelled a sneer.

Arlene's eyes narrowed. "I'm expecting between twenty and thirty," she informed her daughter-in-law icily.

"Oh, lovely." On that note, Gina swept out of the house, her family in tow behind her.

Lovely. Kate's thought echoed the contempt Gina had vocalized. Between twenty and thirty people, frenetic in their deisire to appear imbued with the spirit of the season, laughing too loudly, eating to excess, drinking too much.

Kate shuddered beneath the weight of her covers. What was the spirit of the holiday, anyway? Wasn't it supposed to be loving, giving and peaceful, she mused feverishly.

At that moment, weak in mind and body, Kate was inclined to agree with Trace's attitude as related by Kathy. She needed Christmas like she needed this case of the flu!

Seven

By Wednesday the worst of the viral infection had run its normal course through Kate's system. Though she felt weak, the fever and achiness were gone.

By early afternoon, bored to distraction, Kate pushed back the bedcovers determinedly; she'd had more than enough of staring at the ceiling. Kate was also tired of her own melancholy.

Slipping her rag-tail robe over the flannel nightgown her mother had insisted she wear, Kate slid her feet into mules and scuffed her way into the kitchen, pointedly avoiding the mirror above her dresser. She *knew* she looked like death warmed over. She didn't need confirmation.

The short trip from the bedroom to the kitchen was surprisingly tiring. The simple chore of retrieving the plastic container of beef stew her mother had brought for her the afternoon before drained Kate of her meager store of stamina. After a couple of minutes, perspiration started to dampen her forehead, neck and shoulders. Beginning to tremble, Kate gripped the refrigerator door until the bout of weakness passed.

By the time Kate transferred the stew from the container to the stove and had put the teakettle on to boil, she wasn't sure if she had the strength to eat the meal and drink the tea.

Over an hour was required to complete a process that normally would have taken less than thirty minutes. Finally, after she felt fortified by the thick stew and sweet tea, Kate cradled a fresh cup of steaming tea in her hands and made her way slowly into the living room. She understood why the doctor had adamantly insisted she not return to work until after Christmas. Merely thinking about sitting at her desk sent a quiver through her.

The phone rang as Kate sank onto the sofa in weary gratitude. Carefully placing the teacup on the coffee table next to the phone, she lifted the receiver, biting her lip in consternation at how heavy the object seemed.

"Hello?"

"You sound terrible," her mother declared in a crisp tone. "Are you feeling worse?"

"No, mother," Kate sighed. "Actually, I'm feeling much better. I just got myself something to eat and it tired me out." Even Kate could hear the amazement in her tone. "The beef stew was very good, mother." Studying her trembling fingers with a frown, Kate brought the cup to her lips to sip the hot tea.

"Well, of course it tired you!" Arlene exclaimed in exasperation. "Kate, fighting the influenza infection has depleted your body. You must not overdo or you'll have a relapse."

"Yes, mother." Kate smiled wryly; there was more pedantry in her mother's tone than parental concern. "I promise I won't overdo and have a relapse."

"I should hope not," Arlene snapped. "It would ruin your holiday."

What? Kate shook her head. The holiday! Oh, brother! Aloud she murmured, "I'll be back in fighting shape for the holiday, mother."

"Not if you don't take care of yourself," Arlene retorted.

"I'm going to rest now, mother," Kate said, distractedly glancing at her hand, which was beginning to tremble from the weight of the receiver. "I promise that except for an emergency, like a fire, I won't move from the sofa." Kate silently congratulated herself on the return of her sense of humor; maybe she would live, after all!

Arlene was not amused. "Your sense of humor escapes me! There isn't one thing funny about the possibility of a fire." Her sigh conveyed years of impatience. Her pause invited apology; Kate declined. When Arlene spoke again her voice was sharp with annoyance. "I'll stop by again after work."

"That won't be necessary, mother. I'll be able to manage by myself now." Kate closed her lids over a sudden sting in her eyes. Though she appreciated her mother's evening visits since Sunday, she faced the fact that they had been made out of a sense of duty, not real affection. "This *is* your bridge night, isn't it?" Kate asked tiredly.

"Yes. We're having a little wine and cheese afterward and exchanging small gifts," Arlene sighed. "But, I really feel I should stop by your place and get you a meal."

The "I feel I should" hurt Kate more than if her mother had bluntly told her she didn't want to come. Two warm, salty tears rolled down Kate's cheeks quickly followed by a gathering trickle.

"I had a meal." Kate managed a steady tone. "You and dad go and have a good time. I'll be fine."

"Well, if you insist." Relief was evident in Arlene's tone; the decision had been taken from her. "Now you rest, Kate. I'll call you tomorrow and, oh, yes, I brought in your mail yesterday. It's on the corner of the coffee table."

After replacing the receiver, which now felt like it must weigh at least fifty pounds, Kate closed her eyes and sipped at the rapidly cooling tea. Concentrating on collecting her rattled emotions, she momentarily forgot about the mail.

Why, she chided herself, did she let her parents' disinterest—or forced interest—upset her anymore? Hadn't she faced the reality of their life-style and total self-interest long ago? Kate sighed raggedly. If she ever, ever had a family of her own, she vowed, she'd smother them in love and caring! There would never be any doubt about how *she* felt!

Setting the remains of the tea aside, Kate stretched out on the sofa. The instant her weary body was prone a haunting vision of the last time she'd reclined in exactly the same spot rose to torment her mind. On that previous occasion she had not been alone—not in the apartment, not on the sofa. An excitingly hard male body had warmed her outside; an enticing male mouth had scorched her inside.

Throughout the length of her bout with the flu, Kate had relived the hours she'd spent with Trace. In disjointed, fever-induced scenes their meager time together swirled through her memory in fragmented bits and pieces. Prisoner to the accelerated flow of mental images, Kate had cried his name aloud several times. Now, lucid, she did the same.

"Oh, Trace."

With a sigh that was more of a groan, Kate curled into the warmth of her tattered robe. Immediately, the essence that was uniquely Trace captured her imagination, and he was there with her, enveloping her with his strength.

Kate's slender body quivered as she recalled all the clamoring passion Trace had evoked in her. Weakened by her illness, she lay helpless against memory's onslaught, yearning for the low, enticing sound of his voice, the gentle caress of his hands and, yes, the fulfilling presence of his body, banishing the emptiness in hers.

Depleted in spirit as well as strength, Kate moaned with the certainty growing in her mind. Against all reason, she was very much afraid that she was falling in love with Trace Sinclair. Biting her lip, she prevented the moan from becoming a sob.

How had it happened so quickly, Kate agonized, locking her arms around herself. She hardly knew the man, and yet it was as if she'd known him forever.

Infatuation! Yes, that's what it was; that's what it had to be, Kate argued inwardly. It simply was not possible to fall in love with a man she'd known for such a short period of time.

Infatuation was harmless, especially when the man was almost half a continent away. Heaving a sigh of relief, Kate sat up and reached for the mail that had accumulated since Monday.

There were several business-size envelopes which Kate shoved aside. There were the usual pieces of junk mail which Kate ignored. There was also a stack of greeting-card-sized envelopes. Placing the stack on her lap, Kate settled back into the corner of the sofa to open her cards in comfort.

There were several "get well" cards from the girls she worked with, including a rather humorous one from Lisa, the girl who sat at the desk next to Kate's. There was also a large card, signed by every one of the women that worked in Kate's office. There were three Christmas cards—one from a friend Kate had known since grade school, one from her brother and sister-in-law and one that bore a return address that made Kate's heart skip a beat.

Kate had sent a Christmas card containing a brief note to the same address the week before. Trace had given her the address; it was for his home outside San Antonio. Both the return address in the left-hand corner and her own in the center of the envelope had been typed.

With shaking fingers Kate tore open the envelope and withdrew the expensive greeting card. Her eyes swiftly skimmed the words that wished her season's greetings from the Alamo, and the illuminated scene of the famous shrine. Flipping the card open, Kate ran her gaze over the typed message inside.

I miss you, Kate. I wish you could be here for Christmas, but daddy said you have a family and plans of your own. But I pray every night that I get what I asked Santa Claus for for Christmas.
    Love and kisses,

                                            Kathy

A soft smile curved Kate's lips and tears welled in her eyes as she stared at the painstakingly printed name beneath the one someone had typed for the child. Had Trace typed the message for Kathy, Kate wondered bleakly. Did he know that his daughter had sent return greetings to the young woman who'd cared for the child while she was lost?

The very real possibility that Trace Sinclair hadn't given as much as a single thought to her since his return to San Antonio caused a twist of near anguish in Kate's chest and mind. Cradling the card to her heart, Kate closed her eyes and let the tears of longing and loneliness slide unheeded down her face.

The jarring sound of the doorbell shattered the cocoon of misery Kate was sinking into. Kathy's card clutched in her hand, Kate rose shakily and walked unsteadily to the door.

A middle-aged man stood in the hallway, a large, tissue-wrapped flower arrangement in one hand, the index finger of his other hand poised to push the bell button again.

"Miss Warren?" he inquired politely.

"Yes."

"These are for you, miss." The man placed the arrangement in Kate's hands then, as if he was in a hurry to get on with his deliveries, he turned away.

"Wait!" Kate called, if weakly. "I'll get a tip for you."

"Not necessary, miss," the man said kindly, already striding down the hall. "Enjoy."

Maybe the flowers were from Trace!

The idea struck, hopefully if irrationally, as Kate closed the door. As she crossed the room, she realized that Trace would have no way of knowing that she'd been ill. Still, the flowers *could* be a combined thank you and Christmas gift.

And there really *could* be a Santa Claus, Kate thought dejectedly moments later, biting her lip as she stared at the tiny florist's card, signed simply: Speedy recovery from the benefit fund of Coast To Coast Insurance Co.

Of course, Kate knew about the office kitty. It had been set up for this type of occasion—sending "get well" flowers to a sick coworker. Kate contributed to the fund on a regular basis. And it wasn't as if she didn't appreciate the cheery, seasonal bouquet.

Silently chiding herself for her deep sense of disappointment, Kate discarded the tissue and made room on the low coffee table for the floral arrangement. After positioning the flowers, Kate scooped up the business-size envelopes she'd brushed aside to make room for the bouquet.

Bills. There were four of the long envelopes and, sighing, Kate proceeded to tear open the first one. She was withdrawing the enclosed sheet of paper when her gaze skimmed, then became riveted on, the return address on the next long envelope.

Casting the envelope she was holding aside, she lifted the next one with trembling fingers. The return address had been imprinted and looked very professional. It declared that the contents of the envelope came from Trace M. Sinclair, M.D. and gave what Kate had to assume was the address of his medical office.

If it's a check in payment for looking after Kathy, I'll rip it in half and send it back, Kate thought forlornly, almost afraid to open it. As her hands absently smoothed the envelope's heavy, quality paper, she mused on Trace's middle initial. What did the M stand for? Michael? Mitchell? Martin, perhaps?

Deciding the M stood for Michael simply because she preferred it, Kate turned the envelope over and carefully slid her fingernail under the flap. Managing to unseal the flap without a single tear, she slowly withdrew a small square of paper, folded in half. By its size, the single sheet of paper was obviously not a check. A long, shuddering sigh whooshed through Kate's lips as she slipped her thumb between the fold and flipped the paper open.

Her eyes widening in surprise, Kate noted that the sheet of paper had been torn from a regulation prescription pad; the letterhead at the top was identical to the one on the envelope. A choking gasp tightened her throat as her gaze dropped to the four words written in a bold slash across the center of the paper.

Come to Texas, Kate.

That was it. There was no salutation, no signature, just the exact same words Trace had repeated to her several times in the scant two days they were together. Just—"Come to Texas, Kate."

The paper wavered in her trembling hand, then the script blurred. Sobbing softly, Kate was positive she could hear Trace, his voice teasing, coaxing as he murmured the enticing invitation.

Lord, he was tired! Sighing, Trace leaned back into the plush padding of his high-backed desk chair. Closing his eyes he absently massaged the bunched muscles in his neck.

Long fingers digging rhythmically into the tension-tightened muscles and tendons, Trace slowly worked his hand along the curve of his neck to his right shoulder. Perhaps he should take the time to go to the health club and have a professional rubdown, he thought, wincing when the tips of his fingers dug into a particularly tender spot.

Yeah, sure…but when? Trace scoffed at his own idea.

Right now, he had fifteen minutes all to himself. Trace grimaced; fifteen minutes to rest before Maggie, his nurse-receptionist, ushered his next scheduled patient into his consulting office.

The grueling pace Trace had maintained since his return from Philadelphia over three weeks ago had been killing; at that moment he felt more dead than alive. And, as if the workload he'd taken on hadn't been enough, Trace had spent many precious hours searching the stores for gifts he *hoped* Kathy would like. Since all Kathy would say in response to his repeated requests to know what she wanted for Christmas was, "Santa Claus knows what I want," at best his selections had been hit or miss.

"This whole holiday craziness is a pain in the—"

"I just received notice that your next appointment, Mr. Craig, will be delayed, doctor." Maggie's no-nonsense voice cut across Trace's muttered imprecation against the holiday via the office intercom.

"How long delayed?" Trace shot back irritably.

"His wife said ten minutes, fifteen at the outside," Maggie informed tonelessly.

"Is the patient due to follow Mr. Craig here yet?"

"No, sir."

Trace heaved an impatient sigh. "Okay, we wait." Smoothing the ruffles of annoyance from his tone, he added, "Would you bring me a cup of coffee, Maggie?"

"Certainly."

The intercom went silent. Less than three minutes later Maggie entered the room quietly on rubber-soled shoes, a coffee mug in one hand and a small plate in the other.

"I thought you might like a piece of baklava," she murmured, sliding the plate onto the desk in front of Trace. "It's fresh. I picked it up on my way to the office this morning."

A twitching smile betrayed the stern expression Trace leveled on his amply endowed, middle-aged right arm.

"Baklava?" he groaned, shifting his gaze to the honey and walnut pastry. "In the middle of the day? Are you trying to sabotage my waistline?"

Maggie's snort of ridicule bespoke long familiarity with her employer. Arching one gray-tinged eyebrow, she swept his figure with bright, intelligent eyes.

"I seriously doubt your waistline will be in any danger from this one small pastry triangle," Maggie said dryly. "In fact, as a professional, I'd hazard a guess that your waistline has decreased by some two inches within the past few weeks."

"You're a treasure, Maggie," Trace drawled. "But you do have an annoying tendency to nag."

"That being the case," Maggie retorted, moving silently to the door, "I'm going to offer some unsolicited advice. You must slow down, doctor. You're losing weight...and you're beginning to resemble a haunted shadow."

Trace gave a choking laugh around the bite of pastry he was chewing, "a haunted shadow!" Swallowing carefully, he shook his head. "Where did you come up with that?" A teasing light brightened his tired eyes. "Have you been watching some late-night ghost movies on TV?"

"I never watch TV and you know it," Maggie denied calmly. "But I do tend to watch you. I have for the entire two hundred and twenty years I've been with you."

"Is that what it's been? Doesn't seem a day over two hundred and nineteen," Trace observed mockingly.

Then, his expression sobering, he assured softly, "I'm all right, Maggie."

"You're not, you know." She opened the door, then paused to glance back at him, her face set into lines of concern. "You need to be pampered a little bit by a good, willing woman." Her tone made it clear that she wasn't teasing.

"I don't *need* anything, Maggie." A chill had invaded Trace's tone. "Least of all a woman, willing or otherwise."

"Whatever you say, doctor," Maggie smiled sadly. "You have approximately twenty-five minutes. Try to relax a little." With an almost imperceptible sigh, she closed the door quietly behind her.

Trace stared at the wood surface with a wry smile on his lips. Maggie addressed him as "doctor" in that particular tone only when she was put-out with him. Shrugging, he turned back to the baklava and coffee. Twenty-five whole minutes, he marveled. Whatever will I do with all that free time?

What Trace did, while chewing pastry and sipping coffee, was remember instances he had convinced himself were better forgotten.

A willing woman. Unknowingly, Trace's mouth curved sensuously. Kate had been willing. Closing his eyes, he rolled her name around in his mind. Kate. Kate of the alluring smoke-colored eyes and hair the shiny hue of licorice extract. Kate of the clinging arms and the moist mouth, eager to learn. Kate. Kate of the soft, laughing voice and virginal innocence. Kate. Kate. Kate.

Sudden passion, hot and intense surged through Trace's body. Muffling a groan, he clasped the mug with both hands, as if hanging on for dear life.

God, he wanted to possess that woman!

He didn't *need* Kate, Trace assured himself confidently. But he sure did want her!

Settling into his chair, Trace took a deep swallow of the lightly creamed coffee. Actually, he mused, Kate has a lot going for her. She's intelligent, beautiful, has a terrific sense of humor and a sweetly exciting body. A flashing image of her body, her pale naked skin gleaming in invitation, drew a fine film of moisture to his brow.

Maybe he should have taken her when he had the opportunity. No, of course he couldn't have taken her then; he'd been too hot, too ready. But, damn, if he'd have taken her he wouldn't be sitting here now, getting the sweats from simply thinking about her! Oh, no, he'd more than likely be sitting here really hating himself . . . and still wanting her anyway!

The silent argument was a familiar one to Trace. He'd had it with himself a dozen times since returning from the east coast. A smile of derision quirked his lips. The last time he'd engaged in that inner debate, he'd ended by tearing a sheet off his prescription pad to use as an invitation to Kate to join him in Texas. Naturally, Kate had made no response.

You're a fool, Sinclair, Trace informed himself mockingly. Did you actually think Kate would hop on the first plane west after receiving an invitation that sounded more like a command?

She might have at least sent me a Christmas card; she sent one to Kathy.

Hearing the sound of his own thoughts echoing inside his head, Trace straightened abruptly in his chair. Will you listen to yourself, he demanded silently. You sound exactly like Kathy when she's into her best whining routine! This has got to stop, Sinclair. Kate Warren is a woman, like other women...nothing less, but nothing more either. Get to work and forget her.

Even as Trace issued the advice he was reaching for the prescription pad at the corner of his desk.

By the week before Christmas Kate had a very bad case of cabin fever. Although she had always felt comfortable in her apartment, after two weeks of being confined to the three rooms and miniscule bathroom, she was becoming very antsy.

Despite the fact that merely making the short trip to her mailbox in the lobby left her shaking with weakness, Kate decided she had to get out, if only for an hour.

As Kate dressed to go out, she attempted to convince herself this trip really *was* necessary. Her food supply had dwindled, so a trip to the supermarket was a must. And there were still a few items on her Christmas list to be purchased.

Recalling the usual family plans for the holiday brought a grimace to Kate's soft lips. One of these years, she promised herself for perhaps the thousandth time, she would take her vacation weeks in December and run away—if she could find a place where she wouldn't be saturated with the trappings of the season. Kate knew there were such places, but she also knew that the cost of running to them would be prohibitive.

Deciding to keep her priorities straight, Kate tackled the supermarket first. Three overstuffed shopping bags later, Kate stumbled into her apartment, groaning softly and perspiring profusely. Trembling with fatigue, she stashed the perishables haphazardly into the refrigerator, swallowed the vitamin tablet her doctor had recommended, then fell fully clothed on the bed, consigning the Christmas shopping to another day.

On the morning of the twenty-second of December Kate convinced herself she was ready to face the crowds of last-minute shoppers.

The day was mild and bright, the sky such an intense blue that it cheered her spirits just by looking at it. Kate could have chosen any one of several different malls to shop in. Without conscious thought she found herself parking on the lot of the mall where she'd met first Kathy, then Trace.

Deciding she must have latent masochistic tendencies, Kate headed for the tall tree in the center of the mall like a homing pigeon. Her eyes shadowed with longing, she watching as a few late stragglers, their small faces uncertain, tentatively approached by now a weary looking man garbed in red velvet and fake white fur.

In her mind's eye Kate held a sharply defined image of a small girl, her blond curls shimmering from the excitement shaking through her tiny body, her eyes sparkling with expectation, her sweet face glowing with wonder.

Kate turned from the scene abruptly when her eyes began to sting. There had been no more notes from Kathy, nothing from Trace, not even a Christmas card.

Shaking herself mentally, Kate strode purposely away from the site of her first encounter with Kathy. The incident was over, both the child and the father were out of her life. It's just as well, she reasoned, ignoring the way everything was growing blurry. She'd begun to spin dream castles while convalescing; now it was time to get back to the real world.

Discovering she felt much stronger than just the day before, Kate made a day of her shopping. She had lunch in one of the many restaurants located inside the mall, but not the one that she'd taken Kathy to.

By midafternoon Kate had drawn a check mark on every item that remained on her list; she even had most of the gifts wrapped. She was making her way to the exit when her glance was snagged by a small jewelry store display window. Reluctantly, battling the sentimental emotion that urged her forward, Kate walked to the showcase to stare at the item that had caught her eye.

Cast in a glowing matte pewter, the piece displayed was a replica of the Liberty Bell. It was approximately three inches high and four inches wide. A soft sigh of defeat whispered through Kate's lips as she studied the exquisite detail of the piece. Even as resistance tightened her slender body, she turned to walk into the shop. She was going to buy it. Even if she never gave it to him, she simply *had* to buy it for Trace.

Oddly, purchasing the bell, then waiting while the clerk gift wrapped it, drained Kate to the point of exhaustion. On trembling legs, she walked slowly to her car; with trembling arms and hands, she carefully drove home.

Unceremoniously dropping her coat, purse and other packages onto the chair just inside the door, Kate cradled the brightly packaged bell in one hand and clasped her mail in the other as she crossed the room to the sofa.

Setting the stack of mail aside for the moment, Kate set the bell on the coffee table, then sat staring at it, her bottom lip caught between her teeth.

Did she have the nerve to mail the gift to him, Kate mused. She knew full well Trace's opinion of the holidays; in many ways his opinion coincided with her own. If she did send it to him, would he frown upon opening it? Maybe even send it back to her, along with a sarcastic note? Kate's teeth sank deeper into her lip. Perhaps she'd be better off stashing it in the back of her closet— and hopefully forgetting it.

Yet, in many ways the little bell seemed to symbolize and represent aspects of Trace's character. The traits of independence, confidence, pride and strength were as ingrained in Trace as they were in the symbol of liberty. And, as the bell had been cracked with its first peel, Trace's pride and ego had figuratively been cracked by his first emotional commitment.

Smiling sadly at her own whimsy, Kate smoothed the small package with trembling fingers. Oh, yes, the bell was definitely for Trace...even if she never gave it to him.

Swallowing against a sudden thickness in her throat, Kate pulled her hand from the gift and reached for the mail. Disinterestedly shuffling through the stack her eyes froze on one long business envelope. The return address was the same as on the one she'd received the week before. Her breathing unsteady, Kate tore the envelope open and withdrew the small, folded sheet from a prescription pad. And, as on the one the previous week, the paper contained just four words.

Come to Texas, Kate.

Eight

A gentle smile on his lips, Trace quietly shut the door to Kathy's bedroom. It was the second night in a row that he'd made it home in time not only for dinner but to put Kathy to bed as well.

His smile twisting slightly, Trace strolled into his home office. Due to the excitement of the swiftly approaching holiday Kathy had proved a bouncing handful on both nights. Yet still, when questioned, all the child would say was, "Santa knows what I want."

Going directly to the beautifully carved credenza, Trace splashed whiskey into a glass then dropped in two ice cubes. While sipping appreciatively, he walked to the large desk in front of a window that overlooked Kathy's play area in the yard.

Savoring the smoky flavor of the whiskey, Trace propped his feet on the edge of the desk and let his head rest on the back of his chair. It had been a slow week because, as usual, none of his patients would consider surgery the week before Christmas except in an emergency.

For himself, Trace was in mental conflict over the amount of free time he suddenly found himself with. Trace was all too aware that he was pretty much an absentee father. So, on the one hand he was grateful for the opportunity to be with Kathy. Yet, on the other hand, he didn't relish the quiet moments after Kathy was asleep. The quiet was far too inducive to thoughts, thoughts that persisted in traveling east to a woman with vibrant black hair, and smoke-colored eyes, and lips the memory of which could drive a rational man to drink.

Self-mockery turned his eyes cynical. Gazing into the amber whiskey, Trace cautioned himself against having more than one drink; although he had no surgery scheduled the next day, there was always the possibility of an emergency arising. Just one more day, then he would be free until after Christmas; it was his associates' turn to work a holiday.

"Will there be anything else tonight, doctor?"

Dropping his feet to the floor, Trace swiveled his chair toward the doorway. His housekeeper of six years, Inez Peranza, stood in the threshold, her expression one of patient attention.

"No, thank you." A teasing smile hovered around Trace's mouth. "Is the TV movie a good one tonight?" he asked softly.

"*Si*," Inez nodded her silver-streaked head. "The film *Valdes is Coming* is being shown again."

"Really?" Trace was no longer teasing. "Maybe I'll tune it in. I liked that film."

"I know," Inez grinned, revealing teeth that were still in excellent condition, even after sixty-odd years. "Have a good evening, doctor."

"Thanks, Inez," Trace sighed. "Good night. Enjoy the movie."

Trace's eyes fell on his desk phone as the door closed with a muffled click. When he'd walked into the house late that afternoon, Inez had handed him two phone messages. One message had been from his mother, the other from his ex-mother-in-law. After greeting Kathy, Trace had come to the office. Taut with concern, he'd dialed his parents' number in Hawaii. When his mother answered, he'd bypassed the usual greeting to get to the point.

"Is dad all right?" Though his voice had an acquired note of professional calm, Trace felt fear crawl in his guts. His father, Michael T. Sinclair, had been a noted heart specialist before suffering a massive coronary two years previously. After an almost spectacular recovery, Michael decided he'd rather live than tempt fate by pursuing his career. Within six months of his decision to retire, Michael had disposed of his fashionable Houston home and had whisked his wife to Hawaii. Trace's parents had planned to fly to San Antonio to spend the holidays with their only child and grandchild. Before his mother spoke, Trace knew something had happened to interfere with their plans.

"Dad had a very slight heart attack this morning, Trace," Kathryn Sinclair said bluntly, complimenting her son's intelligence both as a man and a physician. "Doctor Cassiday assured me that Michael is in no danger," she went on firmly. "But he also stressed the inadvisability of a long trip at this time."

"Of course," Trace inserted coolly, releasing a silent sigh of relief. "Kath and I will miss you, but dad's health is more important than the holidays."

Trace had talked with his mother for a few more minutes, then had called Kathy to the phone. Well aware of the opinion both his parents had always had of Annette, Trace didn't mention his former wife's threat of a child custody battle in the near future.

The second message he'd set aside until after Kathy was in bed for the night; the last thing Trace needed was to have the child upset and, intuitively, Trace knew he wasn't going to be happy with whatever it was that Ruth wanted. He dialed her phone number.

Trace's intuition was absolutely correct. Using the same direct approach as his mother had, Ruth came to the point immediately.

"Trace, I realize it's asking a great deal," she began slowly, then rushed on, "but could we have Kathy here for Christmas Day?"

"What?" Trace half laughed, too stunned to believe he'd heard her clearly.

"Oh, Trace, please, just hear me out before you refuse," Ruth hurried on. "As you know, Annette's brother Carl has been working in Japan for his company for over four years now. His twin sons have never experienced an American Christmas."

"I know all that, Ruth," Trace said impatiently. "But, I don't see what that—"

"Carl and his family came home yesterday," Ruth interrupted breathlessly. "And, well, we'd like to have a real family Christmas for them—with all the children together." She paused, very briefly, then continued. "Trace, you've never kept your aversion to the holiday a secret."

"That doesn't mean I don't want to spend it with my daughter," Trace retorted.

"I know, I'm sorry," Ruth murmured contritely, then softly, persuasively, "Trace, I'm being very selfish but, just once, I'd like to have all my grandchildren here on Christmas."

Trace was still staring at the beige phone ten minutes after he'd disconnected. Sighing, he pushed back his chair and carried his glass to the kitchen. It was really a pity he was so fond of Ruth, he thought tiredly. If he'd have liked her less, he might have been able to refuse her request. As it was, now he'd have to pull some strings to get a flight east on Christmas Eve.

Flicking off lights as he went, Trace secured the house for the night. On his way upstairs, he stopped at the archway to the living room and reached for the light switch on the wall. His gaze rested a moment on the six-foot balsam tree framed by the picture window at the front of the house. The tree was beautifully bedecked, waiting for the brightly wrapped gifts to shelter under its branches.

Touching the switch, Trace turned for the stairs, his lips tight, his expression cynical.

"Yes, indeedy," he muttered derisively. "And a Merry Christmas to you too, Sinclair."

Kate held the jewel-toned velvet pants suit in midair and ran a critical glance over its classic lines. Had the spilled drink spoiled it, or could the dry cleaner save its life? Examining the large, stiffened spot more closely, she swore softly. She really should have followed the urge that cautioned her against wearing the suit the night before; she was in a position to know how very sloppy her parents' Christmas Eve "gatherings" could get.

Sighing resignedly, she carefully folded the suit and placed it on her bedroom chair before turning back to her closet. Removing a silky men's-style shirt from a hanger, she slipped it on and tucked it into the narrow jeans that hugged her slim hips; on Christmas Day it didn't matter what she wore to visit her parents.

While applying a light brush of peacock-blue eye shadow that matched the color of her shirt, Kate did a mental postmortem of the Christmas Eve party.

As usual, her parents' split-level home was crowded to bursting with their "intimate" friends of the moment—half of whom Kate didn't know...or want to know for that matter.

And, per usual, the drinks, of all varieties, were flowing like a rain-swollen river. By the time Kate arrived several of the guests were already unfurling their fourth sheet to the wind.

And, as always, Kate felt like a stranger in the house she'd grown up in. And a disgusted stranger at that.

Christmas carols blared from the stereo, voices were raised as people shouted to one another from room to room, and at least a half-dozen children ran around, seemingly in circles, screaming excitedly.

All in all, Kate mused, it was the same old general mess. The absolute topper of the evening for Kate was being backed into a corner by a man easily as old as her father, then having the slob spill his drink down the length of one leg of her pantsuit.

Well, it wasn't a complete disaster, Kate concluded, grinning at herself in the mirror. Being baptized by whiskey and water had given her the perfect excuse to leave.

And now she was going back. Kate's grin faded as her lips curved down. She knew exactly what she'd be walking into. Although the house would have been tidied by now, Kate knew both her parents would be sleepy and dull, even though her father would make a show of Christmas cheeriness.

Kate shuddered. It was always the same. Noting the time was 10:22, she stuck her arm into the closet and withdrew her coat, reluctantly slipping it on as she walked out of the bedroom. She was reaching for the doorknob when the phone rang. Grateful for any delay, however brief, she crossed the room to the coffee table and lifted the receiver.

"Hello, Merry Christmas." Kate wasn't sure why she'd given the greeting. She certainly didn't feel very merry.

"Hello, Kate."

"Trace?" For an instant Kate went completely blank. Then everything accelerated. Her heart beat faster, her breathing became shallow, her mind whirled. "Where are you?" she cried.

"A few blocks away," he said quietly, "in a phone booth." Trace was silent for a moment, then he said quickly, "I don't want to interfere with any plans you may have, but do you have time for a cup of coffee with me?"

"Time? Of course I have time!" And if I didn't I'd have time anyway, Kate added silently.

"Good." Trace expelled his breath audibly. "I'll pick you up in a few minutes. Okay?"

"Yes, I'll be waiting." As she hung up, Kate's hand bumped the elegantly wrapped package that contained the pewter bell. Without giving herself time to consider, she scooped it up and slid it into her capacious shoulder bag.

Trace brought the rented Ford to a gliding stop along the curb as Kate ran down the three steps to the sidewalk. Leaning across the seat he opened the passenger door for her as she circled the front of the car.

Kate ran an encompassing glance over Trace as she slid into the car. He looked tired, thinner, and somehow disillusioned . . . and altogether wonderful.

"Hello," she said softly, smiling tentatively.

"Hello, yourself." The lines radiating from the corners of his eyes deepened with his return smile. "You look like every man's dream of the perfect Christmas present," Trace said solemnly.

"*You* look like you've been working too hard," Kate replied candidly, contentedly joining him when he laughed easily.

"Well, now that we've exchanged compliments," Trace drawled, "shall we see if we can find a place that's open on holidays?"

"I know of only one," Kate said thoughtfully. "The convenience store out on the highway."

Putting the car in gear, Trace drove away. "Just tell me when to turn, honey."

Less than five minutes later, Trace parked the car in front of the convenience store. "You were right," he observed dryly, indicating a large sign in the window promising that the store would be open on Christmas Day from 9:00 A.M. till 6:00 P.M. Thrusting his door open, Trace slanted a quick glance at her.

"Don't go away, honey, I'll be back in a minute with our Christmas breakfast." Slamming the door, he strode into the store.

It was after ten-thirty. Hadn't Trace eaten anything, Kate wondered. And where was Kathy, anyway? For all his talk of disliking the holiday, Kate would have bet a month's salary that Trace would play out the role of merrymaker for Kathy's sake. Suddenly worried, she waited impatiently for him to return.

When Trace came back to the car he was grasping a brown paper bag by the top while balancing the bottom of it in the palm of his other hand. As he opened the door, Kate shot her question at him.

"Where's Kathy, Trace?"

"With her grandparents," Trace said tersely, sliding carefully into the car. "It's a long story. I'll tell you about it while we eat."

Setting the bag on the seat between them, Trace dipped his hand inside and withdrew two plastic-wrapped, iced buns. Dropping the pastries into Kate's lap, he plunged his hand inside again and retrieved two Styrofoam cups of coffee. After handing one of the cups to her, he removed both the lids. Steam rose from the cups, filling the interior of the car with the aroma of freshly brewed coffee.

"Mmm, smells delicious," Kate murmured, inhaling deeply.

"Yeah, the first of the day always does." Trace started to raise the cup to his lips then, hesitating briefly, he held it aloft. "Thank heaven for Seven-Eleven," he drawled, tentatively sipping the hot brew.

A shiver of alarm swept through Kate. There was a weariness in Trace that went far deeper than the surface signs revealed; a weariness that had more to do with the spirit than the body.

Gently blowing on her coffee, Kate studied him over the rim of her cup. Though Trace would probably rather die than show it, he was obviously hurting—at least it was obvious to Kate because suddenly, she was hurting too. Impulsively, she made an offer to help.

"What's bothering you, Trace?" she asked softly, her tone relaying her willingness to listen if he cared to unburden himself.

Trace's crooked smile acknowledged her offer. "This whole holiday razzmatazz," he replied sardonically. He was quiet a moment, observing her contemplatively, then he shrugged. "I never thought I'd feel lonely on Christmas." He smiled derisively. "Yet, lonely was exactly what I felt this morning. I . . . ah . . . appreciate the company, Kate."

A sharp pain shot through Kate's chest making it almost impossible for her to breathe. Trace hadn't shut his emotional door on her—he'd slammed it in her face. Dredging a smile from the tattered edges of her pride, Kate said flippantly, "Oh, you mean I'm a port in the holiday storm?" Glancing down, she toyed with the wrapped pastries. "Happy to oblige."

"Dammit!" Trace muttered the exclamation as he reached out to raise her chin with hard fingers. "That's not what I meant!"

"What did you mean, Trace?" Head up, Kate faced him squarely. "What exactly do you expect of me? Am I supposed to just sit quietly and keep you company?"

"Kate . . ." Trace began.

"Or," Kate went on relentlessly, "did you hope I'd invite you into my apartment and my bed?" Kate sniffed, but refused to allow the threatening tears release. "I must admit, that would be one way to take the edge off loneliness."

"Kate!" Trace reflexively tightened his hold on her chin. "Kate, will you stop this and listen?"

"To what?" Kate shouted. "You're not saying anything!"

"I might if you'd shut up!" he shouted back. "What's wrong with you?"

Blinking rapidly, Kate jerked away from his fingers to stare through the windshield. "I'm afraid," she breathed tightly. "I'm so afraid."

"Afraid?" Trace repeated blankly. Then, incredulously, "Kate! You don't really believe I'd ask to see you this morning to force myself on you?"

"No!" Kate shook her head sharply. "Of course not!"

Trace expelled a sigh of frustration. "Then why are you afraid?" Capturing her chin again, he turned her head. "Honey, tell me."

"You're not going to like hearing it," Kate warned, smiling at the wary look that entered his eyes. Her gaze locked to his, she said clearly, "I'm afraid I'm falling in love with you, Trace."

With an outward calm that masked the uncertainty and hope battling within her, Kate watched as Trace absorbed the shock of her statement. There was a sudden alert wariness about him that touched a chord in her, making her hurt for him even while she was hurting so very badly herself. This man had been raked over the coals of love; every tiny nuance about him warned that he would not willingly step into that fire again. The cynical smile that briefly feathered his lips confirmed Kate's conjecture.

"Do you know what love is, Kate?" Trace asked too softly. "Have you been in love before?"

"No," Kate responded simply.

"I suspected as much." Trace nodded once. "If we had the time, I'd tell you about love, kid," he muttered, squashing the empty cup and dropping it into the paper bag.

Kate's hesitation was barely noticeable. "I have all day." Without conscious thought, she handed her half full cup to him. When he frowned in question, she smiled. "You finish it. I've had my breakfast this morning."

"I wasn't questioning the coffee," Trace said impatiently. "What do you mean you have all day? You were obviously dressed to go out when I called—weren't you?"

"Yes, to my parents' house," she admitted. "But it won't cause any problems if I call and tell them I'm not coming." At the questioning arch of his eyebrow, she elaborated. "I know my parents would much sooner sleep off the effects of last night's party than go through the motions of the day with me."

"Emotional poverty." Trace echoed her statement of weeks before.

"In spades," Kate admitted tightly, swallowing against the thickness in her throat.

Trace was silent for some moments, staring moodily into the Styrofoam cup. Then, without looking up at her, he asked carefully, "Will you come back to my hotel room with me, Kate? Spend the entire day with me?"

The thickness in Kate's throat intensified. On the last day they'd spent together she'd promised him honesty and, if she were merely honest with herself, she had to acknowledge that she'd rather spend the day with him than with any other person in the world.

Observing his taut stillness, Kate knew that Trace expected her to say no. As he'd made no assurance of a "hands-off" attitude, Kate knew she should say no. But then, Kate was sick and tired of doing what she knew she should do.

"Yes, I will," she finally responded decisively.

Trace remained motionless for an instant, then he slowly raised his head to gaze at her in bemusement.

"You continually amaze me," he murmured, shaking his head slowly. "I won't hurt you, you know?"

Kate smiled tremulously. "Yes, Trace, I know."

Trace returned the smile, brightening his features—and Kate's mood. "We'll have dinner together, in my room." His eyes beginning to glow with endearing eagerness, he plucked the pastries from her lap and stuffed them into the bag. "We don't need this junk to ruin our appetites!" Gulping the last of the coffee, he dropped the cup on top of the pastries. Settling behind the wheel, he reached for the ignition key, then paused, his eyes narrowing in thought.

"And, dammit, you're going to have Christmas too!" Startling Kate with the suddenness of his action, Trace flung the car door door open. "Sit tight, kid." He grinned at her surprised expression. Sliding off the seat he strode into the store.

Staring after him in amused consternation, Kate couldn't begin to imagine why he'd gone back into the store. Five minutes later, when he pushed through the heavy glass doors, she began to laugh softly. While still moving swiftly, Trace gingerly grasped a meagerly decorated artificial tree approximately two feet tall. The scraggy thing had to be the sorriest excuse for a Christmas tree Kate had ever seen. Kate loved it on sight.

"Trace! What in the . . ." Kate began laughingly.

"Don't ask," Trace warned, laughing with her as he slid onto the seat and plunked the excuse in her lap. "You wouldn't believe what the manager of that store charged me for this beauty!"

"I didn't even know they sold trees in there!" Kate giggled.

"They don't." Still laughing, Trace started the engine. "It was part of their own decorations." As he drove away, he jerked his head at the store. "That guy came out ahead all the way around. Not only did I give him a ridiculous amount of money for it, now he doesn't have to clear it away after the holidays."

On their arrival at the hotel Trace coolly bore the tree through the lobby, ignoring the looks and smiles of amusement the sight drew from hotel staff and guests.

"Okay, Kate, it's your tree," Trace drawled, closing the door to his room behind them. "Where do you want it?"

Frowning, Kate glanced around the room, which was an exact duplication of the one he'd occupied the month before. "Well," she mused aloud, "if we're having dinner here we can't set it on the table by the settee. So, I suppose you'll have to put it on top of the dresser."

"Right." Grinning, Trace plopped the tree on the corner of the long dresser and plugged the one string of lights it boasted into a wall outlet. "Hmm—" he frowned, stepping back to gaze at the pitiful thing "—it needs something. Ah, I've got it!" Swinging away, he strode to the closet.

While his back was turned Kate hastily withdrew the small package from her purse and placed it under the tree before she could change her mind. Then, suddenly unsure, she walked to the window to stare blindly at the street below. Kate had to force herself to turn back to the room when Trace spoke to her.

"Come over here, Kate."

Despite the softness of his voice Kate was afraid Trace was angry about the gift. Reluctance slowing her movements, she eased around, then walked to join him at the tree.

"Look at me, Kate," Trace ordered, raising a hand to glide the tips of his fingers over her cheek. When she lifted her head, he smiled gently. "Now it looks like Christmas." With a light tug, he turned her face to the dresser.

The sight that met Kate's eyes brought a lump to her throat. There was a smaller package resting beside the one she'd placed on the dresser, its beautiful wrapping almost covered by the large bow on top. Picking the gift up, Trace held it out to her.

"Merry Christmas, Kate," he said softly.

As her hand closed on the gift, Kate held the other one out to him. "Merry Christmas, Trace."

Standing close together beside the ugly-beautiful tree, they opened the packages in unison.

"Oh, Trace!" Kate breathed in delight as she removed the lid from the box to reveal a lapel pin in the design of a shield. It was beautifully crafted in sterling silver. Emblazoned on the shield was an intricately wrought K. "How lovely! Thank you!"

"Kate! This is beautiful!" Trace exclaimed as he carefully removed the bell from its bed of tissue paper. "Thank you!"

Their voices blended as they spoke simultaneously. Then, their gazes tangling as they looked at each other, they exchanged the gift of a happy smile.

"Since we didn't get to go sightseeing last time, I brought one of the sights to you," Kate said, quickly fabricating a reason for choosing the bell.

"It's perfect," Trace murmured, caressing the glowing pewter with his fingers. "I'll keep it on my desk." A teasing light sprang into his eyes. "Have you made the connection between your gift and yourself?"

"No." Smiling back at him, Kate shook her head.

"That's the shield of honor for champions of lost little girls," he intoned. "It's only awarded to the fiercest protectors."

Kate swallowed with difficulty. "Who awards this great honor?" she asked in a whisper.

"Me." Leaning to her he brushed his lips over hers. "And I award it only once in a lifetime."

The exchanging of gifts appeared to open the lines of communication between them. Unhesitatingly, they talked the morning away and all through the light salad and wine lunch Trace ordered from room service. By the time Kate had finished her lunch and was halfway through her second glass of wine, she felt safe in asking the question uppermost in her mind.

"You said you'd tell me about love when we had the time, Trace." Kate drew a deep breath. "Do we have the time now?"

"I knew this mellow camaraderie was too good to last," Trace groaned, grimacing. Nevertheless, he answered her.

"Honey, love is an illusion. A trap." A grim smile touched his lips. "You spoke of emotional poverty. Well, love is emotional slavery. The name of love can rationalize the betrayal of previously held principles, a disregard of reasons, and even the debasement of pride." His brief burst of laughter held little humor. "I've known the illusion, Kate. From now on I'll stick to reality, and I'd advise you to do the same."

Though she wanted to cry, Kate somehow managed a weak smile. "The advice comes too late, Trace." She shrugged helplessly. "I told you that you wouldn't like hearing it."

"But that's the strange part," he murmured, looping an arm around her waist to draw her closer to his side. "I do like hearing it." Lowering his head, he inhaled the scent of her, murmuring deep in his throat when she shivered in response. "I can't offer you commitment, Kate. I won't allow myself to be emotionally enslaved again."

"I...I understand, Trace," Kate lied softly. She didn't understand, didn't *want* to understand; all she wanted was Trace!

"I don't think you do, Kate, not fully," Trace smiled. "You see, although I won't let myself *need* you emotionally, I will admit to a consuming physical need for you." His movements precise, Trace released her and sat back, giving her the opportunity to move away from him if she wished. "I enjoy your company. I can relax with you." He paused, then said distinctly, "I want to make love with you. I can't offer you more than that."

Not looking at him, Kate gave his words the consideration they deserved. Trace had complimented her with his honesty and was now allowing her the time and space she required. Within the last hours, her love for him had become an accepted absolute. Although Kate feared Trace would never change his position on love, she felt a great fear of losing him completely. Lifting her head proudly, she turned to face him.

"I want to make love with you, Trace." Kate spoke as distinctly as he had moments before. "I accept your offer."

Nine

Kate was on fire. Her entire body was burning. Murmuring incoherent encouragement to the man who'd ignited the blaze, she slid her fingers through the silky strands of his hair, urging him even closer to her fiery mouth. His tongue plunged in a rhythm evocative of a more intimate possession, plunged as if seeking the source of her excited murmurings.

Long spangled rays of sunlight angled through the window. It struck blue fire sparks off the black mass of Kate's hair, fanned wildly over the pillow and bathed Trace's sweat-moistened shoulders in shimmering gold. It was not the first time they'd made love that afternoon.

With Kate's acceptance of Trace's offer of a physical relationship he'd stared at her intently before slowly rising to draw her to the side of the bed. His eyes, darkened to deepest green by passion, observed the expressions washing over Kate's face as his trembling fingers slowly unfastened the buttons down the front of her shirt.

Heart pounding, barely breathing, Kate trembled with a combination of anticipation and fear of the unknown as Trace tenderly removed her clothes.

"You're a lovely woman, Kate." Trace whispered the words as he slowly ran his gaze down the length of her quivering body and back to her face. He was not touching her, yet Kate felt that gaze to the marrow of her bones; the heat of it melted the chill of fear.

Swinging her into his arms, Trace gently settled her on the bed, then stepped back to remove his own clothing. Kate watched him until his fingers began working on the waistband clip on his trousers, then she closed her eyes.

"Look at me, Kate." Though soft, his voice held a note of command. When Kate raised her eyelids the trousers were gone. Trace stood before her in navy briefs. "If we are going to be lovers there will be no barriers between us. No dishonesty, or darkness, or even closed eyes." His movements deliberate, Trace stepped out of the briefs, then straightened proudly, his sharp-eyed gaze watching for her reaction to the sight of his aroused manhood.

Kate had seen naked men before, in magazines and films, but they had not prepared her for Trace. Though magnificent in his masculine beauty, he was also rather overwhelming. Her eyes betraying the conflicting emotions tearing at her, Kate stared at him mutely.

His body taut, Trace stood absolutely still; the only part of him that moved were his lips.

"May I join you, Kate?"

Twice previously Trace had asked her permission before advancing. She knew that he would not move, either forward or back, until she answered him. Words were not needed. Kate held out her arms in silent invitation.

Trace came to her gently, but anxiously.

"I'll try not to hurt you, Kate," he said huskily, one long hand drawing shivers in it's wake as he stroked her from shoulder to hip. "But it's been so long for me, so very long, that I'm afraid...for both of us."

Even in her inexperience, Kate knew that Trace had tried to restrain himself almost past endurance. Then, his body trembling, he'd slipped between her thighs, groaning a soft whisper in her ear.

"I know you're not ready yet. Forgive me, Kate, but I must...I must."

Though most of his control was gone, still Trace initiated Kate with gentleness and caring. But, although she felt only a moment of pain and discomfort, the soaring flight of ecstasy was not hers. Yet, when Trace cried her name aloud at his own long-denied release, Kate held his shuddering body close to her own with fiercely protective possessiveness.

With Trace's face buried in the curve of her neck and his body still a part of hers, Kate lovingly stroked his relaxing form and softly denied his harsh self-condemnation.

"I shouldn't have come to you this way," he nearly growled with self-disgust. "It was grossly unfair to you."

"But better than the alternative," Kate chided softly.

Trace lifted his head to stare at her through narrowed eyelids, a smile of amusement twitching his lips. "What do you know about the alternatives?" he scoffed gently.

Kate lowered her lashes. "I know you could have...ah...*used* another woman," she said tightly. "I'm glad you didn't."

"Oh, my beautifully honest Kate!" Laughing, Trace returned his face to her neck. "What did I do to deserve you?"

"Nothing yet," Kate teased. "But, I'm hoping that you'll prove your worth very soon."

Their lovers embrace unbroken, Kate and Trace both drifted off to sleep. Kate had now awakened with the delicious feeling of being bathed by the silken stroke of Trace's tongue.

Her pale body gleaming in the afternoon sunlight, Kate arched herself into the caress of Trace's mouth and gasped his name as his teeth raked gently against her aroused nipples.

"Do you like that?" Trace murmured, repeating the action.

"Oh, yes!" Kate wasn't even certain that the purring moan was her own.

"And this?" Trace continued, trailing his fingers from her breasts to the soft flesh of her thigh.

"Yes, yes!"

"And this?" he persisted, moving his fingers in an erotic pattern. "And this," he went on relentlessly, following the path of his fingers with his hungry lips and circling tongue.

"Yes, Trace, yes!" Then, as his lips sought the honey his fingers had delicately dipped into, Kate stiffened. "Trace, no!"

His hard hands grasping her thighs, Trace raised his head to smile into her frightened eyes. "I said there'd be no barriers, Kate. There is no reason to be afraid. You are beautiful—" moving swiftly, Trace lowered his warm mouth to the heat of her "—all over."

Then, reluctantly, Trace moved away from the area of dissension, his lips leaving a moist trail of fire as he languorously made his way back to her breasts. "There are many ways to make love, darling," he murmured. "Eventually, I want to explore them all with you. I will love you in *every* way." His teeth closed gently on one sensitized nipple, eliciting a sharp gasp of pleasure from her. "And, some day, you may even want to return the compliment." Her gasp turned to a moan as he began to draw gently on her nipple.

Kate was trembling violently from the tremors quaking through her body when Trace finally kissed his way to her mouth.

"Yes," he groaned, his breathing labored. "This is the way it should be." His wine-scented breath mingled with hers. "Give me your mouth, Kate." As his lips brushed hers he moaned deeply. "I want to bury my entire body into yours."

This time Kate was more than ready for him. Burning, burning, and completely wild from the flame, she synchronized her movements to the desperate thrust of his, greedy for him. Then, her head thrown back in tension, she screamed when ecstasy caught her.

"Trace!"

"Kate!" His strained voice echoed with her name.

Exhausted, replete, Kate and Trace slept again, his arms embracing her possessively, her legs entwined with his trustingly.

"Happy birthday, Kate."

A soft "oh" sighed through Kate's lips as she came to an abrupt halt in the bathroom doorway. Her startled gaze had been caught by the flame of a single candle glowing in the dark room. The candle was set in the center of a small, frothily iced cake. Taken by surprise, Kate was oblivious to the appreciative gleam in Trace's eyes as he ran a glance over her freshly showered body. Clad in one of his shirts she appeared both vulnerable and sexy.

"Oh, Trace, thank you!" Kate exclaimed softly, looking up at him with misty eyes. "But, when—how . . . ?"

"While you were showering," Trace replied quietly, "via room service." Walking to her, he grasped her hand to lead her to the table. "I told you I would order dinner." Dipping his head, he inhaled the scent of her still damp, freshly shampooed hair then brushed his lips over her temple. "If I had my way, you'd never wear anything but my shirts." Soft laughter rumbled in his chest. "But then, we'd probably never get out of the bedroom either."

Seating her on the settee, Trace moved the table to her. "Make a wish and blow out your candle, honey, our Christmas dinner is getting cold."

Blowing out a single candle was easy; composing a wish was even easier. With all her heart and mind, Kate wished for a softening in Trace's attitude to love and commitment.

"It's your birthday," Trace said softly, bending to kiss her lightly. "Yet I received the present. Thank you, Kate." His voice grew hoarse. "You are the most beautiful present I've ever received."

"No, Trace." Lifting her hand, Kate caressed his freshly shaven cheek. "The gift is mine. You made me a woman for my birthday." A sensuous smile curved her lips. "A very satisfied woman."

While they consumed a traditional holiday meal, Trace explained the circumstances of his return to the east coast. In turn, Kate told him of her bout with the flu. His reaction was both personal and professional. Amusement sparkling in her eyes, she calmly answered all his questions concerning her health and patiently endured his brief but thorough examination.

After the meal was finished, and they were sipping at their second cup of coffee, Kate voiced the subject uppermost in her mind.

"When are you returning to San Antonio, Trace?" Kate stared into her coffee while waiting for his answer.

"Kathy and I are booked on a flight leaving at twelve-forty tomorrow." He was quiet for several heartbeats, then he murmured, "Spend the night with me, Kate."

Kate couldn't think of anything she wanted more than sleeping curled up in his arms, but she also had responsibilities.

"I have to work tomorrow, Trace," she informed him regretfully.

"If I promise to get you home in time to get ready for work," Trace said carefully, "will you stay?"

Kate spent the night as she'd wanted, curled up in Trace's strong arms; however, she did very little sleeping.

True to his promise, Trace drove Kate home early the next morning. Pensive, quiet, they were within a few miles of her apartment before he broke the taut silence between them.

"I . . . I won't be able to get back to spend New Year's with you, Kate. I'm sorry, but I'll be on call for the man who's covering for me now."

Though Kate tried to hide her disappointment, she was not altogether successful. "I understand, Trace." She hesitated, then whispered, "Do you have any idea when you'll be coming east again?"

"No," he admitted tersely. "I'm sorry," he repeated.

"You needn't be." Kate glanced out the side window to conceal her tear-filled eyes. "You've made no promises."

"Come with me, Kate." There was a sudden urgency in his tone. For one tiny instant, hope flared wildly in Kate; it died painfully with his next words. "Let me take an apartment for you in San Antonio. Let me take care of you."

Kate's head was moving back and forth before he'd finished speaking. "No, Trace. I want to be with you," she confessed, "but not like that."

The sigh that escaped his lips revealed Trace's frustration. "I want to ask you to promise me that you won't see any other man, or *be* with any other man, but I won't." Trace expelled his breath harshly. "I know I don't have any right to ask that of you, Kate."

"I've already granted you the right, Trace." Turning to him, Kate smiled, if sadly. "I don't want to see or *be* with any other man. I love you, Trace. I'll be here for you, always, whether you want me or not."

At that moment, Trace pulled the car along the curb in front of her apartment. After switching off the ignition, he turned to her, a self-derisive smile twisting his lips.

"Oh, I want you, Kate." Reaching out, he dragged her across the seat, crushing her slim body to his. "God, how I want you!"

Trace held her trembling body protectively, compulsively for a long time, murmuring endearments and instructions alternately.

"Take care of yourself, sweetheart."

"I will," Kate whispered.

"Don't forget to take your vitamins, honey."

"I won't," she promised.

"Get plenty of rest, don't overdo, baby."

"I'll try," she laughed, sobbingly.

"I'll call you, love."

"I'll be here."

After parking the car in front of the narrow town house of his former in-laws, Trace rested his head for an instant on the cold steering wheel. How was it possible, he wondered miserably. He'd left Kate at the door to her apartment less than half an hour before, yet already he was missing her to the point of near pain!

Feeling raw, his mouth set in a grimly forbidding line, Trace stepped from the car, mounted the three marble steps to the front door and rang the bell with an impatient jab of his finger. Ruth Parker met him in the narrow, elegant foyer.

"Kathy will be down in a moment, Trace," Ruth smiled in genuine welcome. "Won't you come in and sit down?"

"No, thank you, Ruth," Trace responded tersely. "I have something to say, and I prefer to say it here."

"What is it, Trace?" Ruth asked apprehensively.

Trace didn't hesitate. "You do realize that if Annette persists in going ahead with this lawsuit, I can't bring Kathy east anymore?" he stated unequivocally.

"But, Trace!" Ruth cried. "Kathy's so very young! She'll forget me and her grandfather!"

"Yes, she will," Trace acknowledged stonily. "And I'll be sorry for that. But I can't afford to take chances." His expression settled into unrelenting lines. "Regardless of how a Pennsylvania judge rules, I am not giving Kathy up. If I must, I'll barricade my home and hire a twenty-four-hour guard around it."

Ruth's still lovely face seemed to crumble before his eyes, leaving her looking old and afraid. "Oh, Trace, I know what Annette is doing is wrong! I've talked to her...we've all talked to her, even Carl and Barbara, but she refuses to listen to reason."

Trace hid the surprise he felt at learning that Annette's older sister Barbara had championed his cause; personally, he'd always considered his former sister-in-law even more self-centered than Annette. Casting speculation about the motives of Annette's sister aside, Trace said dryly, "Maybe you've all been talking to the wrong person." When Ruth frowned in confusion, he clarified, "Perhaps you should talk to Randall—" he drawled the name sarcastically "—he's the one pressuring Annette to bring the suit."

Ruth's astonished expression convinced Trace she'd known nothing of Randall's part in Annette's scheme. Instinct assured Trace that before long Randall was going to find himself face-to-face with two outraged grandparents. The smile that curved Trace's lips was not pleasant.

"If you do talk to him," he went on softly. "You can give him a message from me. Tell *Randall* that I said there's absolutely *no* way he'll get my daughter."

The fact that Kathy was unnaturally subdued didn't dawn on Trace until after they'd arrived home. Distracted by memories of the hours he'd spent with Kate, his daughter's odd behavior didn't hit him until she'd finished opening the Christmas presents waiting at home for her. It was her unenthusiastic reception that finally pierced Trace's absorbed thoughts.

"What's the matter, honey?" Trace frowned. "Don't you like what Santa brought you?"

"Yes, I guess so," Kathy mumbled, sniffing. "But he didn't bring me the only thing I asked for and really, really wanted."

Drawing her into his arms, Trace murmured. "But what *did* you ask him for, Kath?" With a gentle finger, he wiped the first of the tears from her soft cheek.

"I asked Santa if I could have Kate for my mommie for Christmas," Kathy sobbed pitifully.

Closing his eyes, Trace laid his cheek against Kathy's shining blond hair. Why not? he quizzed himself, aching all over for the sight of Kate, the sound of her, the feel of her beneath him. Then, coming to his senses, Trace grimaced at his own weakness and chastened his daughter gently.

"I suppose this was as good a time as any for you to learn that we simply can't have everything we want, Kath."

For Kate, life became encapsulated within the intervals Trace could manage to fly east to spend a day or two with her; the rest of her time was mere existence. And those intervals didn't happen very often.

She spent New Year's Eve sitting by the phone, willing it to ring. Trace called exactly one minute after twelve.

"Happy New Year, honey," he greeted her softly. "What were you doing?"

"Watching the ball descend in Times Square and praying you would call," Kate replied with artless honesty.

"Oh, Kate!" Though Trace laughed, it sounded forced and rueful. "You don't know the meaning of the word guile, do you?"

"Oh, yes, I know the meaning," Kate responded steadily. "I just don't see the point in using it. You know how I feel, nothing I say or do will change that."

There were times over the months that followed when Kate wished with all her might that she could somehow fall out of love with Trace. There were times when she'd counted the reasons why she should break it off with him, refuse to see him on the rare occasions he found he could spare the time to see her. But those times were immediately forgotten when he showed up at her apartment, pulling her into his arms the minute she opened the door.

And, when they were together, the only thought in Kate's mind was how very much she loved him.

They had one glorious weekend together in January. The instant Trace arrived, Kate looked at him and knew something had occurred to ease the lines of strain on his face. At her careful questioning, Trace smiled with relief and satisfaction.

"I had a call from Ruth Parker yesterday," he explained, his smile growing into a grin. "Annette got married in Paris on Thursday." His laughter had a young sound. "Since Ruth, her husband *and* her son and daughter all apparently had a hand in convincing Annette's new husband of the futility of a custody suit, I could almost feel sorry for him."

As if infused with new life and purpose, Trace was tireless throughout that weekend. Laughing with the emotional high he was on, he swung her into his arms and carried her to the bedroom.

"What do you think you're doing?" Kate gasped with a startled burst of laughter.

"I want to celebrate." Trace paused in the doorway to her bedroom to gaze at her with eyes greenly opaque with desire. "And, my sweet, the best way I can think of to celebrate is by making love to you until you beg me to make you mine."

Kate's chest grew tight from a sudden lack of oxygen. Her breathing sporadic and almost painful, she curled her arms around his taut neck and brushed her parted lips over his warm skin. The musky-spicy scent of him sent her senses whirling out of control.

"I can't wait," she confessed throatily, stabbing the tip of her tongue into the hollow behind his ear.

"Where did you learn to do that?" Trace groaned, tightening his grip to crush her to the unyielding hardness of his chest.

"Don't you like it?" Kate almost purred, gliding her tongue around the outer curl of his ear.

"Like it!" Trace growled, nipping at her cheek. "Honey, I *love* it!" Entering the room he closed the door with one sharp, backward kick of his booted foot. "And now," he murmured in a deep, dark, sexy voice, "I'm going to love you."

Kate's pulse accelerated into overdrive as Trace slid her to her feet. Her breathing grew shallow as he began to undress her with trembling fingers. When, finally, she stood before him as nature had fashioned her, she shivered from the heat of the fiery gaze. Without conscious direction her hands lifted to his chest and she was brushing the heavy jacket off of his shoulders.

Trace didn't help Kate in her unaccustomed role of valet. Inept though her fingers were, she managed to remove every article of clothing he was wearing. Trace's flanks quivered as she knelt to glide his navy-blue briefs to his ankles and off his feet.

"You did promise me that you were a faster learner," he said unevenly, raspily, as he bent to grasp her shoulders to draw her up to him.

Kate resisted his effort and, clasping him around the waist, fastened her moist lips to his flat abdomen.

"Oh, Kate!" Trace's voice was rough with the need coursing through him. "What are you trying to do?"

"Learn," Kate mumbled, touching him with the tip of her tongue. "Does this please you, Trace?" Once more her tongue flicked out to inflict exquisite sensations on his body.

"Please me! Sweet Lord, love! It drives me crazy!" Trace was now breathing with obvious difficulty. "Oh, Kate!" he moaned when her tongue stroked his sensitive skin. "You don't have to do this, darling." Even as he spoke his body shuddered with pleasure.

"But I want to, I want to help you celebrate," Kate whispered an instant before she tasted him.

Their celebration was an unqualified success.

Trace didn't check into a hotel that weekend. Upon awakening from the nap that had followed their wildly enthusiastic lovemaking, he retrieved his valise from the rented car and dropped it at the foot of the bed where Kate was still sleepily ensconced.

"I'm not letting you out of my sight this weekend," he said adamantly, eyeing her warily as if expecting an argument.

"Good," Kate murmured mildly, smothering a yawn with her hand. Smiling inwardly she watched surprise widen Trace's eyes, and wondered exactly what kind of relationship he'd had with his ex-wife. Aching for the man inside the wall he'd built around himself, Kate slid her body into a sitting position and allowed the smile to reach her kiss-swollen lips. "Were you planning to feed me?" Before he could respond, she chided, "I really must have fortification if you intend to indulge in more bedroom gymnastics."

"Kate, you're fantastic!" Trace's warm laughter flowed over her an instant before his body came crashing onto the bed beside her.

"Trace!" she yelped, giggling as he caught her to him in a fierce bear hug.

"Kate!" he mimicked, sinking his teeth gently into her shoulder. "I definitely will feed you, honey," he growled, working his teeth against the curve of her neck. "But, for myself, I think I'll have you for dinner." Trace proceeded to demonstrate his meaning in the most delightful way possible.

Long, wonderful hours later, after a sumptuous dinner in the most expensive restaurant Kate could think of and followed by dreamy hours held molded to Trace's body while dancing, Kate lay wakeful beside her contentedly sleeping lover.

What sort of relationship *had* Trace had with his wife? The nagging question was the thief robbing Kate of sleep. From their first, glorious loving on his arrival, Trace had appeared to shrug off care like a weight that had been dragging him down. Set free, he was a charming companion, a thrilling lover, a good friend. Yet Kate sensed that he still retained a part of himself. Her fear was that Trace would always retain a part of himself.

Choking bitterness rose in Kate's throat against the woman who had hurt Trace so badly that he was determined never to leave himself open to another woman. For while he had spoken passionately of loving, his words had concerned the physical, not the emotional kind.

Acceptance was a bitter pill but, once swallowed, Kate gently drifted into slumber; she would take whatever Trace offered. She had no choice, she loved him.

In February Trace sent Kate an enormous heart-shaped, elegantly decorated box of chocolates. When she saw the manufacturer's name inscribed discreetly on the bottom of the box, Kate gasped aloud; the gift had to have cost Trace the better part of a hundred dollars. But, though he called at least three times a week, Trace could not arrange to fly east during the entire month.

On the second Friday in March, Trace called Kate at the office to ask if she could pick him up at the airport that evening. Excited, so eager to see him that she could barely sit at her desk the remainder of the afternoon, Kate agonized through the hours until she saw his beloved face as he strode off the covered ramp and into the waiting lounge. Unconscious of the milling people around her, Kate launched herself into his arms and fastened her mouth on his.

"I've missed you, Kate," Trace groaned close to her ear.

"And I've missed you," Kate choked, fighting tears.

And so it went on. Trace managed an overnight stay the last week in March, and an entire three days in mid-April. While they were together they made love often, sometimes with such passionate abandonment it bordered on the violent.

In truth, it was the desperate quality of their lovemaking that initiated the first curls of unease in Kate's mind.

How long could a love affair survive when the lovers were separated by half a continent? Although Kate tried to avoid recognizing the niggling unease, once the question was in her mind, it refused to be dislodged or ignored.

By steeping herself in her love for Trace, Kate had literally withdrawn from her friends, both male and female. Could she continue to function healthily when she was really only fully alive while she was with Trace?

Trace, on the other hand, was apparently having no difficulty whatever with their less than normal situation. He laughed often, loved ardently, and even spoke freely of his work and home life for the first time.

"Kath talks about you incessantly to Inez."

The information came out of the blue while they strolled along Penn's Landing in the warmth of the April sunshine.

"Inez?" Kate frowned; who the devil was this Inez?

"My housekeeper." The way Trace answered, it was obvious he assumed Kate knew the woman's identity. Then he frowned. "I've mentioned her before—haven't I?"

"No." Kate shook her head. "Is...ah...is she pretty?" She hadn't wanted to ask, yet she couldn't prevent the words from spilling out of her jealous mouth.

"Inez?" Trace shot her a look of amazement. He opened his mouth, then closed it again, an unholy gleam dancing in his eyes. "Ravishing," he said fervently, "and she sleeps in, you know." His smile was devilish.

Kate was being had, she knew she was being had, yet she was powerless against the question, or the frigid tone that coated her voice.

"With you?"

"Oh, my precious Kate!" Laughing delightedly, Trace hauled her into his arms with supreme disregard for any onlookers. "Were you afraid that, having given up the vow of abstinence, I was indulging my libido with every available female?"

Kate sniffed disdainfully. Trace kissed her hard on the mouth.

"Inez is a lovely woman," he murmured into her ear. "She is also in her sixties." His arms tightened around her possessively. "*You* are the only woman I sleep with.

The only woman I want to sleep with." Loosening his embrace, he leaned back to stare directly into her eyes. "You satisfy all my wants, Kate."

"And you mine," Kate sighed, feeling ridiculously happy.

While they were together Kate was content. It was during the long periods of separation that she grew restless, uneasily questioning the wisdom of indulging herself and her love.

In early May Trace flew east again, but this time their reunion was different; this time Trace brought Kathy with him.

"Kate!" Kathy's squeal and the way her little face became suddenly animated brought a tight feeling to Kate's throat and chest.

Stooping down, Kate held her arms open to the child. Tears running down her face, Kathy flew into Kate's welcoming embrace.

"Oh, Kate! I hoped and hoped I'd see you," Kathy chattered happily. "But I was afraid daddy wouldn't let me!"

Hugging the child, Kate raised her eyes to Trace, who mouthed the words, "I missed you." Kate didn't reply, but then, she didn't need to, her eyes told him of her heartfelt joy at seeing him.

The two-day visit was an unqualified success. Though there was no time or opportunity for any physical activity of the bedroom variety, Kathy gave Kate and Trace plenty of physical activity of the sightseeing type. Her little body practically quivering with excitement, Kathy insisted on viewing everything Philadelphia had to offer the tourist.

By the time Kate saw Trace and Kathy off at the airport, her affections were secured within the child's tiny hand. At the same time, Kate was also well versed on the many attractions of San Antonio. Brimming with enthusiasm and the wistfully voiced hope that Kate would visit her one day, Kathy sang the praises of the Alamo, the famous walk along the San Antonio River, the Mexican Market—El Mercado, the Spanish Governor's Palace, the Tower of the Americas—or as Kathy described it, "the needle-shaped thing with a restaurant on top"—and King William Street with it's beautifully restored Victorian homes.

Though Kate laughingly told Kathy she'd love to see all the sights the girl had described, in her heart Kate knew the one sight she longed to see was Trace, welcoming her to his home city and his life.

By mid-July, both Kate and Trace were showing signs of the strain inflicted by their unorthodox relationship. Trace "stole" three whole days away from his overloaded schedule that week. Using Kate's car they drove to a small, quiet resort town along the New Jersey coast. They spent the entire three days laying on the beach basking in the sun during the day, and laying on the bed basking in each other most of the night.

In early August Trace made an overnight, surprise visit. Only Trace got the surprise.

Hot and irritable, Kate opened the door for Trace with a scowl and stepped back to avoid his arms.

Eyeing her warily, Trace followed Kate into the stuffy living room, shedding his lightweight summer suit jacket as he walked.

"Don't you have air-conditioning in here?" he asked, undoing the top three buttons on his shirt. "This place is an oven."

"Yes, I have air-conditioning," Kate snapped. "The damned thing died this morning."

Trace threw her a startled look; Kate rarely swore. "Have you called a repairman?" he inquired carefully.

"No, I can't afford it until I get paid next week." Kate turned away impatiently.

"Oh, for heaven's sake!" Trace exclaimed. "If you needed money, why didn't you call me?" As he was pacing the room, Trace missed the spark of anger that flared in Kate's eyes. "Go freshen up, honey, and we'll go shopping. I'll buy you a new air-conditioner."

"No, Trace."

Though her tone was soft, Trace couldn't miss the anger lacing her voice. "Why not?" he frowned. "You'll suffocate in here."

"I don't want you to buy things for me, Trace," Kate said adamantly.

His smile coaxing, Trace walked to her. Raising his hand, he caressed her perspiration-wet face with his fingers. "Why not, honey?" he asked softly. "I would enjoy buying you anything you wanted."

Kate's lips tightened. "And what would accepting your gifts make me?" Kate smiled mirthlessly. "There are several names that come to mind. Mistress is among them."

"Kate!" Trace barked, grasping her by the shoulders. "What are you saying? Do you know?" He pulled her into his arms with angry strength. "I never think about you in that way, and you know it," he said roughly.

"Do I?" Shrugging out of his arms, Kate clasped her arms around herself as if she were freezing in the stifling room. "I still don't want you to buy me gifts."

Trace exhaled raggedly. "All right." Turning toward the small kitchen, he sighed. "Do you have any tools? I'll see if I can get it running. We can't sleep in his oven."

At his last statement, something that had slowly building over the last few weeks finally broke through. Swinging around, she ridiculed, "You're a surgeon, Trace, not an appliance repairman. And, if you're afraid of losing sleep, sleep somewhere else."

"Kate . . ." Trace began in obvious confusion that had a thread of impatient anger.

"As a matter of fact," she cut him off, "why don't you go back to San Antonio. Visit the Alamo. Take a walk by the river. Operate on someone!"

"Maybe I will," Trace snarled, grabbing his jacket from the chair as he strode to the door.

"Trace!"

Trace paused with his hand on the doorknob. "What?"

"Don't come back." Kate stared into his astonished eyes. What was she doing? Why was she doing it, she demanded of herself as she stiffened her spine. Kate knew why, had known it for weeks. She just hadn't wanted to admit to the growing sense of despair that engulfed her every time Trace left her, or face the utter hopelessness she endured after he was gone.

"Kate, honey, what are you saying?" Releasing his hold on the knob, Trace moved to her. "You don't mean it."

"I do, Trace." And in that instant, Kate realized that she did. She loved him so very much. Perhaps too much, because she knew inside that the day was swiftly approaching when watching him walk away from her would kill her soul—if it hadn't already.

"I won't be here for you anymore, Trace."

Trace came to a stop inches from her, his eyes as hard and flat as unpolished gemstones. "I see." His lips curled cynically. "It was a short-lived illusion—wasn't it, Kate?"

Kate opened her mouth to deny his assertion. All that came out was a gasped "oh" as Trace hauled her roughly against him and crushed her lips to his. The kiss was brief and very close to brutal. Releasing her as swiftly as he'd grabbed her, Trace pivoted and strode to the door, yanking it open violently. Before crossing the threshold he paused to glance back at her.

"I can't say I'm surprised because I'm not," he said tiredly. "The surprising thing is that I know I'm going to miss you like hell."

The slam of the door punctuated his admission.

"Trace." Kate's cry was little more than a whimper of anguish; Trace didn't hear it; Kate hadn't meant him to.

Exactly how long she stood, unmoving, staring at nothing, Kate had no idea, nor was she aware of the ache of tension in her taut muscles. All Kate was aware of was the growing emptiness inside, yawning wider and wider, threatening to swallow her up in a black void.

By morning she was not only uncomfortably hot and emotionally drained, but she had a severe headache as well. When her doorbell rang just after noon, Kate answered it frowningly. The way things were running, she thought cynically, it was probably her mother.

"Miss Warren?" The man at her door was wearing a shirt with the name of a local florist stitched on the breast pocket, and he was holding a tissue-wrapped bouquet in his hand. At Kate's nod, he handed the bouquet to her. "These are for you, miss."

"Thank you." Kate accepted the bouquet with a sensation of déjà vu. The difference was, this time she knew the flowers were not from Trace.

Kate was wrong. After tipping the delivery man, she carried the bouquet to the sofa and placed it on the coffee table exactly as she had at Christmas time. Still frowning, she slid the tiny card from its envelope. There were three words scrawled across the card in Trace's now familiar penmanship. Three words that brought a gasp to her lips and a flood of tears to her eyes.

Marry me, Kate.

Kate was staring at the blurred message when the doorbell rang again. Tugging a tissue from the box on the table at the end of the sofa, Kate blotted the tears on her cheeks as she went to the door.

"May I come in?"

Kate's stomach muscles contracted. Dressed in western-style, slim-leg jeans and a short-sleeved cotton knit pullover, Trace was the most appealing man she'd ever seen. His naturally unruly hair was mussed, as if he'd been raking impatient fingers through the deep waves. There were dark smudges beneath his somber green eyes. Deep grooves scored his face from the outer edge of his nostrils to the corners of his mouth. He looked tired and dispirited, and Kate might have given in to the need to fling herself into his arms . . . if that now detested, cynical twist had disappeared from his lips—but it hadn't, and she didn't.

Not answering verbally, Kate turned away and walked back into the room, leaving the door standing wide open. A fatalistic shudder swayed her rigidly held body at the sound of the door closing quietly.

Kate didn't hear Trace move, yet she knew he was standing very close to her. Her senses quivered with the scent and feel of him. Without conscious thought her eyes sought the little card she still clutched in her hand. Trace didn't miss the slight movement of her fingers as they tightened on the note.

"Well, will you?" he asked in a harsh raspy tone.

Kate didn't need time to think; she knew what her answer had to be. "No, Trace, I won't marry you." Kate's nails slashed her palms; knowing what she had to say was one thing, saying it was quite another. When Trace sighed she felt it in her throat.

"Can't you even look at me, Kate?"

Molding her features into an unemotional mask, Kate turned to face him. She immediately wished she hadn't moved. Trace looked angry, frustrated, and even more cynical than before.

"Why not?" Trace unconsciously echoed his query of seven months previously. "We get along well." He smiled that hateful smile. "At least we have up until now. You're obviously fond of Kathy." He smiled again. "We're dynamite together in bed. We could make it work." He drew a deep breath, then added, as if it were an added attraction, "I'd give you anything you wanted, Kate."

Kate smiled in a cynical parody of his. "No, Trace, we couldn't make it work. A month ago, two weeks ago, possibly even three days ago, I'd have said yes without giving my answer any consideration at all."

"Then why..." Trace exploded.

"Because now, today, I realize how wrong it would be," Kate interrupted him calmly. "Don't you see, Trace? None of the reasons you've given me are enough. I thought I could do it." Kate swallowed against the thickness in her throat. "I loved you so much, wanted you so much that I really thought I could be satisfied with what you offered me.'' Kate smiled sadly. ''Now I find I'm greedy. I want it all, Trace. And, if I can't have it all, I don't want any of it.''

Ten

It was after midnight, and it was still very hot and very humid. His movements almost stealthy, Trace let himself into the house by the back door. The only sounds in the quiet night were the muffled click of the lock and the faint rattle of the chain being engaged.

Moving silently through the dark hallway, Trace entered his office, shutting the door before flicking the light on. Crossing directly to the credenza, he splashed a double measure of whiskey into a heavy, squat glass and sank wearily into his desk chair.

Raising the glass, he drank deeply, expelling his breath with a soft whoosh as the liquor left a trail of fire down his throat. The moment he'd tossed back the last swallow of whiskey he got up to refill his glass again.

Why not, he mused wryly. He was on vacation, wasn't he? He could look forward to two whole weeks without a waiting room overflowing with patients or back-to-back operations to perform. Two whole weeks! Trace smiled bitterly.

After nearly a month of maintaining a schedule designed to fill as many minutes as possible in every sixteen-hour day, Trace was bone tired. All he'd needed on the Friday before Labor Day, and his last working day before starting his vacation, was trouble in the operating room. So, naturally, that was exactly what he'd gotten.

Shuddering, Trace relived the moment his anesthetist said, tersely, "The patient's heart has stopped beating, doctor!"

Twelve hours! Trace shuddered again. For twelve hours his own team plus a specialized heart team had worked to revive the patient. They'd succeeded too! Trace felt both gratitude and pride for the heart specialists and his own hand-picked team.

What a way to begin a vacation, Trace grimaced. He'd been straddling the fine edge of exhaustion before he'd walked into the operating room that morning. Then he'd spent twelve hours fighting death on its own ground. Trace didn't feel victorious. He felt drained.

Setting his glass aside, Trace propped his elbows on the desk top and dropped his face in his hands, massaging his eyes and temples with his fingertips. As he raised his head his gaze came to rest on the pewter replica of the Liberty Bell. Lowering his right hand, he stroked the smooth metal.

It hadn't worked. All the countless hours of driving himself to the point of numbness hadn't dulled the tearing pain.

Kate.

Trace grasped the little bell and brought it to his face, rubbing it absently against the taut skin on his cheek. Closing his eyes, he conjured an image of her, her smoky-gray eyes darkened to near black with the passion he'd aroused in her, her pale skin gleaming slickly in the aftermath of that passion. Her beautiful mouth pressed to the pulse throbbing in his throat.

Scenes of the moments they'd shared flickered in his mind like a reel of film on a projector gone haywire: Kate, bristling at him on the day they met; Kate, gazing at him, solemn-eyed and trusting the very next day in his hotel room; Kate, giving herself to him in sweet abandonment on Christmas Day—her birthday; Kate, laughing with Kathy as she answered each and every one of the child's endless questions the day they'd finally gone sightseeing; and Kate, her eyes betraying anguish, her voice sad on the day he'd asked her to marry him.

What if it had been Kate on the operating table that day? Trace thought in sudden terror. And what if he or some other surgeon lost the battle against death?

"No!"

Trace sprang to his feet as the denial exploded from his throat. He couldn't lose Kate! He wouldn't! Not to death, if he could prevent it. And certainly not to his blasted pride!

A rush of adrenaline generated energy through his body as Trace strode from the office up to his bedroom. Refreshed by a stinging hot-cold shower, he threw clothes into his carryon with little concern for neatness. Then, dressed in a summer suit, he carried the case to the window in his office that faced east. Motionless, Trace watched the horizon for the first pink streaks of dawn.

Would the nightmare never end? Would the pain never subside? Pacing a well-worn path from the kitchen to the living-room window, Kate gazed at the wilting signs of summer's demise. The tiny patch of lawn that fronted the house was withered in spots. The trees that lined the sidewalk drooped, the leaves were drained of life.

It was Saturday of a holiday weekend. Her eyes as lifeless as the leaves she stared at, Kate grimaced with memory. She had met Trace on a Saturday of a holiday weekend. After the grinding weeks she'd just struggled through, Kate felt positive she would hate holiday weekends until the day she died.

Determined not to sink into gloom, Kate retraced her steps to the kitchen. She'd been up for hours, yet she hadn't eaten a thing. Food. That was the answer, Kate assured herself for at least the thousandth time over the previous weeks. Food was the best tranquilizer for emotional upset, especially chocolate.

Fifteen minutes later, a steaming cup of coffee cradled in her hands, Kate regarded the chocolate-filled croissant on a plate in front of her with emotional hunger.

By feeding that hunger, Kate had gained seven pounds over the last four weeks. The food had failed to appease the starvation. Breaking a corner off the flaky croissant, she gazed at it unenthusiastically before dropping it back onto the plate.

No, Kate protested silently. She didn't want food, she wanted Trace.

Trace.

The coffee forgotten, Kate closed her eyes, filling her mind with an image of him. What was he doing, now, this minute? It was Saturday so he was probably not in his office. Was he applying his skill in the operating room? Or, as this was a holiday weekend, was he free for a few days? It was an hour earlier in San Antonio. Was he still asleep? Did he ever dream of her?

Raising the cup to her lips, Kate gulped back a sob along with the tepid brew. Would the nightmare of memories never end? Would the pain of remembrance never subside?

Glancing at the clock, Kate told herself to get cracking. She had made a date to go shopping with Lisa, the girl who sat next to her at the office.

While showering, then dressing in a denim skirt, sleeveless blouse and flat sandals, Kate asked herself why she'd ever agreed to the shopping expedition in the first place. As she applied blusher to her pale cheeks, she answered her own question. She'd holed-up inside her apartment far too long. She had to get out, be with people, laugh with someone if she ever hoped to forget each and every moment she'd spent with Trace.

The shopping trip was a complete failure. Though Kate talked animatedly with Lisa, the words were meaningless. Though she laughed often, the laughter was hollow. When she and Lisa stopped for lunch, Kate picked at her food, but drank two margaritas thirstily. When she began to feel maudlin, Kate sagely advised herself to go home.

Trace was waiting for Kate in the hallway. The sight of his lean body propped lazily against the doorframe brought Kate to a dead stop as she rounded the corner into the hall at the top of the stairs. His haggard expression caused a contraction in her chest that robbed her of breath. But even with the look of a man honed to a cutting edge, he was the most attractive male Kate had seen in weeks... four weeks.

"I must talk to you, Kate." Straightening tautly, Trace ran a devouring glance over her, his shadowed eyes revealing stark hunger when they came to a stop on her trembling lips.

Suddenly hot, and cold, and exceedingly nervous, Kate slicked her tongue over her parched lips, swallowing roughly when his eyes narrowed at her unconsciously sensuous action.

"I...ah...all right." Forcing her tongue and feet to move at the same time, Kate closed the distance between them. Her fingers shook uncontrollably as she inserted the door key into the lock. Kate's entire body jerked when his long fingers covered hers to guide the key into the slot. When he removed his hand to push the door open, she rushed into the room, stiffening with tension when door shut quietly behind them.

Not looking at him, afraid to look at him, Kate dumped her impulsively bought, not really wanted, purchases on the sofa. Turning slowly, she drew a deep breath. "Would you—" she paused to swallow "—would you like something to drink?" Without waiting for his response, she started for the kitchen.

"No, Kate, I don't want anything to drink." The rough edge on Trace's tone brought her to a quivering halt. The quiver intensified as he continued, "I said I must talk to you. Please look at me while I say what I have to say."

Distractedly shaking her head, she changed course, moving toward the bedroom. Kate was not consciously aware of either action. She was in retreat. Positive Trace was about to plead with her to resume their relationship, and uncertain of her strength of will or her ability to refuse him, she ran into the bedroom. Trace was right behind her.

"Kate!" Without pause, Trace crossed the room to her. "Will you please just listen to me?"

Her breathing erratic, her heartbeat thundering, every one of her senses drinking in the scent of him, the nearness of him, Kate gritted her teeth against the desire to turn and throw herself into his arms. When he got to within inches of her, she ran into the bathroom, locking the door with shaking fingers.

"Kate." Though muffled, his low groan seeped into the room to stab at her heart.

Leaning forward, Trace rested his forehead on the smooth wood that separated them. Had he waited too long? Trace lowered his blunt lashes against the unfamiliar sting of tears in his eyes. Dear God! Had he indulged his pride to the point of losing her?

"Kate?" Trace made no attempt to conceal the pain in his voice; he was past subterfuge. "Kate, can you hear me?" There was a long moment of quiet, during which Trace held his breath.

"Yes, Trace," she finally responded, unwillingly.

"Kate, please open the door." Trace was oblivious to the hot trickle of moisture that ran down his face. "I have to look at you. I have to hold you. Kate, I need you!"

Stunned into immobility, Kate slowly closed her eyes. Had she actually heard Trace Sinclair use the word need? A sob rose in her constricted throat. Oh, please, please make it true! Suddenly frantic with the need to witness that truth, Kate fumbled in her haste to unlock the door. Flinging it open, she searched his eyes through a misty veil of tears. Her own eyes widened in sheer disbelief at the evidence of tears on his cheeks and lashes. But more astounding still was the pain revealed unashamedly in those green depths.

"Trace?" Kate's tone held awed wonder.

Though his burning gaze clung to hers, Trace made no move to touch her. "I love you, Kate. I need you." The steady tenor of his voice banished all shreds of doubt in Kate's heart and mind. "I need you in my home. I need you in my bed. I need you in my life." He paused, then smiled tentatively. "Come to Texas with me, Kate."

"Oh, Trace!" Kate was now sobbing; her defenses dissolving in a flood of healing tears. "I love you so much, Trace," she whispered. "So very much."

His smile tender, Trace held out his arms. "Come to me, my love." Gathering her body close to the protective warmth of his own, Trace lowered his lips to her hair. Holding her tightly, he absorbed her tremors with his own.

Blond curls dancing on her shoulders, the little girl skipped along happily between the adults that flanked her on either side. As they exited the brightly decorated department store she raised her hands to grasp the two that were extended to her. The early evening air was balmy on the expectant face she lifted to the man.

"Can we eat dinner in town, daddy?" Kathy requested hopefully.

Trace smiled down at his daughter before exchanging a glance with his wife. "What do you think, Kate?" he inquired blandly, his green eyes teasing. "Did this little imp behave herself while you were finishing your shopping? Has she earned dinner in town?"

Gazing down at her stepdaughter, Kate winked conspiratorially; they'd had a delightful day, shopping for Trace's Christmas present. "Yes," Kate nodded decisively. "In fact, she not only behaved nicely, she was a great deal of help. Kathy has not only earned the right to dinner in town, she's earned the privilege of choosing the restaurant."

"Okay, honey, the choice is yours. Where would you like to eat?" Trace grinned. "But let me warn you, if you choose a pizza parlor you're in big trouble."

Kathy grinned back at him. "I want to eat along the river walk so I can look at the lights."

"Mexican?" Trace asked with almost boyish expectancy.

"Of course!" Kathy and Kate laughed as their answering voices blended in unison.

Sitting at an umbrella-shaded table on the lower level of the restaurant's tiered patio, Kate was lulled by the gentle lap of the San Antonio River as it slapped the cement siding walls. Her gray eyes reflecting the enchantment shining from Kathy's face, Kate gazed up at the tall trees lining the river walk. Still in full leaf, the trees were ablaze with lights strung through their branches.

Incredible, thought Kate, smiling as a boatload of tourists waved at the diners as the boat glided by. Back east she, and most of those tourists, would be huddling inside heavy winter wear. While here in San Antonio they were all attired in lightweight clothing. Incredible.

Breathing in the warm, scented air, Kate lifted her glass to sip the tangy margarita she'd ordered. Even the drinks taste better here, she thought, smiling at Trace over the rim of her glass. Or, she mused, was it being with Trace that made the air seem warmer, the Christmas lights brighter, the drink tangier?

"Have you decided?"

Kate blinked herself out of her reverie and into the reality of softly shaded green eyes smiling into hers. "Hmm?" she murmured vaguely, admiring the way his unruly chestnut hair persisted in falling onto his forehead.

"I asked if you have decided what you'd like for dinner." Trace smiled in acknowledgment of her caressing gaze. "The waitress is waiting." Turning his head slightly, he smiled at the patient young Mexican-American.

"Oh!" Kate shifted her apologetic glance to the waitress. "Yes, I'm sorry!"

The young woman smiled in understanding. "It is comforting to gaze out over the river. There is no rush here, *señora*."

Señora. Kate very much liked the sound of the word; it was what Inez called her. After ordering, Kate turned her attention to Kathy.

"The lights are beautiful. Aren't they?"

"Oh, yes!" Kathy sighed, looking up at the trees.

"As beautiful as that huge tree you fell in love with in that shopping mall last year?" Trace teased softly.

"Yes," Kathy nodded emphatically. "That tree was beautiful too, but in a different way."

"And the Santa Claus you whispered to before we left the store, was he as nice as the one you talked to last year?" Trace drawled, arching his eyebrows.

Kate frowned. Though she was positive his question had a definite purpose, she couldn't begin to imagine what it might be.

With the innocence of the very young, Kathy went right to the heart of the matter. "Yes, he was nice. Why?"

Trace shrugged. "I was wondering if you were planning to tell us what you asked him to bring you, or if it is a deep, dark secret like last year."

Now Kate was really confused; what was Kathy's secret last year? Trace answered her question before she could voice it.

"Kathy asked Santa for you to be her mommie last year, Kate."

"Oh, Kathy!" Tears welling in her eyes, Kate reached across the table to grasp the child's hand. "Did you really want me for your mommie, baby?"

"Yes." Kathy nodded shyly. "But Santa didn't bring you. I cried and cried."

"And are there going to be any tears this year?" Trace probed gently.

"No." Kathy set her curls dancing with a quick shake of her head. "I don't think so. I only asked Santa for two things."

Holding the girl's hand, Kate waited for Kathy to elaborate; Trace displayed far less patience.

"Well?" he nudged exasperatedly.

Kathy gazed up at him with wide, trusting eyes. "I asked for a Barbie dollhouse," she said simply, then, very quickly, "and a baby brother."

Kate's eyes flashed to Trace even as his gaze shot to hers. There was an instant of silence, then they both burst out laughing.

"Did I ask for the wrong thing again?" Kathy wailed plaintively.

"No!" Trace choked trying to subdue a fresh peal of laughter.

"Of course not!" Kate soothed, stroking the confused child's hand. "But, honey, I hope you realize that Santa can't bring you a baby brother *or* sister *this* year?"

Kathy's lower lip protruded in a pout. "Why?"

"Well...because..." Kate floundered. How in the world did one explain the time element involved in procreation to a four-year-old?

"Because Kate and I want to have you to ourselves for a little while," Trace inserted smoothly, displaying a new-found sensitivity to Kathy's need of a sense of self-worth. "In time, we pray there will a brother or sister for you, baby," he continued, using Kate's endearment for the child. "But, until then, we have one another—don't we?"

The conversation of that evening replayed itself in Kate's mind at odd moments as the weeks until Christmas dwindled to days. During these odd moments, Kate couldn't avoid making a comparison between this holiday season and preceding ones, especially the last one.

The year before, Kate was feeling empty and very much alone and actually dreading the hype and hyperbole attached to the holiday. While Trace had been bitingly bitter and insensitive to his child's excitement and outspoken in his disgust of the whole thing.

The natural reaction to these moments of introspection was fear; so very happy and content was the Kate of this holiday season, she feared it could not possibly last.

And Kate was very happy and content. Her emotional fulfillment had begun when Trace had drawn her into his arms and whispered, "Come to me, my love."

With those five words, Trace had given her the hearth and home Kate had sought and feared would never be hers. The union of their bodies had always been satisfying physically. In the three months since Trace had made her his wife in a quiet, private ceremony with Kathy by his side, Kate had discovered a richly satisfying union of their minds.

The perfection of their wedding trip had less to do with the lush beauty of the island of Maui, and everything to do with the attitude of her husband.

Kate and Trace had married exactly one week after he'd come to her, heart in hand. During that hilariously frantic week they had cleaned out her apartment, sending the things she wanted to keep to San Antonio, and the stuff she didn't want to a local used furniture auctioneer. Kate gave a week's notice at work. She had also introduced Trace to her family with one breath and informed them of her plans to leave almost at once with him for Texas in the following breath.

Less than two hours after the ceremony uniting them, Kate, Trace and Kathy were on a plane bound eventually for Hawaii and a meeting with Trace's parents.

The elder Sinclairs had accepted Kate on sight. Trace and Kate had spent one day with his parents then, leaving Kathy in their capable care, they'd island-hopped to Maui to spend a few days alone.

Over three months later, Kate still thrilled to the memory of the absolute bliss she'd experienced throughout the entire length of their stay in Maui.

Kate had not expected the honeymoon conditions to prevail once she and Trace had settled into his home outside San Antonio. What she had steeled herself for was a rather bumpy trial period while the three of them adjusted to living together as a family.

On their return to Texas, Kate was pleasantly surprised to discover that no trial period of adjustment was necessary. Kate readily admitted that it was Trace's attitude that was the cementing factor: when Trace Sinclair decided to give of himself, he did so unconditionally.

Kate had slipped into the role of wife and mother as if born to it—as, of course, she'd always known she was. And, if she adored her new daughter, which she did, she practically worshipped her husband. Both by word and action, Trace reciprocated the commitment of self.

For Kate, emotional poverty had been exchanged for emotional wealth. Kate shared her wealth generously. There was laughter in the house outside San Antonio, Texas.

As the clock ticked off the final minutes of Christmas Eve, Kate sat on the floor near the sweetly aromatic, brightly decorated balsam. The house, alive with the joyous sound of happy inhabitants two hours before, was now quiet except for the muted music of the season wafting gently from the stereo in the corner of the living room.

Trace had carried Kathy to bed hours before. Trace's parents, visiting for the holidays, had remained to help Trace and Kate "play" Santa Claus and have a light snack and a final drink before they too retired for the night.

Trace was in the kitchen loading the glasses and snacks plates into the dishwasher. Sitting amid the neatly arranged presents, Kate was once again lost in a reverie of comparison.

So much had happened in the space of one year; so many changes had occurred in that relatively short span. To Kate, it seemed much longer than one year since she'd endured the disillusionment of her parents' annual Christmas Eve circus. And even longer since she'd agreed to Trace's terms of a relationship and allowed him to undress her—quite like someone unwrapping an unexpected Christmas gift!

A soft smile curved Kate's lips at her unintentional analogy. But how very apt, she mused. She had given herself to Trace without qualm on Christmas Day, and in doing so had offered him her most precious gift...herself. Though Trace had made full use of her gift, Kate now knew that his total acceptance had come with the offering of himself in exchange.

"What are you thinking about?" Trace probed gently, settling next to her on the carpet while balancing a glass of wine in each hand.

"You and me and the Christmas tree," Kate murmured, her gaze pensive. Accepting the glass of wine, she tilted it to acknowledge his silent toast before continuing, "And the difference between this Christmas and last year."

"You mean, the difference in me," Trace smiled. "Don't you?"

"Yes." Kate smiled back. "You've been wonderful, Trace. I know how you feel about the holiday, yet you've gone out of your way to make it perfect for Kathy and me. You've been so thoughtful, so considerate through all the hectic activity and I wanted to—" Trace silenced her very effectively with a hard kiss.

"You know how I *used* to feel," Trace corrected her softly when he released her mouth. "I was miserable, honey. Miserable and bitter, and not too bright. I had always loved the holidays before my first marriage." He sighed deeply. "When the marriage ended I closed myself off to everything, every involvement, and cheated my daughter as well as myself."

Setting her glass aside, Kate cradled his face in her hands and drew his mouth to hers. "Oh, Trace, I love you so much!" she murmured passionately, kissing him fiercely.

Placing his glass next to hers, Trace slowly undressed her with trembling fingers. The tremor was mirrored in Kate's hands as she fumbled with his clothing. Then, the glow from the tree lights shimmering on their naked bodies, their whispered endearments blending with the joyful music, they exchanged the ultimate love gift of giving and receiving.

As the clock on the mantelpiece struck the hour of midnight, Kate and Trace lay entwined in a lovers' embrace beneath a tree resplendent with ornaments and lights, their breathing slowly returning to normal.

"I haven't been at all wonderful, Kate," Trace confessed, brushing his lips over her cheeks. "I needed this holiday desperately. I needed the love and laughter you've brought to my life, and my daughter, and this house."

Drawing Kate closer to his muscular strength, Trace caressed her with gentle hands and gazed down at her with eyes filled with a hint of wonder and a mist of tears.

"Happy birthday, honey." His lips took hers in a warm kiss. "Merry Christmas, darling." Again Trace bestowed the gift of his mouth. "I love you, my Kate."

*   *   *   *   *

Emilie Richards

*

SEASON OF MIRACLES

For my children:
Shane, Jessie, Galen, Brendan,
who sometimes have to point the way.

CHAPTER ONE

THE FIRST THING she noticed was the silence. It hovered in the August morning air like a patient vulture waiting for his prey to cease its struggles. Elise had never realized that silence, something she had experienced little of in her thirty-five years, could be so foreboding.

Forcing herself awake she sat up in bed, pushing long strands of black hair away from her face with the palms of her hands. She listened carefully, but the silence remained unbroken. Through sleep-swollen eyes she gauged the time. There was no clock in her bedroom. Sleeping late had been one of the problems Elise had never had to worry about.

The heavy sunlight beating relentlessly through her window told her that the morning was at least half gone. *Why? Is Mama sleeping late too?*

The question triggered its own answer as she became more fully awake. *Mama.* No, Mama would sleep forever. Elise waited for the familiar sadness but this morning she could detect no signs of it. Her mother was gone; Jeanette Ramsey's death was unalterable. Elise Ramsey was alive, possibly for the first time in seventeen years.

And the house was silent.

Swinging her legs over the side of the bed Elise stood, her long cotton gown falling in snowy swirls around her bare feet. She drew aside the curtains at her window and peered out at the sun-dappled avenue. The town of

Miracle Springs was awake, going about its business with slow-moving enthusiasm. Elise stood at the window for long minutes counting cars. One...two... Satisfied that by sleeping late she had missed absolutely nothing, she turned and began to search her closet for the coolest dress she owned. The day was going to be a scorcher.

The dress she chose was one her mother had never liked—not that it had been easy to please Jeanette Ramsey, anyway. But this particular dress had elicited comments about gypsies and dressing to suit one's age and position in the community. It was white with a full embroidered skirt in a style that was never quite in or out of fashion, and Elise felt young again when she wore it. She realized that in her mother's eyes, that had been the whole problem.

Elise fastened the dress and pulled a brush through her long hair, twisting it into a cool knot on top of her head, and wondered fleetingly how much longer she'd be able to get away with the severe hairstyle that did nothing to soften the inevitable signs of approaching middle age. She wasn't much of a judge, never having wasted time examining her appearance for innovative ways of dealing with its flaws. Elise had worn her hair long since she was a child. She loved it. Glossy, still black and utterly unstylish, it was an important part of her image of herself. If it emphasized features that were less than perfect, it also emphasized the high cheekbones and smooth olive skin that she liked to think were her best assets.

As she wandered around the room her movements made little noises, disturbing the intimidating silence and shaping it to suit her. Now that she was wide-awake Elise wondered why something she had longed for all her life— freedom, a chance to think her own thoughts—had seemed so threatening this morning. Undoubtedly, living alone was going to take some getting used to.

"But you will get used to it," she said out loud, "because you're probably going to spend the rest of your life alone." It wasn't a new thought or a particularly sad one. It was something she was just beginning to come to terms with, and like a child reciting a Bible verse, she spoke the thought as often as possible to commit it to memory and internalize it.

Downstairs, Elise stopped to throw open the heavy draperies in the living room before moving on to the kitchen to fix her breakfast. The old frame house was already beginning to soak up the day's sunshine. August in central Florida was as predictable as anything in life could be. It was hot and humid, guaranteed to slow the average person's pace by fifty percent. Most of the inhabitants of Miracle Springs cut their losses by air-conditioning their houses and places of employment.

Elise's house had one small air conditioner in the room that had belonged to her mother. The rest of the house had been left to the ravages of the Florida summer. Now Elise turned on a circular fan that was sitting on top of the kitchen counter and began to slice a grapefruit. She hummed as she worked, keeping the silence at arm's length with her own music.

This day would pass, and with it, the other sultry days of August. September would come, and with its arrival her life would once again be filled with the noise and confusion of teaching tenth grade English at Miracle Springs High. Elise, who had spent most of her life wishing for silence, put down her grapefruit knife and picked up a pen. As she slashed an X through the date on the calendar above the counter, she wondered why that simple act gave her so much satisfaction.

"SO AFTER ALL THOSE YEARS of faking illness, Mrs. Ramsey just up and died last month. Just like that. Nobody even knew she was sick. She complained so much all the time Dr. Mooney didn't do more than give her a quick checkup. Next thing anybody knew, she keeled over in his parking lot. Gone in a minute."

Sloane Tyson sat in his aunt's living room and twisted the brim of his panama hat. The malleable straw crackled and popped as he ruined the shape of it forever. "So what happened to Elise after her mother died?" he asked, his voice a shade more enthusiastic than mere politeness dictated.

"Oh, she's still here. She'll be teaching again this year, I suspect. Best teacher at Miracle Springs High. Prettiest, too." Lillian Tyson looked at her nephew with interest. "Weren't you sweet on her years ago?"

Sloane had forgotten how every detail of life in a small town was collected and stored in the minds of its inhabitants. The system was more efficient than a computer bank and only slightly more personal. Today he had sat quietly and listened to his aunt's recital of the intimate details of the lives of Miracle Springs citizens, not expecting himself to be drawn into the conversation. He should have known better. He should have realized that Elise Ramsey would be on Lillian Tyson's list.

"You remember farther back than I do," he said nonchalantly. But of course, what he said wasn't true. He'd forgotten a lot about Miracle Springs, put it out of his mind as if he'd never lived there, but he'd never forgotten Elise. No, he'd never forgotten Elise.

Lillian would not be daunted. "Well, it seems to me that you went steady with her your senior year."

"That was seventeen years ago."

"Around here, nothing much happens in seventeen years."

Sloane smiled wryly. His aunt was right, and it was precisely the reason he had left the small town of three thousand where he'd been born. He'd left at the first opportunity and never come back—except once, for his mother's funeral.

Lillian Tyson seemed to read his mind. "Are you going to make it, Sloane? Can you stand living here for a year?"

"My choices are limited." Sloane stood and began to pace the small living room that was crowded with old furniture and assorted knickknacks. He was a large man, and he dwarfed his surroundings as well as the old woman who fondly watched his pacing.

"You're like a tiger in a cage," she pronounced, proud of her analogy. "Always have been. Miracle Springs hems you in."

And it was precisely that "hemming in" that had brought him back, Sloane admitted to himself. For the first time he was in need of the sheltering influences of the little town, its slow, easy pace, its acceptance of its own. The last thought made him pause. "Do you think they're going to accept Clay?" he asked.

Lillian watched her nephew and her unfailingly cheerful face remained open and smiling. She didn't have to ask who "they" were. She knew Sloane referred to the citizens of Miracle Springs. "He's your son, isn't he? He's a Tyson. He may have some trouble, but he'll make it here."

"He wouldn't have made it in Cambridge," Sloane said to himself as much as to his aunt. "The kids there would have eaten him alive."

"They may try that here, but he'll be protected."

"I guess that's a start."

The living-room door swung open and a slender young man entered the room, his hands jammed in the pockets of stiff new blue jeans. "I fed your cats, Lillian," he said.

"Aunt Lillian," his father corrected him sharply.

"It's all right," Lillian said, waving aside Sloane's protest. "Clay doesn't know me from Adam. I don't seem like an aunt to him yet."

"He's still got to learn the proper forms of address," Sloane said, his hat brim crackling anew in his hands.

"Aunt Lillian," Clay said pleasantly, stressing the first word. "All this relative stuff seems strange."

"I suspect everything seems strange," Lillian said, a smile directed at her great-nephew. "But you don't seem strange to us. You're the spitting image of your daddy there. Right down to the way your hair swirls off your forehead."

Clay nodded, glancing at his father to see what impact his aunt's comment had made on Sloane. With an insight far beyond his years, Clay suspected that their resemblance was not a source of pleasure to his father.

"Resembles you right down to the ponytail," Lillian said, this time to Sloane.

"Sloane had a ponytail?" Clay asked.

"Nothing like yours," Lillian said, reaching out to tug the brown hair that fell in restrained waves to the middle of Clay's back. "When your dad was growing up around here, nobody'd even seen long hair on a man. Your dad's was short, barely long enough to put in a rubber band, but I'll tell you, it caused a stir in this town you wouldn't believe."

"What happened, Sloane?" Clay turned to his father and monitored his expression again.

"My uncle hauled me off to the barber shop. He was bigger than I was." The ghost of a grin lit Sloane's face.

Clay was encouraged. "Are you planning to repeat history?"

Sloane's expression became serious. "I'm not going to force you to do anything, Clay. It's your hair. I have no opinions about it one way or the other."

"Well I do," Lillian said firmly. "You want to fit in at Miracle Springs High, you get that hair cut before you go the first day. Kids'll like you better if you look like them."

Clay considered her words. "Why would they want me to look like them?" he asked finally. "That doesn't make any sense."

Lillian's jaw dropped a little, and Sloane shook his head. "You've got a lot to learn about teenagers, Clay," he said.

Clay shrugged. "I haven't even seen any teenagers here."

"Hasn't he been to the springs?" Lillian asked Sloane.

"I've been too busy settling in to take him."

"He can go by himself," Lillian admonished. "He's fifteen. This isn't Boston. Fifteen's old enough to go anywhere around here. Do you have a swimsuit?" she asked Clay. At his nod she added, "Do you want to go?"

Clay nodded again.

"Then go home and put it on. You can swim while your dad takes care of business this afternoon. I'll walk you down to show you the way."

Sloane waited until Clay was gone. "Are you sure that's a good idea?"

"He's got to start somewhere." Lillian observed the tiny frown lines on Sloane's forehead. "It's not like

Clay's got something seriously wrong with him. He's going to be fine."

"He's got such a long way to go before he understands what this crazy world is all about. I feel like I'm throwing him to the lions."

"All parents feel that way," Lillian said, trying to soothe him.

"But not all parents are suddenly raising a son they didn't even know existed," Sloane said bitterly. "Not all parents have a son who didn't even know he had a last name until a month ago."

"And not all parents in that situation would care," Lillian reminded him gently.

"I never wanted to be a father."

"Give yourself time. Give Clay time. Give Miracle Springs time."

"Miracle Springs will have to bring me a miracle. I'm afraid that's what it's going to take."

"It's happened before." Lillian stood too and set her frail hand on her nephew's shoulder. "The first miracle was finding Clay; the second one will be really finding him."

Sloane's taut body relaxed under her touch. "I appreciate your optimism."

"I appreciate your coming back here. I may be a selfish old lady, but I'm glad you're home. Even if it's just for a year. You were always more like a son than a nephew."

Sloane's expression softened. "By the time we leave, you may be glad to see us go."

"Not likely."

Sloane put his arms around his aunt and hugged her much as he had as a young boy. There were some things that time and distance and endless mistakes never changed. Sloane knew that his aunt's love was one of them.

Lillian's eyes were teary when the embrace ended. "Don't go getting all soft on me, boy." She stepped back to search Sloane's face. "You know, as much as you dislike this town, you might find some things here for yourself this year."

"Such as?"

"Such as a mother for Clay."

Elise's name lay unspoken between them.

Sloane shook his head, his features fixed in decisive lines. "Clay will have to do with one parent. But then, that's more than he's ever had before."

"Just give this year a chance," Lillian said softly. "Let time take care of the rest."

But Sloane, who had never believed that time took care of anything, was lost in his own thoughts.

As ELISE STROLLED under the succession of canvas and fiberglass awnings that were strung over Hope Avenue's sidewalks she wondered if she'd live long enough to see any changes in Miracle Springs. She had often thought that the only miracle the town had to offer was the way it had avoided entry into the twentieth century. Even if changes occurred, they were so subtle as to be invisible to the human eye.

The sameness of everything was like an opiate to creativity and to growth. It was a potent drug that lulled Miracle Springs residents into accepting the inevitability of their lives.

"This town'll kill you, Elise. It'll sneak up on you and bury you in its sameness until you don't know you're different from everybody else. And you'll die not remembering."

Elise stopped in the middle of the sidewalk and wondered at the voice she had just heard. She wasn't going crazy. There was no doubt where the voice had come from. It was in her memory, locked tightly there for safekeeping. It was Sloane's voice, and the words were some of the last he had ever spoken to her. She hadn't let herself think about that conversation for years.

She shook her head, not to banish the voice, but in distress at her own vulnerability. Seventeen years had passed and Sloane was still with her.

"Morning, Elise."

Elise looked up to see Olin Biggs, Miracle Springs mayor, bearing down on her. "Good morning, Olin."

"Hotter than Hades today. Same as yesterday. Probably the same tomorrow."

Funny. Those had been her thoughts exactly, only she hadn't been thinking about the weather. "It is hot," she agreed politely. "How's Sally?"

"She's doing fine. I think she's actually looking forward to school starting. You wouldn't consider moving up to eleventh grade English, would you? I know she'd like to have you as her teacher again."

Elise shook her head regretfully. "I can't do it. But tell her to come by and see me. She was a wonderful student." Elise fielded Olin's condolences about her mother's death and walked on. By the time she reached the post office, she had encountered two former students and one more parent. The students were now gainfully employed residents of Miracle Springs with families of their own. Elise felt the distinct sensation of middle-age settling over her. All she needed was a cat or two and a few gray hairs, and she'd be the sterotypical old maid schoolteacher. If she wasn't already.

She was sorting through her small collection of bills and advertisements when she heard a familiar voice behind her. "Elise. What a nice surprise."

Her smile as she turned was hopeful. "Hello, Bob. Is Amy with you?"

Bob Cargil shook his head, displacing the hair that was carefully combed to cover the widening bald spot at the center of his scalp. "No, she's at the springs. You look lovely this morning."

"Thank you." Elise smiled again. It was nice to have someone notice what she looked like. "You look like you're feeling fit this morning."

"I can't really complain."

A rebellious voice inside her proclaimed that if Bob couldn't really complain, it was the first time such a thing had happened. She squelched the voice with stern self-control. "How's the book coming?"

Bob shrugged. He was a history teacher at Miracle Springs High School and for the past five years had been working on a textbook for high school classes in Florida history. He had been stuck for the past four. "It's hard to work in this heat," he said.

"I'm sure," Elise commiserated. The rebellious voice reminded her that Bob's entire house was air-conditioned. Once again, she squelched it.

"Is our date still on for tonight?"

"I'm counting on it," she said with as much enthusiasm as she could muster. Then her voice brightened a little. "Is Amy coming?" Amy was Bob's fifteen-year-old daughter and Elise's biggest reason for tolerating Bob's presence in her life.

"No. This one's just us."

"Tell her I said to come by and visit."

"You know she will. She's always pestering me to let her come see you. But I know..." Bob's voice trailed off.

"Bob, I've told you, I'm not in mourning. Having Amy visit is something I look forward to."

"I'll tell her."

"Good." Elise reached out and squeezed his hand. "I'll see you tonight." She watched his retreat. Bob had recently developed a peculiar shuffling gait as if he were practicing for the old age that was still a safe distance away. Although he was ten years Elise's senior, there was nothing wrong with his health that exercise and diet couldn't cure. But Bob enjoyed the aging process and everything that went with it. Not for the first time Elise thought of the similarities between Bob and her mother, and shuddered delicately.

The chimes in the town hall tower announced that it was eleven o'clock. Elise knew that meant it was actually 11:06. The tower chimes had been six minutes off as long as anyone could remember. No one had ever bothered to fix them, and now if anyone suggested it, the town fathers pointed out that fixing the chimes would only confuse people. It was better they reasoned, to leave them alone.

The prospect of a long hot afternoon stretched in front of her, and on the spur of the moment, Elise decided not to spend it at home. There nothing awaited her except silence, unrelenting heat and a few unnecessary household chores. For the first time in her life she was really free to explore other options, and although there weren't many options to explore in Miracle Springs, there were a few. She stopped at the drugstore, bought a turkey sandwich to go and took a shortcut down Faith Street toward the source of the town's name.

There was no silence at the springs. Crowds of teen-agers with blaring radios littered the sandy brown beach. The dock stretching from the beach out over the water was covered with glistening, oiled bodies, and under-neath it small children darted in and out between the piers that had been sunk deeply into the sand. Benches enam-eled a forest green sat in the shade of palm trees and moss-draped live oaks at the beach's edge, and Elise set-tled herself on one to enjoy the clamor.

She wasn't alone for long. Former and soon-to-be stu-dents dropped by to say hello. She had known most of them since they were small children. Some were the sons and daughters of her own high school friends; others she had met at church or in her volunteer work teaching reading at the tiny Miracle Springs library. Elise was as certain of her popularity with the town's young people as she was about anything in her predictable life.

A petite teenage girl with a cap of curly blond hair waved and then came to stand in front of her. "Hi, Elise. I've never seen you here before."

Elise patted the bench, and the girl sprawled beside her, spreading wet sand in her wake. Elise didn't even notice. "Hi, Amy. Where've you been all summer?"

"Here mostly." Amy's face grew suddenly serious. "Dad said you wouldn't feel like visitors because of your mom. But I've been wanting to come and see you. He was wrong, wasn't he?"

"Yes, he was." Elise put her arm around Amy's shoulders and gave her a quick hug. "But he was think-ing of me so we won't be mad at him."

"Like I said at the funeral, I'm sorry about Mrs. Ramsey."

"Thank you." Elise smiled to let Amy know that she didn't have to remain so serious. "Now tell me what you've been doing."

They gossiped for a while and then Elise watched as Amy was pulled away by boisterous friends. It was only as she finished her sandwich and settled back to watch the teenagers' antics that Elise noticed the boy standing underneath a nearby tree.

She had heard Sloane's voice in the middle of a nearly deserted sidewalk. Now she was seeing his image and it was just as clear. She resisted the desire to squeeze her eyes shut. The voice had been a product of her memory. The image was real. And it obviously couldn't be Sloane himself.

Elise watched with fascination as the boy turned slightly, giving her a better view of his profile. She drew in her breath sharply as she cataloged his features. He had Sloane's wide forehead and his golden-brown hair waved back with the same determination Sloane's had always shown. Of course, this boy's hair was much longer, but cut short, Elise knew it still wouldn't settle down neatly. It would always be unruly and the girls would always ache to smooth it for him.

The straight nose was Sloane's; the deep-set eyes were too. Even though Elise couldn't see their color, she'd bet her life they'd be that peculiar shade of pecan-shell brown that almost bordered on gray. But it was his mouth that gave away his relationship to Sloane. It was a perfectly formed mouth, chiseled by a master hand, a mouth that could draw back in a sardonic grin or remain locked shut in an effort to avoid trouble.

Was the boy Sloane's nephew? A cousin? A son? The last seemed the most and the least likely. Elise hadn't seen Sloane in seventeen years, but she'd heard all about him.

There were enough Tysons living in Miracle Springs to keep her informed, although Sloane's mother had died years before. She knew that he'd made a name for himself as an author. In fact, she'd read all his books. She knew that his personal life had been less successful. There'd been one marriage and one divorce a year later. To Elise's knowledge there'd been no child, but even if she was wrong and Sloane had had a son by that union, the boy would only be five or six. This boy was a teenager.

And yet, how could a cousin or a nephew emerge with Sloane's body and face? For that matter, as far as Elise knew, she had met all the Tysons. This boy was new in town.

As if he could feel her stare, the boy turned to face Elise. Even though politeness dictated that she look away, Elise could not. Instead she smiled tentatively. "Hi."

Elise accepted the fact that the boy would probably nod and move away. Talking to strange older women was no teenager's idea of a good time. Instead, he moved closer. "Hello," he responded.

"You're new here, aren't you?" she asked, encouraged by his proximity.

"Yeah. We just got to town last week."

And I've been out of touch, Elise thought to herself. *Or I'd know who you are.* "I'm Elise Ramsey. I teach English at Miracle Springs High. Will you be a student there this year?"

"I guess. If they let me in," the boy said candidly. "My name's Clay."

"I'm glad to meet you, Clay."

He nodded as if it only made sense she'd be glad to meet him. "What grade do you teach?"

"Tenth. What grade will you be in?"

"I don't know yet. They're having trouble deciding what to do with me."

Elise frowned. "How old are you?"

"Fifteen."

"Well, most fifteen-year-olds are in tenth grade. Did your other school hold you back or push you forward?"

Clay smiled. "I've never been to school."

It was an answer Elise hadn't expected. "That's surprising," she said as nonchalantly as possible.

"Yeah, I guess it is." Clay came to stand beside her. "If they put me in tenth grade English, what will I be studying?"

"I put a lot of emphasis on writing," she told him, studying him with undisguised interest now that he was closer. His eyes *were* the color of Sloane's. The confirmation gave her a slight jolt. After all these years she could still remember exactly what Sloane Tyson's eyes looked like.

"What kind of writing?" Clay asked.

"Creative writing. Poetry, short stories, plays. We read a lot, too."

Clay nodded. "I'll like that. I've done lots of writing. I started a novel when I was thirteen but I needed help getting over a hump and nobody at the ranch that year was a writer."

"The ranch?"

"Destiny Ranch, in New Mexico. I grew up there."

The name struck a familiar chord in Elise's memory, but she couldn't decide why. "I think I've heard that name before," she ventured.

"You probably have. They were always writing us up in the newspaper." Clay pointed at a group of kids standing by the water. "Do most of these kids go to the high school where you teach?"

"All of them and more besides. It's the only high school in the county, so kids are bused in from the surrounding area, too. You'll make lots of friends." But even as she said the words, Elise wondered how true they were. With his extravagant ponytail and his curious combination of adult intelligence and childlike candor, Elise wondered if Clay would stand out in a school where standing out was thought to be the worst possible crime.

But Clay had already shrugged off her optimistic prophecy. "I'm more interested in just finding someone I can talk to."

"Clay!" a voice on the other side of the dock shouted. "Clay!"

Without turning, Elise knew whom she would see. Somehow the day had been leading up to this. The foreboding silence that had punished her with images of her lonely future, Sloane's voice on the sidewalk, Sloane's image stamped on the boy sitting next to her. They had all been warnings of a confrontation that was yet to come.

"Sloane's calling me." Clay stood. "I'd better go. He hates to be kept waiting."

Not "Uncle Sloane," or "Dad." Not even the more formal, "my father." "Clay," she said, her courage failing rapidly, "are you talking about Sloane Tyson?"

The boy nodded. The too familiar lines of his jaw were set now, and his body was suddenly tense. "Yeah. See you later."

Elise raised her hand in salute as Clay walked away. She knew that all she had to do was turn her head. A slight rotation of her chin and she would see, once again, the only man who had ever meant anything to her. But it was no surprise to Elise that instead she continued to stare at the sparkling turquoise spring and the raucous children on the beach. No, it was no surprise that she lacked courage where Sloane Tyson was concerned.

Seventeen years had passed, but she, like the town Sloane had hated, was still essentially the same. She could take no risks; she could not reach out for what she wanted. She was no different than she had been the day she told Sloane she would not marry him and leave Miracle Springs forever.

Long minutes passed and finally Elise stood, turning to begin the walk back home. The laughter and shouts from the beach were no longer comforting. They only reminded her of what was missing in her life.

CHAPTER TWO

"I MET A NICE WOMAN at the springs," Clay told Sloane, although Sloane hadn't asked about his day. As a small child, Clay had learned that if he wanted to talk about himself, he had to initiate the conversation and pick an adult who would be receptive. Since Sloane was the only adult available, he would have to do, even if his eyes were shuttered and his arms crossed firmly in front of his ribs as they walked down Faith Street. Clay, a master at reading body language, gave the conversation no more than a fifty percent chance of success. But it was worth a try.

"Good," Sloane replied.

Clay tried again. "She teaches English at the high school."

Sloane nodded but the length of his step increased. Clay, who was tall for his age, had to hurry to keep up.

"Her name's Elise Randall or something like that."

"Ramsey. Elise Ramsey. And yes, I know her."

"I hope I'll be in her class."

This time Sloane didn't even nod. He hadn't been close enough to get a good look at the woman sitting beside Clay on the bench, but his gut level reaction had assured him that it was indeed Elise Ramsey talking to his son. He had had a perfect opportunity to approach her, say a casual hello and permanently loosen the knot in his stomach that formed every time her name was mentioned.

Elise Ramsey, for God's sake. Seventeen years had passed, and he had lived the equivalent of several lifetimes since then. So why was he behaving like an anxious adolescent, letting his reactions build up and submerge his common sense?

All it was going to take was one simple conversation, one short series of pleasantries to put Elise in the proper place in his psyche. The longer he waited the harder it was going to be. She was nothing to him but a woman from a small Florida town, a schoolteacher whose idea of fun was probably dinner at one of the two local restaurants and a drive to Ocala to take in a first run movie. She had undoubtedly absorbed Miracle Springs's value system, and now that she was finally free of her mother, she was probably hunting a husband with the frenzied tenacity of a spinster who sees her biological time clock winding down.

Sloane shook his head at his own conclusions. Why was he trying so hard to convince himself that Elise was anything other than the warm, intelligent, sensitive woman he had known? Of course, she hadn't quite been a woman seventeen years ago. She'd been poised on the razor's edge between adolescence and maturity. He had gone that far with her himself, and by now the years would have completed the transition. There was no reason to believe that all that had been wonderful about Elise had changed.

Nor was there any reason to believe that all that was not wonderful about Elise had changed, either. Underneath the warmth, the intelligence, the sensitivity had been a woman too weak to stand up for herself. In the end she had taken the easiest road. And with a flash of insight, Sloane realized that he had never forgiven her for doing so.

"Sloane?"

Sloane grunted, too lost in his own thoughts to pull himself out of them easily.

"I asked you if you used to go to the springs when you were a boy." Clay's tone was patient. Adults didn't like petulance. In that way he was sure Sloane was no different from any of the dozens of adults who had taken care of him throughout his fifteen years.

Sloane realized he was leaving Clay behind, and he slowed his pace a fraction. "I practically lived there when I was your age. Did you enjoy the water?"

"I didn't go in."

"Why not?"

"I never learned to swim."

Sloane flinched. There was so much he didn't know about this boy, this son who was a stranger. "I guess you didn't have much of a chance to learn in the desert," he conceded. "I'm sorry I didn't realize it before, Clay."

Clay heard the genuine regret in Sloane's voice and it surprised him. "What could you have done about it?" he asked curiously. "Besides, I always figured I'd learn how to swim once I got the chance."

"I'll see about getting somebody to teach you."

"Thanks, but I'll teach myself."

Sloane was intrigued, in spite of himself. "How do you propose to do that?"

"I've taught myself to do lots of things. I have a system." Clay paused. "Do you want me to tell you about it?"

"Go ahead."

Encouraged, Clay began. "First you have to divide everything into parts. Take swimming, for instance. You have to decide exactly what part of swimming you want to learn. If you want to learn more than one part, then you have to decide what order you want to learn the parts in."

"Go on." Sloane realized that Clay was communicating more than a personal theory of learning. He was telling his father about his upbringing, and Sloane wasn't sure he could handle the revelations to come. But how could he explain that to Clay?

"Well, then you have to observe someone swimming. You have to concentrate only on the part you want to learn and tune everything else out. Then, when you can verbalize exactly what that person is doing and memorize it, you try it. But not before, otherwise you can get yourself in trouble."

"What have you learned to do that way?"

Clay hesitated. The conversation had gone so well that he hated to spoil it by talking much longer. "Lots of things. Baking bread, riding a horse ..."

"No one taught you those things?"

"Not those things. Mostly no one wanted to bother. They said if the environment was right, we'd learn without being taught." Clay recited the last words as if he were mouthing sacred doctrine.

"Page twenty-two of the counterculture bible," Sloane said, trying to keep the anger he felt out of his voice.

"It wasn't a bad life." Clay defended his past. "I was happy."

Sloane clenched and unclenched his fists as they walked in silence the rest of the way home. Discussion of Destiny Ranch and what the community of people who lived there had and hadn't done for his son shortened his fuse to the point where it was almost nonexistent.

How had it happened that a son of his—a son he hadn't even known about—had been sentenced to fifteen years of exile in the New Mexican desert with a continually revolving community of dropouts from American society? Of course Sloane had to take some of the blame himself. He had fathered Clay, never considering the fact that Willow, Clay's mother, wasn't using birth control. He had been nineteen at the time, blissfully unaware of the most important fact of life: one always reaps what one sows. He had been drunk on freedom, drunk on the number of women who were his for the taking, drunk on the thought of a life without the fetters of Miracle Springs.

And now he was paying the price. No, that wasn't quite true. Clay had already paid the price. Sloane himself would be witness to that for the rest of his life. Somehow, he'd have to find a way to ease the growing burden of guilt and fury that threatened to overwhelm him every time he thought about his son.

Now he turned down Charity Street, oblivious to the curious looks of his neighbors as he and Clay passed.

"I'll take you swimming myself," Sloane said gruffly as they reached the steps of the house he had rented for the next year. "Tomorrow morning, first thing."

Clay watched his father enter the house and disappear. "That'll be fine," he said, although there was no one to hear his answer. Then he followed Sloane inside.

ELISE WASHED HER HAIR and parted it neatly in the middle. The late-afternoon sun was her hair dryer as she lay outside on a blanket, thumbing listlessly through an old magazine. The backyard was beginning to show signs of the drought that had lasted for more than three weeks. Elise considered turning on the sprinkler, then thought better of it. It would mean moving her blanket, and that seemed like too much trouble.

"Go ahead and burn up," she muttered to the sur-rounding foliage. "I'll just plant cactus."

The elephant ear plant nearest her nodded in the light breeze, and Elise shut her eyes in exasperation. Talking to plants was bad enough; having them answer meant she had hit bottom.

She hadn't felt this low, this abandoned, since the hours immediately following her mother's death. Then she had cried and the release had been welcome. There were no tears today.

How could she cry for something that had ended al-most two decades before? Sloane had been out of her life for years and with him had gone possibility. Now possi-bility had returned, and so had Sloane. There was a message here somewhere, but it was in a language she obviously didn't understand.

Rationally she knew that Sloane's return to Miracle Springs at this crucial time in her own life was a coinci-dence. What else could it be? She had lived her thirty-five years in this little town that had been founded around a miracle—or so the story went—but Elise had never be-lieved in miracles. At least not for herself.

Somehow, whether she believed in miracles or not, it was still as if the hands of fate had reached down to pat her on the head. She couldn't believe that she and Sloane were being brought together. That was too sentimental to be palatable. But it did seem that she was being given a chance to put her past in order, to demythologize it so that she could begin to imagine a new future for herself.

A future far away from Miracle Springs. A future with only the silences I want.

Even the thought of that much freedom shot ripples of fear through her body. The thought of facing Sloane again had the same effect.

Elise rolled over and then stood, lifting the blanket to shake and fold it. Inside, the house seemed cooler as she busied herself getting ready for her dinner with Bob. But nothing could keep her from remembering that she had purposely avoided Sloane at the springs today. And that memory triggered another memory of an evening at the springs when she hadn't avoided Sloane at all.

Sloane Tyson had been a remarkable young man. At least that was the way he was described by the few people in town who saw beyond the cynical smile and the saber-sharp tongue that ruthlessly flayed anyone who crossed his path going in the wrong direction. And Sloane had always been absolutely certain about the right direction. For everyone.

Still, Elise had known, even at sweet sixteen, that there was more to Sloane than intelligence and cynicism and arrogance. He was the only son of a widowed mother who had no talent for or interest in controlling him, and Sloane had always run wild with only the occasional firm hand of an uncle or two to keep him in line. But underneath his wayward exterior Elise had sensed a gentleness that only needed a chance to grow, a sensitivity that had to be hidden behind the facade of a rebel without a cause. She had also known that in order to recognize these parts of Sloane and treat him like the young man she instinctively knew him to be, she would have to face the wrath of her mother who was sure "that Tyson kid was going to ruin his family's good name." She would also have to face the scorn of her goody-goody friends and most of the population of Miracle Springs.

Even then Elise had known herself to be weak. While other teenagers were cheerfully using emotional blackmail to get what they wanted, whether it was a new curfew or the keys to the family car, Elise always swallowed her resentment and did as she was told. She was a dutiful daughter, a fact that brought her little recognition, and she succumbed time and again to pressure from her mother on almost every issue.

The exception had been Sloane Tyson. Years later she could recognize her fainthearted rebellion for what it was: a last-ditch attempt to stand up for herself, even if she had to do it in Sloane's sheltering shadow. But at the time it had been the most significant act of her adolescence. At the beginning of her junior year she had simply decided that the entire population of Miracle Springs could be damned. There was something about Sloane Tyson that she liked, and she had set out to discover exactly what it was.

It hadn't been easy. Sloane himself had shown no interest in her attempts to draw him out. He'd sneered at her friends, made fun of her interests, asked her if he was the September selection for her charity-of-the-month club. But once committed, Elise had refused to accept his hostility at face value. More and more she wondered if his reaction to her was fear that she might not turn out to be genuinely interested in him.

Not that Sloane didn't have girls interested in him. Half the female student body at Miracle Springs High— the wrong half—was rumored to have fallen prey to his restless vitality. In a school where getting close enough to unhook a girl's bra was an occasion for locker room rejoicing, Sloane was known to have moved to a new level of expertise without having to lift a finger. No, some of the girls had loved Sloane, had loved his sardonic good looks and his ability to make hash out of every teacher to cross swords with him. It was the others, Elise's friends, that amorphous group known as the "good girls," who wouldn't give him the time of day. And Sloane would no more have asked them for anything than he would have joined the Marines.

By late fall of her junior year, Elise realized her plan— Be Nice to Sloane and He Will Respond—was not going to work. His only response had been ridicule, and she was wearing down under his barrage of insults. She had decided to switch tactics in one final attempt to make him realize she really wanted to be his friend. With her heart in her mouth, and her reputation on the line, Elise had asked Sloane to be her date at the Miracle Springs homecoming dance. The invitation had been especially meaningful because Elise was one of two junior girls elected to the homecoming queen's court, and they would be spotlighted at the dance.

Sloane's reaction had been devastating to a girl whose riskiest act up to that time had been to pet a stray dog during rabies season. He had laughed at her. He had laughed so hard that he couldn't even answer, and Elise, to her chagrin, had burst into tears and run all the way home.

Her romance with Sloane had begun that night. The sensitivity she had felt in him had actually existed. He had called to ask if she would see him, and Elise had agreed because he couldn't hurt her any more than he already had. They had met at the springs so that Elise wouldn't have to argue with her mother about the company she was keeping.

Sloane was late, a habit that never changed in all the months they spent together, and Elise had become increasingly nervous as she waited. Had he set her up, hoping she'd come while he was off somewhere laughing about her interest in him? More and more certain she was being played for a fool, she had decided to leave when she heard his voice behind her.

"I'm glad you came."

Afraid to turn around, she had sat motionless on the green bench at the edge of the beach and waited for him to join her.

"I really didn't expect you to be here," he said, sliding into place beside her.

"I told you I'd come."

"And I'll bet your word is sacred." There was only a faint hint of cynicism in his voice.

"It is," she agreed. "I like people to feel they can trust me. Is trust one of those things you think is silly, Sloane?"

He hadn't risen to the bait. "No."

Mollified, she tried to smile. "I'm glad."

They sat in silence as the night breeze warmed them. Finally Sloane shifted his weight to face her, and Elise could feel his eyes on her. "What kind of Girl Scout game are you playing with me, Elise? I'm not your type, and I sure don't need to be rescued."

He might not need rescuing, but she did, and on some level, she had realized it, even then. "I know we're different," she said cautiously, too nervous to meet his eyes, "but there's something about you I like, Sloane, although today I've been having trouble remembering what it could possibly be."

"My good manners?" he asked helpfully.

Elise sighed. "I thought I saw something buried deep inside you that obviously isn't there."

"And like the good girl you are, you felt compelled to go for a treasure hunt."

"I'm going home." Elise stood and shook out the full red skirt of her dress. "We're wasting time."

In a moment she was back beside him and his fingers were locked around her wrist. "You're not going anywhere. You've been hounding me for weeks. I want to know what's going on."

"I have not been hounding you!"

"What do you call it?"

"I wanted to be your friend. I was being nice to you, just like I would be to anyone I wanted to be friends with. Now let go of me."

"Just friendship, Elise?" He had moved closer, pulling her arm around his neck as he inched forward. "Or were you hoping the rumors you'd heard about me were true? Were you hoping you'd get a chance to live dangerously?"

She had opened her mouth to protest and in a split second, he had covered it with his own, kissing her with a thoroughness that left her gasping for breath when he withdrew.

"Is that what you wanted?" he asked.

It had been, although she had not known it before. But she hadn't wanted to be kissed with Sloane's taunts still between them.

"Maybe it was," she said, stumbling over the words. "Maybe I have wanted you to kiss me, but I've wanted more than that, too."

"We can arrange that," he said pulling her closer to kiss her again, his hands beginning to wander over her slender curves.

Elise had begun to cry.

"Scared, Elise?"

She had shaken her head, sobs racking her body. She wasn't afraid of Sloane. It had never entered her mind that he might try and force her to do anything.

Surprisingly, he had loosened his hold on her and of her own volition, she had rested her head on his shoulder until she could calm herself. "I'm not scared of you," she said finally. "I'm just tired of your insults. I want to get to know you, and all you do is push me away."

"I was doing exactly the opposite."

"No you weren't." She straightened and slid a safe distance to the other side of the bench before standing. Sloane didn't try to stop her. "I'm going home." She had almost reached the street when Sloane called after her.

"Do you still want me to take you to the dance?"

She could have exacted retribution with a haughty no. Instead she shrugged helplessly. "Only if you'll call a truce for the evening."

"I'll pick you up at seven."

She had turned to give him a watery smile, tossing her long black hair over her shoulder as she did. "I'll be waiting."

And after that she was always waiting for Sloane, sometimes on her front porch, more often on the same green bench at the springs. She had waited for more than his presence. She had waited for him to kiss her again; she had waited for him to touch her, and finally to make love to her. She had waited for him to tell her he wanted her to come away with him, and at the end, when she couldn't go, she had waited for his understanding.

Only the last wait had been without end.

Now, as she dressed for her date with Bob, Elise realized that she was waiting for Sloane again. And what did she hope would happen when they were forced to confront each other with the barriers of seventeen years firmly in place between them? Forgiveness? A chance to ventilate self-righteous anger? The realization that the chapter of her life entitled Sloane and Elise had truly come to a close?

She didn't know. The only thing she knew for sure was that she was scared. And the thing that scared her the most was that Sloane might not even remember her name.

"YOU LOOK LOVELY as usual, Elise." Bob bent to kiss her cheek and then straightened slowly as if his back might be thrown out of shape by the subtle movement.

"Thank you." Elise took the bouquet of exotically hued zinnias that Bob handed her and automatically began to strip off the lower leaves to place them in water. "These are beautiful. I'm surprised they've made it through the drought."

"Amy waters them every day. She sent them for you."

"That's my girl."

"She might as well be. You're the only mother she's ever known." Bob followed Elise into the kitchen as she got a vase out of the cupboard.

"Amy's very special to me," Elise said matter-of-factly.

"Sometimes I think you wouldn't even bother with me if I didn't have a daughter."

Bob's comment was uncharacteristically revealing. Elise felt a flutter of surprise. After thirteen years of a relationship that could only be described as placid, were she and Bob finally going to talk about their feelings?

"Well," she said tentatively, "sometimes I think you wouldn't bother with me if you didn't have her. I've been a handy mother-substitute for Amy, haven't I?"

"You could have been more. I've offered you marriage more than once."

"Yes, you have." Elise ran water in the vase and waited while it filled.

"And you've always said no."

"And you've always been glad I did." Elise turned off the faucet and began to arrange the zinnias.

"That's not true."

"You don't love me. And I don't love you." Elise's tone was still matter-of-fact. "We both tried to make love happen. As lovers, we were complete failures." Without wanting to she thought of the nights in Bob's arms when she had found herself thinking of Sloane Tyson. Those nights had ended years before. A mutually agreeable but unspoken pact had put a stop to them trying to force feelings that weren't there. Elise wondered why Bob was discussing matrimony now. She wondered why she was, too.

"Maybe we don't love each other the way you mean, but I care about you. I respect you," Bob insisted. "Good marriages can be built on less."

Elise was surprised that the word "marriage" had crept into the conversation again. "What are you trying to say?" she asked, her curiosity aroused.

"What I'm trying to say is that now that your mother's gone, Elise, I want you to marry me." Elise turned to face him and watched Bob anxiously smooth back his hair. "I can't stand the thought of you alone here in this big old house. When Jeanette was alive, I didn't worry about you. You had her, and I knew she'd watch out for you."

Elise crinkled her brow, amazed that Bob had ever believed that Jeanette Ramsey had watched out for her daughter. In reality, Elise had spent the last seventeen years of her life watching out for her mother. Everyone in Miracle Springs understood that. Everyone except Bob. "What do you think is going to happen to me?" she asked him.

Bob avoided her gaze. "I just think you'd be better off married to me. We're both getting older. We can take care of each other in the years to come."

"I'm not exactly decrepit."

"Of course you're not," Bob tried to soothe her. "You're still a lovely young woman. But . . ."

"But I won't be for long?" Elise tried to decipher Bob's blank expression. Was there a flicker of fear behind the horn-rimmed glasses? Was Bob afraid for her? Elise abandoned the thought immediately. Bob was not the type to worry unduly about others. He was a good man, but he was tied up in his own little world. And she had always refused to share that world with him.

"If we marry, neither of us will have to be lonely," he said flatly.

"Do you really think marriage can prevent loneliness?"

Bob seemed startled by her words. He recovered quickly. "Obviously this isn't the right time for this conversation. I know you're still getting over your mother's death."

"I'm fine, Bob." She tested his understanding. "In some ways Mama's death is a relief. I'm free for the first time in my life."

His look was disapproving. "You never seemed to mind taking care of her."

"I minded a lot." The strength of her words even surprised Elise. Not because they weren't true, but because she had finally spoken them out loud. Since her tongue seemed to be properly loosened for the first time, she continued. "My mother was never sick a day in her life until the day she died. But I spent seventeen years waiting on her hand and foot, catering to every little whim. Now that she's gone, I feel like a tremendous burden has been lifted off my shoulders."

"She was your mother, Elise."

Elise nodded. "She was. And I gave her a big chunk of my life. But I'm not going to waste any more of it wallowing in sorrow I don't really feel."

"You surprise me."

Since she had surprised herself, too, Elise could only nod.

Bob looked at his watch. "We can continue this later. I made reservations at the Inn for seven."

"I'm ready." Elise set the zinnias on the kitchen table and led the way to the front door.

As they drove along in silence, Elise wondered about the spurt of courage that had allowed her to say things to Bob she rarely had even allowed herself to think. At least part of her reason for being so honest had been to keep him at bay. She didn't want to marry Bob Cargil, but neither did she want to lose his friendship and, more importantly, the friendship of his daughter. Perhaps if he realized she was someone other than the selfless martyr he believed her to be, Bob would think twice before trying to push her into marriage.

They parked in front of the Miracle Springs Inn. The inn bordered the Wehachee River, whose source was the crystal-clear springs further down the road. The inn itself was a century-old ramshackle hotel with Victorian gingerbread outside and a mural in the lobby depicting the legend that had given Miracle Springs its name. It was a story of Indian lovers and untimely death, and the local Chamber of Commerce exploited it without a shred of guilt, as did the inn. It was terrific for business.

Bob and Elise ignored the fading painting as they walked directly to the dining room to claim their reservation. The room was crowded as always, and they were seated before Elise could scan it for friends. It would be an unusual night if she didn't know at least two-thirds of the people around her. She nodded to acquaintances and waited patiently while Bob went to greet one of the town's matriarchs at her table. It was only as she turned idly to examine the rest of the room that Elise realized that Clay and a man in a brown suit were sitting two tables away. The man was staring at her.

He had to be Sloane. So much was the same, and yet so much was different, too. Elise could almost feel her mind whirling as it adjusted to this new image of the boy who had never matured in her mind. Seventeen years. He was thirty-five, not eighteen anymore. His hair was still the same abundant golden brown, his body—at least what she could see of it—still hard and fit. Perhaps when he stood she'd see a protruding belly, a slackness of muscles, but she didn't think so. He had kept himself in shape.

The face was very different. The cynicism had hardened into harsh lines. He had a mustache now, a luxuriant one that drooped over the brooding lines of his mouth, giving him the appearance of a hard-boiled private eye. His nose seemed slightly off center as if he'd had it broken once. Elise didn't find that surprising. Sloane had always been the kind of man who could push others to the boiling point without even trying.

His eyes were unfathomable. Elise could feel their probing even though a table separated her from him. He was examining her intently but his expression was so distant that she couldn't tell if he recognized her. Her eyes flickered to Clay. His expression was unguarded and surprisingly warm. He, at least, knew who she was.

Her reaction took only seconds, yet it seemed to her as if she had sat there for years allowing Sloane his examination before she forced herself to stand and walk to his table. She could feel her hands perspiring, and she wiped them on the full skirt of her dress as she moved toward them.

She spoke to Clay first. "It's good to see you again, Clay," she said with a smile that took a surprising amount of energy.

"Hello, Elise."

She smiled again and then turned slightly to face the man she had not been able to face at the springs. "Hello, Sloane. It's been a long time." Silently she thanked Clay for having said her name. At least she didn't have to introduce herself to Sloane. That would have been more than she could bear.

Sloane stood, dwarfing her as he had always done. "Hello, Elise."

Elise inclined her head. They stood quietly examining each other. Elise wondered what he saw. Did he see the same woman he had known, older but not so old as to be unattractive? Did he remember the things about her that only he knew? Could he read the turbulence of her feelings in the black eyes that he'd written poetry about?

"You've hardly changed at all," he added finally. The words were said with no warmth. Elise suspected that no compliment had been intended.

She shrugged. "We all change. Even in Miracle Springs."

His mouth twisted into a humorless smile. "Funny. I've never been sure that's true."

"I know." She stepped back a little. If she'd had any doubts that Sloane didn't remember her, they'd been put safely to rest. Their simple conversation was charged with unspoken energy. Yes, Sloane remembered, and he'd never forgiven her. "You've changed," she said quietly.

"How?"

She examined his stylish haircut and expensive clothing. "You're more civilized somehow."

"It would be a mistake to think I'm much different," he said, a warning clear in the deceptively soft-spoken words.

Elise nodded. If she'd hoped for a simple conversation to destroy her memories, she had been mistaken. "I'd better get back to my table," she murmured politely. "It's nice to see you again." She turned to Clay. "Have a good dinner." After a nod to them both she made her way to the table where Bob was seated once again.

"I see you've rediscovered Sloane Tyson," Bob said dryly as Elise stared with unseeing eyes at the menu.

Elise heard the disdain in his voice, and it shocked her out of the near trance she had fallen into. "What does that mean?"

"You two were a couple in high school, weren't you?"

Elise nodded. Denial was useless in a town that remembered everything. "But I haven't seen him since the day we graduated."

"I knew he was back."

And Elise understood that those five words explained Bob's latest marriage proposal. At least they explained some part of it. She probed for further understanding. "Does it bother you that seventeen years ago I went steady with Sloane Tyson?"

"You did more than go steady." Bob's words were an accusation.

Elise carefully closed her menu and laid it next to her plate. "Why that should bother you now is beyond my understanding."

"It's always bothered me."

"Go on."

"I don't think so." Bob snapped his menu shut and without it to shield him, Elise saw that he was pouting.

"Seventeen years ago you were a twenty-eight-year-old married man with a wife who adored you. What does any of that have to do with today?"

"My wife isn't sitting in this room."

"Your wife is dead."

"I don't want Sloane Tyson making a fool out of you, Elise."

Elise counted the heartbeats throbbing in her neck. Twelve passed before she took a deep breath to answer him. "I don't think Sloane Tyson is the man in this room who's trying to make a fool out of me, Bob."

"I don't want you to get hurt." Bob picked up his menu and buried his face in it again.

Elise folded her hands in her lap, swallowing angry words. Unwillingly her eyes were drawn to the man two tables away. Sloane was staring into space, his eyes carefully veiled. Elise studied him for a moment before she forced herself to look away.

She wanted to believe that Sloane was not unaffected by their meeting. She wanted to believe that he, too, had felt the hidden energy coursing between them. They would never have a relationship again; the days of their love and their lovemaking were over. But suddenly, irrationally, it was important to know that Sloane was not oblivious to her.

She risked another glance, and this time she found his eyes on her. There was self-mockery in his stare as if he could not believe that he was being drawn into this intimacy. But he did not look away.

Defiantly, Elise stared back. She was not afraid of being hurt or of being made to appear foolish. She was not afraid of Sloane Tyson or even of herself. If she had a fear now it was that the years had wiped away all traces of the girl Sloane had once loved and with them, the one love affair of her life.

As if to reassure her, Sloane slowly lifted the glass of wine in front of him and held it out to her in a sardonic toast. Without thinking, Elise responded with her water tumbler. And for a moment, they were the only two people in the crowded little room.

CHAPTER THREE

SLOANE BARELY TASTED the fried catfish he had ordered and partially demolished. It was overcooked and bony, two trademarks of the inn's seafood menu, and not tasting it was a blessing. Out of the corner of one eye he could see Elise finishing a salad and talking to the man she was sitting with.

Lord, she was still beautiful. He had meant what he'd said to her. She had barely changed at all. It was as if she had been caught in a time warp, suspended like Sleeping Beauty, waiting for someone or something to come along and awaken her to the real world once again.

He gave a cynical snort at the last thought. How could she reawaken to the real world if she'd never been in the real world? Miracle Springs *was* a time warp. There was nothing here to make a person grow older. Nothing but heat and humidity and a mercilessly plodding progression of days that stretched into infinity until . . .

"Sloane?"

Sloane lifted his head to gaze at his son, and for a moment he felt caught in the time warp, too. There he was at age fifteen. The same face, the same color hair, the same lithe body. He blinked and cleared his mind of wandering thoughts.

"How do you like the seafood platter?" he asked, finally.

Clay nodded, surprised his father would want to know. "Well, I like it, but I don't know what I'm eating."

Sloane sighed. Everything was new to Clay, even the very food he ate. His son had survived fifteen years on vegetables and whole grains like a damn milk cow. Before anger could overwhelm him, Sloane allowed the calm voice of reason to intervene. There was nothing wrong with vegetables and whole grains. Most of the country would be better off with just such a diet. He took a deep breath, lifting his fork to point at the different things on Clay's plate. "Shrimp, oysters, some kind of fish—probably catfish—hush puppies."

"Hush puppies?"

"Hush puppies. I'll take you fishing for hush puppies someday, Clay."

Clay, who had already eaten one of the fried cornmeal nuggets and recognized the taste, smiled at his father. He wasn't used to Sloane's warmer side, and he found that he liked it. "You mean I can go fishing in the middle of a cornfield?"

"You're a Tyson. Around here that means you can do just about anything and get away with it."

"That should be interesting."

They lapsed into silence once more, and it continued until the end of the meal.

Several tables away Elise tried to concentrate on Bob's monologue. It was a useless exercise. She was as acutely aware of Sloane's presence as she would have been had he been sitting across the table from her. She could see him out of the corner of her eye, silently eating his dinner. She had noticed one brief exchange with Clay, and then nothing more. Curiosity was the least of the emotions she was feeling, but she did wonder what relationship Clay had to Sloane. Whatever it was, it wasn't a comfortable one.

She had carefully avoided Sloane's eyes again after their impromptu toast. She was sure that he had been able to read the turmoil of her emotions in that one gesture. It would be just like Sloane to assume he had scored a point. She could almost hear his thoughts. *Well, little Elise never married. There she sits, growing older by the moment, just waiting for the right man to come along and claim her. There she is, just ripe for a brief love affair.*

Her own thoughts startled her. Was she imagining Sloane's words or were they her own? Was she indeed waiting for the right man? Was she indeed ripe for a brief love affair?

She continued to nod at Bob at the appropriate moments and smile when necessary, but her mind probed her emotions. It only made sense that seeing Sloan would resurrect the feelings she'd carefully put in storage all those years ago. That did not mean that she was still in love with him; that did not mean that she was even attracted to Sloane himself anymore. What it meant was that she was a woman who had denied herself one of the basic pleasures of life for too long. Feelings long repressed tended to make themselves known eventually. Sex was just one more factor to sort out in the jumble that was her life right now.

Having talked herself into accepting her feelings for what they were, Elise hazarded a glance at Sloane. He and Clay were standing to leave, and Sloane was watching her. There was nothing covert about his gaze. He was daring her to notice him, to respond to him in some way. Without thinking of the consequences, Elise lifted her hand and motioned for Sloane and Clay to come to her table.

When they were standing beside her, she gave them both her warmest smile. Already Bob had stood for the introductions. "Bob Cargil," she said, her voice steady, "I'd like you to meet Sloane Tyson and Clay..."

"Tyson," Sloane supplied. "My son."

Elise nodded as if that only made sense. She would puzzle out Sloane's and Clay's relationship later.

Bob and Sloane shook hands, but Elise noticed that Bob did not extend his hand to Clay. "Sloane's back in town for a visit," Elise continued, her intonation making the statement a question.

"Actually I'm back for the next year," Sloane explained to Bob. Elise knew that the explanation had been for her, however.

"It's nice to meet you," Bob said, his voice coldly polite. "I know most of the Tysons. I went to school with your Uncle Jack."

Sloane nodded. "It's almost impossible not to have gone to school with somebody from my family."

"Jack was a real hell-raiser, as I remember," Bob said.

"One of the three black sheep in the family. My father started the tradition, so I hear." Sloane's voice left no doubt as to who the third black sheep had been.

Elise interrupted before they could go on. "Well, it's good to have you here, Sloane, Clay," she said. "I'll look forward to seeing you both around." She wondered at her own words. They had sounded like an invitation.

Obviously Bob thought so, too. "Miracle Springs is so small, we're bound to run into you, aren't we, Elise?"

She nodded, but she couldn't keep a small smile from framing her even white teeth. Bob as protector. It was a role she was having trouble imagining. She raised her eyes to Sloane's, and for a moment their gazes locked. Then he inclined his head and turned to make his way out of the dining room with Clay following him.

"Black sheep," Bob scoffed as he took his seat. "From what I've heard, Sloane Tyson was the blackest sheep to attend Miracle Springs High. And I wouldn't be surprised if that son of his plans to set a new record."

"Clay seems like a very sweet boy," Elise protested. "Not rebellious at all."

"What do you call that ponytail? And did you see what he was wearing? A Save the Whales T-shirt in the Miracle Springs Inn dining room!"

"Do you really think it was any less appropriate than the way those kids over there are dressed?" Elise pointed to a table where two teenagers sat with their parents. The girl was wearing a flowered Hawaiian shirt and enough brightly colored plastic necklaces and bracelets to add five pounds to her weight. The boy was wearing a conservative blue polo shirt but his hair stood up in neatly arranged spikes all over his head.

"Tourists," Bob said.

Although Miracle Springs depended on tourism for some of its income, the local people looked down on the sightseers who thronged to the area in the summertime. Elise knew that Bob's use of the word "tourist" was one step away from profanity.

"Keep an open mind about Clay," Elise warned, knowing all the while that she was asking the impossible. "He may be in one of your classes this fall. If you let yourself, you might enjoy getting to know him."

The look on Bob's face rivaled Sloane's for cynicism.

CLAY WAS ENDLESSLY FASCINATED with television. Sloane was not. Tonight as Sloane sat in the tiny living room of the house he was renting and listened to the television blare, he thought he would go crazy with unreleased energy.

He had got exactly what he'd bargained for. He'd wanted a safe, small-town environment for his son. Clay needed a secure stopping place between the unreal world of the commune where he'd been raised and the dog-eat-dog world of urban America. Sloane had known that life in Miracle Springs wouldn't be exciting or challenging for himself. But he'd forgotten what it felt like to have the pressure build up inside him until he knew he was a walking time bomb.

What had he done as a teenager when he'd felt this explosive tension? He remembered he'd done crazy things. He'd gone skinny-dipping in the ice-cold water of the springs; driven his uncle's pickup at eighty miles an hour over sandy paths in the turkey oak and pine wilderness of the Ocala National Forest; taken a pup tent and a case of beer to some sweetly scented orange grove south of town and spent the night seeing how much of the illegally purchased beverage he and his buddies could consume. Just because it was something different to do.

Then there had been the other way he'd eased his restlessness. Elise.

"Clay, turn that thing down!" Sloane stood and lowered the volume himself before Clay could even move a muscle. Sloane hit his fist lightly on the top of the television. "I'm sorry," he said contritely. "I think I just need some fresh air."

"Did you want to go for a walk?"

Sloane nodded his head, and Clay stood, his eyes flickering back to the screen.

"You're in the middle of your show. I'll go by myself," Sloane told him. Clay, without a change of expression, sat down again.

Outside, the night air still held the day's heat. Despite the recent drought, the humidity was high and Sloane could feel it shimmer around him. He had grown used to the crisp, bracing air of New England and this steam bath felt strange and unpleasant. As he walked, Sloane paid little attention to where his footsteps were taking him. He crisscrossed Faith, Hope and Charity, grimacing at the ridiculous street names.

Years before, Miracle Springs, to get its share of Florida's billion dollar tourism business, had decided to go all out on a publicity campaign. Sloane remembered that he had been about eight years old when the city fathers had decided to change the street names to attract more attention. In addition to the three main streets downtown there was a Love Lane, and two others roads were called Grace and Mercy. Luckily, the town council had run out of inspiration at that point—or else they had run into opposition from citizens who wanted no part of the sham. The rest of the county had been spared from suffering the embarrassment of the people who lived in the center of town.

Back on Hope Avenue, Sloane began to head away from the springs. His steps slowed and he paid careful attention to his surroundings. There was a house missing here, a new house there, but essentially Hope Avenue hadn't changed much. Mayor Biggs's house had just been painted, a real estate office had been opened in the home of a childhood friend. And then there was Elise's place.

Sloane stopped pretending that he had been going anywhere else. He was standing exactly where he had meant to stand, standing where he had stood countless times before. For a minute he could almost pretend he was seventeen or eighteen, waiting on the sidewalk for Elise to come down the steps and join him. Now there were no parents to disapprove of his visit. Only Elise, who would probably disapprove just as much as her parents had ever done. Sloane looked up at the two-story frame house and considered his next move. He could go home again, or he could walk up to the front door and hope she was home alone.

And then what would he say? *Hello, I just dropped by for a chat? Hello, I thought we could catch up on seventeen years?* Sloane felt a surge of disgust at his own ambivalence. He couldn't remember a moment since leaving Miracle Springs when he'd been so confused. He felt like a teenager; he was acting like a teenager. Sloane Tyson, a man who had no tolerance for weakness in himself or others, stood on the sidewalk and wondered exactly what had brought him to such a state.

THERE HAD BEEN NO PARTING KISS when Bob dropped her at her front door. He seemed to have taken Sloane's presence at the inn as a personal insult, an insult for which he blamed Elise. Considering Bob's mood for most of the evening, Elise hadn't been surprised when he'd taken her key, unlocked her door and said a chilly good-night. Then he had got in his car and driven away.

Now, Elise undressed leisurely in her bedroom with the lights off and the windows and shades wide open to capture whatever breeze was stirring. It was too late to catch the beginning of anything on television, too early to go to bed. She knew if she tried to read, the words would blur in front of her.

She pulled on a long summer nightgown of cool white cotton and sat on the bed, taking the pins out of her hair. It fell almost to her waist, and she brushed it absent-mindedly as she thought about the evening.

She had finally faced Sloane. It hadn't been as hard as she had imagined; she had handled herself with aplomb. She was not a confused adolescent. She was Elise Ramsey, popular teacher.... She could think of no other description that was flattering. Spinster. Old maid. Unclaimed treasure.

What was wrong with her? From what corner of her mind had the self-doubt emerged? She had nothing to be ashamed of. Whatever her life lacked in excitement, she could at least be proud of the respect with which she was held in Miracle Springs.

But somehow, tonight, respect seemed a poor substitute for something else.

Her thoughts were interrupted by a series of knocks on her front door. Elise stood, dropping her brush on the bed, and then reached for the robe that matched her gown. The cotton was sheer, but not sheer enough to be revealing, and she gathered it around her as she hurried down the steps.

Sloane was just turning to leave as she opened the door. For a moment they stared at each other, both surprised. Elise, who'd felt perfectly modest in the gown and robe, now felt unclothed. Sloane, who'd convinced himself he knew what he was doing, felt tongue-tied.

"Well, I didn't expect to see you here," Elise said finally, pulling the robe a little tighter.

"I didn't expect to be here," he murmured, taking in the picture she made with her black hair falling over the gossamer white fabric. His body's reaction was unmistakable and he felt a surge of anger at its betrayal. He forced himself to speak calmly. "Would you believe I was in the neighborhood?"

"That's one excuse that always holds water around here. Everything's in the neighborhood." She frantically searched her memory for the appropriate etiquette. There was none. Sloane seemed to be waiting for something, and finally, she shrugged. "Would you like to come in?"

"Yes."

Elise stepped back and opened the door wider. Sloane brushed past her, and Elise felt crowded by his presence in the hallway. Sloane had always been big, and although her height was almost average, he'd always made her feel tiny and fragile. She wondered if he enjoyed having that effect on women.

"Are you here to pass the time, Sloane? Or did you have a reason for coming?"

"I had a reason." Sloane turned and without asking for an invitation, made his way into the living room. Elise had no choice except to follow. "Are you alone?"

"I always dress this way for company," she chided him gently.

"Bob what's-his-name left early," he said with satisfaction.

Elise felt small flickers of anger beginning to kindle. "That's no concern of yours, is it?"

"Only that I don't want to make small talk with him."

"You never were much good at small talk."

"I never wanted to be."

Elise realized that Sloane was still standing. "Sit down," she said as graciously as she could manage. "Would you like iced tea? I'd offer you coffee, but it's too hot even to think about it."

"Nothing, thank you." Sloane sat on the sofa, and Elise chose an overstuffed chair across the room, arranging her gown and robe around her as she sat. She was suddenly conscious that her feet were bare. That small intimacy left her mouth feeling dry.

"Did you have a nice dinner?" she asked, simply because it was the only thing she could think of to say.

"Does the Miracle Springs Inn serve nice dinners?"

"You have to know what to order."

"Obviously I didn't."

Elise fidgeted in her seat. "How does Clay like living here so far?" she asked after a few moments of silence.

"We haven't been here long enough for him to form an opinion."

This time the silence stretched for a full minute; Elise realized she found it unbearable. Sloane was staring at her and even in her agitation, she couldn't miss the cool, male appraisal. Finally she stood. "This is awful," she said with heartfelt honesty. "Even if you don't want tea, it'll give me something to do while we talk or don't talk." Without another word she marched into the kitchen, and Sloane, with a slight smile, followed her.

"I didn't come to make you uncomfortable," he said, standing in the doorway as she moved gracefully around the old-fashioned kitchen.

"Didn't you?"

"Actually, I lied a little while ago. I don't know why I came."

"Sloane Tyson? Unsure of himself?" Elise heard the challenge in her voice, and it surprised her. All day she'd dwelt on the fact that Sloane had not forgiven her for her actions of seventeen years before. Now she realized that she had never forgiven him either.

He went on as if she hadn't spoken. "I guess I'd like to put the past to rest. We'll be seeing each other; this town is too small to hide in."

Elise nodded. "All right. How do you propose that we put the past to rest?"

"We could catch up on each other's lives."

What a deadly game that would be. Sloane would tell her of his fame, his success, his loves. And she would tell him of endless years of caring for a petulant mother and teaching English. Then Sloane would be vindicated, knowing that he'd been right when he'd told her that Miracle Springs would strangle her, cut off her life's blood and her spirit's sustenance.

And yet she wanted to know about him. She wanted to know what he'd done and who he'd become. She wanted to know exactly whom she would be dealing with for the next year.

"All right," she conceded. "You go first." She held out the glass of tea and Sloane took it politely. Elise leaned against the sink and Sloane leaned against the stove. They measured each other across the narrow space.

Sloane began. "Seventeen years is a long time to cover."

"I know some of it. I heard you got married and divorced. I know about your success as an author." She weighed her next words and decided to go ahead. "I've read all your books. You're very good."

"I'm surprised you've read them."

"Why? Didn't you think people in Miracle Springs might be interested in philosophy or sociology? I particularly liked the one you did comparing the problems of Vietnam veterans and those who resisted the draft. I find your viewpoints stimulating. But then, I always did."

Sloane held out his glass in a mock salute. "Touché."

"No one likes to be patronized, Sloane."

"Was that what I was doing?"

"I think so, yes."

Sloane sipped his tea. "What else do you know?"

Elise shrugged. "That's about it."

"When I left here I traveled out west."

"I know that's what you'd intended." She knew because she'd intended to go with him. Even now she felt a pang at the lost opportunity. Especially with the real Sloane Tyson standing mere inches away, overwhelming her tiny kitchen.

"I hitchhiked for a while and then I ended up with a group of people in the Destiny Community. Have you ever heard about them?"

Elise drew designs on her foggy glass as she tried to remember. "Clay said something about a Destiny Ranch today when I was talking to him at the springs. It rang a bell but I can't remember why."

"Same group. But seventeen years ago they were a traveling commune. They sold food and provided medical care at rock festivals."

"Sort of a hippie Red Cross. Now I remember. And you got involved with them?"

"It was a way to see the country. When we weren't traveling we stayed at one of their five farms. I met lots of different kinds of people. For a kid hungry for new experiences, it was wonderful."

"And then?" Elise looked up.

"I got tired of the whole scene." Sloane smiled at his own lapse into sixties vernacular. "Drugs were plentiful and I got tired of seeing people freaking out. There were always good, stable people with real ideals trying to keep Destiny on an even keel, but there were the crazies, too.

One day I realized I was having trouble telling the difference."

Elise tried to imagine a life like the one he was describing. "It sounds . . . colorful."

"It was that."

"Your books are so knowledgeable about the counterculture. Now I understand where you got a lot of your ideas. It wasn't all impersonal research."

"No." Sloane finished his tea and set it on the stove. "I decided to go back to school when I turned twenty. Goddard College in Vermont had a program that was liberal enough to interest me. I was liberal enough to interest them, and they gave me a good-size scholarship. Then I went on to Boston University and finally Harvard where I was given a job as assistant professor of sociology."

"You're still there, aren't you?"

"I'm on sabbatical for a year. Actually I don't teach many classes. They give me lots of time to write and do the lecture circuits."

"And you like Boston?" Elise wondered just how long she could make her final swallow of tea last. The glass was a useful device for keeping her hands busy.

"I live in Cambridge near the campus. Yes, I like it."

"Where does Clay fit into all this?" Elise realized her glass was finally empty and set it down, folding her arms.

"Now that the conversation is rolling, do you think we could go back to the living room?"

Elise nodded and followed Sloane back through the house. They resumed their original seats, and suddenly they were both wary again.

"Clay," Sloane began, "is my son by a woman in the Destiny community. We had a short . . . relationship, and when I moved on she didn't see any point in letting me know she was pregnant with my child." His voice had turned bitter.

"How could she do that to you?" Elise imagined that the anger she felt was nothing compared to what Sloane must have experienced when he discovered he had a son.

"She didn't do it to me. You'd have to understand Destiny to understand how it happened. Pregnancy and childbearing were thought of as natural functions—impersonal natural functions. Everyone liked the idea of children, although how many people actually liked kids, I can't say. Most of the women there got pregnant at one time or another. The children were raised by the community. Family ties weren't forbidden, but they weren't encouraged. As it happened, Willow, Clay's mother, was a die-hard supporter of the Destiny concept. Since everyone was supposed to help raise the kids, no one thought to make a point of whose child Clay was. He never knew; I never knew. Only Willow knew."

Elise sensed the emotion behind the clipped words. "And how did you find him?"

"Destiny's time came and went. Their numbers dwindled. They sold one farm, then another. Eventually what was left of the community settled on their New Mexico ranch where, as near as I can tell, Clay has been since he was a toddler. Finally, even that property had to be sold several months ago. There was only a handful of people left at the end. Seven of them were kids under the age of sixteen."

"And Willow contacted you?"

"Willow had been gone for years." Sloane put his hands behind his neck as if to ease the tension there. "The authorities were called in, and the kids whose parents weren't on the ranch were put in foster homes. Eventually they traced Willow to California. She's married with a new baby. Her husband's an accountant. He didn't want Clay; Willow didn't want Clay. She told the authorities to find me."

Elise couldn't think of one thing to say. Obviously, however, her eyes betrayed her feelings.

"Yes," Sloane said softly, "it was the surprise of a lifetime."

"I'm sorry. You've been cheated so badly." Elise cast about for words to better console him, but found none.

"Clay's the one who's been cheated. A mother he never really knew, a father who doesn't have the faintest idea how to be a parent."

"Then you're finding it difficult?"

"We're getting by."

"Clay seems like a nice boy. I think he'll be a son to be proud of."

"Your turn, Elise."

Elise was jolted by the back-to-business sound of Sloane's voice. She realized that her sympathy had made him cautious. Evidently the atmosphere had warmed up too much. She tried to sound matter-of-fact. Actually there was so little to say about her life that there was no other way to sound.

"After you left I commuted to the University of Florida and got a degree in English education. I've taught at the high school ever since." She searched for details to make her existence sound less dull. "I like teaching, and that part of my life has been more than satisfying." Damn, why had she said that? She might as well have announced that the rest of her life had been anything but.

"You never married." Sloane's face was carefully blank, but Elise could read his thoughts anyway. There was no point in trying to pretend.

"No. I lived here with my mother until she died last month."

"This house hasn't changed a bit. It's exactly as I remember it."

"Mother got more and more rigid as she grew older. Change frightened her." Elise tucked her feet under the folds of her gown and crossed her arms in an instinctive gesture of self-protection.

The gesture wasn't lost to Sloane. He was torn between wanting to comfort her and wanting to rage at her for sacrificing her life for the whining, peevish woman who had given birth to her. "Did she ever love you for it, Elise?" he asked finally. "Did your sacrifice ever make her love you?"

Elise could feel the blood drain from her face. How could he? How could he take her life and reduce it to a pathetic quest for maternal love? Seconds passed as she tried to force words past the lump in her throat. "I think you'd better go," she said finally. Her voice was as cold as his words had been.

"Not until you answer me. I want to know if staying here was worth it for you. I'd like to think it was. I'd like to think your life hasn't been a waste, that you got something important from remaining in Miracle Springs."

"None of this is your business!"

"I wish to God that were true." Sloane stood and for a moment Elise thought he would leave. Instead, he began to pace the length of the room. "I made it my business seventeen years ago. I haven't forgotten what we meant to each other; I haven't forgotten you."

He heard her gasp and he stopped to search her face. "Don't get the wrong idea," he said with his familiar cynical smile, "I haven't been carrying a torch. When you refused to go with me, it destroyed whatever we'd had. Except..." His voice trailed off.

"Except what?"

"Except that I wanted to be completely free of this place. I wanted to leave without another thought. Instead, you kept a part of me behind with you. I've felt the pull all these years. I've never been able to forget Miracle Springs the way I've wanted to forget it."

"And you blame that on me. Convenient." She was surprised that she was capable of such cold sarcasm. Inside she felt wounded, bleeding.

"You were the only person in this town besides a few relatives who ever meant anything to me."

"You have a funny way of showing me I was once important to you." Elise stood, too. She felt much too vulnerable sitting while he towered above her. "You come into my house and demand to know if I've wasted the last seventeen years of my life. You haven't written or called or visited me in all those years, and yet you believe you have the right to insist on answers."

"We both know I have the right."

Sloane was facing her now, and they were only inches apart. "Get out," she said, as calmly as she could manage.

"Believe it or not, Elise, I want to know you were happy. I'd like to know I was wrong when I told you that you were throwing away your life."

She wanted nothing more than to tell him that he had been wrong. She wanted to pull out warm, happy memories to flaunt in his face. But warmth and happiness had been missing from her life. Except for her students and Amy Cargil, no one had really touched her in seventeen years.

"I'm exactly what you see, Sloane. An old maid schoolteacher living in a house that hasn't changed since you left. My mother died a bitter woman unable to reach out to anyone or appreciate anything that was done for her. I've spent my whole life giving love and not getting much in return." She lifted her head a notch.

"But there's something you can't see, too," she continued. "I've taken more risks than you'll ever take, even though I stayed in Miracle Springs and you went off to see the world. I've given love, with absolutely no guarantee of having it returned. And I don't regret one instant of it. I may be weak. I may be afraid of change. But I'm not afraid to give myself. Can you say the same?"

She had summed up the totality of his life in a few sentences, just as he had done for her. Sloane was shocked at her insight and more shocked that she would use it on him. Perhaps she didn't think that she'd changed, but this one change was obvious to him. The Elise Ramsey he had known would never have fought back so effectively. Silently he applauded her courage.

"No," he admitted, "I can't say the same. I've lived for myself."

"Has that made you a happy man?"

"Does such an animal exist?"

"I'd like to think so."

"That's always been one of the differences between us."

Elise could feel her anger melting away. For a moment Sloane's voice had lost its chill, and she could hear the echoes of the young man she had known and loved. Was it possible that Sloane was still vulnerable? That he too was searching for that elusive something that made life worth living?

"I think if you give up on happiness, you do yourself a great disservice," she said softly. Unconsciously she leaned closer to him. "I'd rather spend my life looking for it and not find it than give up the search and miss it when it's right in front of my nose."

Sloane resisted the temptation to cover the distance between them. He could smell her sweet fragrance, a faint, floral smell that reminded him of orange blossoms and night-blooming jasmine. He felt something twist inside him, something that hadn't moved in years. He'd wanted plenty of women, but this feeling was different. It angered him, and he used his anger to keep her away.

"And if you had to reach out for this so-called happiness, Elise, could you do that now? Could you leave safety to find love?" His voice was cold again.

"You've never forgiven me, have you?" Elise took a step backward. The warmth she had begun to feel died within her. "I was young and afraid. And I felt a tremendous sense of duty to my mother. You never understood fear or duty. We were so different."

Sloane shrugged. "It was a long time ago."

"I've never forgiven you, either." Elise found his eyes and held them. "All I asked for seventeen years ago was a little time. I wanted the summer to help my mother adjust to my father's death. I'd have gone with you in the fall. Nothing would have stopped me."

"I didn't believe it then and I don't believe it now. But why are we torturing each other about an adolescent love affair?" Sloane looked at his watch. Both of them knew the gesture was a ruse. "I've kept you up long enough."

Elise wanted to protest. Now that they had begun, they needed to finish. But she didn't allow her feelings to show. "I won't say I was glad to see you," she said honestly. "I hope the next time we meet we'll have a more cordial conversation."

"I doubt that we'll be having many conversations at all. I'm working on ideas for a book while I'm here, and I'm going to be very busy."

"Then the best of luck," she said with exquisite self-control. She wanted to shout at him, rage at him for running away before they could finally, once and for all, put an end to their past. "Please tell Clay I'll be looking forward to seeing him at school." She turned and found her way to the hall and the front door.

Sloane's face was a mask. He followed her, trying not to notice the graceful femininity of her walk or the sensuous veil of hair that shimmered under the lights in the hallway. Why had he come? Better yet, why had he reacted so strongly to her? He always understood his own motivations, but his reasons for this visit to Elise were a mystery. Miracle Springs was already weaving its cloying spell around him. He'd be damned if he'd be its helpless victim.

"Good night, Elise," he said as he stood in the open doorway. Against his will he searched her face for a clue to what she was feeling. But her face was carefully blank.

"Good night, Sloane." She waited a split second, and then added, "If you ever decide you'd like to finish this conversation, I'll be available." She smiled a little, knowing she had effectively had the last word. Even if Sloane never came back, she had made it clear that she knew he was the one who had lacked courage this time. With a small flourish she closed the door in his face.

CHAPTER FOUR

CLAY FIDDLED WITH THE STRAPS of his backpack, adjusting and readjusting it until its weight was distributed perfectly. "I guess I'm ready."

Sloane was surprised by the hesitation in his son's voice. In the months they'd been together, Clay had shown an inbred self-confidence in every new situation. Whatever his secret anxieties, he radiated a quiet composure and strength of character far beyond his years. But this morning, his first morning at Miracle Springs High, he seemed like the adolescent he really was.

Somehow, Sloane found this reassuring.

"Feeling a little worried?" he asked Clay.

Clay looked up and gave his father a tentative smile. "Yeah."

Sloane allowed himself a moment to run through his private and all too familiar litany of resentments. His son should not have to feel this apprehension. Going to school should be second nature, as natural as breathing. He ought not to have to worry about what he should do, what he should say. About now a gang of teenagers should be descending on the house, hooting on the front porch for Clay to come join them. Clay should be making some parting wiseass remark to Sloane, then standing with both thumbs hooked in the pockets of his jeans, eyes rolling while he listened to Sloane's reprimand. His walk to school should be filled with discussions of girls and football and rock stars. The joys of adolescence.

"Miracle Springs High isn't exactly a prep school for the Ivy League," Sloane said, feeling a strong need to reassure his son, "but it's a good school with some fine teachers. After a few weeks it'll feel comfortable."

"I don't think I can sit still that long every day."

Sloane tried to imagine what it would be like for Clay to be confined to a classroom for hours after the freedom of Destiny Ranch. Clay was right; the adjustment would not be easy. "It's something you'll have to develop. This world is filled with places where you have to sit still."

"Once I was sick for three weeks. I had to stay in bed the whole time. I thought I'd go crazy." Clay fidgeted as he talked, as if to make his point more emphatically.

Three weeks in bed. Sloane swallowed, but his voice was still harsh when he spoke. "What was wrong with you?"

"Nobody ever said."

"Did anybody bother to find out?"

Clay stood very still. "They took care of me. I got better."

Sloane knew it was useless to torture either of them with more questions. Questions didn't change a thing. Questions, especially questions that were accusations, didn't bring back the little boy he would never know. "If you're ready, we ought to go now."

Outside Sloane paused by the car door and debated with himself about driving or walking. Driving would get them there faster, and Sloane had a lot to do that day. Walking would give them a chance to talk, maybe help settle Clay's fears a little. Was parenting always such a balancing act? Whose needs took priority?

"Can we walk?" Clay asked, eyeing the car warily. "I'll be sitting enough today."

"Good idea," Sloane said gruffly, the decision having been made for him. "Let's go by the springs."

They covered the blocks to the springs in silence. The route had become familiar to them both. Sloane had kept his promise to his son and in the past week they'd come every day for swimming lessons. Clay's excellent coordination and uncanny ability to concentrate completely on a task had brought quick results. His strokes were still a little awkward, he sometimes forgot to lock his knees when he kicked, but by and large, he had learned to swim.

But he hadn't learned to enjoy the water.

Sloane could see it in his son's eyes when Clay waded into the icy-cold springs each day to begin swimming the laps he felt he had to do to perfect his skills. Learning to swim was a task. He brought tremendous natural ability and wholehearted participation to it. He did not bring the abandon, the childlike release of inhibition that Sloane remembered feeling at Clay's age. Even now that Clay was safe in the water, able to cover distances without fear and able to submerge himself totally and find his way back up, he still showed no signs of liking the experience.

At the entrance to the springs they stood for a moment at the edge of the beach leading down to the water. Then they turned and continued along Hope Avenue toward Miracle Springs High.

"You've never told me why they call it Miracle Springs," Clay said, turning for one quick look before he followed his father.

"I'm surprised your Aunt Lillian hasn't told you the story."

"She probably thinks you did."

Sloane wondered why he'd never thought to explain the legend to his son. How many other things had he neglected to tell him? "Do you remember the mural in the lobby of the Inn?"

Clay nodded. "The one that needs to be repainted?"

"Either that or wallpapered over. Well, it's supposed to be a depiction of the story about the springs."

Clay tried to summon up the picture. "It had Indians on it, didn't it?"

"It's a very anglicized Indian legend. This part of Florida was inhabited by Indians as early as ten thousand years ago, and by the first century A.D. most of the peninsula was well populated."

"The Seminoles," Clay interrupted. "I studied Indian tribes one year because we had two Ind... Native Americans living on the ranch. They were Hopis."

"Well, you're right about Seminoles being in Florida, but not until much later. Originally the Timucuans inhabited this area. And the tribe in this county was called the Ocali. They were village and town dwellers who hunted and fished and grew corn. They were noted for being a beautiful people."

"What happened to them?"

"They got caught in the cross fire between the English and the Spanish, and they also fell prey to the Creeks, or Seminoles as they were later called, who were invading from the North. What few remained were said to have been taken back to Spain by the Spanish when Spain ceded Florida to England."

"The Timucuans named this town Miracle Springs?" Clay asked skeptically.

"No, the town fathers named the town Miracle Springs back in 1883."

"It's all clear to me now," Clay said, teasing his father.

Sloane smiled. He was enjoying himself. Somehow this conversation seemed free of the tensions that permeated most of their discussions. He wanted to prolong it. "Well good," he teased back. "Then I don't have to explain anymore."

"Go ahead if it makes you happy."

"Have you ever noticed the little island in the middle of the river, just down from the spring?"

"There's a big gnarled mass of roots and a bunch of spiky-looking plants that the water doesn't quite cover," Clay observed.

"That's where the miracle occurs."

"The miracle is that nobody's dug it up so boats can get by easier," Clay said, obviously not impressed.

"The legend says that once, hundreds of years ago when the Timucuans still called this area home, there was a beautiful Indian maiden . . ."

"Let me guess. A chief's daughter."

Sloane smiled at Clay's innocent brand of cynicism. "Right. She was about to be married to a handsome young man whom she had loved since she was a child, but she grew very ill. The chief and the tribal shaman did everything they could to save her, but it was soon apparent that she was going to die."

"So they put her in the waters of the spring, and she was instantly healed," Clay finished for him.

"No. She died."

"Then they should have called it Disappointment Springs."

"Who's telling this story? Anyway, right before she died, the young maiden called her father and her young man to her side. She told them she had asked the sun—

the Ocalis worshipped the sun—to spare her so that she could do good works. She said her life had been too short to do enough good for others, and she wanted a chance to do more. But the sun had withdrawn its rays in answer. Then she fell asleep and had a dream. In her dream the sun came to her and told her to ask her father to place her body on the island after her death. Then, every year on the anniversary of that day, she could return to grant wishes to those pure of heart who asked for her help.''

"And does she?"

"Well, supposedly she died that afternoon and her body was taken out to the island. And every year on that day, May 13th, she comes back and grants wishes to those worthy few who ask for her help."

"Come on!"

"Variations of the story were passed down through the centuries. Some of the stories say it was a young Spanish girl, some say it was an old Seminole woman. Some say May, some say December. The version I told you is the one you'll find in the tourist brochures. Every May the town has a big celebration with festivities at the Inn. Then about an hour before midnight, anyone who wants a wish granted goes down to the beach and waits. About midnight, or a little after, the maiden is supposed to appear in a cloud of vapor. If you see her, it means your heart is pure, your wish desirable, and your chances of having it granted, one hundred percent."

"Have you ever had a wish granted?" Clay asked.

"I never tried. Not even when I was a child. I guess I figured I never qualified."

The story had carried them to the sprawling Miracle Springs High School complex. Sloane turned to face his son. "I'll take you in to meet the principal, then he'll show you where you'll need to go today."

"Thanks."

Sloane wanted to say so much more. Clay looked calm, and except for the ponytail he'd decided not to cut, he looked like any other teenager. A little less gawky, a little more reserved perhaps, but a normal teenager nonetheless. Still, he wasn't a normal teenager. He was going to school for the first time in his fifteen years. He was going to school in a strange town, in a strange state, and with only a strange man who happened to be his father to comfort him. He had shared a little, but what other feelings were hidden under that veiled demeanor?

Elise would know.

Sloane was startled by the spontaneous insight, although in the weeks since he'd come back to his hometown he'd ceased to be startled by the number of times he thought of Elise Ramsey. Elise would understand how Clay felt because her life had been spent trying to understand others, trying to walk in their shoes. If he chose to ask her, she could help him get beneath Clay's surface. Only, asking Elise for anything was a bad idea. The bond between them was already too strong.

"We'd better go," Clay said.

Sloane realized he'd been standing on the sidewalk staring right through his son. Even though they were early, the school yard was filling up fast, and curious looks were being directed at Clay.

"You're right. Let's go."

Sloane led Clay through the throng of gathering teenagers and in the wide, glass front doors of the school. The school had been new twenty years before and except for obvious wear and tear, it was exactly as Sloane remembered it. From an adult perspective, however, it seemed smaller—much, much smaller.

He hesitated at the principal's office. "I spent so much time here," he joked, "that I always thought they'd name it after me when I left town."

"Why'd you spend time here?"

Sloane realized that Clay wasn't kidding. He didn't understand a principal's function. It was going to be a hard year for him. There was so much to learn.

"I hope you never have to find out," Sloane told him, putting a hand on Clay's shoulder. "Now let's go meet Mr. Greeley."

ELISE LISTENED to Lincoln Greeley's inevitable first-day-of-school pep talk and nodded her head at the appropriate times along with everyone else in the room. The fluorescent lights in the ceiling buzzed annoyingly, and the one over Mr. Greeley's head flickered on and off making a flashing neon sign of his shiny bald head.

Bob sat next to her listening intently to Mr. Greeley's speech as if it weren't the same one they heard every year and others before them had heard every year, too. Elise fantasized generations of teachers, women in Gibson Girl hairdos, men with waxed handlebar mustaches, all of them listening to Mr. Greeley's speech.

"And so," he concluded, "it is our duty to carry on the tradition of excellence that was begun ninety years ago in that one-room schoolhouse on the Wehachee. In your hands rests the future of this town, this state and this great country."

Elise applauded politely. Mr. Greeley took out a handkerchief and wiped his forehead. Obviously he, too, was glad to have his first speech of the day out of the way. The faculty stood and filed out row by row in a fashion that would have made the fire marshal proud.

"Same classroom this year?" Bob asked as they waited their turn to exit.

"Same one. How about you?"

"Yes."

Same school, same speech, same homeroom, same boring questions. Elise wondered why she was feeling so dissatisfied. The sameness of her life had often been a comfort to her. Now it was barely tolerable.

Out in the hall she headed for her classroom, smiling and exchanging the inevitable greetings as she went. She was in one of the far wings. The school was designed to resemble a dissected spider. The administration section and auditorium were the body of the tortured insect, and the classrooms were laid out along each of six spider legs with triangles of lawn in between. A parking lot, football field and track had been laid out where the rest of the spider should have been, and there was also a small pond with a resident alligator who was the unofficial school mascot.

The unforgiving Florida sun and humidity had made a mockery of the attempt at architectural innovation. The school board had never had adequate funds to keep up with all the surfaces that needed painting and the grass that needed tending. Like many other things about Miracle Springs, the high school was a well-intentioned failure.

As she passed Mr. Greeley's office, Elise glanced through glass walls soon to be covered with the smudges of countless teenage fingers. Clay and Sloane were standing by the wide counter, obviously waiting for Mr. Greeley. She stopped, debating what to do.

Clay was in her homeroom. She had fought with herself since the night a week before when Sloane had come to her house to put their relationship in perspective. But in the end, she had requested Clay's presence in her English class and homeroom, too. Her relationship with Sloane might be a problem, but Elise knew that she had the capacity to understand Clay and the significant adjustments he would have to make at Miracle Springs High. Not everyone else on the faculty had that capacity. And no one else had the emotional investment in him that she did, as dangerous as it was.

Now she took a deep breath and pushed open the doors that led into the office.

"Good morning, Clay, Sloane."

"Hello, Elise." Sloane's smile was no more than polite, and Elise chastised herself for caring.

"Are you waiting for Mr. Greeley?"

Sloane nodded. Clay fastened his long-lashed brown eyes on her face as if she might unlock the puzzles of the day for him. Elise's heart did a flip-flop. What a beautiful young man he was. "Am I going to be in your class, Elise?"

"Miss Ramsey," Sloane corrected before Elise could answer.

"Elise will be fine outside of school," Elise said gently. "But you'll be accused of being a teacher's pet if you call me that here."

"Teacher's pet?"

"Someone who gets special favors," she explained. "And yes, you're in both my homeroom and my English class."

Clay smiled his thank-you. Elise wondered what it was about the Tyson men that made her insides run together when they gave her that certain little grin. She remembered all too well what effect that same expression had had years before when Sloane had aimed it her way.

The door wheezed open, letting in a rush of warm air from the open hallway, then shut. Lincoln Greeley came in behind the warm air, still mopping his forehead. He looked up and his pug-dog features were transformed into a mock grimace. "Sloane Tyson. Right back where you belong."

Sloane extended his hand and the two men shook warily. Elise watched as they readjusted their relationship. It was always the same. It took time for alumni who returned as adults to come to terms with their new status. Sloane wasn't immune, not even after seventeen years and two best-sellers.

"I'd like you to meet my son, Clay Tyson," Sloane said, stepping back to give Mr. Greeley a full view of the boy. "He'll be a student here this year."

"Glad to have you, son," Mr. Greeley said, extending his hand. His sharp, well-practiced eyes examined this new student for signs of trouble. "Hair's a little long, isn't it?"

"Does the school have a dress code?" Sloane asked politely.

"Not one that covers hair. We got out of that business after the sixties. Keep it clean and I can't say a word." He continued to examine Clay. "How many people have told you you look just like your dad?"

"A lot," Clay answered.

"Did your dad tell you about the time I caught him chiseling the mortar out of the bricks in the library during study hall?" He watched Clay shake his head. "Get him to tell you about it sometime. We haven't had too many like your dad in all my years as principal. He kept me on my toes. Are you going to keep me on my toes, too?"

Clay frowned a little. "Am I supposed to?"

The answer seemed to please Lincoln Greeley. He laughed and slapped Clay on the shoulder. "We've put you in Miss Ramsey's class. She asked for you specially, so you treat her right, son." He dismissed Clay and Elise with a wave. Elise opened the door and ushered Clay through without meeting Sloane's eyes. She wished he didn't know that she had asked to be Clay's teacher. She had done it for Clay, but she wondered if Sloane would see it as an excuse to be closer to him. Then she wondered why she cared.

"First days are always a little chaotic," she told Clay as they walked to the classroom. "Everybody feels strange, so don't imagine you're the only one who doesn't know exactly where he's supposed to be. If you need any help, find me and I'll see what I can do."

"All right."

Out of the corner of her eye Elise watched Clay covertly examine every aspect of his surroundings. His expression gave nothing away, and she was left with nothing but her own projections to help her understand his feelings. Two things were certain, however. It wasn't going to be an easy day for Clay Tyson. And watching him suffer wasn't going to be easy for her. She felt a stab of maternal concern so intense that for a moment it was a physical pain.

Clay Tyson might not be her son and she might not be anyone's mother, but Elise was sure that if she'd had a son, Sloane's son, the bonding could not possibly have been any stronger than what she felt at that moment.

No, it wasn't going to be an easy day. It was, in fact, going to be a very difficult year. For all of them.

ALGEBRA. Obviously, Clay thought, it was a foreign language using numbers and letters. A code, probably related to Egyptian hieroglyphics. Clay sat through his first period algebra class and wondered what the day was like back in New Mexico. Destiny Ranch was gone now, but for the fifty minutes of the class he pretended that when the bell rang, he could stand up and walk out of the school, stick his thumb out on Hope Avenue and get a ride all the way back to Destiny to find it thriving as it had been when he was a young boy. At least at Destiny he'd had some idea who he was. Here, in Miracle Springs, he wasn't even sure of his own name.

Clay Tyson. What was this Tyson bit? he wondered. Sure, he looked like the man who said he was his father. At times he even noticed similarities in the way their minds worked. But what did that mean?

Once a woman named Willow had claimed to be his mother. He remembered her only vaguely. She had been tall, but then he'd been pretty short so how would he really know? Her hair had been long, like Elise's, and dark, if his memory was correct. He remembered running to her once to be kissed and cuddled after a childhood injury. After that he only remembered her from a distance. And then she was gone.

When would Sloane leave him or make him leave? It didn't really matter. He was fifteen and he'd understood how to get along in the world for years. Oh, there might be things he didn't understand, like algebra and how to find his way around this ridiculous building. But he did understand the important things, things like not causing anybody any trouble, and teaching himself how to do what needed to be done. He didn't need Sloane. He wasn't even sure he liked Sloane. At least, once, Willow had picked him up and held him and kissed away his hurts. He couldn't imagine Sloane holding anybody.

The sound of a bell interrupted the teacher's indecipherable lecture. The school operated on bells. The kids were trained to respond, just like Pavlov's dogs. What had that experiment been called? Some kind of conditioning. Well, these kids were conditioned. Everyone jumped when the bell rang. In another week, he'd probably jump, too. Was that one of those skills Sloane had said he needed to develop?

The classroom emptied quickly. Clay followed the group of students out into the hall. His next class was American history. He recognized the teacher's name. Bob Cargil. It was the man Elise had introduced him to at the Inn. The man hadn't liked him, but then the algebra teacher hadn't looked any too pleased to see him either.

Was it the ponytail? None of the other boys had long hair; in fact few of the girls did either. Actually they all looked pretty much alike. Everyone had short asymmetrical haircuts that were molded a certain way and didn't move. They wore blue jeans or bright flowered shorts and oversize shirts. And shoes. Shoes seemed to be a big deal here. He'd watched the kids comparing brand names. High top leather sneakers seemed to have some magical allure, especially if they were made by a certain company.

He found the history classroom just as the bell rang, and slid into a desk at the back of the room.

"Tyson? Third seat on the fourth row. On the double."

Clay stood and found the seat, stooping to stow his books in the metal cavern beneath before he sat down.

"Tyson? I expect you to be on time from now on. Tyson! Did you hear me?"

Clay listened to the giggles of two girls next to him. What was he supposed to say? He shrugged, his face a careful blank. "I heard you," he said politely.

"Yes sir!"

Clay realized that something was expected of him.

"Yes sir!" the teacher repeated a little louder.

Clay returned Mr. Cargil's stare. For some reason, few adults expected someone his age to meet their eyes. He liked to show them they were wrong.

"One more chance, Tyson. Yes sir!"

Clay understood. He was expected to say "Yes sir!" back. He complied amiably. "Yes sir."

"I don't want any trouble with you, Tyson. I've got my eye on you."

Actually, Clay thought, Cargil's eyes weren't really on him at all. His eyes shifted when Clay tried to return his stare. It was funny; he acted like a man with something to hide.

"Say 'yes sir,' " a voice behind him prompted.

Clay complied. "Yes sir," he said again, as pleasantly as before.

The response seemed to mollify Mr. Cargil. He began to list supplies they would need, books they had to read and give a year's overview of assignments. Clay leaned over to retrieve his notebook from under the desk. As he did so he turned to see who had offered him help. The girl behind him was writing fast and furiously, but as Clay straightened, she stopped for a moment and gave him a tentative smile. His momentary impression was of curly golden hair and eyes so light that they were almost silver. She belonged in one of those fairy tales someone had read him as a child. A fair maiden who had rescued him from the dragon. It was a nice twist.

"Thanks," he whispered.

Her smile broadened a little showing the hint of a dimple, and she nodded.

Until that moment, Clay hadn't even realized just how lonely he was.

ELISE WATCHED the group of tenth-graders file back into her classroom for the last ten minutes of the day. Where was Clay? All day long she'd worried about him with the hysterical fear of a mother hen who knows one of her chicks is heading toward the jaws of a hungry fox. There was something so vulnerable about Clay Tyson, she reflected, for all his adult mannerisms and conversation.

She had been relieved when fourth period came and he showed up in her English class. She'd started the kids on a writing project immediately. They were to write ten pages in a journal every week, and today they were to begin with their impressions of the first day of high school.

Afterward she'd collected the journals to take a look at the writing samples. She hadn't had much time, but she had checked Clay's right away, expecting trouble. She had worried needlessly. His handwriting was average, but his writing itself was extraordinary. His control of the language, the depth of his analysis and his unusual perspective made the simple journal entry a small masterpiece. She had seldom, if ever, seen such talent displayed.

His father had kept a journal although no teacher had required it. Elise had known about it and wondered what Sloane found to write about. And then she'd had the chance to find out. Sloane had presented it to her the day he left Miracle Springs. It had been an ironical goodbye gift. She had never opened it.

Now, instead, she was reading his son's.

The realization of Clay's potential had affected her deeply. There had been few moments in her life to daydream. But on the rare occasions when she'd had that opportunity, she'd found herself imagining a child. The child had grown in her imagination until one day she'd realized how unhealthy the fantasy was. Motherhood was never to be hers. A child would never grow inside her, never come to her for comfort or advice, never achieve adulthood because of her efforts.

But if there'd been a child ... If there'd been a child it would have had Sloane's face and her gentleness. The child would have had their love of the English language and their talent to communicate it. It would have had both Sloane's uncanny ability to analyze and her own ability not to judge too harshly.

The child would have been Clay.

Fantasies had been bad enough, but having the flesh and blood child in front of her, and knowing that she could never be more to him than an English teacher, was going to tear her apart.

"Miss Ramsey?"

Elise looked up from her desk and focused on Clay's face. She knew immediately that it hadn't been an easy day for him. He looked tired. No, he looked emotionally exhausted. She felt a wave of anger at all those who had given him trouble. "Stay after class a minute and tell me about your day," she invited.

Clay seemed surprised, as if the simple request was incomprehensible. He recovered his poise quickly. "All right."

"Do you need something right now?" she prompted him.

"I'm supposed to go to the counselor's office and take some kind of test. I got in trouble once today for not having a pass in the hall."

Elise took a packet of blue forms out of her desk drawer and filled in the necessary information. She gave the pass to Clay. "Come see if I'm still here when you're finished."

"Okay."

Elise watched him gather his books and leave. She couldn't miss the stares of the other teenagers, the laughter, the mimicking. Kids were so cruel. It was no wonder they drove each other to find ways of blotting out the pains of adolescence. Anyone who didn't understand drugs and alcohol and teenage sex hadn't been to high school in the eighties.

The final bell rang, and a spontaneous cheer echoed through the building. Elise watched her classroom clear out until, one minute later, it was a ghost town of desks.

She stood, smoothing her yellow flowered skirt around her knees and absentmindedly repinning a long strand of hair that straggled down her neck. Her eyes caught a movement in the doorway, and she realized Sloane was leaning there, arms folded, watching her.

Wouldn't it be wonderful if she could pretend, even to herself, that his presence there meant no more to her than the presence of any other parent of her students? Her hands fumbled with the hairpin and she jabbed it harder, wincing when it dug into her scalp. She waited until she'd inhaled deeply before she spoke.

"Hello again, Sloane."

"I was looking for Clay. Have you seen him?"

"He's down in the counselor's office taking a test, but he'll probably stop by here before he heads home. Would you like to wait?"

He inclined his head in a motion that could have meant anything at all. Elise decided to ignore him, turning to clean the chalkboard so that she could print the next day's assignment.

"Do you really enjoy teaching?"

His question surprised her. It seemed to be a continuation of the abortive conversation they'd had at her house. How was she to answer? Truthfully? In depth? Or just politely?

"Well, sometimes I feel pretty frustrated. I actually get kids who can't read, as impossible as that sounds. They've been pushed through the system or they've managed to fool teachers who wanted to be fooled. I have to start back at the beginning with basics and convince them how important reading is, then I have to stay with them every step of the way. I also get a lot of kids who don't want to read, and I have to spend the whole year trying to make them want to. Then, every once in a while, I get a wonderful student. Like Clay."

"Oh? You can tell after one class that he's going to be a wonderful student?"

"You teach. You should understand that."

"But I don't get as involved as you evidently do."

"No, I don't suppose you would," she said evenly. She finished wiping the chalkboard before she turned, dusting off her hands.

Sloane had moved closer. He was restless, and his energy seemed to vibrate through the small classroom. "Why did you ask to have Clay as your student?"

"Because I'm the best this school has to offer." Elise lifted her chin as she said the words. "And because he's your son, although that was almost as much a reason not to ask for him."

If Sloane was surprised by her honesty, it didn't show. "Clay will be fine. With or without your help."

"It's going to be a tough year for him, Sloane. He's not like most of these kids. He's way beyond and way behind at the same time. He needs all the help he can get."

"Elise Ramsey. Rescuer."

"Sloane Tyson. Cynic." Elise realized she was feeling the effects of a long and emotional day. She really wasn't up to trading insults with her teenage lover. And Sloane was hitting entirely too close to home.

"Don't get too involved, Elise. We'll be gone by June. The boy doesn't need one more person flitting in and out of his life."

"What the boy doesn't need," Elise said sharply, "is a hands-off policy. He's flesh and blood, unlike his father. He needs love, just like the rest of us humans do, and even if that love is short-lived, it's better than holding him at arm's length."

"You always did get overly emotional."

"And you always did put me down for it."

"Don't play games with my son!"

"Then you play games with him, Sloane. Somebody needs to. This year is going to kill him if somebody doesn't show him they care!"

They stood glaring at each other. Elise wondered if either of them really understood what their fight was about. The real fight seemed to shimmer under the surface of their angry words, just out of reach.

"I'm going to have him removed from this class. I don't want you clinging to Clay."

Elise knew the color had drained from her cheeks. Even Sloane looked pale, as if he couldn't believe he'd said what he had.

"Only you," she said finally, "would think that of me. And you most of all, should know how untrue it is."

"Me most of all?"

"I loved you once, yet I let you go. Would I do less for your son?"

Sloane passed a hand over his eyes as if to wipe away any feeling that might show at her words. He straightened. "Elise," he began.

Elise shook her head. "I'd like you to go," she said. "You can wait in the office; you can even change Clay's schedule while you're at it."

"Elise . . ."

"Not now, Sloane. Not ever. Please go."

She turned back to the chalkboard, effectively shutting him out. Then she began to write the next day's assignment in tiny, precise letters. When she had finished, Sloane was gone.

CHAPTER FIVE

SILENCE AGAIN. It should have been welcome after a day of noisy teenagers. But it wasn't welcome at all because the silence didn't affect the little voice inside her. As clearly as if her brain had faithfully made a videotape, Elise played and replayed her confrontation with Sloane that afternoon.

She had thought she was beyond being hurt that badly. She had been wrong.

The kitchen of the little two-story house heated unbearably as the oven cooked her frozen dinner. Halfway through the suggested time on the package, Elise turned it off and left the dinner sitting on the oven rack, still frozen inside. She wasn't hungry, and the good sense that always made her eat no matter how she felt was inoperative tonight. She settled for an ice-cold glass of lemonade and took it into the living room.

She ought to redecorate. The house still belonged to her mother; Jeanette Ramsey's mark was everywhere. Perhaps if Elise cleared out the fussy, overstuffed furniture, the frilly curtains and the knickknacks, she'd feel more like a real person.

She had the money. They had lived frugally all these years, not because they had to, but because Jeanette had been such a miser she'd refused to spend a cent she didn't have to. Elise's father had left a large life insurance policy and a pension. The untouched insurance money had sat in the local savings and loan for seventeen years collecting interest. Now it was Elise's money.

"I ought to take it and go around the world," she said, breaking the silence with her own voice. "Have an affair or two in every country in Europe." She set down her lemonade and leaned back, her hands behind her head.

What was stopping her besides the lack of inclination to do anything so ridiculous? She really was free to leave Miracle Springs; she could pack her bags and move anywhere she wanted. And Sloane was providing the impetus once again, although in a different way than he had once before. Seventeen years ago he had tempted her to follow him, even in the face of her duty to her mother. Now he was tempting her to get away from him. Sloane's purpose in life seemed to be to shake her loose from everything she held dear.

Good old Sloane. Tonight nothing seemed dear enough to make her want to stay in Miracle Springs and spend a year avoiding him. If he really did remove Clay from her classes, it would be easier. But avoiding someone in a town of three thousand was just about impossible. That was why people here treated each other as well as they did. Who wanted to come face-to-face with the enemy every day at the post office, the grocery store or the gas station? God bless small towns, thought Elise, even if Sloane had never had much respect for their rules and regulations.

The house was stifling. Elise had thrown open all the windows and there was a faint breeze stirring the humid summer air. But nothing would begin to make the mercury drop except central air-conditioning. Elise was tempted to go for a drive. She could open all the windows and feel the breeze blow through her hair. Nearby there were green rolling hills covered with thoroughbred

horse farms, miles and miles of picturesque wooden
fences and pastures, lush and emerald-hued. There were
orange groves, too. Miracle Springs was a little too far
north to be considered safe for citrus crops, although
there were those who tried to grow the fruit with varying
degrees of success. But just to the south, within easy
driving distance, were geometrical patchwork quilts of
orange trees that spread as far as anyone could see.

By the time she left Miracle Springs behind her, however, darkness would extinguish her view of anything except the road in front of her and the pattern of her own
headlights. It was too late to take a drive, too early to sit
in the frowsy living room and count the beads of perspiration forming on her forehead. Too late to find solace
in the meditative motion of the car, too early to find solace in sleep.

Elise stood. She refused to be trapped by the heat and
her own restlessness. There had been other nights like this
one, nights when she'd felt she might go crazy from the
unreleased tension that haunted her now. Miracle Springs
might not have much to offer, but it did offer the source
of its name. She'd put on her swimsuit and walk to the
springs. There was a place farther down the Wehachee
where she'd be almost guaranteed to find privacy. The
cold, clear water would revive her and help wash away the
humiliations of the day.

"DO YOU WANT to go for a swim?"

"I've got homework to do."

Sloane smiled sympathetically at the tone of Clay's
voice. The boy sounded bewildered that he should be
forced to suffer the indignities of schoolwork at home.
"Do you need help?"

"It's just reading and answering questions for history. You can do the algebra for me if you want."

"I never understood algebra," Sloane admitted.

Clay shrugged. "The guidance counselor said I'll probably be moved to remedial math tomorrow anyway. Evidently no one has ever scored as low as I did on the math part of that test she gave me."

Sloane had spoken to the counselor himself. Clay wasn't kidding. Nor was he telling the whole story. The test, a basic IQ and achievement test, had indicated that Clay was going to have a tougher time than any of them had thought. His education had been so sporadic and dependent on the whims of the adults in his life that he didn't have too many of the skills of an elementary school student. The test had also indicated that the boy's intelligence was easily in the superior range. The counselor had been enthusiastic. More testing would follow, but she intended to have a conference with Clay's teachers immediately to motivate them to help this strange, gifted child achieve his potential.

The guidance counselor saw Clay as a marvelous challenge. Elise saw him as a boy badly in need of affection. Sloane saw him as a stranger with his own face, a son he didn't know how to raise. He wondered how Clay saw himself.

Tonight, watching him struggle with the homework that was so foreign to his experience, Sloane wanted to offer his son the love that Elise seemed to think he needed. He just wasn't sure how to do it. "You could do your homework when we got back."

"You go on. I'm pretty tired."

Clay did look tired. He looked as if the day had stripped something important from him. Sloane wondered if sleep alone would replace it.

Tentatively Sloane reached out to touch his son's shoulder. "All right. I won't be home late."

He changed into his swimsuit and pulled on a pair of jeans before heading toward the springs. His last vision of Clay was of the boy, head bent over his books, looking as if he wished he could be anywhere else.

In a matter of weeks an evening walk might be pleasant, with soft breezes cooling the dampness of his skin. But tonight, even with the sun gone below the horizon, the air swirled around Sloane's body like the steam from a hot shower.

It had rained earlier that afternoon, ending the drought that had curled foliage and burned grass right down to its roots. But the ground had been so dry that the water stood in puddles seeping drop by drop into the thirsty earth with a torturing slowness. And the heat was turning much of the water into humidity.

The smells of summer hung suspended in the air with the fine droplets of mist. There were the scents of jasmine and freshly cut grass, the faint tinge of sulphur water brought from deep within the earth by a droning pump to water a lawn—and the fragrances of pine, cedar and a few late roses.

Nostalgia at his age. Didn't that start later? Sloane asked himself. Wasn't he supposed to experience, not re-experience? Wasn't he too young to be so overwhelmed with memories of other summer nights when he'd headed down Hope Avenue to the springs? Nights when he'd smelled these same smells? Nights when his body had been tormented by the sensuality of a Florida summer?

There had been one place in particular where he had always gone to swim. The beach was often populated, but farther downriver had been a spot he and Elise had found together. It was a treacherous walk through palmetto and trees draped low with clinging Spanish moss, but the riverbank itself had always been clear enough with a huge fallen oak blocking the growth of underbrush and providing comfortable places to perch.

The tree would be gone, dissolved by time into the verdant Florida earth to help nourish it and begin a new life cycle. But the riverbank and that peculiar shelf of crystal sand leading out to deeper water would still be there.

And memories would be there, too. Memories of velvet nights and the smooth satin skin of his teenage lover. Memories of water so cold it left your body tinged with ice-blue tones of the water itself, water so cold and yet never cold enough to cool the passion he had felt for Elise.

The riverbank was sacred ground. Elise had lost her virginity there, and although his had been long gone before she entered his life, he had lost something there also: his aloofness, his solitude, his heart.

He had lost his good sense too. He had known from the beginning that he and Elise were two different animals. She was home and duty and kindness. He was restlessness and curiosity and hard-edged insight. They had never had a chance, but his insight had not been hard-edged enough. He had wanted to believe otherwise.

The spot on the riverbank might still be there, but Sloane knew it would not be the same. And that was as it should be. He reached the beach and his eyes drifted over the water. He could see that the springs itself had drawn others who wanted to drown the day's heat. Tonight he wanted no company.

The smells changed as Sloane walked down the beach and began to make his way through the moonlit jungle that surrounded the civilized portion of the springs. Florida had a way of reminding a person just how close to nature he still was, even if man had done his best to destroy his environment and create an illusion of civilization. Tie up so-called civilized man for a hundred years then set him free to examine his world, Sloane speculated. Florida would be a wreathing mass of vines and moss, insects and reptiles. Hurricanes would have blown away half the scenery-destroying condominiums and shopping centers that Florida builders loved to erect; humidity and heat and relentless sunshine would have taken care of the rest.

Now Sloane inhaled deeply. The smells were savage here; there was nothing civilized about them. Rotting vegetation, a fresh, unexplainable tang from the river, the occasional stark sweetness of some exotic blossom. The smells were as primal as the earth itself, and they did nothing to still the aching need of his body.

The path he followed was faint, just barely discernible in the pale light of a moon not quite full, but Sloane could tell it had recently been used. Others had discovered the special place. Sloane only hoped that on this night he would be alone.

The path took a sharp turn toward the riverbank. Seventeen years had passed, but his feet had turned before he'd even noticed the path changing direction. The river was calling to him, welcoming him home, inviting him to immerse himself in its depths far from the civilized waters of the springs.

Sloane stood at last on the sand- and bark-covered riverbank, stripping his shirt over his head with one hurried movement. Moonlight scampered over the surface of the gently flowing water, creating a pattern of sparkling diamonds and deepest ebony. Framed by the lacy shadows of moss-draped trees on the opposite bank, Sloane could almost believe that the river was inviolate. No one had ever penetrated its depths; no one had ever found its secrets.

But as he watched, the water was split by a human form. He felt a sharp stab of disappointment, like a man who has risked his life to climb an unscalable mountain only to discover a broken soft drink bottle at its peak. Sloane chastised himself for his sentimentality. The river was large enough to accommodate more than one swimmer. It did not belong to him. He had, in fact, rejected the river right along with everything else when he left Miracle Springs.

He watched the lone swimmer, debating whether to join this unknown person or vanish back into the jungle. But as he watched, he realized the person was swimming toward him.

His eyes narrowed and he concentrated on the form approaching. It was a woman. She was swimming on her back, and her body cut through the water with graceful, feminine strokes. As she reached the shallow shelf and stood, wringing the water from dark, waist-length hair, he knew immediately who she was.

Sloane realized that somewhere, deep inside him, he had wondered if Elise would be here tonight. He hadn't been able to admit it. If he had, he wouldn't have come. And yet on some level his thoughts of her had led him here to this place where they had once shared everything. Her back was still turned to him and she stood, staring up at the moon and stars as if their light provided her with a sustenance that daily living never could.

Images too poignant to bear examination flooded through Sloane's body, making him remember more than he wanted to remember. Much, much more.

A boy and a frightened girl, alone on the riverbank on a night like this one. The girl's voice was a soft plea. "Sloane, I don't know if we should. I don't know if I want to."

For once the boy had not taunted her for her lack of courage. He had understood her fears. He had kissed her gently as he explored the contours of her body through the clinging one-piece bathing suit. "I know, Elise. Just trust me, we'll stop when you want to."

He, the boy, had believed his own words; only soon there had been no hope of stopping. Even Elise's fears, the guilt inbred in her by a puritanical mother, had not been able to extinguish the innate sensuality that had flared in her that night, sensuality that had flared brighter and brighter until it had become a brilliant flame enveloping them both. Each new intimacy, each new revelation had shone in her eyes like the starlight reflecting on the crystal sand.

Undressing her had been easy. The swimsuit slid down her sleek young body inch by easy inch. Sloane had touched her breasts before, but never had he seen them. They were small and brown-tipped, and they responded to the firm pressure of his hands in a way that surprised him. Sloane had known all about male arousal, but he had never cared enough to pay attention to what happened to a woman when she wanted a man. He had been astonished when he saw the way her nipples hardened and peaked, just as a part of him was doing at the same moment. He had been astonished and oh, so proud.

Elise had made a sound somewhere between a moan of surrender and a demand for him to stop. He had soothed her, teased her by dropping small kisses all along her chin and cheeks as he continued to fondle her breasts. He had whispered words of comfort and encouragement. He had plunged his tongue into her mouth as the swimsuit slipped lower, and when he had reached the place she was protecting by crossing her legs against his intrusion, he had told her how much he loved her.

He hadn't been lying. He had loved her. At that moment with her trembling body given up to his keeping, he had meant every word. Never had he known this fierce desire to protect, to explore, to join. It was so much more than just wanting to sheath his jutting arousal in the tight warmth of her body; it was so much more than just wanting another sexual experience. This was Elise, a girl-woman who had touched him in ways no one else ever had.

The swimsuit had been stripped away along with his own, and patiently—if a seventeen-year-old male could be patient—he had run his hands over every inch of her flesh. He had taken her hardened nipples in his mouth in spite of her protest and shown her what pleasure they could give her. But he hadn't taken her as his own until, finally, she had surrendered herself to him, shown him she was ready by opening herself and clasping him to her body to give him the gift she could only give once in her life.

He had hurt her. His control had been much less than perfect in those days. But almost as if she welcomed the pain, she had clung to him, inviting him to come deeper inside her. And then there had been no pain. Only an intense pressure that had built inside both of them until his found its release in a storm of passion that left him almost senseless when it ended.

She was still shaking with need when he was finished. It was the first time in his experience with the opposite sex that he realized he had failed somehow. He had held her close and kissed her eyelids even though all he wanted was to fall asleep in the moonlight. He was shaken with guilt and with his own response to her. He wanted to help her, give her back some of the pleasure he had taken from her, but he hadn't known how.

Slowly she had calmed, as ignorant as he was about how to gain her own satisfaction. They had lain quietly together in the moonlight, and finally he had said the only thing he knew to say. "I think it'll be better next time."

She had giggled then, a musical gurgling sound that mimicked the river. "You take a lot for granted, Sloane Tyson. What makes you think there'll be a next time?"

He had expected tears, not the playful, joyous sound of her voice. His guilt had disappeared, replaced with a burning desire to discover how to make it up to her. "There are going to be many next times," he had told her cockily. "More than you can count. And you're going to love every one of them."

"It wasn't what I expected." She had sat up, pulling her long hair over her shoulders to hide her breasts from his gaze. "I knew it would hurt, but I thought after that I'd feel something else."

"What did you feel?"

She had frowned, and the moonlight had traced the lines in her forehead in molten silver. "Like I wanted to explode."

"Do you still feel that way?"

"A little," she had admitted.

"Come back here." He had pulled her next to him against her protests and settled her in the crook of his shoulder. Then his hands had begun to wander the hills and valleys of her body once more, settling at last on the place that had once been forbidden him.

They had learned together what pleasured her. It had taken time to get it right, but once they both understood, her release had come quickly. Afterwards the tears had come too, mixed with the musical sounds of her laughter.

And proud? God, he had been so proud. Prouder than he'd been the first time he'd taken a more than willing girl in the back of his uncle's pickup. Nothing he'd ever done in life had made him prouder than the pleasure he'd given Elise that night. On the banks of this river. On the crystal sand that led out to the water where Elise now stood, her face turned up to the stars. Eighteen years ago.

Sloane was so lost in memories that for a moment he wanted to call out to her, tease her as he had that night when he'd helped her slip on her bathing suit and beach robe before he walked her home.

And perhaps she wouldn't find it strange if he did. Perhaps she too was lost in her memories as the moonlight bathed her face and reminded her of another star-filled night.

Shaken with the desire to go to her and yet knowing that he should disappear back into the jungle behind him, Sloane stood on the riverbank and waited.

Elise stretched her arms to the sky and slowly twisted back and forth, her hair brushing the bare skin of her back. The stars were cascades of fire tonight, and she could feel their brilliance inside her own body. They fed the ache in the core of her being, just as the warmth of the summer breeze and the feel of her hair tickling her wet skin fed that same ache.

The icy temperature of the river had done nothing to help release the tension inside her. She knew she could swim the length of the Wehachee and she would still feel this restless energy. It promised to keep her awake for the length of one hot Florida night.

Where did you run when there was no place thought didn't follow? And memories? She had run right to the memories. Why had she chosen as refuge the place where she had first lost herself in Sloane's arms? It had been no accident. She had come here in the years that Sloane had been gone but never on a night like this one. Never to torture herself with reminiscences of the moment she had become a woman.

She had come tonight because the pain of stifling that memory was worse than giving into it. Today Sloane had destroyed what they had once had together. And so tonight she must remember, and then put the past behind her forever. It was the only way to live with his presence in the coming year. She must desensitize herself, tear down the shrine to the past that she had erected. Then, newly emptied, she could move on with her life.

But it was so hard. Tears she hadn't known she still had to cry sprang to her eyes. Until this moment she hadn't realized just how tenaciously she had clung to a memory of a boy and girl in love, making love on a riverbank of sparkling sand with cold, cold water lapping at their feet.

Sloane had been so gentle. All the things she had believed about him had been true that night. He had been sensitive to her feelings, eager to give as well as to take, lost in wonder as her secrets had unfolded to him. And she? Well she had been lost, too. Lost in doubt and uncertainty until she understood that he loved her. She had known for months that she loved him, but he had never told her until that night.

And he had loved her. She still believed it. The man, Sloane Tyson, was a creature who seemed to have forgotten the meaning of that word. But the boy, ah, that had been a different story. The words had been wrenched from deep inside him, and he had never called them back. Only when he made love to her had he been able to voice them. But she had never doubted just how much he meant those precious syllables.

Elise crossed her arms behind her head and lowered her gaze to the opposite riverbank. Life, she decided, was like swimming across the Wehachee. Even if she turned back to find a place she'd once been, it was not the same. The water flowed on, changing everything. She could remember her first night in Sloane's arms. She could remember subsequent nights. But nothing would bring them back; life and the river flowed on, and if she turned back to her past she would find that it had disappeared in the current. It was better to keep swimming and not to flounder in the cold, clear depths looking for something that wasn't there.

A single tear trailed down her cheek. She bent to splash water on her face, and her tear mingled with the river. She took a shaken deep breath and then another. Finally she turned to find her way back to the bank.

A man was standing on the sand watching her and for a moment Elise knew fear. But a moment later, even from a distance in the moon- and starlit darkness she recognized the shape of Sloane's body and the way he held his head. He had stood that way as a boy, legs spread slightly apart, hips jutting out and shoulders thrown back. It was a cocky stance, one that had always said so much about Sloane Tyson. It had been just one of the things she had loved.

How was she to forget him when he was everywhere she was? How was she to erase memories of the teenage Sloane when the adult haunted her every footstep? Elise felt a whiplike anger crackle through her body. Sloane taunted her, accused her of clinging to him through his son, and yet he stood watching her on the riverbank where he had taken her innocence. Her anger carried her through the water to stand in front of him.

"What are you doing here?" She was proud of herself for not bothering with the amenities. What was between them was too long-standing, too elemental for false politeness.

Sloane took a deep breath, forcing the air out of his lungs with measured precision. Did she know that he was so out of touch with reality at that moment that he wanted to reach out to her and pull her against him as if all those years had never existed? He knew she was angry, that his behavior earlier that day and his unannounced presence on the riverbank had fueled a fire inside her. He also knew that her anger was a good thing. It could keep them apart, keep him from mistaking her for the seventeen-year-old girl he had once made love to on this beach.

But if that was true, why couldn't he say the words that would turn her anger into a raging inferno to burn away their past and sever the bonds between them?

He stared at her. She was still so lovely. Maturity had blessed her as it blessed few women. To look at her was to know that she was no longer a girl, no longer truly young. To look at her was not to confuse her with the Elise Ramsey he had taken on this riverbank, but rather to know something else. This Elise Ramsey, the one who stood in front of him with eyes like a Florida thunderstorm, was a woman of power, a woman whose mature body could hold a man in captivity while her tongue assured him that he was free to go anytime he chose.

"Sloane, damn it, I asked you a question. Stop staring at me!" Elise slapped her hands on her hips and straightened her spine.

He could not stop himself. He reached out and touched her hair, wrapping a long strand around his hand. "I came to swim. And to remember. I think I knew you'd be here."

She recoiled as if he'd struck her. "Don't say that."

"You didn't want the truth?"

"Don't taunt me. We both know your command of the language is better than mine. You don't have to prove it."

"I wasn't taunting you." He wrapped her hair around his wrist again, like a fisherman with a prize fish on his hook. "I came here to swim. And I stood on the riverbank and remembered the first time we made love and how you felt beneath me."

She shuddered, closing her eyes. "Don't."

"Why not? Have you forgotten?" He stepped a little closer. There were beads of water on her face, and they shone in the pale light of the moon. Gently he traced them with his index finger, connecting them like a child connects dots in a magazine picture puzzle.

Elise tried to turn her head, but his hand still held her hair. "I've remembered so much about you, but until today I'd forgotten how cruel you could be."

"Until today, I was never cruel to you."

"You shut me out of your life."

"There are those who would say that was kind."

"Perhaps they'd be right." She stopped trying to pull away and waited for him to free her.

"I don't know why I tried to hurt you today. I wish I could take back my words."

She was surprised by his apology. The Sloane she knew never apologized; he was always sure he was right and that he had the right to say anything he chose. She opened her eyes to examine his face. There was an expression there that she'd never seen before. Regret. And on his face it was oddly attractive. She tried to harden her heart, to think about cold river water changing and flowing, destroying the past.

"But I wasn't trying to hurt you when I told you I stood here remembering another night," Sloane continued. "I wasn't trying to hurt you then."

"What do you remember?" she asked him softly. "A foolish girl in love giving in to a boy who had no intention of keeping his promises?"

"I promised to take you with me. I never promised to stay in Miracle Springs."

"I would have gone if you'd given me time."

"No. You wouldn't have. I understood that even if you didn't."

"Did you care? Wasn't it a relief to be free of everything—including me?" She stepped a little closer, imploring him to tell her the truth, to ease the guilt she still carried over her own lack of courage seventeen years before.

"Free?" He laughed, but the sound was bitter. "I was never free. Not for years and years. There were always other women, some who looked like you but weren't you, some, like my ex-wife, who were your opposite in every way. No, Elise. I told you before. You kept a piece of me here with you, and I never got it back. I was only free again when I learned to function without it."

"Why are you telling me this?" she asked, her eyes wide with pain.

"Because you asked. And because tonight I can't remember who I am and who you are and what year it is." His hand wound further into her hair and he pulled her closer. "Help me remember," he said, his breath warm against her cheek.

"Sloane, don't. Things are bad enough as it is."

"Or good enough." He breached the final distance between them. "It was good. Do you remember how good it was?" His lips nudged her earlobe as he whispered the words.

She jerked away from the length of his body against hers, but he stalked her, his free hand holding her still as his body found hers once more. Elise knew she was trembling, and she knew Sloane could feel it. But more than that, she knew she was no longer resisting. Past and present were united by moon and stars blending one into the other as Sloane's body blended with hers.

"So good," he whispered again. Then his lips trailed along her jawline, finding their way to her mouth. The soft brush of his mustache was different, and the feel of his body, larger, broader, was different too. But everything else about him was achingly familiar. She stood perfectly still, not breathing as his lips neared hers. Then she sighed as his mouth moved over hers, tasting her sweetness like a man who has been so long denied his desire that he isn't sure what to do.

She had expected an onslaught of passion, a skillful exhibition of his prowess. She had expected him to try and prove just how many years had passed and how much she had missed. Instead the kiss ate away all her defenses with its genuine hesitation. Elise understood instinctively that Sloane was as moved as she was by the night and by their past. The kiss was not to conquer, not to belittle. The kiss was simply a tribute, a reminder of something beautiful that was no more.

She felt herself relaxing in his arms. Her body softened against his, and her hands rested lightly on his bare back. His skin was warm and smooth, still firm and muscle-padded. His mouth was familiar, his smell, his taste, familiar too. She wanted to know more, to deepen the kiss and lose herself in the knowing. But she was hesitant, just as he was.

He pulled his mouth from hers without letting her go. His eyes searched hers in the near darkness. "Kissing you doesn't help. I feel like I never stopped."

"But you did."

"I'm trying to remember that. I'm trying to remember that we have to stop now." He untangled his hand from her hair, smoothing it back from her face. "We're not the same people we were."

"Who are you trying to convince?" Elise moved her fingertips lightly along his spine. She wanted to prolong the moment, to create another memory.

"I didn't come back to Miracle Springs to start this all over again."

"I never thought you had." Her hands traveled around his chest, smoothing a path to his shoulders where she rested them lightly. "I wasn't even sure you'd remember my name."

"I remember everything." Sloane stepped back, and Elise's hands dropped to her sides as he said, "I remember things I shouldn't."

"It was all so long ago." She tried to smile.

"Just for tonight, turn back the clock with me."

The words were a surprise, just as his presence and his kiss had been. "How?" Her question echoed with vulnerability and secret dreams.

"Swim with me, like we used to do."

"I'm tired, Sloane. I've had enough."

He extended his hand in supplication. "Please?"

"We'll never be seventeen again."

"We'll never be many things we've been, but tonight we can remember."

She could not refuse. Reluctantly she placed her hand in his. "Tonight we'll remember."

Perhaps tomorrow would be soon enough to try to forget.

CHAPTER SIX

SLOANE STOPPED in the middle of the river and waited for Elise to catch up with him. They had moved in silence through the dark water, changing their strokes to suit each other's pace. Now Elise was lagging behind, and Sloane knew that she was tired. He treaded water as she caught up with him.

"Put your hands on my shoulders and rest," he said when she was beside him.

Elise hesitated. The intimacy of swimming side by side with him, their bodies brushing, had been greater than the hesitant kiss they had shared. Here, in the middle of the river, it was harder to put their past in its proper perspective. "I think we should turn back. I don't want to be 'gator bait."

"It's too civilized for 'gators."

"You've been away too long. There are still 'gators in these waters and moccasins too. I rarely swim this far from the springs."

"Why'd you come here tonight then?" Sloane grasped Elise's hand and set it on his shoulder. Then he reached for the other one and did the same.

"I don't know."

"Do you always swim with your hair loose like that? I remember you'd always braid it in prissy little braids before you'd go in the water."

"And you'd unbraid it."

"You were my mermaid with your hair loose floating behind you as you swam." He fingered a long tendril. "I'm glad you didn't cut it."

"I've thought about it. More times than I can count."

"Some things should never change."

"A peculiar sentiment coming from you." Before she realized she'd done it, Elise reached up to trace the thick mustache, beaded now with drops of water. "How long have you had this? I don't remember seeing it in your publicity photos."

Sloane smiled. "You looked at photos of me?"

"I told you I read your books. I couldn't miss the man on the back cover."

"I grew it when I found out I was a father. I decided it would make me look more paternal. What do you think?"

"It makes you look like someone who keeps a gun under his sportcoat and a dagger strapped to his ankle." She traced the gleaming mustache once more. "I like it. Now you look as dangerous as you are."

"As dangerous as 'gators and water moccasins?"

"Infinitely more dangerous." She pulled away to begin her swim back to shore, but Sloane stopped her.

"Don't go yet. We haven't completed the ritual."

Elise knew what was coming. "Nostalgia time is over, Sloane. We're grown-ups now."

"I don't feel grown-up. Do you?" He pulled her against him until her breasts fitted perfectly against his chest and he was treading water with one hand. "Do you remember all the times we did this?"

"Sloane, don't."

"That's exactly what you always said."

"We're going to drown."

"That's what you always said next."

"I mean it, Sloane."

"So do I, Elise. Take a deep breath." He covered her mouth with his and they sank beneath the surface. Elise clung to him for support although there was no support to be had. She was dizzied with the sensation of his warm body in the cold water and his mouth drinking the breath from hers. When she thought her lungs would explode, he propelled them both to the surface.

She tore her mouth from his to gasp for air. "You could never resist that, could you?" she said when she could talk again.

"I could never resist you. Not from the first moment you turned your ladylike attentions on me." One hand cupped the back of her head and his mouth traveled over hers again as they treaded water together, their bodies moving in unison.

Elise shuddered. There was nothing hesitant about Sloane's kisses now, nothing hesitant about the hardening of his body as it brushed against hers. Immersed in the water and in memory they clung to each other. Sloane coaxed her to open her lips, demanded this further intimacy and Elise, with a sigh, complied. Her body was laced with quicksilver flashes as their tongues united, stroking, exploring, retreating only to renew their quest with more passion.

She was so hungry for this; it seemed that her body had been starved for years, denied of all satisfaction by a life led far away from this man. A few kisses in the water couldn't begin to quench the ache inside her that had grown and grown until it felt as if it might never be assuaged. Sloane was leading her somewhere she would soon be helpless to turn back from. He had always been able to do that; seventeen years of absence had changed very little.

"No more, Sloane." She turned her head from his, fighting to free herself.

He pulled her closer, forcing her to tread water with him so that their legs tangled repeatedly. "Put your arms around my neck."

"No. Let me go."

Sloane could feel the softness of her breasts press against his bare chest, and he was overcome with the desire to touch her. He wanted to slip the simple one-piece suit down and fit his hands around her breasts to feel the smooth fire of her skin and the response of her nipples. He wanted to grasp her waist, then plunge his head under the water to seek the hidden contours with his mouth. Just thinking about it turned the chill of the water into a bath of fire.

"Don't fight me," he murmured. "You're going to drown us both." He hooked one finger under the strap of her suit and began to slip it over her shoulder.

Elise jerked at the new intimacy and struggled harder. "Stop it, Sloane."

Sloane knew he should do as she asked, but he was drunk on the feel and smell and taste of her. He wanted more than he had a right to ask for. And he didn't care. "I want you," he muttered against her cheek. "Damn it, Elise. You can still make me want you."

"What are you trying to do to me?" To her chagrin, she knew her eyes were filling with tears. "I'm not seventeen anymore. I know what year it is, even if you don't." Without another word she pushed hard against his chest, and when she was free she swirled in the water and began to swim back to the shore. Once there, she grabbed her towel and clothing from a low-hanging branch and disappeared into the jungle.

Sloane remained in the middle of the river, watching her retreat.

AFTERNOON HOMEROOM was just a way to make sure the students who started the day in school also finished it. Elise checked the last name off her roll book and passed out the latest stack of mimeographed notes to her students. Announcements were still sounding over the intercom when she sat back down at her desk. It was the end of the second week of classes, and the students were beginning to settle into the routines of high school. As soon as the last announcement was finished, the room filled with the excited buzz of prisoners who knew they were about to be released.

Elise began to grade a quiz that she had surprised her classes with that day. The surprise test was a favorite technique of hers, a way to see if anyone was paying attention. The students didn't know it, but such quizzes really figured very little in their ultimate grades. By the time they realized that, however, the year was half over, and they'd learned how to listen. It was sneaky, but it was a lot less painful for them than getting a bad report card, she reasoned.

Elise divided the quizzes into two simple stacks: good and bad. She would look at the bad ones to see if there was any pattern to the way those students were seated, possibly moving them away from others who had also failed. As she worked, she kept an eye on her homeroom to make sure that the end-of-the-day horseplay didn't get out of hand.

Watching the social groupings of a roomful of teenagers was a fascinating thing. Now that a week had passed, the kids had begun to form cliques. There were the losers or the "late bloomers"—as Elise liked to think of them—who were too fat or too awkward or too shy to be friends with the popular kids, so they became friends with each other. There were the rebels, a select few who proclaimed their individuality with punk-style haircuts and angry facades. There were the neatly dressed good students wearing polo shirts with the correct emblem on the pocket and discussing student council business, and there were the popular kids who rarely wore the same outfit twice in the same month and spent their time discussing who was going to represent the sophomore class at the Get Acquainted Dance in three weeks.

And then there was Clay.

Certainly there were students who drifted from group to group; the boundaries were not yet so fixed that there wasn't room for change. But Clay was the only student in her homeroom who didn't seem to fit anywhere at all. Clay was an observer. He was the most entrenched loner that Elise had ever known to exist in a group of teenagers. He seemed totally unaffected by the commotion, the maneuverings, the joys and sorrows of adolescence.

Elise wasn't a big fan of the social climbing of the teenage animal. But neither was she stubborn or blind enough not to see the practice's value. Adolescence was a series of experiences designed to teach preadults how to get along in civilized society. Part of that was learning how to function in a group. Clay was not functioning in the group because he had separated himself from it. It wasn't just his ponytail or the fact that he was new in a school where most of the kids had attended elementary and junior high together. It was his obvious rejection of the whole experience that was causing the problem.

Elise had heard the whispers. She knew what was said about him behind his back and more and more often now to his face. He was that "different" kid, the most insulting thing one teen could say about another. The few times anyone had reached out to him in her presence he or she had been met with a polite but blank gaze. Only in his journals and in his poetry could Elise detect echoes of the pain Clay was hiding.

The bell rang and the students raced to the door. Clay was last, as if going home held no more joy for him than staying in a school where he was destined to be a perpetual stranger. Elise had avoided personal contact with him since Sloane's accusations, but today she found herself beyond caring what Sloane might think.

"Clay? Can I see you for a minute?"

He came to her desk and stood quietly, his hands clasped behind his back. Elise allowed herself the inevitable reaction to him. Yes, he was Sloane's image. Yes, it would have been wonderful it he'd been her son instead of the son of some commune member with no maternal instinct. But he wasn't. She was only his teacher and his friend. It was as the latter that she spoke.

"Clay, I'm worried about you. You don't look happy."

A new expression flickered over his face. Elise could have sworn it was amazement. Did the boy find it so strange that someone would notice how he was feeling?

Clay's face quickly resumed its careful mask. "Thank you, Miss Ramsey, but I'm fine."

"I don't believe you." Elise stood and came around to perch on the edge of her desk so that she could be closer to him. "If I were you, I wouldn't be happy. I'd be wishing I'd made some friends, or wishing I didn't have to work so hard to catch up, or even that I was back in New Mexico."

"There's nothing there to go back to."

"But you've wished you could."

His nod was slight but perceptible.

"It's hard to make so many changes at once. I'd like to help, Clay. And I'm sure all your other teachers feel that way."

"Mr. Cargil wants to help so much that he's trying to send me back to ninth grade." As soon as he'd said the words, Clay clamped his lips shut as if he wished he hadn't opened his mouth.

Elise didn't let Clay see the anger she felt at his words. "Mr. Cargil is giving you a hard time?" she asked softly.

"It's all right. I can handle it."

Elise suspected that nothing was further from the truth. Clay Tyson had entirely too much to handle in his life as it was without having to absorb the venom of a man who looked at him and saw his father. "Tell me what he's doing to you, Clay."

Clay shrugged.

She used a tactic she didn't like but knew would be effective. "Shall I ask the other students in your class? They'll be glad to tell me."

"He's just after me," Clay conceded. "I've had people after me before. I know how it feels."

"What does he do? Insult you? Pick on you? I could talk to him."

"If you talk to him, it'll only get worse. Besides, other than announcing every day that he's got my number and won't take any funny business, most of what he does is subtle."

"Like what?" Elise said, fuming at the idea of Clay being singled out as a troublemaker before he'd had a chance to prove himself one way or the other.

"He asks me questions he knows I can't answer. He sticks to the reading assignments with the other kids, but with me he hops around to other areas and quizzes me on them. He seems to love making me look stupid. Then he shakes his head and rambles on and on about my terrible education and how I shouldn't be in high school, that junior high might even be too difficult.''

"In front of the other kids?"

"He calls me up to his desk, but they hear."

The terrible thing about what Clay was saying was that Elise could believe it. Bob Cargil was generally a rather harmless hypochondriac with limited understanding and sensitivity. But there was a streak of something darker inside him. If he felt threatened, he was capable of fighting back with any weapon. And for some strange reason, Bob saw Sloane and Clay Tyson as threats.

"I'll see he stops," Elise said, her mouth set and her chin tilted.

Clay's face relaxed a little, but he shook his head at her words. "Once, when I was about seven," he said, "a new kid came to live in the dome where I was staying."

"Dome?"

"Geodesic dome. Destiny had seven big ones. I lived in one of them until I was ten, then I moved into the big house. Anyway, this kid was older than I was, but he liked to pick on me. So every chance he got when nobody was looking or the person who was looking didn't care, he'd do something to me. Once he hit me with a big stick and I fell and lost a tooth. At first I just tried to stay away from him, but finally, I couldn't take it anymore. So I went to Jeff, the guy who was in charge of everything, and I told him what was going on."

Elise was amazed at the atypically long reminiscence, and she nodded, afraid to break Clay's spoken thoughts.

"Jeff got the kid who was bothering me off to one side and gave him a long lecture about how to treat people. It was a good lecture. Afterward the kid had to shake my hand and promise not to bother me anymore. And as soon as everyone's backs were turned, he redoubled his efforts. Only by then, everyone was sure it had been taken care of, so whenever I complained they told me to bug off.''

Elise didn't know what to say. She wanted to cry.

"He kept after me for two more years until his parents moved off the ranch and took him with them."

Elise swallowed the lump in her throat. "And you're afraid that if I talk to Mr. Cargil, he'll pretend he's going to stop. Only then he'll make it worse for you."

Clay looked relieved that she'd understood. "It just wouldn't help me any."

"Then what can I do?" She picked up a pencil and bounced it on her knee. "You may be right about what'll happen if I interfere, at least at this point, but you can't handle this by yourself. Not with everything else you've got going on."

"I'm just studying harder, trying to catch up with everything I've missed."

"You didn't have much history at Destiny Ranch, I take it."

"The founder of Destiny, Jeff, the guy I was telling you about, didn't believe in history. He said it was all lies. He said the only truth was in the present."

"What do you think about that?"

Clay smiled a little, and for a minute he looked like a fifteen-year-old boy was supposed to look. "I'm not sure the present has much truth in it either."

Elise restrained herself from giving him the fierce hug he deserved. Why couldn't this boy have been hers to love? He needed so much, and she had so much to give. "Clay, I want you to come to me if this gets any worse. I'll have the principal interfere if he has to, but in the meantime, I have an idea. We're going to get you a history tutor.''

Clay was suddenly the image of his skeptical father. ''What good would that do?''

''You can read all you want, but you need somebody to help you select what's important and question you on what you've read. Another student would be best because he'd know what someone your age is expected to have learned by now.'' Elise was pleased with her idea. If she could get the right person to help Clay, she might be helping him find a friend too. It was certainly worth a try.

''I'd rather not.''

''Will you just try it for a little while? I think it could help.'' Elise could see Clay struggling. He liked her, and she knew he didn't want to ignore her advice. But the idea of having someone help him was against his better judgment. Clay had received so little help in his life that the concept was as foreign as American history.

''I'll give it a try,'' he said finally.

''Good, I'll let you know as soon as I find someone for you.''

''Are you going to tell Sloane?''

''It would be better if the news came from you. I'm sure he'll approve.'' Elise watched Clay leave, raising her hand in a slight wave as he vanished through the doorway. Then she stood to gather the rest of her quizzes to take home and grade.

Tell Sloane? She allowed herself a self-ridiculing grunt. No, she wouldn't tell Sloane she was trying to help his son. She hadn't seen him in the days that had passed since their moonlight swim, and she intended to continue trying to avoid him. What was it that Clay had said? History was lies and the present didn't have much truth in it either? The statement might not apply to everything, but it certainly applied to her relationship to Sloane.

Where Sloane Tyson was concerned history and memory and present experience were a curious blend that could be absolute truth or complete lies. And as Elise turned out the light and closed the classroom door behind her, she knew she was much too confused to tell the difference.

That evening Elise put the finishing touches on a chicken and artichoke casserole and popped it back into the oven. The casserole was one of Amy Cargil's favorites and one of the few things Amy's picky father would eat without complaining. Elise stepped out into the dining room and checked over the table setting. She was rearranging a display of lavender hibiscus when the doorbell rang.

"Hi, sweetie." Elise gave Amy a big hug, then stepped back to examine the striped, low-waisted knit dress that showed off Amy's nicely developed figure to perfection. "You look wonderful. We made the right choice."

"Thanks for helping me pick it out."

Elise offered her cheek for Bob to kiss and patted him on the shoulder. "I'm glad you could come," she told them both.

"We wouldn't miss it," Bob said gallantly. "Your cooking beats mine any day."

Actually they all knew that Bob seldom cooked. Either Amy made something for them or they ate out. Bob seemed to feel that domestic skills were strictly in the female domain. For Amy's sake, Elise tried to have them to dinner as often as possible.

"Well, I made something you both like," Elise said. "Bob, why don't you fix yourself a drink while Amy and I finish the salad?"

Bob settled in the living room with his eternal Scotch and water and the national news, and Amy followed Elise into the tiny kitchen. "Elise," Amy started when her father was out of earshot, "I've got a date tonight after dinner. Will you help me get out of here without a fuss?"

"Is your daddy giving you trouble about the boy you're dating?"

"No, it's Gregory Thompson, the pharmacist's son. Daddy likes him as well as he likes anybody. I think he just doesn't like me leaving him alone. He doesn't want me to go out with anyone."

Bob seemed to be becoming more rigid, more irritable all the time. Elise thought of her conversation with Clay earlier in the week, and she thought of her own mother. Jeanette Ramsey had got worse as she'd grown older. Whatever positive qualities she'd had seemed to disappear with the passing of the years. Elise had taken the brunt of her moods. She was determined not to let the same thing happen to Amy.

"I'm on your side, sweetie. I'll keep him entertained while you're gone. I might even let him beat me at Scrabble."

"Thanks, Elise. I knew I could count on you."

"Can I count on you for something?" Elise asked, turning to face the girl who was like a daughter.

"Anything!" Amy said with heartfelt enthusiasm. "Always!"

"I need to find a history tutor for Clay Tyson. He's not doing well in one of your daddy's classes, and I think a tutor is just what he needs."

"Clay Tyson?"

"Do you know him? I know you're not in my English class together."

"Actually I'm in his history class. He sits right in front of me."

Elise tried to read the tone of Amy's voice, but she was unsuccessful. "His father and I were friends many years ago," she explained carefully. "I like Clay a lot, and I want him to do well in school. He's very intelligent."

"My father can't stand him. He's picking on him in class."

There had been a part of Elise that had wondered if Clay was imagining Bob's harassment. Now she felt a return of the anger she had experienced when Clay had described Bob's behavior. She tried to be fair. "Does Clay give your dad a reason to pick on him?"

Amy shook her head. "Not that I can tell. He's a quiet kid, hardly says a word. He acts like he's from another planet." She picked up a carrot and took a sizable bite, crunching it with small, pearly teeth. "But he doesn't do anything that would bother anybody. Just listens and tries to answer when he's called on. I've helped him a few times when he doesn't seem to know what to do."

"Thank you, Amy. Clay needs friends."

"Oh, I'm not his friend. I don't think he wants friends. And he's not shy or anything, because he always meets your eyes. He's just…just off by himself. You know what I mean?"

"Only too well."

"It's too bad, too, because he's cute." Amy punctuated her sentence with another crunch.

So Amy thought Clay was cute. Elise couldn't believe she hadn't thought of Amy as a tutor for Clay. Who better to work with the boy than the daughter of the man teaching his history class? Certainly Amy would know exactly what information Clay should have. Elise broached the subject with all the caution her enthusiasm would let her muster.

"Amy, I just had a brilliant idea. There's only one person who's right for this job. And I happen to know that person would like to earn a little extra spending money so she could buy a certain designer dress for the Get Acquainted Dance."

"Me?"

"Got it." Elise opened the oven door and bent to lift out the casserole. "What do you think?"

"He's cute, but he's so strange, I don't know if I can help him."

"Are you afraid of what your friends will say?"

Amy crunched the last of her carrot. "Sure. A little."

Elise appreciated her honesty. "Is 'a little' too much to keep you from doing it?"

"He'll pay me?"

Elise nodded.

Amy visibly struggled with her answer. She wasn't as much a victim of the high school herd mentality as some, but peer pressure had its effect on her, too. Finally she nodded. "I'll give it a try. But not at my house. I probably won't even tell my dad unless he asks where I'm going."

"If you think it's going to be a problem with your dad . . ."

Amy giggled. "He's always telling me how important hard work is and how I've got to earn my way in the world. If he finds out and says anything, I'll tell him I did it for him."

Elise tried to stifle a smile. "I'm never going to have to worry about you. You're going to be all right, aren't you?"

"Sure am," Amy agreed blithely.

"WHEN'S YOUR FRIEND coming, honey?"

Clay met his great-aunt's eyes and shrugged. "Sometime around four."

"I baked brownies. It's not often I get to have two young people in my house for the afternoon. I'm glad your father's over in Gainesville on Wednesdays doing his research." Lillian Tyson dropped an affectionate kiss on Clay's head. "I'm glad you're going to be studying here."

Of all the adjustments in his life, Clay decided that the most pleasant one was getting to know this great-aunt who seemed to care about him no matter what he did or didn't do. It was so strange knowing that in her eyes he was accepted just because he was a Tyson. Certainly she was the only person he could ever remember who had felt that way.

No, that wasn't quite true. Elise Ramsey seemed to care about him, too. For some unknown reason Elise seemed to understand his feelings and want to help him. And her concern didn't seem to be based on how he did in her class or whether he told her what she wanted to hear. She just seemed to care. Period.

He supposed that on some level Sloane cared, too. Once he was over the shock of being presented with a son who was obviously going to be a problem, he had tried to do his duty. That was caring in action as they would have called it at Destiny. Love was what you did for others, not what you felt. If you clothed or fed someone, that was caring.

Sloane did those things for him, and he didn't have to. He could have denied paternity, relinquished any rights over this stranger who was said to be his son. No one would have blamed him. He supposed he was really lucky that Sloane had saved him from the foster home where he'd had to stay until the child welfare people untangled his background. But at least in the foster home someone had been paid to take care of him. He wondered what reward, if any, Sloane was getting.

"Clay? You were staring into space like a zombie."

Clay pulled himself back into the present. "Sorry." He wondered if he dared ask his great-aunt if she knew what he could do to make his presence a little easier on Sloane. There must be something he could do to soften the grim expression that so often crossed Sloane's face when he looked at him.

"Don't be sorry, boy. Tell me what you were thinking."

Clay shook his head. "Just about my homework."

The doorbell chimed. "Well, that'll be your friend," Lillian said cheerfully. "Why don't you get it?"

Clay rose obediently and crossed the room. Amy Cargil was standing on the front porch, her books clasped in front of her. She was wearing a pale-yellow shirt and shorts to match. Clay thought she was just as pretty on the front porch as she had been the first day of school when she rescued him from her dragon-father.

"Hi, Clay. Am I late?"

Clay shook his head. "No, come on in." He waited until Amy was inside, then introduced her to his aunt.

"Glad to have you help Clay here," Lillian's voice boomed. "Now I'll leave you two youngsters alone. There are brownies in the kitchen when you get hungry. And soda pop."

"I didn't think I was going to be fed, too," Amy said after Lillian had left the room.

"Lillian ... Aunt Lillian," Clay corrected himself, "likes to feed people till they burst."

"Do you live with your aunt?" Amy asked curiously.

Clay shook his head. "No, I live with Sloane, down the street a ways."

"Is he your brother or something?"

"My father."

"You call your father by his first name? My dad would eat me alive if I tried that."

"What do you call your father?"

"Daddy, or Dad sometimes now that I'm older."

Clay tried to imagine calling Sloane either of those things. He smiled a little.

"Do you think that's funny?" Amy asked with an edge to her voice.

Clay realized she thought he'd been making fun of her. "No. Not at all." He didn't know what else to say.

"Maybe we'd better get started," Amy said. "Where do you want to work?"

Clay pointed to the table where his books were all spread out.

"Good grief! You've got the whole library there."

"Just the history section." Clay sat down and motioned for Amy to take a seat.

"You don't have to read all these books, Clay. If you do you'll know more than my dad, and he'll dislike you even more." Amy bit her lip as she realized what she'd said. "I'm sorry," she said softly. "That was awful."

Clay frowned. "What was?"

"Saying that thing about Daddy."

"It wasn't awful. It was the truth. He does dislike me."

Amy was quiet for a moment as if she had to adjust to his words. "Well, doesn't it bother you?" she probed.

"Sure. Nobody likes to be picked on. Not even that 'strange kid from New Mexico.'"

Amy winced at the direct quote. It was a title for Clay that she'd heard more than once from more than one person. "I wish people wouldn't say things like that. They don't really mean it."

"Sure they do." Clay looked up from the table where he'd been clearing a space for them to work. "People almost never say things they don't mean. They may not tell the whole truth, but when they say something they're telling part of it."

Amy was becoming increasingly uncomfortable with Clay's unflinching gaze and his direct words. She was used to her friends hedging when a subject was controversial and to boys who rarely met her eyes for any length of time. Clay was so different. Already their conversation had been more honest and more serious than any conversation she'd ever had with anyone under twenty. "Do you always say whatever's on your mind like that?" she asked. "It's kind of unsettling."

"Why? I always think it's unsettling not to know what someone is thinking." He thought of Sloane. "In fact, I hate it when people play games with me."

"What kind of games?" In spite of her discomfort, Amy wanted to find out what he meant.

"If somebody's feeling something about someone else, he ought to tell the other person. That's the only way that person is ever going to understand. At school it's so different. Everybody plays games. They pretend they like somebody and then they talk about them behind their backs. Or even if they do like somebody and nobody else does, they won't talk to that person because they're afraid of what other people will think. It's weird." Clay examined Amy's face as he talked. She looked utterly flabbergasted. Maybe Amy wasn't really any different from everybody else.

"We'd better get to work," she said finally.

Clay shrugged. "All right. Where do you want to start?'

Amy wished she had the nerve to tell Clay where she really wanted to start: with a full explanation of where he had come up with these ideas and more importantly, where he had got the courage to talk about them. Why was he so different? Most boys couldn't manage a sentence unless it was about football or their favorite rock group or what kind of skateboard they were getting. Clay really was "that strange kid from new Mexico," and at that moment, Amy didn't know if she liked him or not. But one thing was certain, he was sure more interesting to talk to than anyone she'd ever met.

Clay watched Amy stare at him, and he wondered if he ought to tell her she could go. Obviously they weren't going to be able to get anything important done. But as he watched, she smiled a little and seemed to pull herself together.

Amy sat down and opened her book. Then she lifted her eyes to his. "Clay, you're a very different kind of person." She gave him a wide, brilliant smile that did funny things to the muscles in his chest. "But you know something? This may turn out to be an education for both of us."

CHAPTER SEVEN

ELISE SAT OUTSIDE on the rusty front porch glider and waited for Bob's arrival. The early October air was mixed with a gray drizzle that promised to get heavier as the evening wore on. She shut her eyes and pictured all the Miracle Springs High School girls who were at that moment trying to figure out how to keep their hairdos intact on their journey to school. It was the night of the Get Acquainted Dance, an annual event that was already old when Elise herself had been at Miracle Springs High, and along with Bob, she had agreed to be a chaperone.

It was traditional for the weather to be bad this time of year. Summer was officially over, but the air had not yet begun to turn cool with autumn's arrival. The drizzle presaged the change. It would probably go on for weeks as the thermometer dropped one degree at a time until the temperature was bearable.

The bad weather didn't matter to Elise. It matched her spirits. As the weeks had passed, she had sunk into a depression so utterly foreign to her that she had no idea how to pull herself out of it. She had been unhappy before, but rarely had she felt this listlessness, this apathy toward what life had to offer.

Maybe it was her mother's death catching up with her. Maybe it was the fact that she was thirty-five with little to show for all her years. Or maybe it was the fact that she was starving for the feel of a man's arms around her—Sloane's arms.

The last thought didn't even shock her out of her malaise. She had grown so used to the realization that she needed what only Sloane had ever given her that she was no longer surprised when the thought resurfaced. She was starving, starving for the feel of his arms, the touch of his mouth and the moment when they became one. Sex was a natural part of life; Sloane had taught her that. Years of abstinence were unnatural, and those years were taking their toll on her spirit.

Of course Sloane wasn't the only man in the world. There were probably plenty of men who would be glad to oblige her. But she remembered only too well what it was like to slip into lovemaking with a man she didn't really want. She had tried so many times to find pleasure with Bob, and had rarely succeeded. She had only felt gratitude when that part of their relationship had died a natural death, and she had been in no hurry to try again with another man.

But Sloane was back now, reminding her every time she saw him of what was missing in her life. Oh, he didn't say anything provocative; in fact he rarely said anything at all. He just looked at her as if he saw straight through to her soul—and nodded his head in greeting.

The simple gesture was enough. She was so aware of him, of the masculine strength of his body and the enormous attraction she felt that she froze each time she encountered him. The night in the river had destroyed the part of her that could pretend the year could be got through safely. Her defenses were toppling and now all her energies went toward making sure they didn't tumble to the ground. If she was depressed, that was why. She had absolutely no energy left over for daily living. Her entire body, mind and spirit were caught up in the battle that was going on inside her.

She pictured a hundred miniature Elises shoring up stone after stone of a wall that was being steadily shaken by earthquakes. No wonder she was emotionally exhausted. If the rest of the year continued with this output of energy, she'd be a true mental case by the time Sloane left town.

The sound of a car stopping in front of her house alerted her to Bob's arrival. She stood and peered through the drizzle. She could see Amy's silhouette in the back seat and as she watched, Bob's door opened and a big black umbrella pointed toward the darkening sky. She straightened the skirt of the black and white dress that made her look properly imposing as a chaperone and waited for him.

"All ready?" Bob temporarily closed the umbrella and shook the water off it, then turned to Elise. "You look very nice in that dress."

"And you look nice in that suit." She smiled a little and stepped forward to straighten his tie. "Ready to face a gym full of cavorting adolescents?"

Bob grimaced. "How'd we get into this?"

"By being responsible, dedicated teachers. And by being in the wrong place when Lincoln asked for volunteers."

"Next time he gets that certain look on his face, let's head for the hills."

"Let's." For a moment Elise tried to imagine what it would be like if she tried once again to have a relationship with Bob. They did have things in common. They were both lifetime residents of Miracle Springs, they both enjoyed teaching, they both loved Amy. And in their own ways, they both needed someone. Good relationships were built on much less, she mused. With difficulty, she tried to concentrate on what Bob was saying.

"I wish you'd talk to Amy. I don't know what's getting into her, but she's gone all the time lately." Bob's tone was whiny, and it snapped Elise out of her speculations immediately. *I must really be lonely and repressed,* she thought, *to consider a life taking care of Bob Cargil.*

"She's a teenager, Bob," she said, trying hard to control the rise of temper she had felt at his words. "She's not your caretaker."

"What's that supposed to mean?"

Elise sighed. "I'm sorry. I'm edgy tonight. We'd better get going."

"You've been edgy for weeks," Bob said huffily. "Does Sloane Tyson coming back to town have anything to do with your behavior?"

The pointed remark was so close to the truth that Elise couldn't even summon up the energy to tell Bob to mind his own business. She just shrugged. "I don't intend to stand on my front porch and pass the time talking about my feelings."

Bob's expression was the same as a child who's just discovered that throwing a temper tantrum doesn't get him another cookie. "You really have changed, Elise."

"If so, it's the first time in thirty-five years," she said heavily. "Come on. Amy's waiting."

The rock band made up of students from a nearby community college was still setting up when they arrived. Amy, wearing the new dress she had bought herself, left to repair her damp curls, and Bob went to help the band haul in more equipment. Elise wandered around the crêpe-paper-bedecked gymnasium talking to the students who were already there and commiserating with the chaperoning parents. More students arrived until the huge gym floor no longer looked empty, and finally the band, after numerous sound checks, began to play.

Elise watched from the sidelines as the students selected partners and immediately began to gyrate around the gym. Amy was dancing with Greg Thompson, and to Elise's jaded eye, she was the prettiest girl there. Her pale-golden curls set off her clear skin and light-gray eyes, and she had a smile that most girls her age would die for. Just four weeks into the first term, Amy showed signs of being one of the most popular girls in her class. She hadn't been chosen to represent the sophomores tonight, but Elise had been there when the votes were counted. She knew just how close the totals had been.

Bob came to Elise's side and stood with her watching the teenagers dull the finish on the handsome maple floor. "We're supposed to let them dance for a while, then I'm going to announce a ladies' choice."

"That's hopelessly old-fashioned. The girls are already choosing the boys." Elise pointed to the other side of the room where a girl was leading a boy onto the dance floor where they were waiting for the music to start again.

"I'd better not see Amy do that."

Elise couldn't tell if Bob was kidding. She wasn't sure if he knew, either. But just as she opened her mouth to comment, she saw Amy cross the room and disappear into a cluster of boys who were standing by the gym door. She reappeared holding Clay Tyson's hand.

Elise wasn't sure what surprised her most, the fact that Amy would ask Clay to dance or that Clay would even be there. She knew that the tutoring sessions were going well. Every once in a while Amy let slip some remark about Clay, although most of the time she seemed to be guarding her comments about him. Elise knew that Clay was rapidly outdistancing his tutor and that Amy couldn't believe how smart he was or how much he re-membered. She even knew that Amy was now spending three afternoons a week with Clay rather than the two they had originally agreed upon. What she didn't know was how the tutoring sessions were affecting their personal relationship. Obviously she was going to find out tonight.

"Who is Amy dancing with now?" Bob asked, squinting across the room.

"Clay Tyson," Elise answered, preparing to do battle.

"He's got nerve asking my daughter to dance."

Elise's vision clouded with anger. "For your information, your daughter asked him to dance."

Bob's answer was a growl that was easily interpreted. "Why would she do that?"

"Because she can see what a nice kid he is, even if her father can't."

"What are you talking about?"

"I know you're picking on him in class, Bob. I've heard it from more than one source. I can't imagine a teacher doing that to a student, but obviously Amy doesn't share your prejudices."

Bob ignored everything but her last comment. "I don't want her hanging around with some hippie trouble-maker."

Elise replied as calmly as she could. "He's not a hippie, and he's not a troublemaker. He's a kid who's having a confusing year and needs a friend. How can you object if Amy shows him the kindness you've taught her?"

"I still don't like it."

"It's one dance, Bob. They aren't eloping."

But it was more than once dance. Seemingly oblivious to the angry stares of her father, Amy danced with Clay so many times that eventually most of the rest of the boys stopped asking her. She chose him whenever she could, and Clay, obviously reticent at first, began to ask her to dance whenever she was free.

Clay was a marvelous dancer. The fact surprised Elise, but she supposed that dancing was one of the things he had picked up at Destiny just like he had picked up wonderful writing skills and a knowledge of poetry that was outstanding. His education might have been unbalanced, but he hadn't spent his fifteen years doing nothing. And apparently he had spent some portion of them dancing.

Someone dimmed the lights, and then the band chose a slow tune. Students who had begun the evening acting shy cuddled up to each other and swayed in time to the music. Elise hummed along; it was an old Beatles tune, a surprise in the midst of a set of songs with questionable lyrics and a driving beat the folk song hero John Henry could have laid a railroad track to. But this song was dreamy and much too familiar.

"Yesterday," she whispered, as she remembered the song's title. The last time she had really listened to the song she had been locked in Sloane's arms and they had been drifting dreamily around this same floor. Then, interested only in tomorrow, the song had been nothing but a lovely melody with words she could sing along with. Now it forced her to remember her own yesterdays.

Elise caught sight of Amy and Clay. Amy's head came just to the bottom of Clay's ear, and she was leaning against him, arms wrapped loosely around his neck as they moved around the room. They were a good-looking couple. Clay looked particularly handsome dressed in dark-brown slacks and a yellow oxford shirt with a dark tie; Amy's pale-rose dress set off her lovely coloring. But nothing they wore compared with the smiles on their faces. They were happy to be together, obviously thinking about their tomorrows just as she and Clay's father had done. Elise wanted to go to them, to tell them to step carefully, to cherish this time in their lives. Young love was so fragile; tomorrow was so fragile.

Elise blinked back tears, ashamed of her own sentimentality. She was standing at a high school dance letting the past drain all that had once been satisfying out of her. If she didn't take care, she would find herself doing something stupid just to feel alive again.

The band seemed to sense the mellow mood of the crowd and swung into another chorus of the song to give the boys a chance to pull their partners a little closer. Elise's gaze followed Amy and Clay. They didn't seem upset that they would have to dance a little longer. Someone else did seem to be upset, however.

As Elise watched, Bob strode on to the dance floor and clamped his hand on Amy's shoulder. Even though she was across the darkened room, Elise could tell that Bob's expression was angry. He said something to Amy and Clay, and Clay said something back to him. Amy's hand flew to her mouth and she turned and fled across the room and out the wide gym doors.

Clay started to follow, but another sophomore boy who had been dancing nearby and had obviously heard the whole thing grabbed his arm to detain him. Bob said something else to Clay and then melted into the crowd of spectators on the sidelines.

Elise knew where her duty lay. She wanted to confront Bob and find out what he had said to cause such a commotion; she wanted to question Clay, who was now the

center of attention. Most of all, she wanted to comfort
Amy who was somewhere outside in the gray drizzle. She
turned and followed Amy's path, calling her name.

"Amy?"

Amy was nowhere in sight. Had she decided to walk
home? It was unlikely, since her house was a good three
miles away. Elise tried to imagine what she would do under the same circumstances. Where could you go to sit
and be alone at Miracle Springs High? Elise tried the
parking lot, peering into Bob's car, and when that didn't
bear fruit, she walked to the portico behind the school
where students waited for buses. There, on one of the
stone benches, she found Amy in a forlorn huddle.

Without a word, Elise sat down and put her arms
around her. Amy sighed, wiping tears off her cheeks. She
leaned her head against Elise's shoulder.

Elise brushed Amy's curls back from her forehead.
"Do you want to tell me what happened?"

Amy sniffed. "My father behaved like an ass."

Elise let the small lapse in vocabulary pass unnoticed.
"I saw him stop you and Clay while you were dancing."

"He's been glaring at me all evening, but I never
thought he'd do something so dumb."

"Did he tell you to stop dancing with Clay?"

"Worse! He pulled us apart and told Clay to get his
hands off me, that I wasn't some kind of floozy for him
to maul."

Unfortunately Elise could imagine Bob saying just
that, archaic language and all. What was the right thing
to do now—explain Bob's feelings? Should she attempt
to patch up this quarrel between father and daughter to
the best of her ability? Or should she simply tell the truth,
that she too thought Bob had behaved like an ass?

Elise finally compromised. "Your dad was wrong to say anything to you, but he did it because he was worried."

"He wasn't worried!" Amy sat up straight and glared at Elise. "He was furious! He doesn't want his little girl to have a life of her own, especially one that includes Clay Tyson. He hates Clay. I don't know why; I wish I did."

"I'm afraid that's my fault," Elise said softly.

"What's your fault?"

"My fault he hates Clay."

"Why?" Despite herself, Amy's voice lost some of its angry edge.

"It's a long story, but it involves Clay's father. In a strange way, I think your father is jealous of something that happened years ago. Clay looks like his father and so he's a constant reminder to your dad of the past."

"He calls him that 'hippie kid.' I don't even know what he really means by that, but if it's true, I like hippies!"

Elise smiled. "I didn't know you and Clay were such good friends. Didn't that happen kind of suddenly?"

"I don't know." Amy dug her teeth into her lower lip. "I guess," she admitted finally. "At first I thought he was really strange. He's not like anybody else I've ever met. But after I got used to him, I decided I liked him. We've been eating lunch together, and I've been tutoring him. Last Saturday I met him at the springs, and we went swimming with some other people."

"So he is your boyfriend?"

"No. Nothing like that. We're just friends," Amy protested.

Now Elise understood why Clay had been looking happier. He no longer seemed to be as haunted, as detached. He still didn't take part in the horseplay going on around him at school, but he no longer seemed to be so completely alone either. Once or twice Elise had seem him exchange words with other students, and once, after she'd read one of his poems aloud in English class, she'd seen two or three other kids stop to praise him before they left for their next period. Amy's acceptance of Clay had made him more acceptable to the others.

Faced with Bob's bullheadedness, Elise tried to decide what to do. She didn't want to make the situation any worse, but neither did she want to keep Amy from facing the truth. Silently she damned Bob Cargil for causing this trouble. Then she spoke. "Your father isn't ever going to approve of Clay, Amy. Not even if you remain 'just friends.'"

"I don't care! Clay's my friend. I'm going to keep seeing him whether Dad approves or not."

"That could be pretty tough," Elise cautioned. "On both you and Clay."

"If he keeps bothering Clay, I'll go to Mr. Greeley myself," Amy vowed. "I'll tell him my own father is picking on a student!"

They both knew she wouldn't visit the principal, but Elise was still pleased by Amy's spunk. Amy would never fall victim to her father as Elise had fallen victim to her mother. When the time came for Amy to make the break from Bob, she would.

"Well, before it gets to that point," Elise said, "let me talk to your dad. I'll try and straighten him out for you."

"Could you?"

"I can try."

Amy put her arms around Elise's neck and gave her a hug. "Thanks."

"Now, let's get back inside. I'll say something gentle to your father like," she cleared her throat and made her tone menacing, "Bob, if you cause another scene Amy and I together will pull every remaining hair out of your head." Elise smiled at Amy's giggle. "And in the meantime, until I can really talk to him, no more slow dances with Clay unless you stand a good foot apart. Deal?"

"Deal," Amy said with a sigh. "I just wish my dad didn't teach here. I wish he laid bricks, or worked on the *Banner*, or raised racehorses."

"We'll do what we can to make it easier."

After another quick hug they both rose to their feet and began their walk back to the gym.

Inside, Elise skirted the edge of the floor until she was standing beside Bob. She watched as Amy defiantly sought out Clay to ask him to dance with her. Elise could feel Bob stiffen next to her. She didn't even look at him. "Bob," she said under her breath, "if you so much as move one foot in Amy's direction I'll follow you and make a scene like none this school has ever known."

"Stay out of this, Elise."

"I won't. I'm the closest thing to a mother that girl has ever had, and as such, I'm telling you that if you keep this up, you're going to lose her for sure. She likes Clay; he's not doing anything he shouldn't; and the more you make of it the more they'll make of it." She faced him. "You're picking on Clay because once, a long time ago, his father and I were lovers."

"That's ridiculous!"

"It's the truth." Elise turned back to the dance floor. "Sloane may be back in town, but he has nothing to do with you and me. And Clay has nothing to do with you and me. Don't make him a scapegoat."

Bob was silent, and Elise imagined she could feel the tension emanating from his body. But the evening passed without another confrontation, even when Clay and Amy danced the last slow dance together.

Finally the long night ended. Kids streamed out to the parking lot to find their cars or to wait for their parents. Amy and Clay stood by the door saying goodbye, and Elise demanded that Bob help her thank the chaperoning parents until she saw that Clay had gone.

With obvious reluctance, Amy joined them. "I'm ready to go," she told Elise, refusing to acknowledge her father.

To his credit, Bob looked a little sheepish. Faced with Amy's withdrawal, he seemed to reconsider what he'd done. "Let's go out for ice cream," he said with false joviality.

"No thank you," Amy answered coldly. "I want to go home."

"Elise, how about you? Wouldn't you like some ice cream?"

Elise was tired. The emotional scene with Amy had taken its toll. She felt unstrung. She could not face being the buffer between father and daughter anymore that night. They would have to be left alone eventually; it might as well be now. "No. In fact, I think I'm going to walk home. You two go on without me."

"But it's raining," Bob objected.

Suddenly Elise didn't care about anything except getting away from everyone who made demands on her. "I like the rain."

"Your dress..."

"Is cotton and will wash nicely," Elise finished for him. "Thanks for the ride over." She bent and kissed Amy's cheek. "I'll see you on Monday," she told her. "Have a good weekend." Without another word to either of them she headed for the gym doors.

SLOANE WAITED while Clay slid into the front seat of the car and slammed his door. Then he pulled out into the steady stream of cars heading down Hope Avenue. "How was the dance?"

"All right."

Sloane searched for a way to prolong the conversation. "Got your eye on anyone in particular?"

"No."

Sloane wondered if Clay had danced at all. It had surprised him that the boy had wanted to go. He had showed no interest in any other aspect of high school social life. Other than his tutoring sessions, he seemed to have no contact with any of the teenagers in town. According to Aunt Lillian, however, Clay's relationship with Amy Cargil was progressing nicely enough to make up for whatever other friends he lacked. Perhaps Amy was the reason that Clay had attended tonight's dance, even if he wouldn't admit it.

"Look! There's Miss Ramsey." Clay pointed ahead of them. Sloane realized his son was correct. Elise, with neither umbrella nor raincoat, was hiking along through the light rain.

"What on earth is she doing out in this?" Sloane passed Elise, then slowed down and pulled over to the side of the road just ahead of her. He opened his door and stood beside the car. "Elise, get in. You're getting soaked."

"I want to get soaked," she muttered, without so much as a glance in his direction.

Sloane caught up with her, getting splashed by a passing car as he did. "Elise, this is crazy." He caught her arm. "Are you all right?"

"No, I'm not all right." Elise pulled her arm from his grasping fingers. "I'm not all right at all." She faced him, raindrops beaded on her forehead and in her eye-lashes like tiny diamonds. "I'm going to do what *I* want to do for once. I'm going to walk home even if the heavens open any moment and drop hail as big as golf balls. Then I'm going inside and I'm going to fix the world's largest hot toddy and drink myself witless. And then, if I haven't had too much to put me out for the night, I'm going to lie awake until dawn and fantasize about what my life would be like now if I'd left this god-awful place years ago when I should have!" Without another word she turned and continued down Hope Avenue.

Sloane watched Elise go, torn between picking her up and putting her in his car and following her to try and talk some sense into her. In the end he did neither. He walked back to the car and slid under the steering wheel.

"She doesn't want a ride?" Clay asked, a worried expression on his face.

"I think she needs to be alone, son," Sloane said. "Something's upset her."

Clay wondered if Sloane realized he'd just called him son. The word had sounded so strange, almost like an endearment. An endearment from Sloane? It was just one more puzzling thing in a puzzling night. He sat back as Sloane started the car and pulled carefully back on to the avenue.

ELISE TOOK HER TIME getting home. The heavens did open, although it was sheets of silver rain that deluged her, not hail. She hadn't gone walking in the rain for more years than she could remember.

Her father had been the one to introduce her to the pleasures of rain and splashing in puddles. He had been a true outdoorsman, happy in any kind of weather, as much—and Elise had known it even then—to get away from his nagging wife as for any other reason. He had taken Elise with him whenever he could, although he'd never had the energy to stand up to Jeanette Ramsey when she refused to let Elise go. But Elise had treasured their few times together. She had loved her father, even with his weaknesses, and it had devastated her when he had been killed right before her high school graduation.

The accident had been senseless. Her father had been fishing; someone else had been poaching alligators. Her father had got in the way. The poacher had never been found, but there had been no suspicion of foul play. It had just been one of those freak things that happened. One stray bullet—one life had ended and others had changed. Her own life had never been set right again.

Sloane had understood her sorrow, but he had not understood her need to help her mother by staying in Miracle Springs for the summer. Perhaps he had seen the truth more clearly than she. Perhaps he had realized that she was going to end up with all the life sucked out of her and all her dreams buried too deeply to retrieve. Perhaps it was fear of watching her slow disintegration, rather than his own restlessness, that had made him jettison his birthplace the moment he was free to go.

At her house, Elise stepped on to the front porch and shook herself like a Labrador retriever coming out of a lake. Drops of water flew and the wet skirt of her dress clung to her knees. She slipped out of her shoes and flung the door open, leaving it that way as she walked through the house. She wanted to hear the rain.

In the kitchen, she opened the back door too, oblivious to the threat of mosquitoes and flies. As she warmed up milk she stood staring at the backyard. Her fingers found the pins that were holding her hair in a restrained chignon, and she pulled them out, tossing them on a counter. The wet length of her hair blanketed her back as she turned to the stove and tested the milk. She poured it in a cup and completed the toddy with a dollop of honey and a double shot of Jack Daniels.

Without changing into dry clothes she found her way to the front porch glider and rocked, listening to the rain, as she sipped the warm drink.

The night and her walk home had done one thing for her. They had shaken her out of her depression. Depression was an absence of feeling, a blue-gray haze that dulled all of life's glories. No, she was no longer depressed. She was sad. She was angry. She was bone-deep lonely. She was so many things that they were all tied up inside her trying to fight their way loose. Elise wasn't sure which was worse, depression or this writhing, jumbled mass of emotions. She took another sip of the toddy and closed her eyes.

She had no idea how long she'd been sitting that way before she heard footsteps on the porch and the sound of a man's voice in front of her.

"You didn't even change your clothes."

Without opening her eyes, she knew who was there. "Go away, Sloane. Even I'm entitled to be miserable once in a while." Elise felt his warmth beside her and the heaviness of the glider with two bodies on it. She ignored him, taking another long swallow of the toddy.

"You always did have a temper, only it was so well hidden I was one of the few who ever got to see it."

"You deserved to see it. You were rotten, selfish and totally unforgiving." She drained the rest of the toddy with one big gulp.

"I was all those things. I was also madly in love with you."

Elise snorted.

"You doubt that?"

"My memory doesn't extend back that far." She opened her eyes. "Why are you here?"

"I was worried about you."

"That's a first."

"I thought you didn't remember back that far."

"Go away, Sloane."

"You're not all right, are you?"

She turned her face up to his. "No, I'm not all right. I haven't been all right since our friendly little moonlight swim, and I probably won't be all right until you leave town. There, do you feel happier knowing that?" She stood, opening her arms for his examination. "What you have here, Sloane, is a sexually frustrated middle-aged woman pining for a fantasy lover. It's a nasty situation. Truly nasty." She spun around and stalked back into the house, ending up in the kitchen where she poured more milk in the pan to warm.

"Why are you frustrated? Are the men in this town blind?" Sloane was standing behind her, but Elise didn't turn at his words. "I can't believe all of them, single and married, aren't beating a path to your door."

"Did you see a path?" Elise put her hands on the edge of the stove and leaned against it, staring at the burner. "Do you want the truth? You'll find it hysterically funny. It's been years since I've made love to a man, and there's only been one since you left town."

"Cargil?"

"Does it matter? I'm just a dried-up, unhappy old maid. I'm just what you said I'd be if I stayed in this town. You've been vindicated, Sloane. You were right; I was wrong."

"Elise." Sloane didn't know what to say. He was shocked and sick at this waste of a wonderful woman. He was furious that she'd given herself to that oaf, Cargil, and more furious that she hadn't found someone worthy to love her. He put his hands on her arms and felt her stiffen, but he didn't move away. "Why, when you have so much to give?"

"Nobody but you ever saw that," she said, her words punctuated by peculiar little gulping sounds.

"I'm sure that's not true."

"Sloane, the comforter. This is hard to believe."

Sloane rubbed his hands up and down her arms in a soothing gesture. "What happened tonight to upset you?"

"Nothing that should make me act like such a fool." Elise watched the milk bubble around the edges of the pan. It was time to turn it off, but she couldn't make herself move.

"You're not acting like a fool. You're upset. Hurt."

"Let's not forget lonely. Do you know what that word means? Do you know what it feels like to be a tiny little part of lots of lives but not important to anyone?"

Sloane reached around in front of her and switched off the burner. Then he put his hands on her shoulders and turned her to face him. "You're tired, cold, wet. Look, you're shivering. Go upstairs and change. I'll make you another hot toddy. Then we can talk."

"I don't need talk."

Sloane felt Elise's words burn right through him. Her eyes were wide with emotion and her control seemed to have completely vanished. "What do you need?" But even before she spoke, he felt his body stir in response to the inevitable answer.

"I need to be loved. Right now. Will you love me, Sloane?"

CHAPTER EIGHT

ELISE SEARCHED SLOANE'S FACE until she could find no undiscovered clues. She dropped her gaze to the ground and suffered waves of humiliation as she turned back to the stove. She wanted to ask him to leave, but her mouth was so dry she was afraid she wouldn't be able to enunciate the words. She picked up the milk with a shaking hand and poured it into her cup. This time the whiskey flowed without prior measurement. She just poured until the cup couldn't hold another drop, and she didn't even bother adding honey.

"I don't know what to say," Sloane said from behind her.

"I got my answer. Please go."

It took two hands to lift the cup to her mouth. Her first sip was straight Jack Daniels since she hadn't bothered to stir the drink. It burned a fiery path down her throat and through her chest, and she swallowed convulsively to keep from coughing. She waited for the sound of Sloane's retreat, but the house remained silent.

She felt his hand on her back, stroking her hair, and as if he'd given a signal, her eyes overflowed. Now, in addition to pleading for lovemaking from a man who obviously didn't want her, she was crying. She wondered what she could do to bring herself any lower.

"I don't need your sympathy," she snapped at him, her voice unsteady.

"You've never had it. My anger, my passion, yes, but never my sympathy."

"If you're not feeling sympathy, it must be pity. God, I've sunk so low!"

"Stop it, Elise." Sloane's fingers gripped her shoulders, and he shook her lightly.

"Get out of here!" Elise slammed the half-filled cup on the stove top and turned to face him. Her fists beat on Sloane's chest. "Get out of my house!"

He stopped her assault by pulling her tightly against him and crushing her to his chest. Elise cried out, trying desperately to pull away, but he wrapped his arms around her and bent her backward, muffling her mouth against his cheek. Elise struggled, flailing her arms uselessly at her sides where Sloane had them pinned. Whatever was happening was something she had driven him to, not something he had chosen. She wanted no sacrifices, no concessions.

"Stop fighting me." Sloane held her imprisoned as his mouth bathed her face in kisses. "Calm down and stop fighting me."

Elise knew she was beyond self-control. She continued to struggle, hoping that he would grow tired and release her. She lifted a knee and aimed it where it would do the most good, but Sloane was too quick for her, thrusting his own leg between hers and clamping it tightly to block her. His arms tightened around her and his mouth continued to soothe her heated face. She managed to inch her hands up to his chest to push against him, but it was like pushing at a wall. She pulled at his clothes, trying ineffectually to scratch him, but her hands were too tightly pressed to his body.

Even in the hysteria that gripped her, Elise realized that Sloane was not going to release her until she stopped fighting. She continued to struggle against him, but the hopelessness of it was apparent to them both. When she was finally exhausted she relaxed against him, her tears soaking the collar of his shirt.

He held her as she cried until there were no tears left. His hands slipped under her hair and covered the length of her back, kneading and stroking it as she leaned against him, her breath coming in dry sobs until the sobs were gone, too.

"How many years have you needed to cry that way?" Sloane rested his cheek against her hair. "How many years have you needed someone to hold you while you did?"

Her anger was gone. She was empty of emotion, and Sloane's quiet caresses had completed the purge. "Forever," she whispered, not even sure if the words were loud enough for him to hear.

"Lise, you turn yourself inside out giving to everybody else, and you never take anything for yourself. Not even a good cry. I had to wrestle it out of you."

She was startled at the nickname; it had been seventeen years since she had heard it.

"I'm all right now." She pulled away and Sloane let her go. Elise turned to look for something to repair the damage to her tear-streaked face, but Sloane beat her to the sink, soaking the edge of a dish towel with cold water.

"Come here."

She shook her head, but he ignored her, reaching out to pull her closer. Gently, beginning with her forehead, he rubbed the wet towel over her face. Elise shut her eyes, letting him do as he wished. She could imagine what she looked like, although she was much too drained to care. She could feel the rough terry cloth slide over her nose and around her eyes. He mopped at her cheeks and her chin and then started all over again.

"You can go," she said when he seemed to have finished. She commanded her voice to be steady and rational even if inside she felt anything but. "I'm sorry I caused such a scene, but I really am all right now."

"I'm not going anywhere." Sloane leaned back against the sink and crossed his arms in front of his chest. "I was issued an invitation, and I haven't heard a withdrawal."

Elise hadn't met Sloane's gaze since she had asked him to make love to her. Now her eyes shot up to his face in surprise. "Consider it withdrawn."

"I don't think so."

Elise forced a bitter laugh. "Wouldn't that be something? You'd make love to me, and I'd be so pathetically grateful it would make you feel like God. It would be an experience to remember."

"It would be an experience to remember."

"Look, Sloane, I don't know what got into me to ask you such a thing, but whatever it was is gone now."

"Is it?" He reached out, and before she could object he grasped her hand. "Funny, I want you more than I ever have."

"You didn't want me. You made that obvious. Do tears and tantrums turn you on?" She tried to pull her hand from his but he wouldn't let her.

"Didn't want you?" He laughed softly. "I can't remember not wanting you. Are you talking about the night at the river? Didn't I want you then? Or how about the night I came here to settle our past and you greeted me in a sheer white robe with your hair streaming down your back? Didn't I want you then so badly that I had to get out of here before I lost whatever sense I had?"

"Sloane..."

He brought their clasped hands to her mouth to silence her. "Or tonight? Spitting at me like a drowning cat, that dress clinging to every curve of your body until my insides went liquid. Didn't I want you then?"

She turned her head. "Don't."

"Is that what you really want to say, Lise?"

"I practically threw myself at your feet, and you didn't say a word!" Elise felt a resurgence of anger, but it died quickly when she looked in Sloane's eyes.

"I felt like someone was choking the words out of me. Here you were offering me exactly what I wanted, and I knew you were only doing it because you were distraught. What could I say?"

"Yes."

Sloane shook his head. "Do I want you hating me when you wake up tomorrow? You don't give yourself to a man easily. What would it have done to you to give yourself like that?"

Was he handing her a good line or was the concern she saw in his eyes genuine? "Well, now you won't have to worry."

"You're right. Because now when I make love to you, you'll know it's my idea, too. It's what I want." He pulled her inexorably closer. "Not that you're not going to want it."

Elise could feel her heart stop, then begin to pound so fast that the beats merged into one rolling crescendo. "No. Not like this. Not because you know it's what I need."

"Have you ever known me to be charitable? I need it, too. I've never forgotten what it feels like to sink inside you and feel your life pulse around me." He dropped her hand and dug his fingers gently into her waist, pulling her ever closer. "We owe each other this night."

Only this night? Did she need to be loved that badly? "We don't owe each other anything."

"You're right. 'Owe' is the wrong word. It's not a debt; it's a gift freely given. I give myself to you, taking what I need in return. You do the same."

Elise reached up to touch Sloane's cheeks. She smoothed trembling fingertips over the faint roughness of his skin and down over the luxuriant mustache. Could she let Sloane feed this ache inside her until once more she sated herself on the only taste of heaven she'd ever known? Would one night be enough to help her get on with her life?

"Lise?"

"No one but you has ever called me that." Elise traced the fine lines around Sloane's eyes, her fingers memorizing the new additions to a face that was still very much the same. She stroked her thumbs over his eyelids when he closed them. His eyebrows were wiry, and she smoothed them, watching them spring back to life immediately. His hair was of a wiry texture, too. Her fingers fanned out to tangle in it. It was not quite curly, not quite straight. It had a resiliency that wouldn't change, not even, she suspected, when the few silver strands giving it character turned to many.

It would be so easy to forget everything. . . .

Sloane's fingers swept up and down her spine. When the rain-cooled wind from the open back door whipped through the kitchen he opened his eyes. "You're shivering. You need to get out of those wet clothes."

Elise debated what to do. He was offering her solace, warmth, pleasure. She was an adult and perfectly free to take him up on his offer; she had in fact begged him for this night of loving. So why the hesitancy? Why the doubts?

"I'm all right," she said, shivering again.

"You're asking for pneumonia."

There was not one rational reason to say no. She needed this, and Sloane said he needed it too. They were two consenting adults who—at least on some level—cared about each other. She knew Sloane would be a magnificent lover. She had spent her whole life being afraid to take what she wanted. Tonight, just for this night, she would.

She shivered again, and then laughed a little at the warning in Sloane's eyes. She felt suddenly much too shy just to invite him to her bedroom. And yet her decision seemed to have been made. They were going to make love. Even saying the words to herself increased the throbbing inside her. What should she do? Go upstairs and change into something dry, then come downstairs only to go back up again later with Sloane? She wasn't very good at this. She and Sloane had only made love outdoors or in the back seat of his mother's car. The times she had made love to Bob had been at his house when Amy was away with friends. What was the protocol now?

"I'll tell you what we'll do," Sloane said softly, as if responding to spoken words instead of thoughts. He brushed his index finger over her cheek and around her ear. "I'm going to take you upstairs and find your bathroom. Then I'm going to run a hot bath for you."

"And then?" Her eyes focused somewhere right below his.

"And then I'm going to make love to you. And it's going to be very slow and very gentle and very, very right." His finger lodged beneath her chin and lifted it a little so that she was looking right at him. "For both of us."

Elise wasn't sure that slow and gentle was what she needed. Already she could feel her body's response to his words. Her nipples tightened against the wet fabric of her dress and bra, and she felt a heated rush in the very core of her. If he could do that with only a few words...

"But first I'm going to kiss you, just the way I've wanted to kiss you all evening." His fingers spread into her hair, and he tugged gently at her chin until her mouth was close to his. She could feel his warm breath against her lips, then his lips hovering against hers, not quite making contact. The first brush of his mouth was so soft, she wasn't sure it had even happened. Inadvertently she sighed, parting her lips a little as she sought more pressure.

He pulled back to slow their pace and brushed his mouth against hers again. "Do you want more?" he asked.

"You always were an awful tease." Elise opened her eyes without moving away. "An awful tease and an awful flirt."

"And you always were so easy to do both with. How could I help myself?"

She smiled a little, aware that Sloane's words were having just the effect he had clearly intended. She was already less anxious. "You could do anything you wanted with me. I never knew how to stop you. I never wanted to stop you."

Sloane bent toward her. "I was always too out of control to take it slowly for long." This time his mouth found hers with more passion. He wet her lips with his tongue then slid it into her mouth to trace the straight line of her teeth.

Elise clung to him, parting her lips to give him easy access. Up against the full length of his body she could feel him stir to life as one kiss melted into another. Any doubts she'd had about his involvement, his desire, were put to rest. Sloane wanted her; this was not charity. Their lovemaking might be slow and gentle, but it wouldn't be passionless.

He sucked lightly on her full bottom lip, then took it between his teeth and tugged gently. Elise could feel the tugging deep inside her as if everything was connected, one part of her a conduit of sensation for another.

"What are you smiling about?" Sloane asked, pushing away from the sink so that they were standing straight but still touching.

Elise slipped her arms around his neck and pulled his head back down to hers. "I was wondering how anyone could top the miracle of the human body."

Sloane laughed and scooped her into his arms, swinging her feet off the ground as he did. "Even soaking wet you don't weigh as much as you did when you were eighteen."

"You're just stronger."

"Let's go upstairs."

He held her off the ground, walking to the steps where he set her down. Obediently Elise turned and began her climb, then returned to the bottom to grasp Sloane's hand and pull him up with her. "After telling me we were coming up here, were you waiting for an invitation?"

"Exactly."

She realized he'd been giving her one more chance to back out. She was surprised at his patience. Sloane had never been patient, and she was grateful for this new sensitivity. It strengthened her resolve and heightened her desire. "I only issue one invitation," she said, her voice provocative.

"But that one wasn't specifically for your bed."

Elise squeezed his hand. "You're right. I'd intended to knock you to the kitchen floor and have my way with you between the sink and the refrigerator."

In the second-floor hallway she paused outside the bathroom door. The idea of a hot bath was a good one, but she wondered if the time away from Sloane would give the doubts she was suppressing a chance to reassert themselves. "I'm warmer now," she said hesitantly. "I don't think I need a bath. I just need to get out of these clothes."

"We're going to do both."

She shivered at the promise in his voice, but she pushed on. "I don't want to leave you right now."

"I'm not going to leave you, I'm going to get in with you." Sloane entered the bathroom, still holding her hand. His eyes took in the old-fashioned claw-footed bathtub. "Perfect."

Elise had to remind herself to breathe. She watched as he bent and pushed the rubber stopper into place, then turned on the water and adjusted its temperature. He straightened and faced her. Even though they weren't touching now, Elise felt as if Sloane were stroking her body. Her hand went to the top button of the bodice of her dress and froze there. She looked down at her own long fingers wrapped around the dainty mother-of-pearl button. She couldn't move.

Sloane's hands covered hers. He pried her fingers from the button and unfastened it himself.

"What would your mother say if she knew what we were about to do in her bathtub?" Sloane whispered in her ear.

It was the last thing in the world Elise had expected him to say. She felt a surge of laughter start at the tips of her toes and progress up her body. She couldn't speak, she couldn't do anything except give in to it. How had Sloane known that the same thought had crossed her mind?

"I've never even kissed a man in this house," she told him when she could.

He unfastened the next button and caressed the newly revealed skin with his thumbs. He smiled at the noise she made deep in her throat. "I could never understand how you could be such a perfectly proper daughter and still have a streak of sensuality as deep as the Wehachee running through you."

She trembled with anticipation as the third button was undone. She was grateful for Sloane's conversation. He had sensed her fears, and his voice was soothing. He was talking to her like the old friend he was as he undressed her like the ex-lover he was. The combination was irresistible. She lowered her eyes and watched his hands as she answered him.

"Split personality. I learned to cut one off from the other, at least when I was around you. I never needed to do it any other time."

He unbuttoned two more; now the dress was open down to her waist. His fingers brushed the soft skin of her stomach as he reached behind her under the dress and unhooked her bra. "Such a waste." He stepped closer and his mouth nuzzled her neck. "All these years, when I allowed myself to think about you, I'd imagine you married to some lucky Miracle Springs businessman who didn't deserve you. I pictured you having your mama over for Sunday dinner and running over here every night to be sure she'd taken her pills or tucked herself into bed properly. Then I pictured you going home to your husband and shedding your clothes and your inhibitions in his arms." Reluctantly he abandoned the smoothness of her back and his hands came out of the dress to settle on the dainty linen collar. Slowly he pulled the fabric down over her shoulders, over her arms, until it was free to her waist. "I never thought of you alone. Why did you let that happen?"

"You spoiled me for anyone else." Elise reached behind him and locked her fingers in his hair. "I tried. With Bob."

Sloane snorted against her ear.

"I dated others. Every time a man would get close, I'd realize he wasn't you."

"I'm surprised you didn't think that was a recommendation."

"For a while I did. But when it got to the point where it was either full steam ahead or breaking away, I broke away. In my own naive fashion, I think I was being faithful to you."

Sloane was shaken by her admission. His hands tightened spasmodically, and he pulled her closer against him. "Lise, did you think I was coming back?"

She sighed, and her head dropped against his shoulder. "No. But I had this dream of coming after you."

"Why didn't you?"

Elise wondered what there was about standing almost naked against a man that loosened her tongue so. "I almost did once."

"What stopped you?" he asked harshly.

"Fear. I knew you were in college by then, at Goddard. I bought a ticket to fly to Boston. But when the time came for me to get on the plane, I couldn't do it." She pulled her hands from his hair and placed them lightly on his shoulders. "What would you have done if I'd showed up at your door?"

Sloane truly didn't know. He shook his head in response.

"I knew it was too late for us," she said, her hands falling to her side. "But I should have come anyway. Then I would have known. I could have got on with my life."

Sloane reached around behind her to hook his fingers under the scrap of lace that had bound her breasts. The bra fell to the floor.

His eyes closed for a moment, but watching him, Elise knew it was not disappointment that held him in its grip. A curious strain seemed to settle over him. "You should have come." He opened his eyes once more. Almost hesitantly he reached up and stroked one breast with his fingertips. Elise could feel her flesh tighten. "How can you still be so beautiful? And so responsive?" He shook his head.

Elise unhooked the black leather belt that held the dress at her waist and felt the fabric billow around her feet. She slid her fingers under the elastic of her half slip and pants as Sloane watched her, and pulled them down over her hips until they were lying with the dress. Bending slightly she rolled down the tops of her thigh-high stockings until they were off, too. She straightened to face him, her hair falling over her shoulders like a veil.

She knew she had changed. Years didn't pass without changes. She had neither borne nor suckled children to mark her body with those wonderful signs of transition, but age had still left its imprint on her. Nothing was as firm or as smooth as it had once been. The straight planes of her body were softer now; she was rounder in the hips and thighs, her breasts no longer tilted perkily to the sky. She was thirty-five, not seventeen, but she was curiously undisturbed that Sloane would see her this way. She was still the same woman, even more of one than the teenage lover he remembered.

Sloane reached behind him to turn off the water, but his eyes never stopped traveling the length of her body. He drew a deep breath as she lifted her arms to twist her hair and sweep it into a thick knot on top of her head, fastening it with a barrette that had lain on the counter over the sink.

He stepped forward and settled his hands at her waist, then lifted her and turned to place her in the tub. She gasped as the heated water stung her skin, but she settled down into it and turned to watch him undress.

Elise had seen Sloane clad only in swimming trunks, and she had tried to ignore the response of her body to the firm, hair-roughened skin and the broad expanse of his shoulders. But now there was no reason to ignore anything. She let her eyes drift slowly over each part of his body as it was revealed to her. Sloane was older too, and yet the changes in his body were good ones. He was broader, more padded, but the padding was muscle and firm, supple flesh. He was stronger, more solid. If possible he was more desirable. She felt a wave of internal heat at the realization.

"Feeling warmer?" Sloane asked, one corner of his mouth lifting in a smile as if he could read the response of her body in her eyes.

Elise could feel the heat travel to her cheeks and she knew she was blushing. Thirty-five and she still blushed like a virgin under his gaze. "Not warm enough," she said, holding out her arms to him to counteract her response.

If he was surprised by her invitation, he didn't show it. He stepped over the edge of the tub and slid into the water behind her. Then he slipped a leg around each side of her and cradled her body between his muscular thighs. The intimacy, the sheer luxury of being surrounded by a man, by Sloane, destroyed whatever shyness she'd felt. She was too alive with feeling, too suffused with waves of desire to feel anything else. Elise leaned back against Sloane's chest and moaned softly as his hands settled at her breasts.

"You fit my hands so perfectly. You always did," Sloane murmured in her ear. He cupped the warm water and drizzled it slowly over her breasts, then smiled at the small noise Elise made in response. "When I was seventeen I thought that was no accident. I fantasized an understanding being somewhere in the skies who'd created us to fit together so well."

Elise leaned more fully against him and began to stroke the tops of his legs with her palms. The hair-covered skin against the smoothness of her hands was a homecoming. How well she remembered this feeling. How she had longed for the special freedom of exploring a man, knowing every inch of his body intimately. Even as she thought the words, she knew it was not just any man she had longed for. Only this one.

The tips of her fingers sank lower in the water to discover the sleek softness of his inner thighs. His response was immediate.

Sloane's hands tightened on her breasts and his thumbs brushed against her nipples. Elise's breath caught in her throat.

She felt Sloane's lips against her shoulder. Slowly he nuzzled his way up to her ear. His teeth caught her earlobe and tugged lightly on it. Then his tongue traced the graceful whorls, dipping inside to send sparks through a body that was already on fire.

As he played with her ear, his hands slid lower, skimming the taut satin skin of her abdomen to rest at the juncture of her legs. With a measured cadence he began to stroke the soft black curls he found.

It was only then that Elise realized how great was her need. She caught her breath and held it, fighting back the instant response to his touch. Her hunger embarrassed her, humiliated her. What would Sloane think? They'd only just begun.

She turned a little so that her side was against him and she could see his face. She felt she had to explain, to apologize. "Do you know what this is doing to me?"

Sloane suspected. He nodded his head in response.

She was ashamed of her needs, ashamed that she had let them build until they were driving her to rush something she'd wanted for years. "I feel like I'm coming apart inside," she mourned.

"That's what it's supposed to feel like." He bent his head and found her lips, turning her around with his hands at her waist until she was lying across him, her breasts rubbing against his chest. "Has it been that long, Lise?"

"Too long. God, much too long."

There was no more reason to talk, to rehash a past that had cheated them both. They were starved for each other and for forgetfulness. Sloane explored her water-slick body as he explored the tastes and textures of her mouth. Elise pressed against him, forgetting to be careful, to be afraid. Sloane was hers for this evening. That was more of him than she'd ever dreamed of having again.

She tried to know each inch of his body. She wanted to remember it all, to be able to pull out and cherish the sensation of his skin against her fingers, her lips, her breasts. Frantically she drove herself to make memories. If this was to be a reprieve from her loneliness, let it be complete, she prayed. Let it be a moment caught in time.

Sloane's response was immediate, although he seemed to hold himself back as if he were afraid to give in to the depth of his desire. "Lise, I want to be gentle," he said finally. "If it's been such a long time for you it might hurt ..." He tried to push her away, to slow down the passion that had ignited so fully.

Elise ignored him, seeking the probing evidence of his desire for her. She'd done little to excite him directly, yet he was completely ready for her, hot and hard and more than willing. She couldn't believe he really wanted to wait. Grasping his hardened flesh with her fingers she lowered herself over him, bringing him home where he belonged. Her cry was exultant. Sloane was truly hers once more.

He shut his eyes and clasped her against his chest. He could feel the shudders run through her body. He knew it would take very little to turn them into full-blown quakes. "We never had any control," he apologized as she moved against him again.

"I don't need control. I need you." The ecstasy she felt at his presence inside her was so overwhelming that it surprised even her. Her body, set free to pursue its goal of pleasure, ignored all the warning signals from her brain. It carried her along like the tumult of a rising river, and she could only go with it. Each time she moved, each time Sloane moved, she experienced such an intense agony of sensation that she knew she was going to explode.

Yet she didn't. Sloane was holding back as if he were afraid his own passion would hurt her. He had promised her slow and gentle lovemaking. He seemed determined to uphold that promise no matter what it cost him.

"Don't you want me?" she asked him finally, her words as heated as the sensations flooding her. "Have you forgotten what it's like to want me?"

Suddenly she could feel his control slip. His fingers dug into her and he turned her slightly so that he could plunge deeper into her flesh. "I never forgot. Never."

She gasped at his words and at the increase of pressure. She felt herself spinning away from him even as he held her closer. He thrust once more and she came apart against him, crying out his name. He thrust once more and joined her.

Afterward they lay in the cooling bath, their breath mingled and slower. Elise rubbed her hand over Sloane's chest to spread the beaded droplets of water and watch them condense. She was strangely embarrassed to meet his eyes. She had orchestrated this, rushed them to a conclusion that should have taken much longer. But she had needed him, wanted him so badly. And that need and desire had been communicated to him. She felt painfully vulnerable.

"Let's get out of here before you get chilled again," Sloane said finally. He sat up straighter, bringing her with him. Elise pushed away to stand and step out of the tub. She was numb with uncertainty. Did she dress again? Did he? She turned to see if she could read an answer in his eyes. She saw in them a duplication of her own doubts.

She turned and took a bath towel off the rack on the door and began to dry herself, carefully avoiding any more direct glances at Sloane. She wanted only to maintain whatever dignity was left to her. She heard Sloane get out of the tub and then felt him tug the towel from her fingers. He dried her, using long, gentle strokes. Then he unpinned her hair and used the towel to blot the moisture from the long strands. When he was finished, he dried himself, then lifted her chin and forced her eyes to his.

"I don't know what to do," he told her. "I want to stay the night. Will you let me?"

Elise wondered if she had misread Sloane's feelings. Or perhaps she hadn't, and he was being kind. She had certainly made her needs clear enough. They were needs most men would be glad to oblige for a night, Sloane included.

"What do you want, Sloane?"

"This night. With you," he said, stroking the soft skin under her chin.

Elise knew a clearer statement of his intentions would never be issued. He would give her this night, even enjoy the giving, but he was warning her that it was all she could expect, no matter how powerful her own needs. It was what she had known all along and what she had feared.

"Lise?"

"What about Clay?" she hedged.

"Clay's staying at Aunt Lillian's for the night because I have to get up early tomorrow and head over to Gainesville. No one will know if I spend the night here."

"That's not exactly true, not with your car parked outside. The whole town will know."

Sloane stiffened and drew away. "That would be a problem, wouldn't it?"

It would be a problem. Short affairs in a small town were grist for the gossip mill. Elise could imagine the speculations of her neighbors. They would know just exactly what she had given Sloane. They would also know how little it had mattered to him.

"I have to live here," she countered quietly. "What people think matters to me."

"How about what I think?"

Elise lowered her eyes. "I know what you think."

"What's that supposed to mean?"

The humiliation she had successfully suppressed came rising to the surface. "I threw myself at you tonight. Completely. I imagine it was flattering and scary as hell at the same time. But you don't have to be scared, Sloane. I know what tonight was, and I know what it wasn't. I just don't want the whole population of Miracle Springs to know the same things."

"What do you mean, what it was and what it wasn't? It hasn't had time to be anything compared to what it could be."

"Tonight was a one-night stand. I'd rather not share that piece of news."

"Fine." Sloane reached for his clothes and began to dress. "In other words, now that I've served my purpose, I can get the hell out of your house before your neighbors begin to speculate that you're really flesh and blood."

She wanted to protest, but Sloane was turning toward the door, one hand buttoning his shirt as he did. "I won't be back," he said, "even if you get all charged up again and invite me. I won't be used like some kind of gigolo to relieve your sexual discomfort. I thought we could have something different, but I was a fool. You're no different than you ever were. You put everybody else's needs and opinions before your own because then you don't have to make decisions. You're a coward, plain and simple."

"What do you mean?" she asked, suddenly afraid that she had misjudged him. "Tell me what you mean!"

"Figure it out by yourself. I've got to go move my car!" Sloane slammed the bathroom door and the explosion resounded through the silent house. Elise leaned against the sink with her eyes closed and listened to the angry sound of his retreating footsteps.

CHAPTER NINE

AMY TURNED UP THE COLLAR on her gray wool jacket to cover the back of her neck and pulled the front zipper a little higher. It was hard to believe that only a few weeks ago she'd been wearing shorts to school. The change in temperature that had begun the night of the Get Acquainted Dance was now firmly established. It was truly autumn. She could only be grateful she didn't live farther north, where blizzards had already been reported.

Amy tucked each of her hands under the opposite arm and stomped from foot to foot to keep warm. Kids streamed past her on their way home to seek shelter. Amy nodded her head in response to their comments, barely registering what was said to her.

The first wave of students had come and gone before she saw Clay appear in a cluster of boys walking in her direction. Yes, it was definitely Clay, deep in conversation with some of the kids in his homeroom. So deep in fact that he almost missed seeing her. Just as Amy was beginning to feel irritated at his lack of interest, his head lifted, and he looked directly at her and smiled.

That smile. She could forgive him anything for that smile. Why had it taken her so long to notice Clay? Really notice him, that is. Sure, she'd noticed—in passing—that Clay was cute the first time she'd seen him. But lots of guys were cute and worth noticing. Only a few guys were worth paying serious attention to. Clay was one of them, and it still bothered her that it had taken her so long to realize it.

"Amy!" Clay lifted his hand in greeting, then turned back to his friends. "Catch you later." In a moment he was at her side.

The November sun spilled over everything, refusing perversely to warm the earth with its rays. It glinted merrily off the golden highlights in Clay's hair, and Amy reached up to smooth a short strand that had fallen over his forehead.

Clay made an approving noise low in his throat. "If I'd known how often you were going to do that, I'd have cut my hair weeks ago."

Amy giggled, dropping her hand immediately. "If anyone had suggested you cut your hair weeks ago you would have looked at them like this." She stared at him without expression for a long moment, then giggled.

The corners of Clay's mouth lifted in a smile. "Well, weeks ago, you probably weren't available to cut it."

"When I was finished with you last Friday, you wished I hadn't been available." Amy started down the sidewalk.

"As a barber, you're a great history tutor." Clay walked beside her.

"What did you expect? You were my first customer."

"And your last. The real barber told me if I ever came in with such a mutilated mess again, he'd toss me out on my ear."

"I thought you looked like a British rock star."

"Wouldn't your father have loved that?"

The teasing comment had the effect of sobering them both. In the two months of their friendship, they had covered almost every possible subject. The one subject that was still difficult for both of them was Amy's father.

"You never did tell me what your father said about your hair," Amy said, trying to change the subject.

"Nothing much."

"Does he ever say much to you?"

"No. He stares at me a lot when he thinks I'm not paying attention. I think he wishes I'd tell him it's all a mistake, and I'm really someone else's son."

Amy was beginning to distinguish the fine gradations in Clay's tone of voice that expressed pain. Clay would never admit it, but the distant relationship he had with Sloane made him unhappy.

She tried to lighten the heavy mood they were falling into. "Maybe he just doesn't know what to say. Besides, you could be lucky. Most of the time I wish my father wouldn't say anything. What if Sloane starts talking to you and you find out he's a nerd?"

Clay rested his arm on Amy's shoulders and moved closer so that their hips brushed as they walked. "The world needs people like you, Amy."

"It needs people like you and me," she amended. "But I'm not sure it needs people like our fathers."

As if to punctuate the end of her sentence, a horn blasted on the road beside them. Amy turned to see her father beckoning to her from the front seat of his car. "I thought Daddy had a faculty meeting," she said forlornly, "or I'd have just met you at your aunt's." She waved back. "I'd better get this over with."

Clay stood on the sidewalk and watched Amy walk slowly to the car as if she already knew just what was going to occur and her feet were protesting the inevitable.

"Hi, Daddy." Amy opened the door but didn't move to sit down on the seat.

"Get in."

"Daddy, I'm going over to Clay's aunt's house to help him with his history homework. Mrs. Tyson will be there the whole time, and she'll drive me home when we're finished."

"Get in. You're not doing any such thing."

Amy's normally amiable expression vanished. Her jaw clenched and her eyes narrowed until she was glaring at her father. "Why not?"

"Don't question me, young lady. Get in!"

Amy took a deep breath. "No."

"What!"

"I said no. I'm not doing anything wrong. I'm helping a friend with his homework. When I'm finished, I'll be home. In plenty of time, I might add, to do the cooking and all the chores I do every day of my life. Without fuss," she added for good measure.

"How dare you talk to me like that!"

"I'm sorry, Daddy, but I'm right this time, and you've always told me to do what I know is right."

"Who do you think you are?" Bob slid toward her, as if to haul her down to the seat beside him.

Amy backed away. "Your daughter. A very good daughter who never gives you trouble. But I am going to Mrs. Tyson's house. I've been going three times a week for months now and I'll keep on going!" Amy straightened and turned to walk back to Clay.

"Three times a week for months?" Bob's voice was apoplectic. "Whose idea was this?"

"Elise's." Immediately, Amy wished she hadn't revealed the truth. There was little question what her father would do next. Elise was in for it.

"I should have known!"

With her back still turned, Amy heard the revving of the car engine and the squeal of tires. She had a sick feeling in the pit of her stomach, and she wasn't sure exactly why. Was it because she'd stood up to her father at long last? Because she had just condemned Elise to suffer her father's wrath? Or was it knowing that she and Clay might never be allowed to be together again after this afternoon?

Clay seemed to understand immediately what she was going through. He put down the books that hadn't fit in his backpack and reached for her when she joined him again. "It's going to be all right, Amy," he reassured her. "You were in the right. You didn't do anything wrong."

Amy leaned against Clay, and she knew immediately what bothered her most. She didn't want to be separated from him. More than anything, she didn't want that. "He's going to make sure you never see me again," she whispered against Clay's navy-blue jacket.

"We won't let him do that," Clay said evenly. Hesitantly he smoothed his fingers under her chin and lifted it slowly so that Amy was staring at him. Then he lowered his mouth to hers and took it with firm, steady pressure. For a first kiss, it was wonderfully effortless.

Amy blinked back tears, and her eyes shone with something else when Clay finally drew away. "If that's the way you say goodbye," she said breathlessly, "I could get to like going away."

"That's the way I say hello," he said with a shy smile. He kissed her again, an exuberant, quick kiss. "Hello, Amy."

"Hello, Clay." Amy raised her hand and let her fingers trail lightly through his hair. Then she stepped away from him, turned and began to run. "I'll beat you to your aunt's."

Clay watched Amy sprint down the sidewalk, and he suspected she was right. She was going to beat him. Amy might be able to run, but his feet felt strangely unattached to his legs. He would just float to his aunt's house. With a grin he followed her path.

ELISE RARELY DROVE her car to school. Unless she had an errand to do she walked the mile or so each way. Other women might do aerobic dancing or take up tennis to keep their weight down, but Elise walked everywhere she could with the same results.

This day was one of those rare occasions when she had reluctantly been forced to drive. She was so low on groceries that she had been compelled to eat freezer-burned waffles for her dinner the night before. Malnutrition had less appeal than eating—although neither appealed to her much. She had sat over her tasteless meal making a grocery list.

Now, one canceled faculty meeting behind her, Elise packed her little car with three bags of nutritious food and turned toward home. She had brought enough groceries to feed a family of four. She supposed her shopping spree reflected a secret desire to do just that. She liked cooking; she hated cooking for one person. On the occasions that she had a guest over for a meal, she lavished attention on her menu and cooked difficult dishes with only the freshest ingredients. When she cooked for herself she could hardly be bothered warming up fish sticks.

It said something basic about her life. She was a giver. As long as there was somebody to give to, she was happy. Of course, she was happiest if that person appreciated what he was getting. She hadn't been happy giving to a mother who had always found fault with her efforts. And she wasn't happy giving to Bob, who seemed to feel it was somehow his due. But on the occasions in her life when she had been given credit for what she did, she had been filled with happiness.

As if her mind had to take this latest realization to its obvious conclusion, she thought of Sloane. Sloane had always appreciated what she did for him. As arrogant, as impatient as he could be, Sloane had always been grateful for whatever she chose to give him, whether it was the gift of her body or something more trivial.

Sloane had always been the one to point out how little she asked for herself. He had been right. It was his biggest failing. He was almost always right. He had been right about her lack of courage. He had been right about her attempts to get approval from the wrong people. He had been right about her inability to make demands on others. Only about her reasons for rejecting him he had been wrong.

She was beyond caring what anyone in town thought of her virtue. Miracle Springs could be damned. If Sloane truly wanted her and claimed her for his own in front of the whole town, she wouldn't give anyone else's opinion a second thought. She would give him her hand and go with him gladly.

What she hadn't wanted was to suffer the humiliation of knowing he didn't want her and knowing that the town knew the same thing. She knew she had been suitable for a one-night stand, but there had been no indication on Sloane's part that he wanted anything more, not until he had blasted her with the ice-cold anger that made the weather outside today look like blazing summer. He had not understood her fear of being left high and dry, of seeing him day in and day out and longing for him with this newly awakened desire that was gnawing away her insides.

And now he would not understand her other fears. Sloane moved through life without looking anywhere except straight ahead. Not for Sloane the long reminiscences and emotional replays of the past. He had left her once without so much as a glance backward. Then he had probably put her out of his mind like a little boy's forgotten teddy bear, traded in for baseballs and roller skates. He would do the same thing the day he left Miracle Springs again. And what would she be left with? Memories?

She already had enough of those to last a lifetime. Memories were fine...if you enjoyed tormenting yourself. What joy would there be in remembering a year of love when she had to live the rest of her life without it?

Immediately, another part of Elise's mind accused her of being too careful, too controlled. It was caution mixed with a sense of duty that had kept her in Miracle Springs in the first place. Other women could abandon themselves to the future and take what came their way. Not Elise Ramsey. She opted for the secure, the known.

And with them had come a life of servitude.

Elise stopped unloading her groceries from the trunk of her car and realized just where her thoughts were leading. Being careful, taking no chances, she realized, had led her exactly to her present situation. She was a lonely spinster, unloading three bags of groceries she would never finish eating, spending every spare ounce of energy trying to convince herself that she'd made the right decisions.

If her decisions had been good ones, she'd know it. She'd feel it inside her and neither Sloane nor any other human being would be able to shake her faith in her own judgment. But she didn't feel that way. She felt bereft and angry at her own cowardice. She felt used, used by everyone in her life except Sloane Tyson and the children she had taught and loved.

"Elise!"

She had been so caught up in her self-discovery that she hadn't heard Bob's car pull in behind her.

She turned and wearily waited for him to come to her side. She put her emotions on hold; with a touch of self-pity she realized she'd been doing just that for years.

"Elise, I want to talk to you."

She sensed Bob's anger immediately. His words were clipped, and he was standing straighter than usual as if his anger had literally carried him to new heights. Irreverently Elise decided that whatever was enraging him had made him forget his affected stoop.

"Go ahead, Bob," she said calmly. "Here, make yourself useful." She balanced a bag of groceries in front of him and waited for him to grab it. When he did, she handed him another one. Since she never asked him to do anything for her, the gesture momentarily disconcerted him. Elise saw him blink. She wondered if it would be enough to make him forget whatever was bothering him.

Inside, she got her answer. He moved through the hallway and into the kitchen with a purposeful stride she hadn't seen him use for a long time. Elise decided that anger agreed with him somehow. Maybe Bob's life had been too settled to be good for him. Like hers.

"Just what do you mean by setting Amy up with Clay Tyson?"

"You must be talking about their tutoring sessions." Elise took the bags of groceries from his arms and set them on the counter. She unpacked as they talked.

"Tutoring sessions. Is that what you're calling it?"

"Yes." She stopped and studied him, her eyebrows lifted. "What are you calling it?"

"I just found out about it, so I—unlike you—haven't had time to give it a name."

"Try calling it tutoring sessions, then," she said lightly. "It fits beautifully. Amy helps Clay with his history, Clay pays her for her time, and they both benefit. It's the American way."

"This is serious. You don't have to be flippant!"

"And you don't have to be angry. There's nothing wrong with what's going on. In fact, if you hadn't taken out your prejudices on poor Clay in the first place, the sessions wouldn't have been necessary." Elise shoved a bag of sugar in Bob's direction. "Here, fill that canister behind you."

"How dare you blame this on me!"

"Who should I blame it on? Frankly, I didn't even know you were still in the dark about the sessions. What did you think Amy was doing all this time?"

"She said she was studying."

"So she was. I bet her history grades will reflect the work they've been doing."

Bob continued to clutch the bag of sugar. "You knew I didn't want her associating with that Tyson kid. You saw what happened at the dance."

Elise could feel her temper rise. It didn't take much these days to make her angry. Just one request too many, one criticism she didn't deserve, one blow to the underdog. *Midlife crisis,* she decided. *Premenopausal syndrome, if there is such a thing.*

"The only thing I saw at the dance," she said, enunciating every word distinctly, "was a man so wrapped up in his own selfishness that he couldn't even let the daughter he purports to love dance with a harmless boy she was attracted to."

"Harmless!"

She faced him, clasping her hands to steady their trembling. "The only reason you don't like Clay Tyson is that he looks exactly like Sloane. And you don't like Sloane because he had me first. Not that you want me! Not really! But what I felt for Sloane might affect your plans for my life. God forbid, I might stop taking care of you!" Elise knew she was shouting, but she couldn't make herself lower her voice.

"Calm down. You're screaming like a crazy woman!"

"I am a crazy woman. I've been crazy for years. Crazier than anyone I know to put up with you and your demands and your hypochondria. No more! And it has nothing to do with Sloane Tyson, so leave Clay out of it!"

"He's a troublemaker. I'm going to make sure he never goes near my daughter again if I have to call in every favor anyone's ever owed me!" Now Bob was shouting. "I'll have him put back in ninth grade. I can do it, too! And I'll make life so miserable for him that he'll leave Amy alone just to get me off his back!"

"You couldn't make his life that miserable because Clay's not a self-serving sniveling bastard like you are!" Elise drew a deep breath and clamped her lips shut. She couldn't believe the words that had just come out of her mouth. And she had meant every one of them.

They both stood in shock, staring at each other. They were two people who had never known any kind of passion together. Neither had any idea how to handle the storm that had just passed over them.

"I shouldn't have said that," Elise said finally. It was the best apology she could manage.

"Why not? You meant what you said."

"I did when I said it. And if you carry out your threats, Bob, I'll mean those words again. You have no right to interfere in Clay's life."

"Amy is my daughter. I have a right to do what's best for her," he said coldly.

"Then do what's best. Leave her alone."

"We disagree." Bob turned to go, dropping the sugar on the counter as he did. He was almost at the door before Elise's words stopped him.

"If you make trouble for them, Bob, you should know two things."

"What?"

Elise sounded regretful. It wasn't difficult. If her words failed to move Bob, she would regret them always. "I'll step out of your life and Amy's life totally. I won't be a party to this injustice, and I won't pretend to Amy that I think you're doing the best thing. You can raise Amy by yourself. You can pick out her clothes, answer her questions about her body, help her try new hairstyles, give her advice about how to act on dates. You can do it all. If you shut me out of this decision, she's yours to raise. Alone, Bob."

"You love her too much to do that to her."

"I love her, yes. But I'm not going to help you with her unless I have some say in her life. I won't be your yes-man, I won't be the person who carries your load with none of the responsibility for what's really important." Finally, she played her trump card. "And Bob, if you do one thing to Clay, I'll go to Lincoln and tell him you're harassing a student because you're jealous of his father."

"You might as well run your dirty linen right up the school flagpole!"

"That wouldn't bother me at all." Elise realized she was telling the truth. She really didn't care what people knew about her and Sloane. Years ago most of them had suspected their love affair anyway. She imagined there would be a few raised eyebrows and more than a few yawns. People would watch her and Sloane carefully to see what was going on now. They would give the sleepy little town something to talk about. She would be doing Miracle Springs a favor.

Bob was silent, but Elise could almost hear his brain whirring. She knew she must let him save face if she was to get him to agree to leave Clay and Amy alone. By now he probably wanted to, considering the consequences. But even Bob had his pride. She swallowed her own.

"You know I don't want to hurt you. We're both upset, and we've both said things we regret. I care about Amy, and I care about you. That's why I don't want to see you make a mistake. I know you'll realize I'm right if you just think about this a little."

His answer was a grunt.

"Will you think about it?"

This time his answer was a shrug. Elise realized the gesture was Bob's way of telling her she had won. She would never get a clearer message, but she suspected that the vendetta against Clay Tyson was over. Bob would probably lecture Amy, ground her for not telling him about the tutoring sessions, but in the end, he would allow the two teenagers to see each other, and he would not persecute Clay.

Elise realized that she would never know if it had been her threats or her logic that had been the deciding factor. But she would always have her suspicions. "Will you tell Amy

I'm still planning on our trip into Ocala on Saturday?''

Bob left without giving her an answer.

ON THANKSGIVING MORNING Sloane stretched his arms out high, and then folded them under his head. He listened for the sounds of Clay's stirring, but the house was quiet. More and more Clay's life was beginning to take on the rhythms and patterns of a normal teenage boy's.

Sloane remembered their first months together. Clay had risen at dawn to prowl Sloane's Cambridge apartment with restless energy. He slept little, always alert and curiously tensed as if he were waiting for some signal that his life was going to change yet again. The city itself had simultaneously fascinated and frightened him. Sloane, who was so used to urban living that he scarcely gave its problems a second thought, had begun to realize that Boston and Cambridge were producing a sensory overload in the impressionable young man who was his son.

Miracle Springs had been a much better choice for Clay's first year away from Destiny Ranch. Yet even here it had taken a long time for Clay to begin to feel secure. Now Sloane could see that Clay was beginning to make friends at school, beginning to fit in. He mentioned names, told an occasional story. Sometimes the neighbor boys dropped by to get homework assignments or to play video games on the home computer Sloane used as a word processor.

Clay slept better now. He allowed himself to get tired. He didn't seem to worry that something was going to happen to change his life if he gave in to sleep. The prowling restlessness of before had been tempered and with it some of the boy's watchful intensity that had so worried Sloane. Clay had even cut off his ponytail. And to Sloane, there was no clearer symbol of his son's adjustment than that.

Clay was not yet an all-American boy, nor did Sloane care if he ever became one. But slowly, slowly, Clay was adjusting to life outside Destiny Community. His own intelligence and strength of character would carry him through this difficult time and on into adulthood.

Sloane wished he could be of more help. He wanted to reach out to his son, but he didn't know how. Other than providing the proper environment, the proper equipment, he was at a loss. They never discussed anything personal. When they did talk, Sloane spoke and Clay listened. The boy rarely volunteered anything and when he did, some internal mechanism seemed to stop him after a sentence or two. He seemed convinced that Sloane didn't really want to hear what he had to say, and no probing on Sloane's part could change that.

Sloane knew he would just have to be patient. He'd been cheated out of fifteen years of Clay's life; he would not ruin his chances of getting to know his son by pushing too hard. He would take it slow and easy. Eventually they would become closer.

He wished there was somebody to talk to about Clay, somebody who could understand and sympathize with what he was going through. He'd never needed a sounding board before. Even during his divorce he had felt no need to bend anyone's ear. The divorce had made sense, for both him and his ex-wife. The marriage had been wrong from the beginning; ending it had been right. His lawyer had been the only person he'd wanted to talk to. But now he needed someone to confide in.

Elise. He hated it, but he needed Elise. She was the only person he knew who would understand, the only person with both common sense and sensitivity. She was drawn to Clay, seemed to understand his struggles. In many ways, Sloane could see that Elise and his son were very much alike. She would be able to help him understand Clay.

But even as a confidante, he couldn't have her; the problems between them were legion. Elise kept a part of herself walled off and she didn't want him to break through that wall because then she might have to confront the problems in her own life. And she didn't have the courage to do that.

As he lay in bed, hands still folded behind his head, Sloane heard noises from downstairs. It was Thanksgiving Day. He and Clay would be going to Aunt Lillian's house along with the other Tysons from around the county. It would be Clay's very first family holiday and Sloane's first in a long time. He must be getting old; the idea of a family reunion was actually appealing. He liked the thought of people he was connected to all sitting down together for a turkey feast. The bird itself would have been shot by one of his cousins, the pumpkins grown in a family pumpkin patch. It was a shame that the family was short on teenagers now; Clay was the only one in the whole group. But there would be younger cousins and married cousins. The gathering would give Clay a sense of belonging and continuity. And in some strange way, Sloane realized it would give him the same thing, even though he's spent most of his thirty-five years refusing to believe he needed it.

He showered and dressed to go downstairs and eat breakfast with Clay. He found his son in front of the television set watching the Macy's Thanksgiving parade. Sloane settled beside him with a bowl of the granola Clay faithfully made once a week. "This is good," Sloane complimented him. "It tastes different than usual."

"I used cashews instead of peanuts. It costs more, but I like to vary it."

"What do you think about the parade?" Sloane asked between crunches.

"I'd like to see it in person."

"Maybe we could someday. I never have."

"Yeah."

Sloane tried again. "Are you looking forward to Thanksgiving dinner?"

"I always liked Thanksgiving best of all the holidays at Destiny. We'd have a huge feast with every kind of food you can imagine, except meat, of course. Then afterwards someone would light a bonfire and there'd be dancing until everyone was too tired to dance anymore." Clay's nostalgia for the familiar celebration was evident.

For once, Sloane could listen to the memory of Destiny Ranch and not be mute with anger. The boy had a right to his memories; they were sacred to him. Sloane put aside his own sense of loss for all the holidays he had missed with his son. "I was at the Destiny farm in Vermont one year for Thanksgiving," he recalled. "We did pretty much the same thing except that there was no bonfire. Only a fire in the fireplace. But we danced."

Clay's ears seemed to perk up. "I forget sometimes that you used to be part of Destiny."

"I never was, not really," Sloane said gently. "I was an observer. I always knew I'd move on."

"Did Willow know you were going to move on?"

Sloane was surprised by the question. He and Clay had never discussed Clay's mother except in the most cursory of ways. "Yes," he said honestly. "I think that's why she chose me to father you."

"And you didn't know."

"Not until I got the phone call six months ago."

"I asked Jeff once who my father was. He said my father was Destiny."

Sloane swallowed more than his granola. He could barely speak for a moment. Then he cleared his throat. "In some ways he was right, but only because I was never given the chance to be your father, Clay. I never would have left you there if I'd known."

Clay inclined his head and shrugged. "I was happy."

"Were you?" Sloane set his bowl on the coffee table in front of him. "I have dreams sometimes about a little boy who needed a daddy and a daddy who needed a son but didn't know it. In my dreams the little boy isn't happy."

Clay looked away. "I was happy at Destiny."

Sloane knew better than to push. Clay was not ready to repudiate the only home he had known for fifteen years. "Are you happy here, Clay?" he asked instead.

Clay focused his eyes on a spot across the room. "Yeah."

"Really?"

Clay realized he could be more honest than he had originally thought. Sloane was surprisingly mellow this morning. "I'm getting happier," he amended. "Some things are working out real well."

Sloane settled back against the sofa cushions. "Like what?"

"School. I've made some friends."

"I understand from your aunt that Amy Cargil has become a good friend."

Clay smiled a little and turned back to his father. "Don't they call this the third degree or something?"

"You're catching on."

"Yeah, Amy's a friend, especially now that her dad is..."

"Her dad is what?"

Clay considered whether to tell Sloane but surprisingly, Sloane seemed genuinely interested. He filed that fact away to consider more deeply at another time. "Well, her dad was picking on me. Amy says it's because I look like you and Mr. Cargil doesn't like you because of Elise."

Sloane frowned. "What does Elise have to do with anything?"

"I don't know. That's just what Amy said. But it doesn't matter because Mr. Cargil isn't bothering me anymore."

"What changed his mind?"

"Amy says Elise talked to him. He's been leaving me alone in class ever since. Amy's allowed to see me after school, too. Things are a lot better than they were."

"Why didn't you tell me this before?" Sloane asked.

"What could you have done?"

"Talked to Cargil myself. I won't have anyone picking on my son." Sloane stood and picked up his bowl to take it into the kitchen.

"Would you really have talked to him?" Clay sounded surprised, and the tone of his voice made Sloane turn to look at him.

"Of course I would have. That's one of the things fathers do. I think I could have managed that much. Don't you?"

"I never thought about it before."

"Think about it, son." Sloane disappeared into the kitchen.

Clay turned back to the television set and watched a giant helium balloon of Garfield the cat float down a New York avenue. He wondered if there was more to this father-son business than met the eye.

CHAPTER TEN

ELISE STRIPPED OFF her gloves and unzipped her short coat. Anyone who thought Florida was sunny and warm all year around should be in Miracle Springs on this particular Thanksgiving Day, she reflected. The sun was shining. That part was correct. But it was anything except warm outside. Fall had only just arrived, but already it felt like winter. Elise had just completed an errand in record time, anxious to stay indoors for the rest of the day.

With her winter garb carefully stowed in the closet, she walked through the hallway into the kitchen. The room looked just like a kitchen was supposed to look on Thanksgiving. There were pots and pans that needed washing, dinner ingredients that needed to be put away, leftovers that needed to be wrapped. It was funny, really. Here were the remnants of a Thanksgiving feast, and she hadn't eaten a bite all day.

At this moment two elderly widows who lived out on Mercy Road were enjoying her cooking, as they had every year for as long as Elise had known how to cook. It was one of those acts of conscience that Elise truly enjoyed performing. Mrs. Waid and Mrs. Furman counted on her to make the holiday special, and she never disappointed them. In return, they served her peach brandy and regaled her with tales of Miracle Springs sixty years ago. It was an hour of folklore that Elise wouldn't miss for anything.

Usually she came home to put the finishing touches on the rest of the meal so that when Amy and Bob came for dinner late in the afternoon she could just sit and enjoy being with them. This Thanksgiving, for the first time in ten years, Amy and Bob were eating at home, alone. Elise was eating alone, too.

She supposed it was for the best. She had invited Bob as usual, and he had stiffly declined. There was no question why. He was still angry with her for interfering in his handling of Clay and Amy. She didn't regret her interference, not one little bit. But today, faced with the remnants of a Thanksgiving feast that she would have to eat by herself, she did regret the change it had made in all their lives.

What was lonelier than a banquet for one? She knew she was responsible for her own loneliness. Whatever she was, it was because of choices she'd made. Whatever she became would be because of the choices that were left to her. Her life probably wasn't even half over. She could turn it around, fling her arms open wide and embrace opportunity. She deserved happiness—and could make it happen.

So why was she staring at the holiday dinner like a lost little waif? Elise smiled wryly at her own vulnerability. She had great intentions, but today even a little thing like a kitchen filled with uneaten turkey and dressing could bring her down quickly. She was going to have to learn how to be courageous. It was going to take time.

Halfway through repackaging the turkey into freezer bag-sized portions, she heard the knock on her front door. ''I hope it's somebody who'll take some of these leftovers," she muttered to herself, wiping her hands on a dish towel.

Sloane stood at the front door, dressed in a wool jacket the color of his eyes. He was the last person she had expected to see. "May I come in?"

Elise stepped back, and Sloane brushed against her, bringing the smell of autumn air and wood smoke with him as he stepped into the hallway.

The fragrance of turkey and Thanksgiving greeted him. Sloane sniffed appreciatively. "Obviously I'm interrupting dinner."

"Not really."

"You've eaten already?"

Elise shook her head.

"Then I have interrupted."

"Actually, I was just putting it away."

"Without eating?"

"It's a long story." Elise turned back to the kitchen. "Do you mind if we talk while I finish up?"

Sloane watched the gentle sway of her hips as she moved away from him. Elise had a natural grace to her movements that sometimes haunted him when he was away from her. He wouldn't be thinking of her; she would be the furthest thing from his mind, and then suddenly, he'd be struck by a memory of her body in gentle motion. It was disconcerting when he saw such mental images, for it was as if his unconscious mind was waiting for exactly the right moment to surprise him, the moment when he least expected it and his defenses were down.

He followed her, hopelessly entranced. He had not come to renew a relationship that could never be renewed; he had not come for intimacy. He had tried that once, and it had only led to a new distance between them. No, today he had only come to say thank-you.

So why hadn't he said it and left?

In the kitchen Sloane looked around and his eyes narrowed. "There's enough food here to feed the world's hungry."

"I know. I guess I got carried away."

"Who's coming to dinner?"

"Nobody. I cooked for a couple of ladies from my church and this was left over." Elise waited for Sloane's lecture. He would put her down for her unselfishness, ask her what she got from performing these endless acts of charity, and condemn her with a look that neatly said it all.

"Well, they were lucky ladies," he said instead. "This looks fabulous. If I hadn't just eaten at Aunt Lillian's, I'd tackle some of this meal myself."

Like a dog who's expecting a kick and gets a pat on the head instead, Elise didn't know how to react. Sloane had missed a chance to give her a hard time. "Yes, well ..."

"Lise, you ought to eat some of this before it gets cold. I'll sit with you while you do."

Too surprised to respond, Elise watched as Sloane opened the cabinet, got a plate and began to dish up the food for her. He piled the plate with turkey, then stuck a finger in the dressing and shook his head. "It's cold. Will this dinnerware go in your oven?" He turned the oven dial as he asked the question.

He had taken over so quickly that Elise hadn't made a move to stop him. She wanted to tell him to forget about her dinner, but suddenly she realized just how hungry she was. She nodded, and was treated to the full power of one of Sloane's disarming grins. For a moment she wondered exactly what she was hungry for.

Sloane finished dishing up and then held out the plate for her approval. "Good enough?"

"Fine." Elise watched as he slipped it inside her oven and adjusted the temperature. Then he straightened. "Now, how about a drink while we wait?"

"You really don't have to stay to make sure I eat."

"I want to stay. May I?"

Elise could have worked up the courage to send him away if he'd been belligerent or arrogant. But this concerned man was someone she couldn't be rude to. "What would you like to drink?"

"Something light."

"White wine?"

"Perfect." Sloane watched as Elise poured them both a glass and took his when she was finished. Then he followed her out of the kitchen and into the living room. "I could help you finish putting everything away," he offered.

"I'll do it later, after I've eaten." Elise sat on the sofa and took a sip of her wine. It hit her empty stomach like an icy blast of autumn air.

Sloane sat beside her. "How have you been?"

Elise set her glass on the coffee table and folded her hands primly in her lap. "You didn't come here to ask me how I've been," she said, more sharply than she had intended.

"No, I didn't," he agreed easily. "But I'd still like to know."

"I've been fine."

"If you've been fine then why are you having Thanksgiving dinner alone?" he countered gently. "Where are Cargil and his daughter?"

"At home." She lifted her eyes to glare at him. "If it's any of your business."

"Evidently it is my business. Clay told me today that you stood up for him with Cargil."

"That's right."

"Obviously it's had an effect on your relationship with him."

Elise shrugged.

"Cargil's a fool."

"Now you're talking like the Sloane I know." Elise reached for her wine again and swirled it around in the glass for something to do.

"I mean he's a fool for letting this come between you. You're the best thing in his life." Sloane put his hand on Elise's shoulder. "But I didn't come to insult him. I came to thank you for what you did for Clay. I had no idea what was going on until he told me this morning."

"I'm surprised he never mentioned it." Elise remembered what had happened at Destiny Ranch the one time Clay had asked an adult to help him. She sighed a little at the memory. "I guess I'm not surprised," she amended. "Clay doesn't believe that adults will really do anything for him. I'm sure he felt if he mentioned Bob's persecution to you, you either wouldn't help him or your help would make things worse."

"He must have trusted you or he never would have told you."

Elise was surprised by the hurt hidden in Sloane's words. "The truth slipped out with me," she assured him. "He didn't want to tell me, and then afterward he insisted that I stay out of it. The only thing I was allowed to do was arrange to have Amy tutor him. Even after the scene at the dance he..."

"What scene?"

Apparently Clay had not told his father everything. Elise found herself feeling sorry for Sloane. "Bob got angry because Clay and Amy were dancing together. I had to...to straighten Bob out. But even after that, Clay refused to let me do more. Actually, Bob was the one who finally brought things to a head, and when he did, I was able to say what needed to be said to him."

"What did you say?" Sloane sat back and took his hand from her shoulder.

"I just told him if he didn't leave Clay alone, I'd make life difficult for him." Elise took another sip of her wine and then set it down. She had to eat.

"You threatened him?"

Elise smiled a little at the memory. "Sort of."

Sloane watched her and he didn't miss the smile. Elise might be sad that Cargil was angry, but she wasn't sad that she'd stood up to him. He felt a rush of pleasure at her reaction.

"I won't ask you exactly what transpired." Sloane stroked the smooth sides of his glass, and he watched Elise relax at his words. He'd seen that she was gearing up to tell him to mind his own business. He waited until she appeared completely relaxed again before he continued. "But I will ask why Cargil's been picking on Clay. Clay says it has something to do with us."

So far they had managed to keep their conversation fairly impersonal. Elise didn't want that to change. "Clay's different, and Bob doesn't like people to be different. I think it frightens him."

"And?"

"And what?"

"And what do you and I have to do with it?"

She realized Sloane wasn't going to let the subject drop easily. Her best defense was to answer quickly and simply. "Bob's jealous because he knows you were my first lover."

"Well, well." Sloane drained the contents of his glass. "Territory. Is he afraid I'm back to take you for my own?"

Elise was surprised how much Sloane's words hurt. He made the possibility sound ridiculous. "I suppose," she said, hiding her hurt feelings. "Silly, isn't it?"

"Silly, considering how clear you've made it that you wouldn't consider such a thing." Sloane stood. "I'm going to check on your dinner."

He was in the doorway before Elise's words stopped him. "Would *you* consider such a thing, Sloane?"

"What are you asking?" He faced her, leaning casually against the doorframe.

Elise had known Sloane wouldn't make this easy for her. She'd thought if she ever had the chance again to put things right between them, she'd do it with courage, ignoring his scorn. Instead she stood, nervously smoothing the folds of her plaid wool skirt. "I'm not sure."

"Then how can I answer?"

She reminded herself that it was Sloane who had come to her. She remembered their angry words weeks before, but she also remembered the distinct impression she'd had when he stormed out of her house—the impression that she'd made a terrible mistake. She knew this was her last chance to reach out for what she wanted and to hold fast to it.

She put her hands in her pockets to still their nervous movement. She lifted her chin. "Sloane, I know you didn't come back to claim me as your own—that's Bob's little fairy tale. I know you'll be leaving town in June, and I won't be. But is it so silly to believe that you might want me while you're here? Was he wrong about that?"

"I answered that question the last time I was in this house," Sloane said, almost hissing the final word. Suddenly politeness and gratitude were forgotten and weeks of repressed anger poured out. "You knew I wanted you that night. The signs were unmistakable. You were too worried about what Miracle Springs would think to consider more than a quick screw."

"You're wrong about that."

He was at her side in a moment, her dinner forgotten. "What am I wrong about?" he demanded.

"I was scared." Elise saw her own hand leave its shelter and reach out to touch Sloane's cheek. It surprised her.

"Scared? Of what?"

"Of doing just what I wanted, without worrying about the consequences. Can you understand that?"

He shook his head, but he reached up to cover her hand with his to keep her from withdrawing it. "Explain it to me."

"I thought you only wanted me for that night. Afterward, I couldn't bear the thought that I'd be seeing you day after day, continuing to want you and knowing that I couldn't have you again."

"You thought I wanted to make love to you once just to get you out of my system?" Sloane's laughter was harsh. "How little regard you have for either of us." His hand dropped to his side, and Elise withdrew hers.

"What did you want, Sloane?"

"Believe it or not, I hadn't drawn up a contract with exact terms. I wanted you. I knew that feeling well enough to know it wasn't going to go away after one night together. And I knew us both well enough to know that when June came, I'd leave, and you'd stay behind. Beyond that, I didn't know anything."

"And now?"

"Now there's nothing left to know. You made it clear to me that you didn't want me in your orderly existence. I bowed out as gracefully as I could."

"There was nothing graceful about it. You ranted and raved."

"That was as graceful as I could be!"

He looked so fierce, and yet, once again, Elise could sense the pain behind his words. She swayed toward him and her body was heavy with longing. She had been convinced it was too late, or perhaps she had convinced herself because she was always afraid to go after what she wanted. But now she was faced with a chance. It was a small one. Sloane looked as if he'd like to pick her up and shake her. He was fed up with her cowardice, her excuses. She could feel him slipping away from her as she stood in front of him, trying to put her doubts behind her.

"Sloane..."

"Don't apologize. I don't need your apologies."

She focused her eyes resolutely on his. This was the man she had loved so long ago. Inside of him was the boy who had taught her all she knew about her own body. It was to that boy that she spoke.

"Make love to me, Sloane. Now, and for as long as you desire me. I won't be afraid anymore."

He shut his eyes, and suddenly he looked tired. "Don't, Elise."

She understood his response. She had offered herself before, and then afterward she had sent him away. The miracle was that he was in her house again. She reached up to stroke his cheek once more. Even with his eyes shut, he flinched at her touch.

"I want you, Sloane. And you want me. We care too much about each other to want to inflict any more pain than we already have. Love me now. When it's time for you to leave, I'll let you go. And I'll cherish the months we had together."

Sloane felt the gentle slide of Elise's fingers over his cheek. Until that moment, he hadn't realized just how much he'd wanted to know her touch again or hear the words she had just spoken. He could feel the floodgate of his desire that he had so carefully locked burst open.

"What about the town?" he asked.

"What about it?" Elise smoothed her fingers around each of his eyes and then into his hair. "I won't lose my job if we're the slightest bit discreet. Beyond that, I don't care what people know or think they know. I want this for myself. For me. Just for me."

Sloane opened his eyes and gathered her close in a painfully tight hug. "This is crazy," he whispered against her hair. "I'm crazy. You're crazy."

"It's crazy to resist," Elise whispered. She could feel Sloane's body stir to life against her. She had months of wonderful closeness, this anticipatory pleasure ahead of her. It would be enough. It would have to be.

"Can we make it to your bed this time?"

"If you promise to ignore the rug on the landing."

"That's going to be hard."

Elise broke away from Sloane's arms and took his hand. The trip to her room was a blur. Later she would remember only the steady pressure of his fingers wrapped around hers and the moment when he scooped her up and fell on the bed with her.

He undressed her slowly, one piece of clothing at a time, covering each inch of her body with his hands and mouth. There was nothing patient in the way he touched her. His need was powerful, and he focused it on each movement, each caress, building their excitement into excruciating mutual arousal.

Elise was no less needy than she had been weeks before, but this time she knew Sloane would not disappear. She let him fan the flames of her desire, knowing well where it would end. She trusted his passion. She knew he would take and take and give in the taking.

She arched against him, crying out as his mouth fitted itself over her breast and tugged at it. She dug her fingers into his flesh, first pushing him away, then pulling him toward her. Her body was no longer under her control. Her legs wrapped around him, urging him on. Their skin heated and became slick; she felt the boundaries between them soften and disappear until she was no longer sure where she began or ended.

This time Sloane held her back from premature completion. When they were naked together he lay half on top of her, cherishing the smoothness of her skin and the ripe softness of her breasts. They didn't talk, but there was no need for conversation. Everything they would have to say for the next months had already been said. They had only to feel, to know, to accept.

Elise met each of his movements with one of her own. There was nothing obscure about the gift she was giving him. She was giving herself, her softness, her warmth, the very center of her being. That gift was apparent in every stroke of her hand, every sweep of her lips and tongue, every twist of her body. They melded together, changing forever what they had been before.

Finally Sloane pulled her under him, sliding deeply inside her. Elise wanted more. She strained to gather all of him within herself, the indefinable essence of him, the whole person. She loved him, had never stopped and never would. Sloane Tyson, her teenage lover, now a man. Her love was ageless and without boundaries. Sloane set her free, and in her freedom she could turn back to him and give him everything.

She did. She vibrated to the rhythm he set, meeting each of his thrusts with one of her own. Each time she gave, her own pleasure increased. Wasn't that the way it was supposed to be? Always?

Elise squeezed her eyes shut and let the rhythm accelerate, let the faster tempo eat into her control until what little had been left vanished altogether in a wild burst of heat and color and primitive sensation. She could feel him explode too, his release part of her own and yet different. She wrapped trembling arms around his back and pulled him to rest against her.

Sated and content, they lay entwined, exploring each other's bodies without haste and with more control. Elise lazily traced the ridges of Sloane's muscles, the curve of his ribs, the tapering curls. She leaned over him and the black silk of her hair, which he had unpinned, fell over his chest. She watched his eyes widen in pleasure, and she bent forward to kiss him. "That was spectacular," she congratulated him. "Amazing what a few years did for your skills."

Sloane laughed and affectionately patted her rump. "Two can play that game. Shall I tell you what a few years did for yours?"

Secure in the pleasure she had given him, Elise nodded, then kissed his nose. "Tell me."

"Absolutely nothing. You were always the best lover a man could want. That hasn't changed at all."

She was surprised by the tears that sprang unbidden to her eyes at the compliment. "That's lovely," she said huskily.

"It's true." Sloane pulled her to rest on top of him with her head cradled on his shoulder. "I've never met anyone who had your capacity to give and receive love. That's true in bed, too."

"Just how many people have you met in bed, young man?" she asked in her best schoolmarm voice.

Sloane laughed and hugged her tight. "Enough to know."

Elise lay against him and basked in the warmth of his embrace. There were few times in her life when she'd felt she was exactly where she was supposed to be. This was one of them.

"After you left," she said softly, "sometimes I'd lie in bed and remember just exactly what this felt like. Then I'd pretend that wherever you were, you were remembering, too. There were times when I actually felt like I was communicating with you, that somewhere, you were listening."

Sloane slipped his hand under her hair and kneaded a path along her spine with the palm of his hand. "Sometimes," he admitted, "I'd be in the middle of something—important, or not important, it didn't matter—and out of nowhere I'd start thinking about you. Other times I wouldn't even have you on my mind—not consciously anyway—and the next thing I knew I was turning around, expecting you to be there."

"I probably was there, at least a part of me was."

"It wasn't enough for me," Sloane said with a trace of bitterness.

"Hush." Elise lifted her head to look at him and she put one finger on his lips. "We can't change the past. And if we could, who knows where it would have led? Were you really ready for a wife at eighteen? You had wild oats to sow. I would have held you back. Wasn't there relief mixed with regret when I told you I wouldn't come with you? Wasn't part of your rush to get out of town because you were afraid I might change my mind after all?''

Sloane opened his mouth to protest, then closed it abruptly. He had sometimes wondered the same thing. "We were both immature," he said finally. "I was a volatile mixture of emotions I can't identify now. Neither of us can.''

"And neither of us will ever know what would have become of our relationship if we'd left here together. Perhaps we wouldn't have this much left of it." Elise smoothed Sloane's hair back from his face and kissed him. "I'm through with regrets. Tell me you are too.''

"I'm through with regrets," he repeated. Then his eyes warmed, smoldering with new heat. "But I'm not through with you." With one quick twist he turned her over onto her back and covered her body with his own. Elise gave herself up totally to the present. There was no more past and no future. She had the man she wanted. Time was no longer important.

"TURKEY TASTES BEST as leftovers," Elise said later. She and Sloane were sitting on the living-room rug, feeding each other bits of Thanksgiving dinner with their fingers. Elise wasn't sure which she liked best, the food—the first food she'd put in her stomach that day—or Sloane's fingers, when she got to lick them clean. "But didn't I hear a rumor that you already ate your dinner?''

"I think I worked off enough calories to deserve this," Sloane said, swallowing a morsel of dressing that Elise had dropped into his mouth.

"More than enough," she agreed.

"You should have a family of ten children to cook for," Sloane said, refusing another bite. "I can just see you stuffing their little bodies until somebody would have to roll them to school."

Elise laughed, and then she realized that Sloane was frowning at his own words. "What's wrong?" she teased him. "Did the mashed turnips catch up with you?"

"Elise, are you using birth control?"

She licked her own fingers and wondered at the stab of pain his words had given her. Obviously he was hoping her answer was yes. But then, of course he would. He was still trying to adjust to one surprise son. He was a man who said quite frankly that he'd never expected to have any children.

"I don't need to, Sloane. Didn't you ever wonder why I didn't get pregnant when I was seventeen? It wasn't those condoms you occasionally remembered to use. I rarely ovulate. Without medical intervention—fertility pills, hormones—my chances of conceiving a child are infinitesimal."

To Sloane's credit, he didn't breathe an audible sigh of relief. "When did you find that out?"

"Years ago. Bob asked me to marry him, and frankly, I'd wondered for years why I'd never got pregnant when you and I were together. So I went to my gynecologist for tests. He explained my problem, and when I told Bob, he was overjoyed. Turns out he didn't want another child— my child—anyway."

"And that was the reason you didn't marry him?"

"I'd like to think I wouldn't have anyway. But honestly, I don't know. If I could have had children with him, I might have felt it was worth it."

Sloane surprised her by putting his arms around her and pulling her close. "You'd be a wonderful mother."

"I know. But I've devoted all that maternal instinct to my students. It's made me a better teacher. I have the satisfaction of knowing I've changed lives."

"Clay certainly thinks the world of you."

"He's a beautiful young man. I love him."

"So do I."

Sloane's voice was so full of emotion that Elise turned in his arms and put her hands on his shoulders. "Of course you do," she soothed him.

"I don't know how it happened," Sloane said, almost as if he were detailing a crime he had committed.

Elise smiled a little. "Hadn't you ever thought you could love a child?"

"Not this way. I feel like I could lay down my life for him. I have nightmares of something happening to him and not being able to help. I wake up feeling like I'm fighting my way out of a black pit."

Elise understood. "You have to tell yourself that you're there for him now. That you'll always be there for him as long as you live."

"How do I make him understand that?"

Elise tilted her head and drew a line from his brow to the tip of his nose. There was so much that Sloane understood about the world and so little he understood about human emotions. Especially his own and Clay's. "Have you told him?"

"Not in so many words. What would they mean to him? He's never been loved before. A parent's love is as foreign to him as white bread and roast beef."

Elise smiled a little. "Well, he eats white bread and roast beef now—even if he was probably healthier without them. What makes you think he won't get used to the idea of being loved by you, too?"

Sloane shrugged in answer.

"I think you're afraid."

Sloane stiffened, but Elise's fingers massaged his shoulders until he had to relax again. "I don't know," he finally admitted. "Maybe."

"Don't be afraid, Sloane. He'll love you back. You need each other."

Elise let Sloane pull her down to the rug, and she nestled against him as he began to cover her face with kisses. Clay wasn't the only one who needed what Sloane had to give. But if there was a small part of her that envied Clay the love of his father, she pushed it resolutely away. She had as much of Sloane this moment as she would ever have. She could not begrudge the boy she also loved having more.

Afternoon turned into evening, and Sloane reluctantly dressed to go pick up his son. Elise stood in the doorway to watch him walk to his car. He stopped and turned, lifting his hand in farewell. She saw him touch his fingers to his lips in an unusual gesture of affection. Then he was gone.

For the first time in seventeen years she knew he would be back. As she closed the door behind her, she reminded herself that it was more than she had ever hoped to have. It would have to be enough.

CHAPTER ELEVEN

"I DON'T BELIEVE what you're humming." Sloane stood in the doorway between Elise's kitchen and living room, a glass of eggnog in his hand. He was watching Elise and Clay put the finishing touches on a Christmas tree.

"I can wish, can't I?" she said, stretching on tiptoe to rearrange one of the god's-eye decorations Clay had made for her.

"'I'm dreaming of a white Christmas'?" Sloane taunted her.

"Are you?" She turned a little and shot him a smile. "You're so sentimental."

Sloane laughed and watched as the two of them completed the task they so obviously loved. Everything seemed so natural, so right, that it was hard to believe only a month had passed since he and Elise had become lovers again. It seemed like a lifetime. "The tree's crooked," he pointed out, after the last ornament had been hung.

"Have you no sense of tradition? It's not supposed to be straight. If there was a Christmas tree in Bethlehem, it was crooked." Elise came to stand beside him and Sloane pulled her close. They examined the tree together. "Actually," she admitted, "it's a little more than crooked. Horizontal might be a better word." She poked her elbow in Sloane's ribs when he laughed at her. "It's just like you to wait until the tree has been decorated before you point out its problems."

"Actually, I like it," Sloane said, finishing his eggnog. "I'm thinking of starting a pool. The person who comes closest to guessing the exact minute when that tree hits the dust wins a dinner for two at the Miracle Springs Inn."

"Ebenezer Scrooge. Making profit off the misery of the world."

Sloane's arm tightened around her. "You do realize where you're standing, don't you?"

Elise smiled. She had wondered how long it would take Sloane to get around to the obvious. "No. Where?"

"In the crook of my arm with my fingers dangerously near your armpit." He tickled her a little to make his point.

"Such a romantic!" Elise squealed. "You'd rather tickle me than kiss me?"

"Kiss you? Why would I want to do that?"

"Because I'm standing under mistletoe and so are you!"

"I've been meaning to discuss that with you." Sloane brought his face down to hers. They were a scant inch apart. Elise shut her eyes. "Are you a druid?" he asked.

Elise opened her eyes and glared at him. "What?"

"A druid. That tree, the mistletoe, the holly on your dining-room table. All druid traditions."

"No, I'm just a crazy woman who invited you and your son for Christmas Eve dinner." She shut her eyes again. "Kiss me if you're planning to be fed."

"Such bribery." Sloane met her lips for a kiss that lasted as long as propriety would allow. Then he straightened. "You don't taste like a druid."

"How does a druid taste?"

"Different." Sloane lifted his hand and tucked a long strand of hair into the braid that trailed down to Elise's waist. "Very, very different."

"That's reassuring." She gave him a bright smile, then turned back to Clay who was staring at the tree. "What do you think, Clay? Other than the angle, don't you think we did a great job?"

The Scotch pine was covered with dozens of small god's-eye ornaments. Each ornament consisted of two crossed branches wrapped in an intricate design of different-colored yarns. To go with them Elise had wired hangers on small glitter-dipped pine cones and hung them beside the god's-eyes. At the last minute, she and Clay had examined their attempt at decoration and then run out to the store to buy strings of miniature flickering lights. Sloane had taken one look at the resulting mixture of technology and homespun charm and disappeared to buy a bright gold star for the top.

"It's interesting," Clay answered tactfully. "Unique."

"My son has a way with words," Sloane said proudly.

Clay looked at his father and grinned. Elise thought her heart would burst. For tonight, the peculiar tension that seemed to hover in the air between Clay and Sloane had dissolved. They seemed to have forgotten about roles and expectations, and they were thoroughly enjoying each other. During the past month Elise had seen this absence of tension very rarely.

"Ignore him," Elise counseled Clay. "Come help me check the pie."

"Actually, if you don't mind, it's past time for Amy to get here. I told her I'd wait outside for her."

"Better hurry then. She might beat you." Elise and Sloane together watched Clay spring for the front door.

"Remember?" they said together, then stopped.

"You first," Sloane said, playing with her braid.

"Remember the Christmas Eve I waited for you out on the front porch after my parents went to bed?"

"That's what I was going to say." Sloane tossed the long braid over his shoulder and wrapped his arms loosely around her. "You were blue by the time I got there."

"You were always late."

"I never wanted you to know how anxious I was to see you." He kissed her forehead.

"We gave each other presents."

"I gave you a Beatles album."

Elise smiled in remembrance. "I still have it."

"You gave me a pocket watch."

"Who says I'm not practical?"

Sloane put his cheek on her hair. "I still have it. It stopped ticking years ago, but I never did throw it away."

"Such an old softie." She put her arms around his waist and leaned against him, wrapped in memory. "You kissed me out on the front porch, and your lips were ice-cold."

Sloane was still remembering the watch, silent for so many years. "I ought to take it to the jeweler's and see if it can be fixed."

That possibility gave Elise a surge of pleasure, although she didn't know why. "I wonder what Clay and Amy will give each other."

"They're younger than we were. Not as serious."

"They're both older than they should be. That's one of the things they share. And they're just as serious as we were."

"If that's true, we'd better keep our eye on them. I'm still adjusting to having a son. A grandson would be too much."

"Bob's got his eyes open, believe me. Amy's so well chaperoned that she'll never have a chance to get into trouble." Reluctantly Elise pulled away and turned toward the kitchen. "About that pie."

"Why do you suppose Cargil let Amy come to dinner over here?" Sloane asked.

"I'll bet he has a date."

Sloane grabbed her arm and stopped her. "A date?"

Elise laughed and slapped Sloane's hand away. "Do you want this pie to burn?"

Sloane followed her, standing with his arms crossed as Elise lifted the pie from the oven. The sudden heat brought roses to her cheeks, and wisps of hair around her face curled delicately. He admired the softening effect for a moment before he spoke. "Who's he dating?"

"You're playing Miracle Springs's favorite sport. I'll warn you, professor, you may leave here with a small-town mentality." Elise set the pie on top of the stove and wiped her forehead with the back of her hand.

"Who?"

"Carol Groves. She's a widow. Lives down by the railroad crossing. They've known each other for years."

"And she mellowed him enough to let Amy come here?"

"More likely Carol invited Bob to dinner by himself. It's hard to carry on a romance with a teenager staring you down."

"We're managing nicely," Sloane said, putting his arms around Elise's waist and pulling her back to lean against him for a moment.

Elise understood the difference, even if Sloane didn't. Bob and Carol had all the time in the world. She and Sloane had to make memories to last a lifetime. She relaxed against him and moaned softly as his hands crept up to her breasts. A month had slipped by. More months would come after it, each one taking on the frantic pace of a river nearing its destination. In no time Sloane and Clay would be gone. She dismissed the thought. This month had been the best in her life. There were more coming. That was what she had to think about—that and each precious moment as she lived it.

A HALF MOON lit the tropical winter landscape, re-splendent with poinsettia in full bloom and tall ever-greens that screened Elise's house from those of her neighbors. Clay watched Amy, her arms filled with packages, climb out of her father's car and shout good-bye as he drove off. Then the boy stepped off the porch and joined her on the sidewalk. She set down her pack-ages, and as naturally as if they'd always been together, they melted into each other's arms.

Clay lowered his mouth to Amy's and greeted her with a kiss. She wrapped her arms around his neck and stood on tiptoe to kiss him back. For a minute they were obliv-ious to everything else.

"Merry Christmas," Amy said, when she could talk again.

"Merry Christmas."

"I've missed you."

"I'm glad you're here." Clay watched as Amy re-trieved her presents, then he put his arm around her waist and they began their walk to the house. "I was surprised your father said yes."

"I think he was glad I had a place to go. He's having dinner with Carol."

"Again?"

"Yeah. That makes three times since school let out." Amy giggled a little. "I think he'd marry her if he thought he could talk her out of keeping her Peking-ese.''

''Maybe he'll get used to it.''

''Maybe. Carol's a good cook, and she loves to wait on him. He always comes back looking relaxed and happy.''

''Do you like her?''

''She's okay. She tries to be nice to me, but she talks to me like she talks to her dog.'' Amy raised her voice three octaves. ''Amy sweetie pie, have just one more bite of your pork chop. There's a good girl. It's so-o-o-o good for you. Do you want me to warm it up? Cool it down? Chop it up? Put it back together?'' Amy giggled and resumed her normal tone. ''She's perfect for Daddy.''

They reached the porch and Clay leaned against a pillar, pulling Amy against him to delay their entrance into the house. ''Why didn't your father discover her sooner?''

''Elise. I think he's been hoping for years that...'' her voice trailed off.

''That she'd marry him?''

Amy nodded. ''I hoped the same thing. She already feels like my mother.''

''I don't know what a mother feels like,'' Clay said with a tiny smile, ''but I suppose if Elise married my father, I'd find out.''

''Are they going to get married?''

''I don't know. They never say anything about it.''

''Are you still leaving in June?'' Amy transferred her packages to one arm and smoothed back an errant lock of Clay's hair.

''Sloane has to go back to Boston. I guess I'm going too. If he still wants me.''

''He's your father. Of course he wants you,'' Amy said indignantly.

"Amy, just because he fathered me doesn't mean he wants me. Haven't you figured that out yet? How many kids do you know who actually live with both their parents?"

"But that's divorce, not ... not this!"

Clay kissed her forehead. "Sloane thought he was doing the right thing by bringing me to live with him, but he's not getting anything out of it. Eventually, when people don't get something out of whatever they're doing, they stop doing it. He's playing father now, but he'll get tired of it. Then he'll find another place for me."

"But he's your father!" she repeated.

"That doesn't mean anything," he explained patiently. "The only person you can ever really count on, Amy, is yourself."

"You can count on me."

Clay laced his fingers through Amy's short curls. "I hope we'll always be friends."

"But you don't think we will be."

"People change."

"You sure were raised funny." Amy stood on tiptoe once again and kissed Clay's nose. "You've got a lot to learn."

The front door opened, and Elise stepped out on the porch. "Are you two ready for dinner?"

"I'm always ready for dinner," Clay told her, pushing away from the pillar and catching Amy's hand.

Inside, the house was fragrant with the smells of pine and baked ham, cinnamon and bayberry candles. Amy took a deep breath. "Now this is what Christmas is supposed to smell like. Elise, you never had a tree before, did you?"

"No. My mother thought they were much too messy. If we put up anything, it was always one of those ten-inch ceramic trees with blinking lights."

"I like this better."

"So do I," Elise said fervently.

"I haven't had a tree since I left home," Sloane said, coming to stand next to her. "I'd forgotten how sentimental it can make you feel."

"We always have a tree," Amy said. "An artificial one. One year I sprayed it with pine air freshener to make it smell real and Daddy sneezed every time he walked by. I guess I overdid it."

Clay laughed and squeezed Amy's hand. "We always had a tree at Destiny. Not pine, usually—they were scarce—but whatever we could get. Everybody made decorations—paper chains, popcorn and cranberries. Then, on Christmas night, we'd stand around it and sing carols."

"Sounds like you had the most authentic celebration," Elise said, laying her hand on Clay's shoulder. "And I'll bet you made god's-eyes for the tree, didn't you?"

Clay nodded. "It was always beautiful."

Elise looked at Sloane and saw the regret in his eyes. She shook her head in warning. One thing she was sure of, Clay would not understand Sloane's sadness and it was better for Sloane to keep his feelings to himself. Clay had his good memories; they were important to him. It was better that he didn't know the effect they had on his father.

Dinner was a festive affair. Elise was in her glory cooking for the people she loved most in the world. She had planned the menu for weeks, like a new bride serving dinner for the first time to her in-laws. There were baked ham and sweet potatoes rich with butter, brown sugar and spices. There were green beans, overcooked the long, slow Southern way and delicate yeast rolls. There were mincemeat pie and a *bûche de Noël* made from sponge cake and mocha cream frosting with marzipan mushrooms to make it look like a real Yule log. And finally there were groans from everyone and protests that they could not eat one more bite.

Afterward, Elise and Sloane relaxed together on the sofa while Amy and Clay did the dinner dishes to the loud strains of rock music interspersed with an occasional carol.

"Nothing could point out how unusual those two are more than the fact that they offered to do the dishes," Elise told Sloane.

"I never washed dishes," Sloane admitted. "Not once in all the years I was at home."

"You were a rotten teenager. You should have had one just like you were as punishment."

"Clay's too good to be true. It's like he's always aware of what adults want from him, and he goes out of his way to give it to them." Sloane pulled Elise to rest in the crook of his arm. He stroked her hair. "I'd be happy if he'd argue with me once in a while or yell at me or throw things."

"I'm sure he thinks if he did, you'd toss him out on his ear."

"I wouldn't."

Elise turned a little so that she could brush Sloane's cheek with her fingertips. "Then tell him. Tell him you love him and plan to keep him no matter what he does. It would relieve his mind enormously."

"It's not that simple."

"It's a start."

"I'm not sure I understand love, but I understand what it's not. It's not pretty words. It's what you do for somebody."

Elise thought about Sloane's comment. She traced a line down his nose and smoothed her finger over his mustache. Finally she brushed his lips lightly. "I'll bet that in fifteen years, no one has ever told that boy he's loved. You should be the first."

"The last time I told someone I loved them was seventeen years ago." Sloane caught Elise's finger between his teeth and bit it lightly. Elise withdrew it. "I believe I was in the throes of passion at the time."

Elise was shocked at Sloane's statement. "What about your wife?" she asked.

"I didn't love her."

"Why did you marry her then?"

"She was pregnant. She lost the baby right after the wedding."

"I'm sorry."

"I wasn't. She would have made a lousy mother, and I had no desire to be a father. We were both relieved, as awful as that sounds."

Elise tried to understand. "But you married her? You must have felt something."

"Duty. And just barely that. Neither of us had any illusions about the potential our marriage had. It was strictly to give the baby a name. I resented her for being careless about taking her pills; she resented me for being in the right place at the wrong time."

"You love Clay. You would have loved the baby, too." For some reason, Elise wanted to believe her assertion was true.

"Lise, haven't you noticed? This is not top-notch parent material you're sitting next to. Clay snuck up on me, grabbed me by the gut when I least expected it. But a baby? I don't think so. As much as I regret the years I lost with Clay, I can't be sure it wasn't for the best. If I'd had him with me all that time, maybe I wouldn't love him now."

Elise wanted to believe that Sloane was just being hard on himself. She knew he was still adjusting to parenthood, trying to come to grips with the sudden onslaught of emotion he felt for his stranger-son. But there was something that rang true in his words. She couldn't imagine him tenderly holding an infant, walking the floor at night while the baby teethed or screamed from an earache. Clay was a real person with ideas. But a baby? What was a baby other than a mass of nerves and sensations it couldn't interpret? A baby took patience, endless unqualified love and faith that your efforts would be rewarded with a healthy, happy human being farther down the line. Elise wasn't sure that Sloane had those qualities. But she wasn't sure he didn't, either. Sloane was always a puzzle.

"It's funny we should be having this talk now," she mused. "Tomorrow is all about birth and hope and love."

"And miracles."

"Sometimes the biggest miracle is finding out that we have more inside us than we thought."

"Always the optimist."

"Always the pessimist." Elise leaned over and covered Sloane's lips with her own, then she drew back. "You loved me seventeen years ago because I saw more in you than anyone else did. Maybe I still do. And maybe I see more than you do."

"What do you see?"

What did she see? A man who for all his academic titles and success still didn't truly believe in his own value as a human being? A man who was afraid to reach out, a man who wanted to share himself with his son but didn't know how? A man who for seventeen years had not uttered the three most precious words in the English language to anyone?

"I see Sloane Tyson. A man who has so much to give that those of us who love him would never be able to take it all if we had a millennium to try."

"Lise . . ."

She put her finger against his lips to stop him. "I love you, Sloane. I'm not ashamed of it, and I'm not trying to bind you to me. I just want you to know I still do. I don't think I ever stopped, and I don't think I ever will." She rested her head on his shoulder.

"And what happens when I leave?"

"I go on loving you." There was a commendable lack of self-pity in her voice. "And we both go on with our lives, glad for the time we did have together."

Amy and Clay came out of the kitchen, arm in arm. "All clean," they said together as if they'd rehearsed it.

"Terrific." Elise tried to sit up and fell back groaning. "I can't move."

Sloane gave her a push and watched as she finally got to her feet. It amazed him that she could act so naturally after what she had just said to him. She had told him she loved him as if it were the most normal, everyday kind of thing to tell someone. He wondered what it said about the depth of her feelings. He wondered what it said about his own reluctance to say the same words.

"It's time to open presents," Elise announced. "Under the Christmas tree." She turned back to Sloane and extended her hand to help him off the sofa.

"Can you lower me to the rug under the tree or shall I call for a crane?" he asked, laughing.

Sloane let her pull him off the sofa. He filed away her words and his thoughts about them to examine another time. He had always been good at living for the moment.

When everyone was sprawled around the tree, Elise passed out packages. "Amy, you go first."

Amy opened Elise's gift, exclaiming over the blue and gray sweater she had once admired when they shopped together. Clay was next, opening one of Sloane's gifts. He was genuinely thrilled with a beautifully bound book from a multivolume encyclopedia that was waiting for him at home. Elise would have throttled Sloane, who had been stubbornly determined to give his son something so impersonal and academic, except that she knew that along with the encyclopedia there was also going to be a new stereo for Clay on Christmas morning.

Elise went next, opening a monogrammed leather wallet from Amy, and Sloane followed with a large volume of e.e. cummings's poetry from his son. Then they began again. Amy rattled Clay's present, frowning. "I can't tell what it is."

"You're not supposed to be able to tell," Clay said helpfully. "If you could tell, I wouldn't have had to wrap it at all."

Amy stuck out her tongue at him and began to rip off the wrapping. Inside the small box was a silver and turquoise pin in the shape of a tiny bird. "It's beautiful." She leaned over and kissed Clay on the cheek. "Thank you."

Clay just smiled. Amy handed him his present next, and he performed the rattling ritual before he opened it. It was a colorful plastic watch, exactly like the ones every other student at Miracle Springs High had. "Because you're usually late," Amy informed him.

"Is he?" Elise asked with interest as Clay kissed Amy in thanks. "It's obviously in the Tyson genes."

Sloane grunted in protest as he handed Elise her present. She unwrapped it slowly, sadly aware that it was the last Christmas they would spend together. She wanted to draw out each moment. She opened up the box from an expensive boutique in nearby Ocala and shook out the burgundy silk that lay inside. It was a blouse, richly detailed with cutwork and lace and Victorian in style. "It's beautiful. Thank you."

Sloane stole his own thank-you kiss and then reached for his present. He opened it with no ceremony, just ripped open the wrappings and stared at the contents of the box. "Where did you get this?" he asked finally.

"Don't you remember?"

Sloane shook his head.

Elise covered his hand with hers. "You gave it to me seventeen years ago. Right before you left town. I've kept it all these years. I'm glad I did."

"What is it, Sloane?" Clay asked curiously.

Sloane held up his old journal. The cover was smudged with ink and the corners were torn away. Even with the smell of Christmas dinner hanging heavily in the air, the journal gave off the pleasant, musty scent of the past. "I kept this from the time I was your age until I turned eighteen," he told Clay. "I guess it has every feeling I felt in it, every single thing I did."

"And you gave it to Elise?" Clay asked. It was obvious he wanted to know why.

"Did you ever read it?" Sloane asked, turning to her.

"No. I couldn't."

Elise was sure Sloane understood. He had thrown it at
her in anger the day he had come to say goodbye to her.
"Read this if you ever get lonely," he'd said. "It's all
you're ever going to have of me if I leave tomorrow and
you don't."

And she had been lonely for him. So lonely sometimes that she'd picked up the journal just to feel his
presence. But she'd never read it. She'd never wanted to
suffer that much. And the day she'd decided not to fly to
Vermont to see him once more, she had packed the journal in the attic and never looked at it again. Not until
yesterday when she had unpacked it and wrapped it in
Christmas paper.

"I'm not sure I'll be able to read it either," Sloane admitted, staring blankly at the cover.

"It's the past," she reminded him. "And now is now.
That's why I'm giving it back to you."

"Thank you." Sloane's eyes caught hers and held her
gaze.

Amy and Clay got to their feet. "I'm going to walk
Amy home," Clay informed them.

"She lives a long way from here. I'll drive you,"
Sloane said, still looking at Elise.

"We're walking." Clay took Amy's hand. "I'll be
home late."

Elise smiled at Clay's show of spirit. She could see that
Sloane appreciated it, too. "Fine," he said, giving in
gracefully. "I'll see you later."

There was a flurry of goodbyes and thank-yous, then
the two teenagers departed. Elise stood at the living-room
window and watched them disappear down the street.
She felt Sloane's arms slide around her waist, and she
leaned against him.

"Two gifts, Lise. You gave me two gifts."

She knew immediately what he meant. "My love and our past," she said.

Sloane was silent, but he pulled her closer.

"Both were freely given," Elise told him. "No strings."

"You're coming over tomorrow?" he asked after a long silence.

"I still have to give Clay the book I bought for him."

"Come early. I'll make us brunch." Sloane's hands worked their way up her sides to her shoulders. Slowly, he turned her around. "Are you in a hurry to get rid of me now?"

Elise shook her head.

"How do soft carols, another glass of eggnog and me under the Christmas tree sound?"

"Like the best Christmas present of all." Elise lifted her hands to the top button of his shirt. "But let's save the carols and eggnog for later."

"Much later," he agreed, bending his head until his lips were a fraction of an inch from hers. He began to tug her blouse out of her skirt until his fingers grazed the soft skin of her stomach.

"Much later," they said together. And then they didn't say anything for a long, long time.

CHAPTER TWELVE

ELISE TUCKED THE PLAID NAPKIN over the basket of food she was carrying and swung it to the crook of her left arm. She opened the front door of Sloane's house and poked her head inside. "Sloane? Are you up? If you aren't I'm coming to get you!"

Sloane stepped out of the kitchen, wiping his hands on a dish towel. "If I'd known that, I'd have stayed in bed. Want me to go upstairs and pretend?"

"Is Clay here?"

Sloane pointed to the ceiling. "He's getting dressed."

"Then no, we'd better stay down here," Elise answered regretfully. She stepped over the threshold and into Sloane's arms. They had made leisurely love the night before, but they kissed as if they were starving for each other and had been for years. Finally Elise pulled away. "Are you sure Clay's here?"

Sloane smiled. "He's been moping around the house all morning because he can't see Amy until lunchtime. Her father's making her clean house."

"Bob's been in a foul mood ever since Carol started dating the man who owns the male Pekingese she bred hers to. He's not speaking to anybody."

"Obviously he's speaking to Amy." Sloane guided Elise into the kitchen and settled her at his table. "Coffee?"

She nodded and Sloane fixed it just the way she liked it. There was something wonderfully intimate about watching him add cream and sugar to the cup without having to give it a second thought. For a moment, she let herself pretend that this kind of familiar sharing wasn't going to end soon.

"I can't believe you're going to the celebration with me today," Elise said after half a cup was finished in comfortable silence.

"I can't believe it either. I have written proof upstairs that I once vowed I would never do this."

"You said you'd never come back here, period," Elise reminded him. Without thinking she reached out and stroked his smoothly shaven jaw. "You've been reading your journal, haven't you?"

"Last night. What a passionate creature I was."

"Passionate. Sensitive. Intelligent." Elise lowered her voice to a whisper. "Obnoxious."

Sloane grinned at her. "You won't get an argument from me on that. I was worse than obnoxious. I was prejudiced, small-minded, totally set in my ways. All the things I accused this town of being. How did you stand me?"

"Well, I never saw you that way. I guess I saw a boy whose feelings ran deeper than anyone I'd ever known. That was the part of you I fell in love with."

It was the first time in months that they had mentioned their past. With Christmas Day as a new beginning they had lived only in the present. They had spent every spare minute together, laughing, loving, building onto a friendship that had begun so many years before. Their time together had to be carefully orchestrated. Sloane had Clay to worry about, and Elise had her reputation in the community. But they had seen those obstacles as challenges, and they had found ways around them.

January had included a weekend in Miami where Sloane was supposed to be researching his next book but instead, had thoroughly researched Elise. February, a month too short on days, had been long on leisurely evenings by Sloane's fireplace while Clay studied or slept upstairs. In March, over Easter break, they had explored nearby Disney World. There Sloane had immediately scrapped the nebulous ideas for his next book and begun an impassioned sociological study of what Mickey Mouse had and hadn't done for Central Florida. And in April, more than once, they had visited the riverbank to wade in the icy Wehachee and watch it awaken to the glories of spring.

Now it was May. In a month, Elise knew that Sloane would be gone.

"I got a letter from the couple subletting my apartment in Cambridge today," Sloane said, as if he were reading her thoughts. "They're moving out two weeks earlier than they'd intended. It means I can leave a little sooner than I'd planned."

"When will you be going?" Elise forced herself to meet his gaze.

"Right after school ends. There's a summer program for gifted high school students at Boston University. I talked to a friend who teaches there and he wants Clay to attend. He'll meet some kids in the city, and it'll help him get ready for school next year."

Elise kept her tone neutral. "That sounds like a good idea. I'll send a recommendation if you need one. I know he's still struggling with math, but he's absolutely brilliant in English."

"Science is a puzzle for him. He told me yesterday that his biology teacher says he knows more biology than any student he's ever had. Then he told me that until he was twelve, he didn't know that man had ever been in space. He can identify all the stars in the heavens, put a car engine together with his eyes closed and explain Darwin's theories better than Darwin could. But he's never heard of an ion, a proton, or a neutron."

Elise wondered why they were talking about the peculiarities of Clay's education when what they really needed to talk about was the fact that Sloane was leaving in less than a month. But the reason for the evasion wasn't too mystifying. She suspected that Sloane, like herself, didn't want to face their parting.

She chose to continue talking about Clay, too. "Clay's going to miss the friends he's made here. I hope you'll let him come visit Lillian from time to time."

"Actually, he wants to stay and finish school here." Sloane's voice was emotionless.

Elise imagined the hurt behind Sloane's carefully guarded expression. She wanted to comfort him, but she knew there was little she could say. Even though Sloane and Clay had lived together for almost a year, they were still strangers in the most important ways. Sloane rarely discussed it, but Elise knew how much he yearned for his son's love.

"Have you considered letting him stay?" she asked, reaching out to cover Sloane's hand with hers. "He could live with me if Lillian isn't up to it."

"I want him with me."

Elise nodded, relieved at his answer. Sloane wanted to continue trying to be a good father. He had no intention of giving up. "Good."

"Maybe I'm wrong."

"Maybe you're not." She laced her fingers with his and brought them to her cheek. "He needs you more than he needs to stay here."

"I'm not sure Clay needs anybody. Except Amy, maybe."

"Didn't you need a father when you were Clay's age?" she asked gently.

"I always needed a father."

"Clay's no different. He just doesn't know how to let you know."

"Sometimes I think I'd know what to do better if my own father had lived and I'd grown up with him." It was a rare moment of vulnerability for Sloane, and Elise squeezed his hand in tribute.

"Hi, Elise." Clay's entrance was heralded by the clatter of his topsiders on the stairs. He headed straight for his father. "Can we pick Amy up on our way to the Inn? Mr. Cargil said she could leave at noon if she was finished, and she is."

"I don't know how she finished, considering the two of you spent most of the morning on the telephone," Sloane observed. "But I think we're about ready to go."

"I packed a picnic lunch." Elise patted the basket, which she'd set on the table. "We can avoid the food at the Inn."

Clay peeked under the napkin. "You made your own bread!"

"Just for you. I used your recipe."

"And it made enough for an army," Sloane guessed out loud. "It took Clay three months before he figured out how to cut down his granola recipe for the two of us. We were eating it for breakfast, lunch and dinner. I gained three pounds."

"If I flunk out of that fancy New England prep school you're planning to send me to, I can always get a job as a cook in a health food restaurant," Clay said nonchalantly.

"What's this about a prep school?" Elise asked Clay.

"Sloane's got his eye on the Ivy League."

"Sloane?"

"You know," Sloane teased, "one of those places where Clay'll have to wear a coat and tie all day except when he's out on the field in his rugby uniform."

"You wouldn't!" Elise slapped the table in front of her.

"Actually it's a military academy."

"Sloane!"

"How about a private coed Quaker school that concentrates on small classes and individual learning?"

Elise smiled and relaxed. "That sounds wonderful."

"Convince my son, then."

"Don't you want to go, Clay?" she asked, turning back to the teenager who was rummaging through the picnic basket approvingly.

"I don't know."

Elise recognized Clay's answer for what it was. An attempt to avoid telling the truth. Pretending indecision was better than saying yes when he didn't mean it and not as good as saying no. As much as she wanted to ease the strain between father and son by getting them to talk to one another she decided not to push. "Well, I know a certain man—a man who is sitting at this table in fact— who would have loved to go to such an institution at your age. Correct?" she asked Sloane.

"At Clay's age I didn't know such a place existed. But yes, I would have loved it. I think Clay will, too. If not, we'll find something he likes better."

Clay abandoned the basket and faced his father. "Really?"

Sloane's voice showed his surprise. "Really. Did you think I was going to stick you somewhere and leave you? You'll be living at home; we'll talk. If you hate it you can tell me."

"And you'd listen?" Clay sounded as if he wanted to make sure he understood.

"Don't I listen now?"

Father and son were staring at each other. Elise wanted to disappear under the table and leave them alone. All she could do was remain perfectly still.

"I don't know if you listen because I don't say much," Clay said finally. Then he turned to leave the kitchen. "I'm going to call Amy and tell her we'll be over in a few minutes." He was gone before Sloane could say another word.

THE INN HAD ENDURED its yearly sprucing up for the Festival of the Miracle. The grounds were as neat as the proverbial pin with all the shrubs trimmed to immaculate perfection and the grass cut so that each blade was identical. Summer annuals bordered the Inn's front porch and hanging baskets of shocking-pink petunias and lilac lantana decorated the rafters. Even the Spanish moss on the trees seemed to have been arranged in lacier designs.

Church groups and local entrepreneurs had set up booths and tables all over the grounds. Behind the Inn where the long yard sloped down to the Wehachee, blankets were spread and family groups sat at makeshift picnic tables enjoying the late spring sunshine.

The temperature was a not-so-subtle reminder of the blistering heat that would follow in the months to come, but everyone had dressed accordingly in shorts and cool summer dresses. The air was redolent with the smells of spring and coconut sunscreen.

Elise and Sloane, followed in the distance by Amy and Clay, spread two quilts side by side and began to unpack the picnic basket. Sloane inventoried out loud as he set the food on the quilt. "Deviled eggs. Chicken sandwiches. Celery stuffed with cream cheese. Brie. Brie? The Piggly Wiggly is carrying Brie these days?"

"I bought it in Ocala. Keep going. I'm starving."

"Homemade bread." Sloane sniffed the bread. "Raisin bread." He looked up and grinned. "How much is at home in your freezer?"

"Six loaves. That's why we're having chicken sandwiches. I had to take out two chickens to make room for it."

"You have to cut all of Clay's recipes in half."

"I did." Elise pushed Sloane playfully to one side and finished unpacking the basket herself. "Marinated mushrooms. Artichoke salad. And," she waved the last item in front of Sloane's nose, "fresh blackberries."

"My sweet little yuppie Florida cracker," Sloane crooned, planting a big kiss on her willing mouth. "You can pack a picnic for me anytime."

"Just remember to order well in advance so I can drive into Ocala." She picked up a stalk of celery and stuck it in Sloane's mouth. "Do you know how many people just saw you kiss me?"

Sloane crunched on the celery thoughtfully. "What happens if I do it again?"

"They'll read the banns next Sunday at church."

"Everyone knows we're sleeping together."

"Everyone suspects," she corrected him. "They're just looking for a shred of firm evidence."

"Has anyone said anything to you?"

Actually she had been innundated with tactless queries, but Elise didn't want to burden Sloane with that knowledge. She had become adept at evading questions. She would evade this one, too. "Well, sure. Mrs. Barlow said hello this morning, and Marion, the cashier at the grocery store, asked me how I was when I bought mayonnaise for the sandwiches."

"Is your job in jeopardy?" Sloane asked, cutting through to the heart of the matter.

"No."

"You could find a job in Boston."

Elise met his eyes. "I could find a job anywhere."

"Do you want to leave this place?"

Elise had no idea why Sloane had asked the question. A part of her leapt in hope that it was his way of asking her to go with him. Another part drowned in despair because the question seemed so casual. He might as well have asked her to pass another piece of celery.

"Sometimes leaving here is the only thing on my mind," she said carefully. "And sometimes I realize I'm lucky to live somewhere where I'm held in high esteem. Teachers in big cities are just part of the scenery. In a town like this one, we're part of people's lives."

Sloane seemed contented with her answer. "I could never live here. Even now, with my departure right around the corner, I feel so constrained and hemmed in that I think I'm going to explode."

"I haven't sensed that." Elise felt a surge of pain at his words.

"I don't feel it when I'm with you," Sloane reassured her. "I've never felt it with you. I'm going to miss you, Lise."

"I'm going to miss you, too." More than you could ever imagine, she thought as she leaned over for the second forbidden kiss. Probably more than she could imagine herself.

Clay and Amy joined them a few minutes later and the afternoon became the makings of a bittersweet memory. Each of them knew that the time for finding simple joy in each other was coming to a close. They took the time remaining to them and colored it with laughter and kisses and poignant conversation.

After stuffing themselves with Elise's picnic, they strolled to the front of the Inn and visited the festively decorated booths. Elise and Amy had their fortunes told, and although Clay and Sloane laughed at them, the two males were discovered a few minutes later gambling all their spare change on a balloon-busting dart-throwing contest. They drank fresh lemonade, cakewalked and applauded Amy, who was brave enough to have a glittering butterfly painted on her cheek. They watched little girls in lipstick and tutus perform a ballet to the music of *Swan Lake* and little boys in green derbies tap-dance to "The Sidewalks of New York." Afterward, they sat on the riverbank with a crowd of others and fished from numbered cane poles to try and land the largest catch of the day.

No fish, three volleyball games and four hot dogs later, they stood on the riverbank and watched the sun disappear behind the bald cypress, tupelo and water oak that lined the Wehachee. Frogs in the thick underbrush of cabbage palm and button bush began a symphony and a screech owl joined in with its mournful wail. The night was damp and velvet dark before they gathered their quilts and headed back to Sloane's car.

"Now to see the maiden," he said. "We have plenty of time. Would you like to go home first?"

"I'd like to change out of these shorts," Elise admitted. "It'll be chilly by midnight."

"Can you drop Amy and me at the springs?" Clay asked. "We told some people we'd meet them there."

"I guess that'd be all right."

Elise watched Clay slide out of the back seat and extend his hand to Amy. Amy took it as naturally as if she'd always held it. Clay and Amy were more than teenagers in love. They were kindred spirits. There was so little of the moody, exhilarating highs and debilitating lows of young love in their relationship. They were enchanted with each other, obviously emotional in their responses, but there was a steady quality, a certainty about their feelings that set them apart.

"Clay and Amy are going to feel like they've each been torn in half when Clay leaves," Elise observed, her head back against the seat of Sloane's car as he drove to her house.

"For once I'll understand exactly how Clay feels."

She smiled a little. "And I'll be able to sympathize with Amy. I'll remember just how it felt." She didn't add that she'd be feeling the same way again. It was part of the bargain she had made with herself and, unconsciously, with Sloane. She had no right to make him feel guilty about leaving. She would not tell him of the devastation she was going to feel when he walked away for the last time. It would serve no purpose; it would only spoil their last days together.

Minutes later Sloane and Elise were alone in her front hallway. "Do you mind if I help you change?" he asked, his hands already laying claim to her body in a way that announced that he expected no resistance.

Even as a lustful teenager, Sloane could not remember being this insatiable. It seemed to him that he always wanted Elise. He could make love to her, fill his body with the total peace that comes after good sex, and then an hour later—alone in his own bed—he would begin to crave the feel and smell and taste of her all over again. His fingers would tingle with the urge to stroke her smooth olive skin and feel it heat with her response. He wanted to smell her subtly exotic perfume of orange blossoms and jasmine, the fragrance of a hot Florida night that drifted around her when she moved. He wanted to taste the rich cream flavor of her skin, feel it linger on his tongue until she seemed a part of him.

He would lie in his bed and try to remember the little noises she made when he touched her, the sighs, the moans, the words of love she'd murmur. But it was never enough. Not nearly enough. His heart constricting, Sloane realized it never would be. When he left Miracle Springs, his longing was going to explode within him. She was staying behind; he was leaving. It was inevitable, as inevitable as the calm, sure flow of the Wehachee. If he asked Elise to come with him, history would repeat itself. In seventeen years, neither of them had changed enough to challenge fate.

Away from everything she knew, Elise would be like a bird raised in captivity who is set free to roam the skies. She would be stricken with fear, unable to fly in strange territory. Eventually her freedom would be her undoing. She would long for her cage, perishing without it, and she would never know the joys of the new gift she had been given.

But oh, how he wanted it to be different. How he wanted to challenge her to come, to defy the inevitable, to dare her to fly far and free.

"Sloane? You asked me a question, I answered it and you've been staring at me ever since." Elise frowned and stood on tiptoe to wipe parallel vertical lines from his forehead.

He pulled her close in a bone-crushing hug, and he knew that if his life depended on letting her go at that moment, that he could not. He held her and felt his eyes fill with tears. He never cried.

"Sloane?" Elise's arms crept hesitantly around his waist. She could feel him tremble with emotion. "What's wrong?"

He swallowed hard, banishing the moisture from his eyes. He wanted to tell her that he didn't want to leave Miracle Springs without her. He wanted to ask her to come. But he couldn't do that to either of them. He would not watch what they had together die in new surroundings. Instead he told her only a tiny part of the truth. "I was just thinking how lucky we've been. You've given me more happiness in these months together than most people get in a lifetime. I'll never forget them."

"Don't forget me," she whispered. "Don't ever forget me. Promise me that much."

"I won't forget you. I couldn't, not even if I wanted to."

He picked her up and carried her to the sofa. Their clothes were abandoned and their movements were, too. They made love, completely aware of each other as they searched for the response they needed to make the act of love perfect. It was a long time before they dressed again and walked in silence to the springs.

The springs was silent, too. The same boisterous crowd who had romped and laughed at the Inn's festivities had settled on every square foot of sand of the beach. There were only the hushed tones of an occasional voice to augment the sounds of a star-filled Florida night. Sloane and Elise found Amy and Clay near the water's edge, and they joined them on their quilt.

Now was the time of meditation, of crystallizing wishes until—if the maiden appeared—the wish would be so clear that it could be granted. Now was also the time of searching hearts for purity. No one on the tourist commission had ever defined exactly what a pure heart was, but each person on the beach had his or her own understanding of what that meant. Even those who had come to scoff fell into the mood of contemplation and wondered what their greatest heart's desire was and what they had done that year to prevent it from being realized.

There were already mists rising from the water. The temperature had turned cool enough to scare away mosquitoes and the air hummed only with expectations, crickets and frogs. Elise leaned against Sloane and closed her eyes. She had no idea if she qualified as having a pure heart. She knew she had tried to live up to her own beliefs. Finally, after much thought, it wasn't her own purity she questioned, but her wish. Like the cowardly lion in a different fable, she wished for the courage she knew she didn't have. She wished for the words to tell Sloane her feelings. She wished she could ask him if she could come with him. She wished for the fortitude to withstand his inevitable answer, his apologies, his sympathy. She wished that just this once—even knowing she was doomed to failure—she would reach out for what she wanted most in the world. And when that effort was unsuccessful—as she knew it would be—she wished she might have the courage to leave Miracle Springs anyway, to begin a life somewhere else, a life rich in possibility and growth.

Sloane felt Elise sigh, and he tightened his arm around her. He wondered what she wished for. Was it the impossible? Did she fantasize that life could go on always as it had in the last incredible months? If she did, it was close to his own deepest wish. But Sloane knew better than to put his faith in Indian maidens and tourist commissions. His wish tonight would be simpler and entirely plausible. He would wish that his parting with Elise would be quick and as painless for both of them as possible. He would take nothing of her back to New England, and his wish was that she would keep nothing of him here with her.

AMY STROKED CLAY'S HAIR. He had pillowed his head in her lap and the sensation was intimate and very special. Their parting lay before her, and it was all she could think of as she waited restlessly for the Indian maiden to appear. It wasn't fair. Clay had come unexpectedly into her life, and soon he would be gone. She would stay behind in a town that now seemed filled with restrictions and people who were nothing but strangers. Her wish was simple. She wished that the years would pass quickly and that someday she would find Clay again as an adult, free to live the life she chose.

Clay absorbed the pleasures of Amy's hand stroking his hair. When she touched him he could feel the effect all over his body, and he wondered what it would be like to feel all of her against him. The forbidden thought shot through him, translated into sensation. Someday he would be an adult. If he had any wish at all it was that when that day arrived, somehow Amy would be there to share his life with him.

Amy bent her head and put her mouth to his ear. "You'd better sit up or you won't see anything."

He did so reluctantly. They sat holding hands and watching the wisps of mist play over the water of the springs. The sliver of moon disappeared behind a cloud, and the frogs quieted until the sound that was dominant was the whisper of trees at the water's edge as a light wind blew in from the south. The mists danced, scampering over the water like small children. They formed and reformed, tantalizing the people on the beach with their antics. Near the island the mists gathered, covering and obscuring the palmetto and cypress knees until the island itself was wreathed in vapor and seemed a part of the river.

Midnight came and went. There were soft rustling sounds from the beach as some people left. Elise wondered if they were leaving because they had seen the maiden or because they had given up. She never wanted to leave. The sensuous beauty of the night, the comforting feel of Sloane's arms around her, the shared longing of humans—skeptical and not skeptical—who waited for a miracle, all blended together to fill her with a peace she had seldom known. She could sit there for hours, absorbing it into her soul to sustain her in the days ahead when she would need tranquillity most.

But as she watched, the mists on the island parted. The moon came from behind its cloud and grew in power until the island was brilliant with its beams. From the cypress knees and palmetto an iridescent wraith uncurled. It was vapor illuminated by moonlight, one delicate, human-shaped spiral of mist that looked strangely unlike mist at all. It moved to the edge of the island, a woman with her arms outstretched, and then as Elise watched, it floated above the island and was absorbed into the surrounding vapor. She felt the sting of tears in her eyes and then the wetness of her cheeks.

Sloane's arm tightened spasmodically around her. Suddenly he wished that he'd been less practical. Given the chance for a miracle, he'd chosen only to ask for a comfortable parting. He wanted to shout for the maiden to come back. He wanted to shout his sorrow to the heavens and ask for another chance.

"Did you see her?" Elise asked softly. "She's gone now. Tell me you saw her."

He took a deep breath and wondered at his own response. "I saw something."

"Amy, Clay?" Elise whispered. "Did you see her?"

She saw their heads nod in the darkness. Silently, with no need for more conversation, they all stood together. Sloane picked up the quilt and they found their way across the beach to the road.

No one else moved. Those still on the beach sat quietly, still waiting to see the maiden.

CHAPTER THIRTEEN

ELISE STARED at the telephone receiver until a loud buzzing informed her that the other party was no longer on the line and the phone had been off the hook long enough. She replaced the receiver gently and then stared at her hands, finally letting her eyes and her hands travel to her abdomen. The words she had just heard still rang in her head. *"The test was positive, Miss Ramsey."*

Positive? The doctor's words had been clear and precise, but how could she have heard him correctly? Still, he had warned her of this possibility at her annual checkup earlier that day. The telephone call had only been a confirmation of their earlier conversation. She'd thought of nothing but his warning since she'd left his office.

"I told you you'd have great difficulty getting pregnant. I didn't tell you it was impossible. These things can change as a woman grows older. It was years ago, but I'm sure I must have pointed out that if you wanted to be absolutely safe, you'd have to use birth control."

Elise shook her head as if to rid herself of the truth. Pregnant. Six weeks along, he had estimated. Hadn't she wondered when her period was late?

No, she hadn't. Sloane and Clay were leaving in a matter of days. Her periods had been late often enough, especially when she was under stress. She'd had no reason to worry about pregnancy and no symptoms that couldn't be explained by her unhappiness. She had not considered the fact that a child might be growing inside her. Sloane's child. Clay's brother or sister.

Why hadn't she postponed her appointment until Sloane was gone? Her decision now would be easier. She'd considered it. She hadn't wanted to make the drive into Ocala and miss an afternoon with him. But her doctor was popular and the appointment had been made months before. She had decided to go, using the traveling time to try and figure out how to say goodbye to Sloane when he left on Saturday.

The trip back home had been a nightmare. If what the doctor said was true, saying goodbye would be easy compared to telling Sloane he was to be a father again. She had refused to accept the doctor's diagnosis until the test was completed, but she had known at some deeper level that the phone call would confirm his prediction.

Sloane would not believe she hadn't done this on purpose. And perhaps he was correct. Wasn't it Freud who said there were no accidents? Had she hoped that Sloane's seed would find its way deep inside her and give her a part of him to keep forever? Against the odds, had she hoped for the miracle of life, for the miracle of joining herself with Sloane in the unmistakable commitment of a child?

She would never know. She had believed she would never conceive. But she had taken no additional precautions to insure it. She had left the final decision to fate.

A baby. Hers to love. She had loved and let go, loved and let go all her life. But this time she would not have to let go. The child would be hers forever. He or she would grow, move away and live its own life, but there would be a bond that would never be broken. Her child.

Sloane's child. The man who never wanted to be a father. The man who had admitted to relief when the wife he hadn't wanted to marry had miscarried. But also the man who yearned for the love of his teenage son, the man who felt cheated because he hadn't known Clay as a child. A man often at war with himself.

Elise stood and smoothed her skirt nervously. Sloane was coming for dinner. She was faced with two choices. She could tell him about the pregnancy—as his ex-wife had done—accept his obligatory offer of marriage and prepare herself for a life of one-sided love and resentment. Or she could refuse to tell him—as Willow had done—and deny him the chance to learn to love his own child.

Neither possibility was tenable. She could not bear trapping Sloane into marriage, nor could she bear cheating him out of knowing his son or daughter. And as she realized that both choices were impossible, her third choice became obvious to her.

She would tell Sloane, but not until the baby was born and she was established somewhere else. She could not live in Miracle Springs any longer. That was definite. Unmarried mothers did not make role models for the youth of the town. She would lose her job, her prestige, her place in the community. She had to leave town, and she had to do it before her pregnancy began to show.

She would move to another part of the country, find a job outside of teaching and set up a good situation for her child. Then, when her life was in order, she would tell Sloane. He would not be obligated to offer her marriage, and he would still have the option of getting to know his son or daughter. The choice would be his. She would not push or plead. If it was beyond him to love another child, she would understand. This child would have all her love; she could be father and mother to it.

There was a knock on the front door, and Elise realized just how long she had been standing in one place, contemplating her future. As she walked to the door she realized something else. She was no longer in shock. She was terrified at the coming changes, but more important, she was elated. Growing inside her was the child of the man standing on the other side of the door. Sloane would leave, but no matter where he went, no matter what happened in the future, she would always have a part of him in her life.

When she opened the door, her smile was genuine. She put her arms around Sloane's neck before he could say a word and kissed him. Then she drew away, and she knew that doing so was the more significant act.

"Let's pretend I just knocked," Sloane said, stepping forward to catch her by the waist before she retreated farther. "Instant replay." He bent and joined his mouth to hers. He encouraged her to part her lips and his tongue tasted them before it moved beyond to meet hers. Elise sighed and allowed him to pull her closer.

"Any man worthy of the name would kill for a greeting like that," Sloane said finally, after reluctantly pulling his mouth from hers.

"I'm afraid it was the highlight of the evening," Elise apologized. "I haven't gotten dinner started yet."

"Let me take you out."

"No." She stepped away and held out her hand. "I don't want to share you with crowds."

"We could go somewhere romantic and intimate."

"We'd have to drive miles to do that. Come help me." She led him into the kitchen.

"Hard day?" Sloane asked as they rummaged through the refrigerator.

She bit her lip to keep from blurting out an answer she would regret. "We only had a half day of school today, and I had an appointment in Ocala," she said finally. "I got home later than I'd intended."

Sloane took lettuce and cucumbers from her hands and set them on the counter.

"These tomatoes are fresh," she said, changing the subject. "The father of one of my students grew them in his garden. I've got peppers, too."

"What kind of an appointment?"

"Doctor's. Routine. How does steak sound? We can broil it."

"Are you all right?"

Elise felt her heart stop and start up again at double speed. She wet her lips and told him the truth. "I've never been better."

Sloane took the peppers and tomatoes out of her arms and lifted her to stand against the open door. "Dinner sounds great. Why don't you put some potatoes in the oven to go along with the steak?"

"That'll take a long time," she warned.

"My intentions exactly." He drew her toward him and shut the refrigerator.

And since she had never needed him more than she did at that moment, Elise went willingly into his arms.

"YOUR FATHER WON'T let you stay with your aunt and go to school here next year?"

Clay brushed Amy's curls with his fingertips. They were sitting in the front seat of his father's car. Clay had turned sixteen on the twenty-seventh of May, and Sloane had taken him for his driver's license the next day. The resulting sensation of power was overwhelming. "He wants me to come with him."

"I want you to stay."

"He's promised I can come here for Christmas."

"That's seven months away!"

"I can count, Amy."

Amy lay her head on Clay's shoulder and turned her face up to his. "I'm sorry."

Clay hugged her against him. "I'm not anxious to leave. You know that."

"My father says it's a good thing you're going."

"That doesn't surprise me. What else does he say?"

Amy hesitated and then giggled. "Something about a chastity belt."

Clay grinned. "Maybe he's not so out of it after all."

"He's going to be out here any minute to drag me inside."

Clay took the hint and turned her so that he could reach her lips. She ended up on his lap with the steering wheel pressed against her back.

"What a difference sixteen makes," Amy teased finally, pushing Clay away. She slid off his lap and straightened her clothes. "Maybe my father's right. Maybe it's a good thing you're going."

Clay fingered one bright-gold curl. "I'll miss you."

"We can write."

The front door of Amy's house slammed, and Amy swiveled to watch her father stalk down the sidewalk. She opened the door before he reached the car. "I was just coming in, Daddy."

Bob Cargil peered through the window. "You've been out here long enough!"

"Mr. Cargil?"

Bob frowned at Clay, his obvious dislike barely in check. "What?"

"We both care very much about her. We do have that much in common."

Clay could see the effect the simple statement had on the older man's face. Little by little Bob's frown disappeared until the resulting lack of expression was like a chalkboard wiped clean.

"You're a hard kid to figure out," Bob said finally.

Amy slid across the seat and stepped out onto the sidewalk. Bob slammed the door, and together he and Amy watched Clay drive away.

THERE WAS ONLY ONE PLACE to say goodbye. Only one way.

On Friday night Elise stood in her bedroom, adjusting the fit of the bathing suit she had bought for the occasion. Her old suit, a sleek black maillot, had emphasized the slight fullness of her stomach. The faint bulge was barely noticeable—she hadn't thought about it herself until the doctor's diagnosis. Still, someone who was familiar with every curve of her body might be able to tell the difference. Naked, she looked very much the same, but the clinging black fabric might point out the truth about her pregnancy to Sloane.

To compensate she had got a new suit, a dark blue and red Hawaiian print in a sarong style that softened the lines of her abdomen and the riper curves of her breasts. It set off her perpetual tan and the glossy length of her hair, and she covered it with a beach dress in the same pattern.

She was halfway downstairs when she heard Sloane's knock. He was early for once, and when she opened the door to greet him, Clay was standing by his side. She kissed them both, one more passionately than the other, and drew them inside. "Where's Amy?"

"We'll pick her up on the way."

"I've got everything packed to take."

"I picked up drinks."

"Champagne," Clay added.

Elise met Sloane's eyes without flinching or showing her distress. "Bon voyage."

"Something like that." He reached out and smoothed a lock of hair back from her face. The champagne had been an afterthought, and he wished he hadn't brought it. Tonight felt like anything but a celebration. And yet it would do nothing but harm to treat the occasion like the funeral it was.

"It's a good thing there's a graduation dance at the Inn tonight. The springs would be packed otherwise." Elise made her way into the kitchen and began to load Sloane and Clay with food to carry out to the car.

"Actually I thought we could go down the river to a spot I know," Sloane told her. "But I didn't realize you were packing all this food."

Elise knew just what spot he meant. "Well, you're going to be sitting in a car for days. You can use the exercise to get yourself in shape."

They managed to take all the food to the car in one trip. Amy was waiting for them in front of her house. Sloane had handed the car keys to his son at Elise's, and he and Elise had climbed into the back seat. Now they watched as Clay got out to open Amy's door.

"Polite boy, your son," Elise murmured. "Much politer than you ever were."

"Everything a father could want."

"He's the brightest student I ever had. If he decides to write, he's going to be well-known someday."

"I hope he's going to be happy someday," Sloane said cryptically.

"He's happy now."

"He tolerates his life. He wants to be free."

"Don't we all?" Elise laced her fingers through Sloane's and squeezed them tight. "Growing up is realizing you're never free and learning to live with your restrictions."

Sloane wondered if she was talking about herself or Clay or all of them. "Maybe growing up is learning to rise above restrictions," he parried.

"We've had this argument before."

"Continuously," Sloane said with a touch of bitterness.

"Don't." Elise withdrew her hand. "I thought we'd accepted our differences."

"I'm sorry. This is no time to fight."

No, this was the time to pretend that everything was fine. Elise accepted his apology with a nod.

Clay covered the miles to the springs with confidence. He was a good driver, careful, patient, thoughtful. Elise admired his skill and told him so. At the beach they unpacked, distributing the food into four loads. Then Sloane led them down the path to the riverbank.

"This is great," Amy said with enthusiasm. "How come you never showed us this before?"

"I thought every teenager in Miracle Springs already knew about this place," Elise told her. She spread the quilt she carried on the narrow strip of sand. There was just enough room.

"They've been keeping it private," Clay told Amy, dropping to the quilt to take off his shoes. "Race you to the water."

In a minute he and Amy were chasing each other into the river.

Sloane watched Clay play. He swam now as if he'd been born to the water. Best of all, he obviously enjoyed it. It was just one of many changes.

"Why didn't we show this place to them?" Sloane asked. He sat next to Elise and opened the small cooler, pulling out the bottle of champagne.

"Because we didn't want them doing what we did here. They're not old enough yet."

"How old do they have to be?"

"Old enough to realize how much they could hurt each other."

Sloane stopped work on freeing the plastic stopper from the bottle neck. "Did we hurt each other?"

Elise stretched out next to him and rolled to her side. "It's been worth any pain it caused. All of this has."

"Are you going to be all right, Lise?" Sloan set down the bottle. "Be honest."

"You don't have to worry about me." She wrapped her fingers around the open lapel of his shirt and pulled him down beside her. "I have no regrets."

"None?"

"None I want to talk about." She put one finger on his lips to silence his questions. "Do you remember Thanksgiving?" She went on without letting him answer. "I told you then that when it came time for you to go I'd let you. No tears, no recriminations. I've known this day was coming. I'm prepared."

Sloane kissed her finger then brushed it aside. "You have a standing invitation to visit me in Cambridge."

"Maybe I will." Neither of them believed her.

"Clay wants to come back for Christmas." Sloane couldn't stop himself from continuing the subject although Elise had obviously tried to bring it to a close.

"That would be nice."

Sloane frowned at her lack of enthusiasm. "I might come too."

What could she say? That next December she would be in her eighth month of pregnancy and settled somewhere far away? That if Sloane came, he would not find her here? "It's easier for me to believe this is over than to grasp at straws," she said at last.

"That's like you."

"And it's like you to criticize me for it." Elise sat up and grabbed her knees, staring at the river. "You're trying to start a fight. It'll be easier for you to leave if you're angry with me. I'd suggest you rise above the inclination."

Sloane sat up, too. He put his hand on her shoulder. "Is that what I'm doing? Maybe I'm genuinely upset to be saying goodbye."

"You don't have to say it, Sloane."

"What does that mean?"

Elise clamped her mouth shut and shook her head. What was she saying? With all the complications between them, why was she confronting him now?

Sloane's hand tightened on her shoulder. "What are you saying?"

She shook her head again and wished the conversation had never gone this far.

"I have to say goodbye. I can't stay here. My life is in Cambridge."

"Don't you think I know that?"

"Then what are you saying? That you'll come with me?" He cupped her chin and turned her face to his.

"Do you honestly believe you'd be happy living away from everything you know and care about?"

Elise wondered how Sloane could have made love to her all these months and not realized that *he* was what she cared about. He clung to the belief that she was still the eighteen-year-old girl who had refused to leave her home for him. It was easier because then he could avoid thinking about making a commitment to her. He was a man who wanted no commitments. It was that part of him that made it impossible to take the final step with Clay—and that part of him that would hate knowing he was a father yet again.

She decided, having gone this far, that she owed him some of the truth. "I could be happy living anywhere with a man who loved and wanted me always. We both know that man isn't you."

In the twilight, Sloane's expression was difficult to read. Elise thought she saw anger, chased closely by regret. But she couldn't be sure.

"Maybe it's easier for you to believe that than to reach out for something you say you want." He removed his hand and turned back to the water. "I'm going for a swim."

"We can eat when you get back."

He stripped off his shirt and shorts and walked to the water's edge. Then he turned and held out his hand. "Come with me."

She wanted to refuse. She needed the time away from him to put everything back in perspective. But even as she was about to say no she stood and took his hand.

"I don't want this night to be spoiled," he said.

"Neither do I."

They walked into the water together, passing Amy and Clay who were on their way out. "Go ahead and start on the picnic," Elise encouraged them. "Just save us some."

Clay watched Elise and Sloane swimming toward the middle of the river. "They had a fight," he said.

"How can you tell?" Amy handed Clay a piece of fried chicken. "Do you want a Coke?"

He nodded. "Watch the way they swim. They're three feet apart, and they aren't talking."

"It's hard to talk and swim at the same time."

"Not when you're in love."

"Do people their age fall in love? I always thought they got together because they were lonely or something."

"I think they've always been in love. At least Elise loves Sloane. I'm not sure Sloane can love anybody." Clay punctuated his sentence by turning the Coke can bottom up and drinking most of it in one long swallow.

"He loves you."

Clay set down his can and began on the chicken. "Are you going to date other people while I'm away? I want you to."

Amy respected the abrupt change of subject. "Yeah. Did you think I was going to sit around and mope for two years?" she teased. "And you. Are you going to find yourself another girlfriend at that fancy school you're going to?"

"Probably three or four, now that I know how."

"I like the three or four bit. Just don't get too serious about one."

"I'm already serious about one."

"Do you think? . . ." Amy finished her chicken as she contemplated how to ask her question. "Do you think we'll still love each other when we're old enough to?"

"We're old enough now."

"That's not what I meant exactly. I don't feel old enough, not for... well, you know."

Clay smiled. "It's funny. The moment I turned sixteen I felt old enough for that."

"Well if that happens on *my* birthday, it could be a problem. I'll turn sixteen while you're away."

"There was a guy at Destiny who always used to lecture everybody about the beauties of self-denial. He was kind of a nut. Everybody listened to him and then went right on doing what they pleased. Maybe he had a point, though."

"Will you wait for me?" Amy wiped her hands on a napkin, taking great care with each finger, not looking at Clay. "I want to be your first. I want you to be my first."

Clay swallowed hard. "When?"

"When we're ready. We'll know, won't we?"

"I guess we'll know. I just hope we don't both get ready when we're living in different places." He reached out and covered Amy's hand.

She met his eyes. "Just make sure you get Sloane to let you come back to visit as often as you can."

"I will."

Amy giggled. "That shouldn't be too hard. He and Elise are going to want to see each other."

"I don't know. They went seventeen years without seeing each other. Who knows, maybe it'll be another seventeen."

"What is it that keeps them from getting married?"

"They're both afraid."

"That's dumb. They're so happy together."

Clay and Amy turned to watch the two adults who were treading water in the middle of the river. "I sure hope when we're that age we'll have more sense," Amy said, as Sloane kissed Elise and they disappeared under the water's surface for a moment. "I don't ever want to be that messed up."

ELISE CAME AROUND to the driver's seat of Sloane's car and leaned through the window to give Clay a goodbye kiss. "I'll miss you," she said, her eyes bright with tears. "Write me."

"I will." Clay's voice was husky.

She stepped back and watched as he drove away. Sloane stood on the sidewalk. When Elise joined him he picked up the empty picnic basket and the quilt and started up the walkway to her house. He paused on the front porch. "Do you want to say goodbye here?" he asked without turning to look at her.

"We've been saying goodbye for weeks now. One more real goodbye won't hurt either of us."

Sloane turned and held out his hand for her key. In a moment they were inside. He leaned against the door. "I wanted to make love to you at the river tonight. I've never wanted anything that badly before."

Elise tossed her hair over her shoulder. "And how do you feel now?"

"The same."

The corners of her mouth curled up in a tiny smile. "Will my bed do?"

"The hard floor would do."

Elise started toward the stairs. "Let's be comfortable."

Upstairs they undressed each other slowly. Their agreement was unspoken. Both set out to make their lovemaking last as long as it possibly could. They traced each inch of skin and covered each other with kisses. They teased and played and brought each other to the brink of pleasure time and time again only to withdraw.

Finally, even knowing that it was their last time, they could not hold off any longer.

"Now," Elise commanded, wrapping her legs around Sloane to take him inside her. "I need you now."

It was over too soon. With her release came tears. Elise pillowed her head on Sloane's shoulder and allowed them to fall.

"Don't cry, Lise." He held her tight.

"It's all right. It was just so beautiful." She almost choked on the words. "It's been so beautiful."

"It doesn't have to end. Come with me."

The room was silent.

He had said the words she most wanted to hear. She had taunted him at the river with his inability to ask her to come. And yet, he had no idea what her coming would entail. Even with the fierce flame of hope burning off her common sense, Elise knew that this was not the time to tell him about their child. Not when they were entwined, body and soul, and unable to think rationally. If she did and he still said he wanted her, she would never know if it was duty, passion or love that had made the decision for him.

"Not now." She turned on her side so that she could trace his jawline with her fingers. "I love you, Sloane. I've loved our time together. But we both need a chance to see this more clearly."

"You're afraid."

She was. "Yes."

"Again." His voice was bitter.

"Yes." She kissed his cheek.

"God, it's a repeat of last time."

"No, it's not. Please trust me. It's not the same, Sloane."

"Then what are you afraid of?"

"Of making a mistake."

Sloane sat up and swung his legs over the side of the bed. He rose and began to look for his clothes, slipping on his shorts, obviously angry. "Then it is the same. You won't take the risk. You're opting for the comfortable, the familiar."

"I'm just asking for some time."

"Funny, I've heard you ask for that before."

Elise could say no more without telling him the whole truth. She got out of bed and came around behind him, pressing her body against his. It flashed through her mind that their child was right between them. "This time you need the time. Think about us, Sloane. If you still want me, I'll be waiting."

"Don't hold your breath." He turned and placed his hands on her shoulders, shaking her. "Do you know how damned hard it was to ask you to come with me? I knew you'd say no again."

"I said not now."

"The first two letters of both words are N-O."

"Is this where you throw something at me and tell me it's all I'll ever have of you if I don't come?" Elise lifted her chin and stared unwaveringly into his eyes.

The tension left his body. He dropped his hands. "No, this is just where I tell you I'll miss you."

She relaxed too. "Then maybe we have grown up."

"I still feel the same inside."

"I'll miss you, too." She bent and picked up his shirt, fingering the soft cotton. She resisted the desire to smooth it against her face. She held it out, and he slipped it on. "Will you do me a favor?"

He shrugged.

"Will you kiss me once and then get out of here before I say something stupid?"

His arms locked around her and the kiss was fierce. When Elise finally opened her eyes, Sloane was gone.

CHAPTER FOURTEEN

DECEMBER 15TH: I miss Florida. I miss the storms that blew in suddenly, leaving just as suddenly with the air cleansed and fresh behind them. I miss the passion of those furious clouds, the golden split of lightning, the smell of the rain just before it drenches the earth. Most of all I miss the peace that comes afterward.

Here in Cambridge there are no thunderstorms— not this time of year anyway. There is snow and the cold snap of air as it bites at your skin. In the New England countryside there must be peace after the blizzards. Here there are only the sounds of the snow plows and salt trucks and then the rhythms of a city once again.

At home, with Sloane, there is no storm; there is no peace. There is only waiting. I think I lost my patience for waiting the day I turned sixteen.

Clay looked at the words he'd just written and shook his head. Keeping a journal was a habit he'd acquired in Elise's English class. Now, even though he was usually loaded with homework, he still found time each day to write a few paragraphs. It had become as necessary as breathing. It was the one chance he had to express his feelings now that he and Amy were so far apart.

Closing the journal he stood, in no hurry for what was ahead. He pulled on his jacket and gloves and slung his backpack over his shoulder. The walk to Sloane's condominium from the Harvard library wasn't a short one, but he preferred it to taking a bus. These days he preferred anything that got him home late.

Forty-five minutes later, he stripped off his gloves and blew on his fingers to restore circulation. No matter what he wore, no matter what precautions he took, he could not keep out the bone-chilling New England cold. He suspected it was going to get worse before it got better.

He reached in the pocket of his slacks for the key to the front door of the gray stone four-plex and pushed it in the keyhole. In a moment he was standing inside at the foot of the stairs that led up to Sloane's apartment. Someone had set up a Christmas tree at the side of the bottom steps. It was small, not up to the job of making the cold, empty hallway a festive sight, but Clay appreciated the gesture. It was a reminder that the holiday season was here and that soon he would be flying back to Miracle Springs.

Sloane would not be going with him. Clay trudged up the steps, his backpack less heavy than his spirits. He hoped that Sloane had worked late; he hoped that the apartment would be empty when he unlocked the door. He hoped he would not have to face his father at all that night.

He was not to have his wish. He was greeted by the sound of soft classical music and the sight of Sloane, a drink was in his hand, staring into sputtering flames in the fireplace. "You're late."

Clay closed the door behind him. "I stopped off at the library. I've got a research paper due, and I needed some more information."

Sloane nodded, still staring vacantly at the flames.

Clay went into his room and unpacked his book sack. He had his report to finish, and he was tempted to begin it immediately. But he was also growing, and his stomach was rumbling to confirm the fact. He changed out of his school uniform and into comfortable jeans. He liked his school. He was constantly challenged, and he had been accepted by the other kids immediately. But he also liked the end of the day when he could just be himself again. Of course he would like coming home even better if Sloane didn't make him feel so unwelcome.

Back in the living room he took stock of the situation. Sloane hadn't moved. The same drink was in his hand, his eyes were still trained on the flames. It was the portrait of an unhappy man. Clay wondered if Sloane was this way all day or only when he was forced to come home and face the son he didn't want. Something clenched convulsively inside him, but he ignored it and resolutely faced his father. "What are we doing about dinner?"

"I stopped and got Chinese. It's in the kitchen. You can heat it up in the microwave."

"Have you eaten?"

"No."

Clay went into the kitchen and took down plates for both of them, dishing up food from various cartons and shoving it into the microwave, one plate at a time. When it was ready, he took it to the dining-room table, pulling silverware out of a drawer in the buffet on the way. "It's ready."

Sloane looked up as if he were surprised he was not alone. "You go ahead."

Clay shrugged and began to eat. He would never think of this time in his life without tasting the exotic tang of soy sauce and M.S.G. He figured that in the last six months, he and Sloane had averaged four nights a week of shrimp-fried rice, moo shu pork and egg rolls.

"How is it?"

Clay was surprised by Sloane's question. Whenever Sloane spoke to him nowadays it was a surprise. "It's okay."

Sloane wandered over to the table, picking up his egg roll. He looked at it as if it were a radioactive isotope and dropped it back to the plate. "I was nineteen before I had my first Chinese food."

"You've made up for it."

Sloane's eyes narrowed, and he regarded his son. "Is that a complaint?"

"Would it do any good?"

Sloane was surprised at Clay's flippant answer. He sat down and leaned over the table. "I asked you a question."

"So you did." Clay leaned back, his eyes never flickering. "You'll have to excuse me, I'm out of practice at answering."

"What does that mean?"

Clay sighed. "It means whatever you want it to, Sloane. Look, I've got to get busy on my report. It's due before I leave for the holidays." He stood, then looked in surprise at his arm. Sloane's fingers were wrapped tightly around it.

"Sit!"

Clay sat, and Sloane released him.

"What did you mean about being out of practice answering?"

Clay leaned back in his chair. "What did you think I meant?"

"Obviously there's some truth to what you say. I'll have to give you a refresher course on how to respond. You don't ask another question. You give an answer, a sentence with a period at the end. Now, what did you mean?"

Anger flickered across Clay's face. "I meant that you never ask me anything."

"I ask you how school is going."

"That's true. Sometimes you do ask me that. You did last month in fact."

Sloane had the grace to look sheepish. "Has it been that bad?"

Clay shrugged. "I'm used to it."

"I don't mean to be so distant."

"Don't you?" Clay picked up a fork and began to toss it from hand to hand.

"No, I don't. I've been…preoccupied. I haven't meant to ignore you."

"It seems to me that people always mean to act the way they do. I figured that out when I was about five and somebody apologized for spanking me. It could have been Willow, I don't even remember. It was a woman. She said she didn't mean it. She did. She enjoyed it. And you mean to be distant."

"What makes you think so?"

"I'm not stupid, Sloane. I'm not a little kid either. I know what's going on. I know you want me out of here."

Sloane exhaled with force. "No, Clay…I—"

For the first time in a long time, Clay told the adult in charge what he wanted to tell him, not what that adult wanted to hear. "Stop lying to me! You don't want me." The fork clattered to the floor. "You haven't wanted me from the first moment you found out you had a kid. You think you're supposed to want me so you try. Why don't you just stop trying, Sloane? I don't want you. I don't need you!''

Sloane felt a surge of fury at Clay's words. He didn't need this now. He wove his fingers together to keep from slapping Clay's face. "I think you'd better go to your room."

"If you recall, that was my idea in the first place." Clay pushed back his chair and slammed it against the wall behind him. He was gone in a second.

Sloane shut his eyes. The momentary rage that had crackled through his body was gone. He sagged against his chair and wondered if it was humanly possible to feel any lower.

He had always thought of himself as a winner. Through sheer determination he had won his heart's desire: freedom. Now freedom seemed a petty goal if it meant the absence of all the ties that made life worth living.

He stood and went back into the living room. He bent and stoked the fire, then he returned to the chair where he had spent so much of the evening. He wasn't a winner. He was a loser. He had lost Elise; now he knew he had never even had Clay. He was a man alone.

How do you set things right when you're incapable of communicating with the people you love most? He loved Clay, and yet somehow he had neglected to let Clay know. And Elise? Elise was gone, had been gone since September, and he had no idea where to find her. The past months had been like living in the middle of a nightmare.

In August, after a cocktail party where he had imbibed more than his usual limit, he had called Elise just to hear the sound of her voice. She had said nothing about leaving Miracle Springs, and of course, he hadn't asked. Their call had been friendly and impersonal. He had hung up feeling lonelier than he'd ever felt. He hadn't wanted to repeat the experience, but he hadn't wanted to lose touch with her either. In September he had tried to call again, only by that time her phone was disconnected.

He had assumed the recorded message telling him to check the number was just trouble with the phone lines. Elise would not leave the town of her birth. He was as sure of that as he was of anything in the universe. But the next day he had gotten a chatty letter from his Aunt Lillian containing all the news of Miracle Springs. The biggest story had been Elise's disappearance.

Evidently Lincoln Greeley, the high school principal, had known she was leaving because when the academic year started, there was a new teacher for tenth grade English. But no one knew where she had gone or why she had left. Lincoln, a master of small-town politics, had refused to discuss the matter. All Aunt Lillian knew was that Elise's house was up for sale and a nice young couple was probably going to buy it. Did Sloane know anything about it?

Sloane had gone through the month of September telling himself that when Elise wanted him to know where she was, she would tell him. At first he'd been pleased that she would spread her wings so mysteriously and fly away from everything that was familiar and dear. He half expected her to land on his doorstep. The thought gave him pleasure. He was beginning to admit just how much he missed her, beginning to realize what she added to his life—beginning to believe that there was hope for them after all. But by the end of September, he was beginning to worry.

Where was she? By mid-October he was frantic. He was working harder than he'd ever worked, writing, teaching his classes, lecturing at nearby colleges and universities. All the work didn't even begin to make a dent in his fears. How could he ever have thought that he and Elise had no future together? Why hadn't he told her he loved her?

Why hadn't he realized he loved her?

He did. More than his freedom. More than his pride. More than his fears. He loved her. He wanted her. And for the first time he realized that it was his own fear that had stood between them this time. He had been afraid to ask her to come. He had been so afraid that when he finally asked, it was only at the very end of their time together, when she couldn't say yes without worrying about how genuine his request was.

He had been afraid to tell her he loved her. Love bound people together. He had been a man who wanted no ties, no boundaries. He was a man, but he had acted like the boy who could not wait to leave the town of his birth and its restrictions. He was a man, but he had acted like the boy who wanted to punish the girl who spoiled his grand escape. He had been reacting.

He had been a fool.

By November, Sloane had humbled himself to the point of calling Bob Cargil and begging him for information about Elise. Bob had refused to tell him anything. If it was possible to gloat over the telephone, Bob had done it. Still Sloane sensed when he hung up that Bob had known no more than he did.

Lincoln Greeley had known. Sloane called him, explained his desperation and pleaded for Lincoln's help. With no explanation, Lincoln had refused. He could not be swayed. Elise's realtor pleaded confidentiality and hung up on him.

Now it was December. Once, at the beginning of the month, a phone call had come late at night. Sloane had picked up the receiver and when he held it to his ear he could hear the peculiar crackle of a long-distance connection. There had been no voice, only a click and then, later, the buzz of a dial tone. Every night now he waited for the phone to ring again. This time he would pick it up and call her name before she could hang up. He would make her know he wanted her, needed her, loved her. He would make her know that no matter what problems stood between them, he would find a way to make them all right.

If she didn't call before vacation started, he would spend his holiday looking for her.

Now Sloane had a more immediate problem, but it stemmed from the same source. He had never had the courage to tell his son the one thing he needed to hear, just as he had not had the courage to tell Elise the same. It was time to make the final commitment to Clay.

Sloane stood and walked down the hallway to Clay's room. He listened, undecided about how to approach the conversation that was long overdue. After a deep breath, he knocked on the door. "Clay? Will you come out here, please?"

There was a long interval. Sloane remembered well what it was like to be a teenager. He remembered well the heady feeling of power that comes from knowing an adult is waiting for you. He was surprised it had taken Clay this long to learn the same thing. Finally the door swung open.

Clay lounged in the doorway, his eyes carefully veiled. He wondered what fancy language Sloane would couch his rejection in. What words would he use to rid himself of the son he had never wanted, the son who had finally told him exactly what he thought? If Clay knew one thing about adults, it was that they didn't want to hear the truth. Sloane wouldn't want to chance having to hear it again. Clay only hoped that when his father found another place for him, that place would be in Miracle Springs.

"I want to talk to you." Sloane turned toward the living room, and Clay followed him. Sloane sat on the sofa and motioned for his son to join him. Clay sat on the far end.

"It's very easy to misconstrue..." Sloane stopped. He realized just how stilted he sounded. Clay was trying to look stoic, but even in his own agony Sloane could see the vulnerability in his son's eyes. He started again. "I've blown it."

Clay just looked at him.

"Look Clay, I've been acting like a jerk. It just never occurred to me that you'd think it had anything to do with you. I'm one hell of a lousy father."

Clay's eyes widened, and his expression encouraged Sloane.

"You see, I never had a father of my own. I never had anyone, really. My mother was always busy, distant. My aunts and uncles cared about me but they weren't usually there when I needed them. I...well, I made it on my own. But I never learned how to tell people what I was feeling. I never learned to be a father either, and I don't seem to have much talent."

"What's this got to do with me?" Clay's voice was still tinged with anger, but Sloane could hear the hurt little boy under the insolence, and he slid a little closer and touched him on the shoulder.

"I've been wrong about one thing. Very, very wrong. Right from the beginning. I've never told you the most important thing you can tell someone. I've never told you I love you. I do. I loved you the minute I set eyes on you." He coughed to subdue the lump in his throat. "I've been torn up inside ever since thinking about all the time I've missed with you, thinking about how lonely you must have been, how lonely I was. I've tried to show you, but it hasn't been good enough. You may not need me, Clay, but I need you. I want you in my life forever."

Clay looked skeptical. Or was it that, having never been told he was loved, he didn't know how to answer? Sloane didn't know, but he did know that telling his son he loved him wasn't enough. He slid closer until he was next to him. Then he put his arms around Clay in a powerful bear hug. "I mean every word of it," he said, and he felt tears wet his cheeks. "And someday you'll know I mean it."

Clay sat in the circle of his father's arms and wondered why he felt he was going to cry too. He hadn't cried since he was a small child. He felt Sloane tentatively stroke his hair and he marveled at how good it felt. Before he knew what he was doing, he was patting Sloane's shoulder to comfort him.

"If you love me and you really want me here, then why have you been so awful to live with?" he asked after Sloane had drawn away a little.

"I promise, it hasn't had anything to do with you."

"Do you need a refresher course on answering questions?" The insolence was gone. It was the voice of the Clay Sloane had known in Miracle Springs, humorous, ingenuous.

Sloane laughed a little, wiping away the tears that had felt so cleansing. "You want me to share my feelings with you?"

"Yeah. I could get to like it."

"I'll make a long story short. I'm upset about Elise."

"Why? She sounds fine. She likes Atlanta; she likes her job."

Sloane froze. "What?"

"It's hard to tell the truth from letters, but I think she's doing all right. She sounds a little lonely."

"What are you saying?"

Clay frowned. "I can't figure out why you're worried. Did she tell you something she didn't tell me?"

"She hasn't told me anything! I didn't know where she was! How do you know?"

"We've been writing ever since I left Miracle Springs. She sent me her new address when she moved. I just got a Christmas card from her yesterday."

"Damn!" Sloane stood and began pacing the living room, pounding his fist into his hand. "All this time."

"Too bad you didn't tell me before."

"Damn!"

Clay wondered just how far he could push Sloane. "See, if you'd told me, I could have saved you all this. I could have told you she's in Atlanta working for some publishing company. I could have given you her address. I haven't seen much of this love stuff but it does seem to me that if you love somebody you talk to them, tell them what's worrying you."

Sloane continued to pace. "Didn't I already tell you I'd blown it? Obviously it was worse than I thought."

"Well, why don't you make a short story long?" Clay lounged back in his seat. "Tell me the rest."

Sloane stopped pacing to shoot a grin at his son. He could almost see Clay relax under its power. "Do you really want to hear this?"

Clay nodded.

"All right, but it might take me awhile to get to the point. I'm still figuring it all out."

"Make it up as you go along. I've got the time."

Sloane began slowly. "Once upon a time there was a man, a hermit, who lived in a cave all by himself."

"A bedtime story?" Clay interrupted. "Aren't I a little old for that?"

"I missed all my other chances. I was cheated out of them. I'll never forgive Destiny Ranch for that!"

Clay was surprised by the strength of his father's words and the detour. "I was happy...." He stopped.

"Were you?" Sloane faced him.

"No."

Sloane shut his eyes and nodded. "I know."

Clay tried to be honest. He realized that Sloane actually wanted the truth. It was a new experience, but one Clay thought he was going to enjoy thoroughly. "There were good things. I see the way kids are raised in other places, and what I had was better than a lot of that. Some of the people who came through the ranch were terrific. I learned so much from them. But I always missed," his voice caught and he swallowed, "I always missed having someone who thought I was special enough to keep with them."

"I think you're special enough." Sloane opened his eyes. "You can do what you want, be who you want to be, but no matter what you do or who you are, you're my son. That can't change."

Clay swallowed again. "Finish your story."

Sloane nodded, knowing that Clay already had enough to contemplate. He began to pace again. "This hermit I was telling you about liked his cave. It was huge and warm and it had a picture window where he could watch the world go by. At night sometimes he'd sit by the fire and write down what he'd seen. He'd send off his writing, and people would read it. They liked what he had to say."

"And then?"

"And then one day, the hermit was forced to go outside his cave. He didn't want to go. He was happy being alone, at least he thought he was. Outside he found out that the real world, the one he thought he'd been writing about was a difficult place to be. One minute he'd feel happier than he'd known he could be and the next minute he'd be in the depths of despair."

"Sounds like a place I've been myself," Clay murmured.

"Then you understand how this hermit felt."

"Anyone who's been there would."

Sloane nodded. "It took this hermit a long time to adjust. He was so used to being alone he didn't know what to say, what to do for other people. He didn't realize he lacked courage, that was something he always accused other people of lacking. But the truth was that he was afraid of all those highs and lows. He kept a big part of himself away from the people he grew to love, just to play it safe. Finally, he couldn't stand it any longer. He returned to his cave."

"But he wasn't happy?"

"No, he wasn't. Because you see, he'd changed. The picture window wasn't big enough anymore. He could see but he couldn't touch or smell or hear. In fact, he couldn't hear at all; his cave was silent. So he tried to go back to the real world again, find the people he loved, but one of them was gone, and he couldn't find the words to tell the other one what he was feeling."

"So he ignored him."

"Exactly."

"And the one that was gone. Why did she go without telling the hermit where he could find her?"

"Because the hermit seemed like a hopeless case, I guess."

"Was she right?"

"No."

Clay smiled. "Then one day, the hermit found a map. At the very center of the map in a kingdom called Georgia was a big X. The hermit journeyed night and day until he reached the spot. There he found the treasure he'd been seeking."

"Yes."

"When are you going to leave?"

"As soon as you take off for Florida. With any luck, Elise and I'll be joining you at Aunt Lillian's for Christmas."

"I don't know. Elise may have too much sense to get mixed up with a hermit again."

"You're a rotten kid!" Sloane tempered his words by ruffling Clay's hair. "*My* rotten kid, and don't you ever forget it."

Clay's smile got bigger. "People don't own people."

"Don't kid yourself. I've been owned body and soul for years, and I just figured it out. And you know what? It feels wonderful!"

CHAPTER FIFTEEN

ELISE LIFTED HER CUP of nonalcoholic punch along with everybody else in the room. She listened as her new boss made a toast to the Christmas season. Mechanically, she brought the cup to her lips and swallowed. It was red fruit punch, the kind the children had been served when she'd taught Sunday school in Miracle Springs. Someone had tried to make it Christmassy by floating lime sherbet in it. The result was a sickly brown scum where the sherbet and punch had blended together, and it took all Elise's fortitude to swallow it. She apologized silently to the baby inside her, who gave a mighty kick in response.

The party resumed. Elise found an unobtrusive spot to set her cup down. The buffet was classier than the punch and she was starving. Ignoring the warning voice that told her whatever she ate would show up when the nurse weighed her at the obstetrician's, she heaped a plate with cold boiled shrimp, salmon mousse and crackers, fruit-cake and rum balls.

"Only a pregnant lady would eat that combination," her boss commented, coming to stand beside her.

"I believe I qualify," she said, patting the huge bulge that preceded her everywhere.

"You look like the Madonna." John Switt shook his head at his own words. "Just don't go having that baby in a stable somewhere."

"At this point, I'd be glad to have this baby anywhere, just to have it."

Mary Jo Switt came up behind her husband and laughed appreciatively at Elise's words. She took his arm. "I remember just how it feels to be that close. How much longer do you have?"

"Three weeks, two days. Give or take a month." Elise smiled at the Switts. They were a handsome couple in their fifties who resembled each other in the way that people long married often did. She envied them their togetherness.

Mary Jo was clucking like a mother hen. "Shouldn't you be on maternity leave? Has John been making your life difficult?"

"Never. I'm just happier working. I want as much time with the baby as I can have afterwards."

Mary Jo nodded. "I don't blame you."

"Southern Pines Press can do without you," John assured her, as he'd assured her every day for the last month. "You're the best copy editor we ever had, but we can make do with free-lancers till you get back. Don't hesitate to take off when you need to."

The baby kicked again, and for a minute, Elise couldn't speak. It was amazing how much a kick could hurt. "You're so kind," she said when she could talk again. "But don't worry, I promise I'm not going to deliver in the office."

"If you do," Mary Jo put in, "John'll know what to do. He almost delivered our last child himself. You'd think I'd have known better, but I kept telling myself the baby was just restless. By the time I realized what was going on, the poor little fellow was already on his way to meet us."

"We got to the hospital just in time for Mary Jo to give one last push," John reminisced.

Elise wanted to hear more, but by the time she had weathered another kick, Mary Jo and John were gone, distracted by other employees. She finished the plate of food and helped herself to seconds on the fruitcake.

She was lucky to have landed this job. Because of her father's insurance money, she had decided to work more for her sanity than her financial stability. Still, even though she hadn't sought prestigious or high-paying positions, few employers had been willing to listen to the plight of a woman old-enough-to-know-better who was unmarried and expecting a child. They hadn't wanted the prospect of instant maternity leave, and Elise hadn't blamed them. But John had listened without making a moral judgment. He had hired her because he had believed she would do a good job, then he had made it clear that his door was always open to her. John and Mary Jo had helped make the adjustment to Atlanta easier.

Elise was pleased with her choice for a new location. Atlanta offered all the things that life in a small town never had. In addition, it offered the one thing she needed most of all: privacy. No one here cared that she was not married to the father of her baby, or if they did, they didn't make a point of it. After the child was born, she would explore all the sections of the city, check into school systems and buy a house where she could raise her son or daughter in peace. She would make friends. She would survive. If she sometimes missed the town of her birth, she still knew that this was better.

Miracle Springs was just a memory now. It was a cocoon where she had lived far too many years of her life. She had traded its comforts, its unchallenging sameness for the adventures of the unknown. Some days she awoke and wept for the ease of the life she had left behind. More often she sat up and stretched, eager for the joys of a new day.

She should have left years before. But as often as not, she put that thought behind her. She had finally made the break. She was free, independent and as happy as she would ever be without Sloane.

Elise realized she was tired. She traded repartee with her fellow employees, made plans to attend Christmas Eve Mass the following week with one of Southern Pine's editors, and then excused herself to head home. The drive through downtown Atlanta's traffic always tired her, but never more than it did this evening. The long day and the baby's activity had taken a toll on her limited energy. All she wanted was a chance to sit in a warm tub with her feet propped as high as she could prop them and a good night's sleep.

No, she wanted more than that. She wanted the impossible. She wanted to go home and find Sloane waiting for her. She wanted to melt into his arms and feel his hands soothe away the constant ache in her back and the pain in her heart. She wanted to hear him ask how she felt and how their child was doing. She wanted to know that in three weeks and two days he would be standing beside her, watching their baby come into the world.

She wanted the impossible. Clay had her address. Sloane would have no trouble finding her if he wanted to. Obviously he didn't. Elise edged her car into the right lane of the interstate and took the exit that would lead to the apartment complex where she was living. It was hard to get behind the wheel of a car now, hard to steer, hard to sit up straight. It would be hard to climb the stairs, hard to undress. Maybe she'd forgo the bath and go straight to bed.

She found a parking place immediately, which was unusual. Apparently some of the sprawling complex's tenants had already gone elsewhere for the holidays. For a moment, she envied them their freedom. She climbed the open stairway, which always made her think of a cheap motel that rented its rooms by the hour, and paused outside her door. She must be tired. The faint strains of Christmas carols had reached her ears, and for a moment, she had almost believed they were coming from inside her apartment. The sound was welcoming, pleasant. Maybe she would leave her radio on from now on so that when she came home, the apartment wouldn't be so silent, so foreboding.

She stuck the key in her lock and turned it. The sound of carols grew louder. She *had* left her radio on. That was funny, she didn't even remember having it on that morning. Inside she felt for the light switch. The resulting brightness made her close her eyes. She stayed that way as a sharp pain shot through her abdomen, and she felt her body bend in protest. She gasped as the pain continued for long seconds and then disappeared. *That was no kick.*

"Lord!" She straightened and opened her eyes to find her way to the sofa and the telephone. She forgot about both when she realized she was not alone. "Sloane!"

Sloane was standing next to the sofa, his face as white as Christmas snow. "What in the hell!"

"How did you get in here?"

"You're pregnant!"

"Did you pick my lock?"

"Why didn't you tell me?"

"That's why I heard carols. You turned on my radio."

"Who the hell cares how I got in and what I did while I waited? Why didn't you tell me?" Sloane's face was no longer completely white. There were two red spots of anger on his cheeks and the muscle in his jaw was jumping. "My God, you're as bad as Willow. You used me like a stud and then took my child!"

"No I didn't! I was going to tell you. I…" She stopped and her eyes widened. "My God!" She bent over again. "Sloane, I can't. Sloane…"

He was at her side in a split second. He put his arms around her waist. "Lean on me, Lise."

"I can't." Her knees began to tremble. Something inside her seemed to give way, and she felt a rush of fluid soak her undergarments. "It's not supposed to happen like this," she said on a moan. "It's supposed to happen slowly the first time. Especially when you're my age. I don't know what to do."

"Let's get you over to the sofa. Then tell me who to call."

She was no help at all. She couldn't move. Sloane finally picked her up, grunting at her new weight and carried her across the room. "Who do I call?" he asked after he had laid her down.

"It's by the phone. This is too soon. I'm not due for the better part of a month!"

"You knew, didn't you? You knew before I left town!" Sloane dialed as he spoke. "You knew, but you didn't tell me." He realized that he ought to stop himself, but he couldn't seem to halt the angry flood of words. "You kept this a secret… Hello? My name is Sloane Tyson, I'm calling for Elise Ramsey. I'd like to speak to," he covered the receiver with his hand. "Who the hell am I calling?"

"Dr. Pinchot." Elise closed her eyes.

"Dr. Pinchot," Sloane continued smoothly. "Miss Ramsey is about to become a mother," he hesitated, "and I'm about to become a father. Again," he said, looking straight at Elise.

The voice on the other end of the line asked him to wait.

"How long have you been in labor?" Sloane asked her.

"I don't know. I thought the baby was just kicking hard."

"How long?"

"Two hours or so."

"Where have you been?"

"At my office Christmas party."

"Did you eat anything?"

"Tons."

"Terrific. Hello, Dr. Pinchot? My name is Sloane Tyson. I'm the father of Elise Ramsey's baby." Sloane watched as Elsie turned her head to the back of the sofa. "She's in labor. Hard labor. Has been for a couple of hours but she didn't know it. She may already be in transition."

Elise's head spun around, and she stared at him.

Sloane covered the phone. "Did your water break?"

She nodded weakly, biting her lip as another pain ripped through her. Sloane looked at his watch and began to time the contraction. "I'd say her contractions are about three minutes apart and they're lasting around ninety seconds or so. But that's just a guess. I just started to time them."

Sloane listened to the doctor as he watched the minute hand on his watch.

"Yeah, she ate. Tons, she says." He covered the receiver. "He wants to know if you've completed the Lamaze childbirth training."

The contraction ended and Elise nodded. "Last week."

"She says yes." He listened again. "We'll meet you there in—" he covered the receiver again. "How long will it take to get you to the hospital?"

"Twenty minutes."

"Twenty minutes," Sloane repeated into the receiver. "Pant and blow? I'll tell her. I've helped before." He hung up. "Come on, Lise. We're going bye-bye."

Elise couldn't sit up. Her whole body was trembling. "This is supposed to take hours."

"Or minutes. Depends." Sloane slid his arms under her back and helped her sit. She bent over as another contraction began. "Come on, love. Do as I say. Now, take a deep cleansing breath. That's right. Let it out slowly." Sloane began to massage her abdomen. "Now light pants, like an overheated Dalmatian. That's good." He could feel the contraction tearing at her until her belly was as hard as a rock. "Okay, three pants and a short blow. Come on, Lise." He demonstrated, and she followed his lead. They continued together until the contraction was finished. "Time to go."

Elise was too weak to stand. "I can't make it. You go ahead without me."

"I'll carry you if I have to."

"Sloane, I was going to tell you."

"When? When the kid needed tuition for college?"

Something purely imaginary burst inside her, and she began to cry.

"That's not going to help. Come on." Sloane helped her stand, and then he lifted her in his arms. "You realize I'm too old for this, don't you? I'll get a hernia."

She sniffed, trying hard to control her tears. "Why are you here?"

"I'm beginning to think I'm here to deliver this baby. Be quiet now. We'll talk later."

"How do you know so much?" They were at the doorway, and Sloane was fumbling for the knob with one hand.

"Destiny. I watched a baby being born once at a rock festival. I held the girl's hand and talked her through it. Later one of the Destiny midwives taught me the Lamaze techniques, but I never got to use them because I left right afterward."

"And you remembered it all those years?"

"You'd better hope I did." He felt her stiffen. "Okay, take a deep breath." They began to pant together.

The trip to the hospital was the most difficult twenty minutes either of them had ever spent. Sloane alternately cursed traffic and panted. Elise felt every bump, every twist of the road. Finally Sloane roared into the parking lot with the speed of an ambulance and ran around the side of the car to scoop Elise out. They were in the emergency room in less than a minute.

"Dr. Pinchot's patient is here, her contractions are two minutes apart and lasting ninety seconds or more," he yelled to the admitting nurse.

"They don't start and they don't stop," Elise corrected him on an indrawn breath.

The nurse, gray-haired and somber, took one look at the man holding the woman in his arms and called for a gurney. "Take her right to delivery," she instructed the orderly who arrived a moment later. "Pronto."

Sloane laid Elise carefully on the hard, sheeted surface, and touched her hair. "Only a little longer."

"We've got to take her up now," the orderly told him.

"I'm coming too."

"Just a minute," the nurse began. "Did Dr. Pinchot give his permission?"

"Of course," Sloane said smoothly. "I'm the baby's father."

"Then you can go to admitting first."

"I already did all the paperwork," Elise said between gasps. "Elise Ramsey."

"We'll have to check. Mr. Ramsey, if you would wait."

"Sloane!" Elise grabbed his hand. "Come with me."

"Of course." He bent and kissed her forehead. "We have to talk, don't we? I'm not going to let you out of my sight until you answer a few questions." He straightened. "I'll be down as soon as the baby's born," he told the nurse. Without waiting for the orderly, he began to push the gurney himself.

"This is irregular . . . !" the nurse shouted.

"Highly!" Sloane agreed. The orderly took his place and Sloane grabbed Elise's hand. "Okay, Lise. This time, start the pant-blow sequence as soon as it gets rough."

She was beyond response. She could only feel the intense pain in her abdomen and the warmth of Sloane's hand around hers. She did as she was told.

The delivery room was icy cold. Dr. Pinchot was already in hospital blues, and he chased Sloane out immediately, insisting that he cover his clothes, hair and shoes before he was allowed to come back in. With a nurse's help, Sloane was back in a minute. Elise had been stripped, garbed in a hospital gown and covered with a sheet. She was gasping for breath.

"No anesthesia," Dr. Pinchot said when Sloane returned. "Too far along and too stuffed with dinner."

The doctor turned back to Elise. "Okay sweetheart. When I tell you, I want you to push. You," he pointed at Sloane, "get behind her and lift her up. Elise, grab your knees."

"I don't know how to push," she wailed.

"Your body's going to teach you how. Just follow its lead," Dr. Pinchot said calmly.

"Sloane, I'm sorry I asked you to come. You don't have to stay. Oh!"

"Try and toss me out! Take a deep breath and hold it." Sloane looked to the doctor for confirmation. "Okay, Lise. Bear down hard!"

The first pushing session went well. Elise welcomed working with the contractions. "How much longer?" she gasped when the doctor told her to stop.

"Depends on how well you do," he said nonchalantly.

"Is the baby okay?"

"No reason to worry."

"Sloane, I'm sorry."

She felt his hands massaging her shoulders. "We'll talk later. Just worry about the baby now. This is Clay's brother or sister you're having."

Elise closed her eyes and waited for the next contraction. When it began, her body took over and pushed for her. All she could do was help it a little. She felt Sloane lift her, and she heard his voice soothing her although she couldn't understand any of the words.

"Good job, Elise. You're that much closer. One more push should do it," Dr. Pinchot told her.

She drew in her breath on a sob. "Sloane. I'm scared."

"So am I." He came around to her side. "I love you, Lise. It's going to be all right."

She didn't have time to absorb his words.

"Okay, Elise. Give it one more good, hard push and then I'll let you hold your kid." Dr. Pinchot stationed himself between her legs. "Looking good. Don't shut your eyes. Look above you in the mirror and watch this baby come into the world."

Sloane wiped her forehead. "Push, Lise. Harder. Harder!"

"Open your eyes!"

Elise did as she was told and watched the biggest miracle of all. She heard a cry: the baby's. She heard a sob: her own. She heard a laugh: Sloane's.

She heard a calm professional voice. "It's a girl. Looks full term. With a mop of black hair and a powerful set of lungs."

Elise felt something warm and wonderful on her stomach. Sloane held her up a little and she saw their daughter, eyes open and staring in her direction. Her skin was mottled and covered with a pasty white film, but she was without doubt the most beautiful baby in the world.

"Oh, Sloane, look at her!"

"Just lie back, Elise. You can hold her as soon as I cut the cord," Dr. Pinchot said cheerfully.

Sloane eased Elise back to the table. "She looks like her mother."

"You can't tell that already."

"She does."

"I wanted a boy who looked like you." Her voice trembled.

Sloane was filled with emotion at her words. He hadn't known he could feel so intensely. His knees felt weak from it. "Don't tell me you're disappointed," he said at last. "I won't have you be disappointed she's a girl. She's perfect."

"What's Clay going to say?"

"He'll be as surprised as I was," he said with irony.

"Okay, you two. Here she is. Not a thing wrong with her either except that she's pretty cold and more than a little mad."

The delivery room nurse who had efficiently hovered in the background cranked up the table so that Elise could recline. Elise opened her arms and held her daughter for the first time. "She does look like me." She touched the wailing little bundle on the forehead with her index finger. "Please don't cry, honey," she soothed. The baby continued wailing as if she were insulted by the request.

"Go ahead and nurse her," Dr. Pinchot prodded Elise. "She can't cry if her mouth's full."

Sloane untied Elise's gown and watched as tentatively she put the baby to her breast. Elise gasped as her daughter grabbed hold and began to suckle like an expert.

"It's good for both of you," Dr. Pinchot explained. "Makes your uterus contract, quiets her, and hopefully it will keep your mind off the stitches I'm about to put in."

"Stitches?"

Sloane bent closer to watch his daughter eat her dinner and distract Elise. "She has my personality. Look at her. She knows exactly what she wants."

"Sloane, help me hold her. My arms are trembling," Elise pleaded.

Sloane reached down and steadied the infant who was ignoring everything except her new connection to her mother.

"When I got off the plane and rented a car, I had no idea what I was getting myself into," Sloane told her. "This is incredible. What a way to spend an evening!"

"You hate me."

"I don't understand why you did it. I expect a complete explanation in about three hours. But no, I don't hate you. I love you."

Elise shut her eyes. "You don't have to say that. This doesn't change anything."

"It doesn't change the fact I love you. It changes just how fast we're going to get married, though." He straightened. "When does she get out of here?" he asked the doctor who was just finishing up.

"Three or four days. The pediatrician will have a look at the baby. If all goes well, it should only be three."

"How long before Elise is on her feet again?"

"She'll be tired for awhile. But she's done real well for an old gal."

Elise opened her eyes and narrowed them. Dr. Pinchot laughed. "Thought that might pep you up." He came around and plucked the baby from Elise's breast. "We've got to weigh and measure her." The baby was quiet as if she felt sleepy already. "I'll have her back in a jiffy, and then you two can go into recovery with her."

"Have you got a name picked out for her?" Sloane asked Elise.

She pulled the gaping neckline of her gown closed, aware that Sloane's eyes were lingering there. "I'm not going to marry you."

"No?" He smoothed her forehead in a gesture that was distinctly humoring. "Why not?"

"The whole reason I did this was to keep you from marrying me out of duty. I'm set up here. I have a job, a decent income. I have my own apartment, my own friends. I even have a woman who'll baby-sit for me when I'm working. I'm free, independent and quite capable of taking care of myself and my daughter. You don't have to worry. I'm not the scared, fragile little girl I used to be."

"And you didn't think I had the right to know anything about my child?"

"I was going to tell you." She grabbed his hand. "I wasn't going to do what Willow did. I just wanted to be sure you believed me when I told you that you didn't have to marry me."

"How long would you have waited?"

"As soon as I'd recovered from the birth."

Sloane picked up a lock of her hair and held it to his lips. "Why did you have to recover first?"

"I didn't want to be weak. Don't, Sloane."

"Are you weak now?"

"Extremely."

He bent a little closer. "Good. Marry me."

She tried to shake her head, but the movement pulled the hair held tightly in his hand. "Sloane, you told me yourself you married once to give a baby a name. You didn't want that baby or that wife. How do I know you want me and our daughter?''

"Because I love you."

"Even if that's true . . . what about her?'' She nodded to the other side of the room.

"I already love her." Sloane saw the disbelief on Elise's face and he smoothed it away. "Look, Lise. When my ex-wife miscarried, I felt relieved. I knew our marriage wasn't going to be a good one. I didn't want to bring a child into it. But I know now there was a part of me that mourned that baby. I tried to ignore it, to tell myself it was for the best, but I was depressed for a long time. In my own blind way, I covered over those feelings. I told myself I wasn't father material. But now I have another chance, another child. And you're the two ladies I want to spend my life with. Don't shut me out of your lives."

"Sloane . . .''

"Marry me. Be my love, my wife, my adored companion, the mother of my children, my heart, my own private miracle.''

It was the last word that convinced her. She was too tired to prevent tears. "When did you decide you wanted me?''

"Months ago. Only I couldn't find you."

"Clay knew."

"Clay and I were hardly speaking."

"Sloane . . .''

"We're speaking now. He told me where you were. I told him I'd bring you to Miracle Springs for Christmas. We'll get married there—unless the thought embarrasses you."

"Do you really love me?"

He nodded.

"And the baby? You want the baby?"

"Try and keep me away."

"I could have made it on my own."

"I couldn't have." He brushed her lips with his, then did it again. "I never want to make it on my own again. Only with you, with Clay and with that screaming little bundle over there." They both listened to their daughter begin a new set of rebellious roars.

"She does have your personality."

"You're going to have your hands full with both of us."

Elise felt a peace she hadn't known was possible wash over her. She shut her eyes and grasped Sloane's hand. "This isn't a dream, is it?"

"Ask me that after three months of wet diapers and midnight feedings."

"It isn't a dream. It's a miracle," she said, bringing his hand to her lips. "The maiden couldn't have done any better."

"We made this one happen ourselves."

Elise smiled. "'Tis the season."

"It's always the season."

Elise heard a rustle, a roar and then a quiet cooing. She opened her eyes and looked up to see Sloane proudly holding their daughter, who had nestled against him as if she knew just exactly who he was. "You're going to make a good father," she said sleepily.

"I am a good father," he corrected her with a grin. "I'm going to make a good husband."

"I believe you will." Elise yawned and closed her eyes again.

"I take it that means you'll marry me."

"That's right."

"I love you."

"I love you."

Sloane watched Elise drift off to sleep. He swayed back and forth with their baby and planned their wedding. It couldn't be soon enough to suit him.

EPILOGUE

CLAY'S JOURNAL: It's Christmas. The second one I've spent with my father. For a present this year he gave me a mother and a sister. After a lifetime alone I'm suddenly overwhelmed with family. It's a funny thing about having all these people who matter to you. At first I wasn't sure there was room inside me for them. I thought that part of me was just inoperative—like a short circuit on a robot. Now I know that's not true.

I called Sloane "Dad" yesterday, and his face lit up like the brightest of Christmas trees. The smallest things seem to give him pleasure now. When I see him holding Rhea and smiling at her, I get the strangest feeling. I wonder what it would have been like to have him hold me that way. He seems to be trying to make up for it though. I haven't had so many hugs in my entire life.

And now Elise is my mother. She says stepmother is an honorable title, that it's the best step she ever took. We're staying at the Miracle Springs Inn, and she and I walked down to the river together this morning before Sloane and Rhea woke up. Elise wanted me to know that as much as she loves Rhea, she loved me first. I told her she could quit worrying about sibling rivalry, and she laughed and kissed my cheek.

Rhea is beautiful. I named her. It's Latin for "that which flows from the earth: the river." Rhea Elise Tyson. Elise says her name is perfect; Sloane says it sounds like something straight out of Destiny Ranch. But he says it with a smile.

Today at two Elise and Sloane are going to say their vows down at the riverbank. They already got married by a justice of the peace in Atlanta so that people here wouldn't talk, but their real wedding is going to be today. Just Amy and me and Sloane and Elise. And, of course, Aunt Lillian and Rhea.

Amy hasn't changed at all. She's still the most beautiful girl I've ever seen. We've both been going out with other people since I moved away, but it doesn't seem to matter at all. When we're together it's like we've never been apart. When I kissed her for the first time in months, it felt like I'd never stopped.

She has more freedom than she used to. Mr. Cargil asked Carol to marry him to keep her away from the man with the male Pekingese. They were married December first. Amy says Carol was smart. Making her father jealous was the only way to get him to pop the question. Now Carol keeps him busy and well fed, and Amy can live her own life. Mr. Cargil has even given Amy permission to spend Easter vacation in Cambridge with us. Amy giggled and said she thinks Carol's going to make him use that time to work on his textbook.

I'm glad to be back here. Late last night when everyone was sleeping I walked down to the springs. Christmas Eve is like holding your breath, waiting for something to happen. The night was very black and very still. There was part of a moon hanging in the sky and the water was a black satin ribbon. I know the date's not right, but as I looked at the island, the mists surrounding it parted. I thought I saw the maiden.

Just in case, I thanked her.

Six exciting series for you every month... from Harlequin

Harlequin Romance·
The series that started it all

Tender, captivating and heartwarming...
love stories that sweep you off to faraway places
and delight you with the magic of love.

◆

Harlequin Presents·
Powerful contemporary love stories...as individual as the women who read them

The No. 1 romance series...
exciting love stories for you, the woman of today...
a rare blend of passion and dramatic realism.

◆

Harlequin Superromance®
It's more than romance... it's Harlequin Superromance

A sophisticated, contemporary romance-fiction
series, providing you with a longer,
more involving read...a richer mix of complex plots,
realism and adventure.

Harlequin American Romance™
Harlequin celebrates the American woman...

...by offering you romance stories written about American women, by American women for American women. This series offers you contemporary romances uniquely North American in flavor and appeal.

◆

Harlequin Temptation™
Passionate stories for today's woman

An exciting series of sensual, mature stories of love...dilemmas, choices, resolutions... all contemporary issues dealt with in a true-to-life fashion by some of your favorite authors.

◆

Harlequin Intrigue™
Because romance can be quite an adventure

Harlequin Intrigue, an innovative series that blends the romance you expect... with the unexpected. Each story has an added element of intrigue that provides a new twist to the Harlequin tradition of romance excellence.

Harlequin Books®

PROD-A-2